PRAISE FOR *WOLF*

T0023354

"In Northern Minnesota, winter is full of dan
hard men, and hungry wolves. Cary J. Griffith brings the menace of all three
into play in his riveting new thriller. Returning to the childhood home he
fled 20 years earlier, Sam Rivers finds himself battling a group of scheming reprobates and struggling against an avalanche of painful memories.
Griffith's intimacy with the territory he writes about comes through in every
line. I loved this novel and recommend it highly. But I suggest you enjoy it
under a warm blanket. Honestly, I've never read a book that evokes the fierce
winter landscape of the North Country better than *Wolf Kill*."

> —William Kent Krueger, Edgar Award–winning author of
> *This Tender Land*

"Griffith's prose makes you feel the winter chill . . . and the twisty plot delivers
a chill down your spine. This is a Minnesota mystery with razor-sharp teeth."

> —Brian Freeman, *New York Times*–bestselling author of
> *The Deep, Deep Snow*

"*Wolf Kill* is a terrific read! The writing is so good that you can feel the frigid
winds blowing through this dark and masterfully crafted novel even as the
suspense heats up. And the wolves are as magnificent and frightening as you
could hope."

> —David Housewright, Edgar Award–winning author of
> *What Doesn't Kill Us*

"I love books where I go on a great adventure, but I also learn something
along the way. *Wolf Kill* does all this and more—it's the beginning of a series
featuring a smart wildlife special agent who takes us into the wilderness and
safely out again. A deeply satisfying read."

> —Mary Logue, author of Claire Watkins mysteries and *The Streel*

"Cary J. Griffith defines the savage, howling beauty of a Northern Minnesota
winter in this taut, compulsively readable mystery. I want more Sam Rivers!"

> —Wendy Webb, author of *The Haunting of Brynn Wilder*

"The deep freeze of a Minnesota winter meets the chilling underbelly of a small Iron Range town in Cary J. Griffith's fantastic *Wolf Kill*. I loved meeting Sam Rivers, the wolf expert and USFW field agent assigned to protect the nation's wildlife, and can't wait to follow Rivers on his next adventure."

—Mindy Mejia, author of *Leave No Trace* and *Strike Me Down*

"Up here in the North Country, we have a bounty of fine mystery writers: Krueger, Housewright, Eskins, Freeman, Mejia, Sanford . . . add to that list Cary J. Griffith, whose *Wolf Kill* thrills for its plotting, superb writing, and unforgettable characters, not least the brutal Minnesota winter. Sam Rivers is not only a fine sleuth but also a complicated man with a complicated history and a fair family grudge. Taken together, he's a force, both on the page and long after you finish reading his story. Good thing there's more of him to go around, and I'll be first in line for the next Sam Rivers novel."

—Peter Geye, author of *Northernmost*

Also by the author

Gunflint Burning: Fire in the Boundary Waters
Opening Goliath
Lost in the Wild

WOLF

A SAM RIVERS MYSTERY

KILL

CARY J. GRIFFITH

Adventure PUBLICATIONS

A version of this novel was originally published in 2013. This new edition has been heavily revised and reedited in anticipation of future Sam Rivers adventures.

Copy editors: Mary Logue and Kerry Smith
Cover design: Travis Bryant
Cover photo: July Flower/Shutterstock

Library of Congress Cataloging-in-Publication Data

Names: Griffith, Cary J., author.
Title: Wolf kill / by Cary J. Griffith.
Description: Cambridge, Minnesota : Adventure Publications, [2021] | Series: A Sam Rivers mystery | Summary: "Special agent Sam Rivers's investigation of a bizarre wolf attack leads to evidence of murder, conspiracy, and shocking family secrets in this wildlife-themed thriller"— Provided by publisher.
Identifiers: LCCN 2020053382 | ISBN 9781647550578 (paperback)
Subjects: GSAFD: Suspense fiction.
Classification: LCC PS3607.R54857 W65 2021 | DDC 813/.6—dc23
LC record available at https://lccn.loc.gov/2020053382

For Nicholas Tristan and Noah Alexander, keepers of the flame

WOLF

A SAM RIVERS MYSTERY

KILL

PART I

Beware of false prophets, who come to you in sheep's clothing, but inwardly are ravening wolves.

Matthew 7:15

CHAPTER ONE

The farmhouse stood 12 miles outside Defiance, Minnesota, at least as the common raven flew. The house was a compact two-story peaked square with peeling clapboard sides and a tar paper roof. Behind the house, a stand of red pines marked a short ridge and the start of wilderness that stretched 20-odd miles to the Canadian border. To the right of the house was a barn where three feeder calves huddled, protected against stray wolves and the deep cold. The field beyond the barn lay blanketed in fresh snow. It was January 26th, one of the coldest nights of the year.

Sheriff Dean Goddard and Deputy Smith Barnes turned into Williston Winthrop's farmhouse drive. The house was lit up like a Chinese lantern. The drive was long and narrow, and they pulled up and parked behind two trucks, an SUV, and Bill Heins's patrol car.

"Looks like a damn party," Barnes commented.

"That it does," Goddard agreed.

As they got out of their cruiser, Heins opened the farmhouse door, stepping into the cold. He was dressed for the weather, which was well below zero. Thankfully, there was no wind and the nearly full moon was high and clear. While Heins walked up the plowed path, the sheriff watched him zip up his policeman's jacket, then his down parka over the jacket. He flipped its hood over his short-cropped gray hair. The sheriff guessed Heins was near retirement; he hoped so, anyway.

"Sheriff," Heins nodded as he came forward.

"Heins," Goddard said. "You know Smith Barnes?"

"Sure," Heins said, nodding at Barnes.

The three men were tense in the cold. It wasn't just the weather, or the corpse beyond the house and barn. Heins, Defiance's town cop, had long made an effort to keep the sheriff out of Defiance's law enforcement affairs, which was fine by the sheriff, who had the rest of the county to patrol. The sheriff's office was 10 miles east of Defiance, in Vermilion Falls. There had been times a crime crossed borders, requiring the two men to work together, which neither did well nor enjoyed.

From the sheriff's point of view, Heins had never quite passed the smell test, and that was one reason why small-town cops were best limited to the narrow confines of their own town's borders, particularly when it was a Minnesota Iron Range town like Defiance. On more than one occasion, the sheriff had received complaints about the graying lawman. But he had been forced to back off when Winthrop interceded. Now that he thought about it, the only thing Goddard appreciated past midnight in cold like this was being rid of that son of a bitch Winthrop, if the reports were true. He would no longer have to worry about pulling his punches with Heins, providing Winthrop hadn't shared their little secret. What made the sheriff edgy was his doubt that the dead man had kept his word.

From up the road, another pair of headlights came over the rise. The three men watched a red Explorer approach and turn into the drive.

"Coroner," Goddard observed.

"You have headgear?" Heins asked Barnes. "It's over a quarter mile to the site."

"I got it," Barnes said.

Goddard was much taller and younger than Heins. He was also a better politician, having just won his second four-year term in a landslide. Barnes was long and wiry, lined in the face and lean in body. He still moved like a man half his age. He was the best investigative deputy on Goddard's staff, which is why he was the first person the sheriff contacted when the call had stirred him out of bed.

"Sounds like a hunting accident at Williston Winthrop's place," Goddard had said, still coming awake. "Not sure I know how to get there. You know the place?"

"I know," Barnes said.

Didn't sound like Barnes had been sleeping. It was almost 11 p.m.

"How bad?" Barnes asked.

"Winthrop's dead," Goddard managed. "I'll be over in 10 minutes."

The second person Goddard contacted was Dr. Susan Wallace, the coroner.

"Dr. Wallace?" he started.

There was a pause. "Hi," Wallace said, surprised and sounding sleepy.

"Business," he said, low. Belinda, Sheriff Goddard's wife, lay in the adjacent bedroom. Although it was late, she sometimes stayed up reading the Old Testament.

Then he told Wallace about Winthrop's accident.

"You don't think he . . . ," she started.

"No goddamn idea. Hard for me to believe a man like Winthrop would take his life. Even with the assistant DA breathing down his neck."

"I'll follow," she said.

He couldn't be sure, but he thought she sounded pleased.

Now Dr. Susan Wallace parked her Explorer behind the squad car. The three men waited while she stepped into the cold and zipped up her heavy down coat, pulling the hood over her head.

"Who's in the house?" Goddard asked.

"The club," Heins said.

"Card club?"

"Gun club, but mostly we play cards."

The sheriff nodded, remembering. "Remind me who's in it," he said.

"There's Hank Pederson, Hal Young, and Angus Moon. We were supposed to play cards tonight, over at Moon's place. Williston hasn't missed a game since I can't remember when. And no one heard squat. So after a couple hands of poker, we decided we'd better come have a look. Found his trail in the snow, his shotgun missing. Followed the trail out to the slough," Heins pointed. A well-trodden path turned around the barn, disappearing into the dark.

Wallace approached as the men looked toward the trail.

"Doctor," Goddard nodded.

"Sheriff," she said. "It's a cold night." She looked at Heins, then Barnes, nodding to each in greeting.

"Yes, it is," Barnes agreed. "You dressed for a hike?"

She nodded. "I guess."

"Let me take that," Barnes said, stepping forward to shoulder her bag.

"Thanks," she said with a smile.

Wallace had been an Iron Range doctor her entire professional career. A year ago Goddard recruited her to be the county's coroner, an effort he came to appreciate more than he'd expected. What he saw, when she wasn't bundled up and looking like a marshmallow, was a fit blonde just past 40 with a professional demeanor he had taken some time to crack. Goddard was still surprised by the absence of judgment that had, over the last six months, put him in the doctor's bed (or, at least on numerous occasions, a bed in the Vermilion Falls hotel), where they had finally decided they had something they could not live without.

The other club members decided to remain in Winthrop's farmhouse. The sheriff asked them not to leave; he'd have some questions later.

Past midnight the crime team hiked out to the narrow slough. Barnes brought along a sled they could use to return Winthrop to the doctor's Explorer for transport to her makeshift morgue. First, they would have to make a cursory examination of the scene and take some photographs.

Moonlight helped, though by the time they reached Winthrop's body, Goddard was ready for a rest. Barnes was barely breathing hard. Goddard noticed Wallace was in the same shape as Barnes, proof you could work 60 hours a week and still have time for exercise, providing you had the doctor's energy. Goddard was comforted by Heins's heavy exhalations, much like his own. Goddard wasn't Vermilion County's only out-of-shape law officer.

"Should have used the Cats," Goddard remarked, thinking snowmobiles would have made hauling the body back a hell of a lot easier.

"It'll be OK," Barnes assured.

Heins explained the scene. Winthrop had been hunting

snowshoe hare and approached the slough after last night's snowfall. There'd been a clear, solitary path to the heavy cover of this ravine, trampled over now by Heins and the others. They'd followed it to the fallen birch, searching for their poker partner. Just this side of the birch, Winthrop's body lay with his back in the snow. The front of his head was a bloody, grisly visage, frosted over and staring faceless into the night sky.

"That's a damn unfortunate accident," Barnes observed.

"Awful," Goddard agreed.

Wallace, familiar with death, had never before seen this kind of massive gunshot trauma. But she didn't look away.

Goddard took a minute to examine the scene. There was a wide area of trampled snow. The shotgun lay on the ground near the fallen birch, in front of Winthrop's body. Winthrop wore a heavy orange-camo down coat with orange-camo coveralls underneath, both frosted over in the cold. Goddard recognized the shotgun and coveralls. He'd seen both hanging in Winthrop's office last Sunday, when they'd had a meeting. Before Winthrop told him why he'd asked the sheriff to visit, Goddard had asked about the shotgun, which was oversized. Winthrop told him there were two, nicknamed the Decimators: 10 gauges handcrafted near the start of the 20th century, one of them missing, though the dead man claimed he knew who had it and swore he would get it back. Now Goddard guessed it didn't matter.

The sheriff didn't like to remember their meeting, where he had betrayed one friend to protect another. Now he might not be losing any more sleep over the dead man, providing Winthrop had kept his secret to himself. Goddard had been robbed of revenge, but under the circumstances he was willing to accept it.

"Did you check the pockets?" Goddard asked.

"We didn't touch anything," Heins said. "Once we saw there was no point."

The sheriff patted down the pockets, felt the outline of four shotgun shells. He felt inside, pulled them out, put them back. He unzipped the heavy down coat and saw a billfold bulge in the top right coverall pocket. He unbuttoned the pocket and extracted the billfold. Deputy Barnes held out a plastic bag and the sheriff dropped the billfold in. The rest of Winthrop's pockets were empty.

The entire scene looked like they'd walked into some kind of deep freeze. It was laid out exactly the way Heins had described it.

Goddard used a pair of heavy tongs to lift the shotgun out of the snow. "Damn big gun," he said.

Barnes helped him crack open the double-barrel and look inside. One shell fired, one ready. He sniffed around the opening. An acrid burn. The safety was set to off.

"One hell of a gun for snowshoe," Goddard observed.

"That gun's been in Williston's family for years," Heins explained. "You get anywhere near a hare, it drops it. The spray's so big only a few pellets usually hit, but it's plenty, coming from a gun like that."

"It's a wonder anything's left of a hare after a shot from a gun like that," said Barnes.

They retrieved what was left of the orange-billed hat from behind Winthrop's body. Barnes took the necessary photos, the brilliant flash illuminating the carnage and the trampled snow.

"You could have been more careful with the scene," Goddard said, turning to Heins.

"Sorry about that, Sheriff. All of us came out to find him. We were practically on top of him before we saw him. Then we rushed to his side before we knew what happened," Heins explained. He wasn't looking at Winthrop. He was contrite and solemn, which Goddard understood, given the presumed accidental death of one of Heins's oldest and closest friends.

There was no reason for Goddard to doubt the events, but it was hard not to feel they were peculiar, given what he knew. It wasn't only the hour, the cold, and the accident. He wondered if his disclosure of the subpoena's contents might have precipitated Winthrop's demise. He wasn't sorry to see the man dead. He was sorry to see the man escape justice. Winthrop, the sheriff guessed, had paid the ultimate price. But Assistant District Attorney Jeff Dunlap would be disappointed. Given the markings the heavy gun made as it slid along the birch bark and Winthrop's bulk lying frozen in the snow, Goddard wasn't going to push it. It was too damn cold, too late, and he was too tired. And when he stared at the body, he could not help but feel some measure of reprieve.

The hat's bill had been torn clean off. Barnes also examined the fallen birch and saw where the barrel had been leaned against the tree before Winthrop stepped over it. The dead man must have jostled the birch, causing the gun to slide across the bark and discharge. Looked like it, anyway. "Damn odd," he said.

"What?" Goddard asked.

"Man like Winthrop setting down a gun like that with the safety off."

"Probably saw a hare jump. Wanted to be ready," Heins suggested, reasonable enough.

"I guess," Goddard said.

"Can we turn him over?" Wallace asked. "I should at least try and figure out when this happened."

Goddard and Barnes bent over the frozen body. It turned over stiffly and awkwardly in the snow, as though they were flipping a fallen log. The dead man fell over with a heavy *whump*.

Goddard checked the back pockets and found three of the dead man's business cards—Williston F. Winthrop, Attorney at Law, with his office address in Defiance. There was nothing else on them. No writing. Nothing. Goddard added them to the bag with the billfold.

Wallace worked a long thermometer needle out of her bag. She tried to insert it through his lower back, trying to probe an internal organ so she could get an accurate temperature reading. She could use the dead man's internal body temperature to determine the approximate time of death. But the body was already frozen.

"Can't get it in," she said.

"Seem reasonable?" Goddard asked.

"In this cold?" she said. "Seems like the body's been here for more than 5 hours. It's like a deep freeze out here. That'd be enough time."

Goddard looked back to the body. "All right. Let's get him in that bag and put it on the sled."

The scene was clear enough. By the time they returned to the farmhouse, it was just after 2 a.m. When they approached, they noticed a Datsun pickup added to the covey of cars.

"The *Gazette*," Barnes said.

"That Diane's truck?"

"Looks like it," Barnes replied.

Diane Talbott, the *Vermilion Falls Gazette* reporter, was already inside the farmhouse interviewing the other members of the club. She'd just about finished when Goddard entered the house.

"Diane," he nodded.

"Hi, Sheriff."

"How'd you find out?"

"Couldn't sleep and I was out. Saw your patrol car. Then I saw Dr. Wallace's car. Looked official. Just a hunch," she said.

Over the last few months there had been too many hunches, Goddard thought. He suspected Diane was monitoring their official radio channel. Scanning wasn't illegal, but if the office knew she was scanning, they'd probably return to a stricter adherence to the use of codes, or start scrambling their signal. "You could get in trouble, following me around."

"Sorry, Sheriff. Just couldn't sleep." She managed a weak smile that told Goddard he'd have to keep an eye out for Diane Talbott.

Diane was one of those women Goddard's father described as "built like a brick icehouse," which meant she was strong and attractive, and had some style and a body that easily fired the imagination. For a woman around 50 who had spent most of her adult life on the Range, she was still surprisingly unaffiliated, which was to say without a man. Not that there weren't plenty of men who had tried. Some said she'd been known to party when she was young. But now she spent most of her time at her job, either for the *Gazette* or writing freelance, covering wilderness issues.

"OK if I take some notes?" she asked.

Goddard thought about it. "Winthrop have a next of kin?" he asked Heins.

"Not really," Heins said. "There was a son, some years back.

Disappeared. And you know Miriam died two years ago. Just us," he added, indicating the four club members in the room.

"All right," Goddard said, turning toward Diane.

Goddard spent the next 10 minutes taking the club members' statements. Hal Young was the local insurance agent. He was the same height as Angus Moon and Heins but different in stature and temperament. Heins was mean, but savvy enough to hide it. Moon was like a wolverine, wild as the woods he hunted, with a temper that could turn on a dime, the few times Goddard had crossed him. Young was a businessman, and other than being a member of the Iron County Gun Club, he was about as foursquare as a white cardboard box. Hank Pederson, an aging, self-professed ladies' man, owned the Ford dealership in Defiance. The four gun club members filled in the details—solemn, perhaps a little nervous, Goddard figured, because their lifetime friend had just met his grisly end, maybe from a self-inflicted gunshot wound, though none of them betrayed that suspicion. Regardless, incidents such as this one were sober reminders of one's own mortality.

They'd assembled for poker. When Winthrop didn't show, they came looking. And found him. They were quiet and grave in the poorly lit front room of Winthrop's farmhouse. They looked tired.

While Goddard spoke with the men, Heins and Barnes loaded Winthrop's body into the doctor's Explorer. Once he was finished in the house, Goddard gave Diane the details she'd need.

"Hunting accident," he said. "Massive head trauma. I'm sure you'll say it using more words, but that's the sum of it."

Diane nodded. "Thanks, Sheriff."

He nodded and turned away.

Once outside, Goddard approached the doctor's car.

"I can drive with you to the office, help you unload him and get him squared away, providing you can give me a lift home."

"No problem, Sheriff."

He thought maybe she sounded a little too eager, if anyone was listening. "Barnes," Goddard turned to his deputy. "Can you take the squad car and follow us over? You'll have to help me with this cargo, at least to unload it. Then you can take the cruiser home and the doctor'll give me a lift."

Barnes nodded. "See you there."

"Get your truck out of the road, Diane. Go home and get some sleep."

But she was already too preoccupied to think about sleep, contemplating the story she was about to write. Goddard knew he'd be reading about Winthrop's accident by morning.

Goddard knew Dr. Wallace hated icy roads, so he offered to drive. They got into their cars and started their engines in the cold. Then they turned toward Vermilion Falls.

For the first mile Goddard and Wallace rode in silence, following Diane's truck. Barnes followed them in the squad car.

"That was a horrible accident," Wallace finally observed, careful not to turn her head, so if the reporter glimpsed them in her rearview, she would think they were driving in silence. "But it could uncomplicate things."

Goddard exhaled as though trapped air were being let out of a bag. "Could," he said tersely, but clearly pleased.

"You think he mentioned it to anyone? Shared that video?"

"No way to know," he remarked, eyes carefully focused on the narrow lane in front of him. They were traveling over back roads. Winthrop's farmhouse was in one of the most remote areas of the county. On either side, dense wilderness closed in on the narrow lane.

"What are we going to do, Dean?"

"You're not going to do anything. I'm going to find that video." He paused, thinking. "If I know Winthrop, it's someplace safe. I'd bet his office or the farmhouse. But it's not going to be easy finding it."

"What about his house in Defiance? Miriam's old place?"

"Could be," Goddard guessed. They drove another half mile in silence. "I guess I'm going to have to sleep on it," he said, his hands gripping the wheel of the doctor's Explorer.

The doctor stared ahead, peering to where the edge of headlights disappeared into darkness. Goddard thought she was pondering the location of Winthrop's evidence when he felt her hand inch over and graze his right thigh.

He could feel the heat of it through his jeans.

"Maybe we should sleep on it together," she said.

CHAPTER TWO

By the time Sam Rivers arrived at the U.S. Fish & Wildlife office, Judy Rutgers's message had already been broadcast to a half-dozen coworkers needing a Monday morning chuckle. Rutgers was a sheep rancher who lived over 2 hours southeast of Denver, Colorado.

"This is Judy Rutgers," she blurted. "Last night one of my ewes was taken. A wolf! I got all the proof you'll need. And I'm sitting here with my rifle, hoping the cocksucker shows its ugly head. When it does, I'll be blowing it off."

There was a pause, during which Maureen, the office assistant, said, "Wait. She's not finished."

Sam's coworkers paused over Maureen's speakerphone.

"I'll give you 'til sundown to get out here and look, Rivers. Then I'm settin' traps." The line went dead.

"Sundown!" Maureen repeated, parroting Rutgers's rasp. The office broke into laughter.

Sam Rivers's appearance caused his coworkers to fade back to their desks.

"Morning, Sam," Maureen nodded.

"Maureen," he nodded back.

His sallow-rimmed eyes told her all she needed to know about his weekend. She'd keep it to business, but like the rest of the staff, she was waiting for an end to Rivers's depression. Or maybe for his transfer back to national field operations. "Judy Rutgers has issues again."

"I heard."

"What should I tell her?"

"Tell her I'll be out after noon. First I need to talk with Kay Magdalen, then finish some paperwork." He had received another troubling email he hoped Magdalen could help him track down. The anonymous emails came from a region and a past Sam thought he'd put behind him a long time ago.

"Should I see if Kay's in?"

"Her Outback's in the lot."

Maureen's ears tracked gossip like a pair of Doppler radars, and she had a mouth like a satellite radio, which is why Sam never shared anything with her. Maureen might have been the one to overhear the news about his dog, Charlie.

"That's two Kay Magdalen visits in less than a week," she said. "You sure you feel OK?"

Maureen was fishing. He almost never visited his old supervisor. "Clarence is a Rockies fan, and I have a lead on some tickets," he lied. When she didn't recognize the name, he added, "Clarence is Kay's husband. He and I go way back."

Truth is he and Kay Magdalen had worked together for more than a decade—when he was a national field agent—and he had never met Clarence.

Maureen nodded. "Oh. OK. I'll let Judy know you'll be there this afternoon."

"Thanks, Maureen." Then he turned and disappeared into his cubicle.

Charged with protecting and managing the nation's wildlife, the USFW had taken Sam Rivers, one of its best national field agents, into places no sane person would want to go. That is until a year ago, when his failing marriage and then his failing best friend—his dog, Charlie—prompted him to step down from the national spotlight to take a job in local investigations.

Five years earlier the *Denver Post* ran a Sunday feature on his work at the USFW, "Saving Endangered Species One Animal at a Time." The article recounted one of his most recent cases. Rare Florida deer were being annihilated from a section of the Florida Keys. Their total disappearance from an area they'd previously inhabited was suspicious. Sam investigated, and after some digging and a few lucky breaks, he discovered a small group of developers who believed concern for the Key deer, which the USFW estimated to number around 800 animals, was negatively impacting their development plans. They'd hired a south Florida hunter to rid the proposed development site of any trace of the small, endangered deer. And they would have succeeded, if the hunter hadn't begun selling Key deer skins, hooves, horns, and venison on the black market.

The article called Sam Rivers "the predator's predator," a moniker that stuck, at least within his office and the USFW. There was a picture of his 6'2" frame standing in front of the south Florida bulldozer he had single-handedly idled. His square shoulders and 195 pounds looked small in front of the huge shovel blade. But his greasy black hair, disheveled undercover clothes, and four days' beard growth made him look like the swamp rats he'd hunted. The article recounted how before it was all over, Sam had to fight his way out of a backwoods bar.

His then-wife, Maggie, had been proud of the *Denver Post*'s coverage. She cut out the photo and taped it to their fridge.

Magdalen was as surprised to see him as he was to be there. "You're coming back," she opined.

"Not exactly. Still thinking about it."

Magdalen was heading up the new interagency task force, and she wanted Sam back on her team. Magdalen had the demeanor of a truck driver and the appearance of a fullback, and she could bull her way through USFW law enforcement bureaucracy unlike anyone Sam had ever seen, which was a rare quality and just one of the reasons he liked her.

"It would do you nothing but good, Rivers."

"I suspect you're right. I just need a little more time."

He reached into his back pocket and pulled out a folded piece of paper, passed it across her desk. "Got another one of these last Friday."

Magdalen opened it. Another email from canislupustruth @yahoo.com. This one was short. "Soon," it said.

"Soon what?" she asked.

"Good question."

Sam had been receiving these messages for the last two years, spread out at least a month apart. They'd started after his mother died. The first he'd almost mistaken for spam. He still remembered it, because it was brief and personal. "Clayton?" it asked, in the subject line. The text of the message repeated the question using his full birth name: "Clayton Evan Winthrop?" That was all.

No one had called him Clayton Winthrop in years. He treated it the way he treated everything else from his childhood; he highlighted the message and pressed Delete. But the email address was interesting. *Canis lupus,* the scientific name for the gray wolf.

And then a few days later he'd received a second message. This one contained a single phrase in the subject line: "Seen this?" There was an attachment with the email. It was a copy of his mother's will, which he had never seen. It left everything to the old man. There was the house, car, the proceeds from a large life insurance policy, and the money Sam's mother had managed to save, a little over $179,000. Sam was surprised, both by his absence from her will and the size of her estate, which he'd always assumed would be meager.

He'd spoken with his mother just weeks before her end. He was comfortable with their parting. Sam always remembered her as an old-school wife. For years she had been largely estranged from the old man, living in separate residences. But there had never been talk of divorce. There was logic to her leaving everything to the old man. But Sam was still surprised.

Over the last two decades he and his mother had seen each other only a handful of times. But the absence of visits hadn't diminished their connection, such as it was. Though she'd been unable to stand up to Williston Winthrop, Sam considered his mother a positive influence in his life. He assumed he would be a beneficiary in her will, though they'd never discussed it. He wondered who had sent the will, and why. He immediately considered the old man, but then excluded him. Coy wasn't the old man's style. There was no good reason for the old man to be secretive or to send him a copy of the will. Why invite trouble, should Sam want to contest it?

Twenty years earlier Sam had fled west, changed his name, and disappeared. It had taken him more than a year to reach back out to his mom. And even then it was only by phone. Eventually he shared his new name and whereabouts, but he made it clear she should keep it in confidence.

He had not seen or spoken to Williston F. Winthrop since the day Sam had wreaked havoc in the heart of his farmhouse, letting the old man know how he felt about the Winthrop family heritage. Then he fled. But not before stealing one of the old man's precious Decimators.

There had been other cryptic messages. He began to wonder about them, so he recovered the first email from his deleted folder. Then, he'd created a folder—named Defiance, the name of the closest town to his childhood home—and dragged the messages into it one by one over the intervening months, where they remained unanswered.

This message, like all the others, was typically cryptic. He had printed off a copy to share with Magdalen. He wanted her to find out whatever she could about the sender. She had solid contacts in the USFW information technology group and he didn't want to draw a lot of attention to it. He just wanted to know about canislupustruth@yahoo.com. Where did he/she live? Where did the message come from?

"Sorry, Rivers," Magdalen said. "Another bizarre message isn't going to change anything. I'm sure it's annoying, but until something more specific happens, like maybe a threat, there's nothing IT can do about it."

She told him what he'd expected. Yahoo guarded the privacy of its members like Fort Knox gold. Truth was, given the ease with which Yahoo email accounts were set up, a person could easily register an email using a bogus name and address.

"IT tells me the only thing that they might be able to tell you," Magdalen added, "would be the identity of the computer from which it was sent. But that would take some work, backtracking through code, IP addresses, proxy servers, and plenty of email traffic, whatever that means. Nothing they'd even think about without a warrant."

"I thought these people were your friends?"

"Colleagues, Rivers. We don't have friends. I know them well enough. And if I wanted to push it, I could probably get them to look into it without a warrant, see what they could find out. But this is personal," Magdalen said. "You know how the service is about using resources for personal stuff."

Her answer was bullshit and they both knew it. The flash of a badge enabled an agent to cut to the head of a line or get some free doughnuts and coffee, and Sam had seen it used countless times, had occasionally used it himself. Magdalen knew what he was thinking.

"The last time I checked," she said, "personal annoyance wasn't enough for a judge to grant a warrant." Then, "What's keeping you from coming back?"

She was dangling a carrot. If he told her he was coming back to national field ops to be part of her interagency task force, she might spend a little of her IT capital to help him.

"Not ready."

She considered him for a long few seconds. "You know what you need?"

"No idea."

"You need to take some time off. Maybe head over to Las Vegas. It's probably been a while since you've had your . . . ," she paused, wondering how to say it. "Your pipes cleaned out. You should take some time. You've got plenty of vacation built up. I've seen your file. If you don't take it before the end of the year, you'll lose some of it."

"Are you telling me I should buy a whore?"

She looked away, a little miffed by his crass characterization. "I think it's more of a rental fee. Personally, I find it morally repugnant. But men feel different about these things."

Truth was, his appetite for sex had left with Maggie. He knew it would return. But hiring a hooker was about as far from his mind as vacationing in Cancun.

"I think I'll pass."

"Just saying," she said, but left it there. Then she handed the paper back.

Sam returned it to his back pocket and stood up. "If I came back on the team, would you use your IT contacts to find out what you could about canislupustruth?"

Magdalen looked at him, considering. "Who knows? Teams are funny things. If a team member is going through a rough spot and it impacts the organization, then from my perspective it makes sense to do whatever you can to help out."

Sam thought about pushing it, but he had his answer. She could get IT to look into it if she wanted, but until he decided to come back and work for her, she wasn't going to expend the capital to get it done. He turned to leave, and then remembered.

"If you happen to run into Maureen down in local investigations and she asks, Clarence and I are old friends and I got him tickets to the Rockies game this coming Saturday," Sam said.

"Rockies? Clarence has never been to a baseball game in his life. You've never even met him."

"I know. And I'm not taking it personally."

She grinned. "Whatever, Rivers. I'll cover for you. Just get your head on straight. We can't wait forever."

CHAPTER THREE

The "dead" man walked out of the cabin and paused, listening for Moon's approach. In his right hand he held a .45 caliber pistol. The first thing he noticed was the cold, probably 20 below in the shadow of these trees. He listened carefully but heard nothing. Maybe a little wind through the pine tops, but you could never tell—they were bunched so tightly here, the cabin hidden in their midst.

The man knew he would hear Moon's approach along the swamp edge. Now he hustled down the path, searching for a place to hide.

Almost 24 hours earlier the man had snowshoed across Skinwalkers Bog. It was a 2-mile hike, and unless you knew where you were going and how to get there, the trip would probably be your last in this kind of cold. He had reached the cabin after dark, let himself in, shook out the cold, and fired up the pot-bellied stove. Then he switched on the CB radio and scanner but heard nothing until the call to dispatch around midnight, from the sheriff's cruiser. There had been two calls: one by the sheriff telling dispatch where he was headed and why, and one on the way back, from Barnes, telling the office they were finished and returning. That was around 2 a.m., but the man only half heard it. By then he was dead drunk, celebrating with three-quarters of a fifth of rye.

Damn good thing Moon was bringing more supplies, he thought.

Now he stepped carefully over yesterday's tracks, weaving through the thick wood for a little more than 100 feet until he stopped again to listen. Nothing. Just wind, at the tree edge. He could see the intense afternoon sunlight through the perimeter's boughs. He stepped forward, using the pistol's barrel to part the branches, and peered across the frozen swamp.

No sign of Moon . . . yet. He leaned back, concealing himself, and waited. It was a full minute before he remembered to cock his weapon. If he waited until Moon passed through the tree edge, the wary woodsman would hear it and be warned. He pulled back the trigger until it clicked and held. Then he listened again, but it was still quiet. Now he just tried to remain still.

The appearance of the vagrant James T. "Jimbo" Beauregard happened less than a week ago. Jimbo's entrance triggered a series of events that happened so quickly that the dead man's head still spun. Since then, he'd been looking forward to spending some time alone at the club's cabin.

The cabin was in the heart of a remote tract of wilderness the Ojibwe had always avoided, probably because it was so covered over by swamp, bush, and mosquitoes that it was no place to hunt. Even deer had trouble navigating there. The Iron County Gun Club managed to build a secret, remote cabin in the center of it. And to keep it secret the club members promoted the name Skinwalkers Bog, reporting that the American Indians stayed out of it because within its 10-mile-square tract of swamp, strange things occurred. Never mind that Skinwalker was actually a Navajo myth from the American Southwest. The club thought Skinwalker sounded a whole lot better than Wendigo, an Ojibwe evil spirit. So they appropriated the name for their own purposes, and it stuck.

In the summer the terrain was impassable. In the winter, not much better.

But by early afternoon the man started feeling stir-crazy. The morning hadn't been a complete waste. He'd spent some serious time contemplating future moves, and he'd come up with something so compelling and perfect that it was an inspiration, in keeping with their latest spate of good fortune. No one had seen Jimbo coming. He'd stumbled into Defiance, broke, freezing, and ready to do anything for a meal and a warm bed. Heins took one look at him and recognized the opportunity.

But no one else would see this opportunity. Jimbo had been a sacrificial lamb. It would take some work and getting the other club members to recognize that his feeder calves could also be sacrificial. What he needed was to make one of them believe it was their idea. And he thought he had figured out how.

Now he stood hidden at the tree edge, his pistol raised and ready, waiting for Moon. Finally, he heard movement across the snow.

Moon snowshoed through the brittle sunlight, skirting a rare stretch of open swamp, searching among the ancient stumps for the dark entrance where the path turned off into tree-covered shadows. Moon didn't like hiking into the bog in the middle of daylight. He preferred coming late in the day, or under cover of darkness.

The club members were careful about approaching the cabin. Starting in the full light of a clear afternoon, even though the temperature had only climbed to −15°, was risky. Someone might see where Moon had turned off the highway onto an old logging road. If they followed the tracks, they'd find his truck more than a quarter mile up the path, concealed in a stand of black spruce. But they'd have to hike it, Moon thought, since he was always careful about relocking the heavy-gauge chain that stretched across the logging road entrance, padlocked at one end. Someone'd need a bolt cutter to remove it, Moon knew, which is why he wasn't too worried about it.

He was more irritated about Winthrop's goddamn calves. Now that Winthrop was gone, the chore of tending his livestock fell on Moon. He had to check on them twice a day. This morning he'd fed them and made sure the propane tank heater was still on and operational. The arctic wind sometimes blew it out and froze the tank solid. He would have to check on it later, on his way back, and Moon didn't much care for the extra labor. Tending to his own dogs was about as much work as the old woodsman wanted.

Few people knew it, but Moon's most ambitious venture involved hybridizing wolf dogs. He'd brought a powerful Arctic wolf down from Canada. The wolf killed two malamute bitches before he took one for a mate.

In some states, breeding wolf dog hybrids was illegal. But in Minnesota, breeding and selling them was a legitimate business, though there were few who pursued it because wolf dog hybrids could be problematic pets, if not outright dangerous. Moon didn't care. He charged the out-of-state breeders $1,500 a mutt but made sure the transaction was confidential. He was careful about his work and happy for the supplement to his meager income. But he chafed against even the minimal work his breeding operation required. Now, for instance, he would have to drop off supplies, have a drink, and then gather himself for the hike out. Calves and dogs, they were pissing him off.

He was familiar enough with the cabin path to snowshoe without thinking. His short, bandy legs knew the way. Besides, he was damn close and getting thirsty. Whiskey'd take the edge off. Now he pushed through a swale of pine boughs, pausing just beyond its edge to let his eyes grow accustomed to the shadows.

When the waiting man heard Moon approaching, he positioned himself carefully amid the tree boughs. He raised the gun in both hands, holding it straight out in front of him. Moon came through the tree edge and stopped.

The man adjusted the pistol's aim so that it focused on the center of Moon's hood-covered head, less than 3 feet away. Then he pulled the trigger.

The hollow metal ping made Moon jump like a snowshoe hare startled by a lynx. He jerked, grunting, and then turned to see Winthrop aiming the pistol at his head.

"You're a dead man, Angus Moon," Winthrop said, laughing.

"You could get killed, pullin' a stunt like that!"

The pistol dropped to Winthrop's side. "I'm already dead," he said.

For half a second Moon's eyes flashed.

Winthrop saw it, and added, "Take it easy, Angus. I was getting bored and needed a little fun."

Moon looked away, still pissed.

"Let's go get a drink," Winthrop said.

Once inside the cabin Winthrop poured them both a full tumbler of cheap rye. They drank it off in one long swallow and Winthrop refilled their glasses.

"So how'd it go?" Winthrop asked. He could see the whiskey was working.

"The paper's out," Moon finally said. "Already got a story."

"The paper's already covered it?"

"That Talbott bitch was at the farmhouse last night, askin' questions."

"With the sheriff?"

"Came after, when the sheriff was out lookin' at the body."

"That's interesting."

"Talbott must've seen the patrol car," Moon guessed.

"Maybe. But that's good. We're ahead of schedule."

Moon pulled the *Vermilion Falls Gazette*, followed by three cans of chili and two more bottles of whiskey, out of his bedraggled pack. Moon got settled and had another good long drink, feeling the pleasant burn.

"Who all checked on the body?"

"The sheriff, Heins, Barnes, and Doc Wallace."

"Sounds like a goddamn convention."

"Heins said everything went off like clockwork."

"Did they take the Decimator?"

"Took the shotgun back to the morgue with Jimbo's body."

Less than a week earlier, Heins had found Jimbo holed up in the abandoned rail station on the outskirts of Defiance. He was a bum, on his way north to work in his sister's café, somewhere up in Canada. Heins liked rolling bums, but the first thing he noticed about Jimbo was his look; except for the face, he could have passed as Winthrop's twin. The face was definitely different, but the club finally figured out how to fix it, and they did. Moon had pulled the Decimator's trigger, removing the front of Jimbo's skull.

"You make sure to get the Decimator back," Winthrop said.

"Course," Moon said.

"Did they check the pockets?"

"Heins said so. Took your wallet and some business cards from a back pocket."

"Perfect. I won't be needing that license anymore. Or the cards," Winthrop laughed. Then he picked up the paper. It was column one, front-page news in the *Gazette*.

Local Attorney Dies in Hunting Accident
Diane Talbott
Vermilion Falls Gazette, Jan. 27

Vermilion Falls—Williston Francis Winthrop, 62, of Rural Route 3, died Sunday evening of a single gunshot wound to the head, the victim of an apparent hunting accident. Winthrop was hunting alone on his rural acreage when he leaned his shotgun against a fallen tree. As he straddled the tree to step over it, the shotgun slid down the log and discharged.

The shooting was reported to the sheriff's office at approximately 11 p.m. Sunday by friends of the deceased. The friends, all members of the Iron County Gun Club, went searching for the late attorney when he failed to appear for their scheduled card game.

Vermilion County Sheriff Dean Goddard and coroner Dr. Susan Wallace said the full coroner's report would be released pending further investigation and consultation with the county attorney's office.

Winthrop was a well-known Iron Range attorney and hunting rights advocate. One of his recent high-profile efforts was ardent opposition to Minnesota's Wolf Management Plan. In several public comment hearings Winthrop argued that wolves had returned to the state in sufficient numbers to have them removed from the List of Endangered and Threatened Wildlife. He noted that wolf depredation of livestock and pets was on the rise, and he believed it was only a matter of time before wolves attacked a human. His most controversial recommendation was to reinstate wolf bounties, a population control method not used in the state since 1965. His suggestion was never seriously considered.

Williston Winthrop was preceded in death by his wife, Miriam Winthrop, also of Defiance. He is survived by a son. Funeral services pending.

He smiled when he reached the end. "Goddamn," Winthrop said. "I'd say she just about nailed it. Except for the part about my suggestion to return to wolf bounties."

Moon had read the article, but quickly, just to make sure there was nothing worrisome. "What?" he asked.

"She got the stuff about being opposed to that goddamn wolf-management plan about right. But she says here my 'suggestion to reinstate wolf bounties was never seriously considered.'" Winthrop scoffed, smacking the paper with his hand. "There are plenty who think it's a good idea. And if I'd lived long enough, I would have seen it through."

"Damn straight," Moon agreed.

"I forgot Talbott knew my son," Winthrop said.

"We wondered about it."

"Nothing to wonder about. The kid doesn't matter. He won't do anything. It's been 20 years. Even if he found out about my death and returned, there wouldn't be a goddamn thing he could do about my estate. Heins'd take care of the boy."

The two men sat for a while, sipping whiskey, talking about plans.

"We still have scores to settle," Winthrop finally said.

Moon grunted, already thinking about his hike out. The afternoon light was starting to settle, and those goddamn calves would be waiting for more feed.

"You tend the calves?" Winthrop inquired, knowing the woodsman hated the job.

"Course," Moon said, displeased.

"They still fat 'n' happy?"

"Big," Moon said. "Eat too much. Sooner we sell 'em, the better."

"They're not quite ready."

In years past Winthrop sold off the animals and used the butchering proceeds to keep the club in beef. But this year was going to be different. "It'll be a while," he answered, reminding the woodsman his labors would not end soon. "Meanwhile you'll need to check on 'em. Twice a day."

"I know it," Moon snapped.

"Morning and night," Winthrop said. "Now that they're just about ready, I don't want wolves coming in to take them."

"Wolves?" Moon knew wolves, and they'd never enter a barn.

"Wolves," Winthrop mused. "Now that no one's around, those vermin might see opportunity."

"No wolves gettin' into a barn."

"Just because they haven't done it yet doesn't mean they won't. You sound like the DNR. Wolves don't give a rat's ass where their meal comes from. If it's easy and available and there's nothing to stop them, they'll take it. They're vile opportunists."

"You know damn well I'm no friend of the DNR. But Williston, wolves don't go into barns and take cows. Just don't happen."

"Yet," Winthrop returned. "If wolves came in and took 'em, one thing's for damn sure. It'd shake up the DNR. And Fish &

Wildlife. Teach 'em these vermin are getting out of control."

"Like to see that."

Winthrop paused. "What if there was a way to lure some in and set 'em loose? We'd teach every tree hugger in the state these wolves are hell-bent on destruction." He waited for the woodsman to catch on.

"Wolves don't lure. Not into a barn."

"It's only a matter of time."

Winthrop let Moon think about it. It didn't take long.

"We should let my dogs have at 'em," Moon said.

And that was Winthrop's plan. Moon's hybrids looked and acted enough like wolves to be the real thing. And Winthrop had witnessed the wolf dogs' work, tracking down wounded deer and keeping them pinned until Moon gave the signal. They were accomplished killers.

Moon considered. "I know damn well what we gotta do." He stood up and moved over to pull his coat off the nearby peg. "First, I'll make sure those fatlings are fed and watered. Then I'll get back to my place. And nail every one of my dogs into their houses. Give them nothin' but water for a couple days. Get them good and hungry."

"Radio forecasts a big storm Wednesday night," Winthrop said.

"Good night for poker," Moon said.

"We could crate them up at your place and take them over to the farm. Then let them loose . . . after poker. If it's coming down as hard as they predict, nobody'll be out in it."

"Except us," Moon said. "And our wolves."

CHAPTER FOUR

J ust after 4 p.m. Sam pulled into Judy Rutgers's gravel drive. The sky was clear, with the sun starting to drop into the distant mountain ridge. Sam recognized the woman's large silhouette in her living room window.

Sam and Rutgers were both members of a citizen wolf-management committee. The USFW created it to provide a platform for ranchers to air their opinions and be heard. Rutgers wasn't shy about sharing her perspectives. But she was disappointed that few of her arguments were sufficient to move anyone at the USFW, or to change service regulations.

Her front door swung open and the substantial Ms. Rutgers, cradling a Marlin 336, stepped out. She wore a faded work shirt over an anemic red T-shirt. The work shirt hung blouselike over her large, barrel-shaped middle. There was nothing fragile about Judy Rutgers. Her arms were as stout as stove wood and her oversized legs disappeared into a pair of well-worn cowboy boots. Carrying the rifle, she looked menacing. But Sam knew it was more bluster than blow.

Sam turned to the cargo space of his Jeep and extracted his camera bag.

"'Bout time, Rivers," she said, her voice like a distant chainsaw. "I called your office this morning."

"Judy," Sam replied, nodding. "Came out as soon as I could. I was under the impression you had plenty of evidence. And we both know a wolf, if that's what it is, wouldn't return in daylight."

"If it was a wolf!" Her round face started to turn crimson.

"Goddammit, Rivers, you know me. You know I wouldn't call if I wasn't 100% certain it was a wolf."

Sam had his doubts, but that would heat her blood to a boil. "You've read the latest wolf population report. U.S. Fish & Wildlife made a careful census of Colorado."

"Don't tell me about that goddamn report," she interrupted.

Sam paused, turning to look at the distant Front Range, hazy in the late afternoon. From here the mountains looked far off, inviting. Rutgers needed time to cool.

The report he referenced was USFW's annual Rocky Mountain Wolf Recovery Report. Since Sam had relegated himself to remaining local, he'd spearheaded the effort to research and write the new report. It detailed Colorado's wolf population, which was practically nonexistent. There were a few places on the western fringe of the state where wolves were starting to repopulate, but those were far from Judy Rutgers's ranch.

Like many livestock owners, Rutgers had an expert's eye for tracking and sorting through the remnants of a kill to determine what had done it. It was possible a wolf, one of those on a walkabout from a western pack, had come into her flock, though its appearance this far east would be unusual. A lone wolf's range could carry it hundreds of miles in just a few days. If she had read the report, she would have noticed that just last year a wolf was struck by a car 30 miles west of Denver. It had been collared, and the most recent tracking data indicated it had covered 446 miles in less than two weeks. Wolves were marathoners of the highest order.

"The report's pretty specific," Sam finally said. Even though her tongue was as coarse as a truck driver's, he liked Judy Rutgers but didn't care for how she felt about his reportorial efforts.

"Goddammit," she said, this time a little softer. "Don't mess with me, Rivers. I've got enough to deal with just runnin' this place."

True enough. A sentiment that plenty in wildlife management were reluctant to admit.

Rutgers stepped around the corner of her house. "Let's go have a look, Rivers."

They hiked out to the gulch. Sticking close to the house, paddock, and barn, sheep grazed in the waning sun. At the ditch's edge Rutgers pointed, then started down toward a small hollow rimmed with scrub oak.

They rounded a bend of head-high brush. They were still 20 yards above the hollow. The side of the hill was open and there were clear signs of a struggle.

"Here's where he took her." Judy pointed to the dry ground.

There were few things that could focus Sam Rivers's attention like a prey site. The grass was broken and the earth torn up in two or three places. There was a dark splash of something that looked like axle grease. Sam stepped carefully to the stained ground and peered at it, suspecting it was blood. He dabbed two fingers onto the spot; it was dry, but sticky. He smelled it. Wet iron. Five feet downhill there was a scrub oak thicket, the perfect hiding place. Sam imagined the predator waiting in the brush until the ewe grazed close, then springing. A big wolf could finish the job in less than 10 seconds. But so could a cougar. He looked for other signs, but found only dirt from the scuffle and blood. "Tell me there's more than this."

"Oh hell yes." Rutgers turned and started down the hill toward the bottom of the gulch. They bushwhacked through heavy scrub oak. When they pushed through the brush edge, their racket startled three birds that rose squawking in the dusk light.

"Ravens," Sam said, watching them rise into the afternoon light. He paused to watch their loping wingbeats carry them over the ridgeline.

"Goddamn scavengers," Rutgers said.

The ravens were a good sign. Ravens were sometimes known to follow wolves. And it meant there was still evidence.

In the narrow opening they found what was left of the ewe. Her gaping throat had the look of a wolf kill, Sam thought. Something had fastened on and tore. Coyotes dart and nip, usually at the flanks or hindquarters. They seldom made frontal attacks, particularly on a full-grown ewe in a flock. Cougars dropped or leaped onto their prey, raking its back while trying to break its neck. This ewe had her under throat torn away in one deep gash. Wolf. He was pretty sure. The hindquarters and entrails were largely missing. Last night's dinner, Sam guessed. Or a very early breakfast.

Rutgers made a wide sweep around the ewe, carefully picking over the ground. "I think you'll find some good prints over here," she said, pointing to the bush edge.

Sam looked down, pulling his camera out of the bag. He took off the lens cap and bent over the prints. There were two pairs, the front and hind paws. The pairs overlapped, as though each foot attempted to step inside the footprint made in front of it. Coyote prints were similar in position, but much smaller: 2.5 inches in length or less. Wolf prints were 4.5 inches in length or more. Certain large breeds of feral dog could approach the size of a wolf's print, but they were usually set much farther apart. Sam had seen hybridized animals, wolves crossed with dog breeds that made them practically indistinguishable from full-blooded wolves. But these prints appeared to be the real thing.

Affixed to the camera was a 200-millimeter macro lens. He paused over each print, focusing the lens. He was almost certain it was a wolf. But he noticed the prints were a little small, and the observation caused his pulse to increase. He reached into his bag and pulled out an 8-inch photo scale. He placed the ruler next to the print, then bent over, focused, and snapped. These prints were just over 3 inches in length, including their claws. He took a couple more shots and placed the ruler perpendicular to the print, repeating the action with the camera.

"That's interesting, Judy."

"What?" She didn't like his tone.

"Any hair?"

She turned around the carcass and pointed to where a tuft marked the sharp end of an oak branch. Sam closed the space between them, reaching into the satchel and extracting a plastic ziplock bag.

"Let's step careful. I think we want this one to return. Any other prints?" he asked.

"Just these. But they should be enough," she said defensively. "We want him back so we can shoot the sucker," she added.

"Take it easy, Judy. I'll issue you a shoot-on-sight permit, no questions asked. And if it's a Rocky Mountain wolf, you have the government's blessing to take the animal down."

"It's a wolf, Rivers," she affirmed.

Sam paused, absorbed in his work. "Yeah," he finally said. "It's a wolf." But he was intent on the hair.

He bent down with the camera, focused the lens on the hair tuft, and took several shots in rapid succession. Then he placed the tuft into the bag, careful to keep it clean. "I have good news and bad news," he said. "Which would you like first?"

"The good news better be full reimbursement. The bad news is the bastard got away."

"That is the good news," he said. "You'll receive full compensation. The evidence is substantial. Prints too big for a coyote, and this hair," he said, holding up the bag in the fading sunlight, examining it. "It's got some red in it.

"Unfortunately, that's a disturbing feature. That, and the prints over there," he said, pointing to the wolf prints.

"What about 'em?"

"A typical Rocky Mountain wolf, particularly a lone hunter on walkabout searching for a mate to start a pack, would have a paw length over 4 inches. Coyotes aren't even close to 3 inches. This one's right in between. Could be a coyote-wolf mix. There is a remote chance it could be a Mexican wolf, slightly smaller than the Rocky Mountain or Great Plains subspecies. A very rare Mexican wolf," Sam said.

Rutgers was just happy it was a wolf. "So what's the bad news?"

"It may be a Mexican wolf."

"You said that."

He looked at her carefully. "There are around 150 of them throughout the Southwest, at least that we know of," he explained. "One this far north and east would be unusual, but not impossible." He continued, watching her. Clearly she didn't understand. "This subspecies isn't threatened," he said. "It's endangered."

There was a pause before recognition and outburst. "Oh for Chrissake!"

"Judy," Sam started.

"I don't give a shit. If that wolf takes another ewe and I'm anywhere near it, it's a dead wolf. A dead Mexican wolf."

"That could be a problem, Jude."

"I don't give a rip, Rivers. And you know I'll do it." She was blistering, her fists clenched.

U.S. Fish & Wildlife was doing everything it could to cultivate Mexican gray wolves. Sam had never heard of one this far north and east. Never in Colorado. But given wolves' loping gaits, long legs, ultrathon capabilities, and drive to find a proper mate, it could happen. Judging from the animal's morphology, it looked promising. But morphology, the art of discerning a species from its physical characteristics, was always dubious. He would have to send a hair sample to the USFW forensics lab in Ashland, Oregon, just to be sure. DNA tests would give him a definitive answer. But it would take time. And meanwhile Rutgers would be waiting with her Marlin 336.

Sam knew Rutgers could cross the line. She didn't give a damn about Mexican wolves, only that they were taking her stock. He liked her, but her perspective on wolves was shortsighted. "You shoot it, you pay," he said evenly. "Might even do some time."

"You mean he gets to live?" she asked, incredulous.

"If he's a Mexican wolf, he's too rare to kill, Judy. We've got to keep him alive. We can use him."

"To make more of these ewe-killing devils?"

"I've got a claim form back in the Jeep," Sam said. "No question about compensation," he added. But Rutgers wasn't mollified.

Before Sam left, he completed the USDA's Wolf Depredation Compensation Claim form. She'd get a check in the mail in just a few days. It would probably be a few days after that before she calmed down enough to thank him. This time Rutgers needed a little extra time to cool.

One of Sam's favorite aspects of fieldwork, particularly when it involved a prey site, was how investigations engaged him. His absorption was instantaneous. His senses calmed and he focused, his blood coming alive. The act itself was one of forgetting, of putting the pain of his recent past behind him, of ignoring headache and heartache until the details of an investigation totally absorbed him.

By the time Sam returned to Yellow Rock, it was after dark. He walked into his unlit townhouse, tired and hungry. After pouring himself a glass of wine, he fired up his laptop and started checking emails.

He read more than 30 messages, mostly office work to be addressed. Then he found two messages that focused his attention like a face slap: an attachment from canislupustruth@yahoo.com and something from dianetalbott@gmail.com. He recognized the name of his mother's friend, but the subject line—Williston Winthrop is dead—sucked all the air out of the room. The old man was dead?

"Sorry for the blunt message. In the event anything happened to your father, your mom wanted me to tell you. She gave me your email address . . . hope it still works.

"It's been a long time, Sam. I'm sure you remember the times you and I paddled your mother into the Boundary Waters for some R&R and a good fish dinner. I have missed her these two years. She was a great friend with a heart the size of a kettledrum and enough kindness for the whole world and everything in it—even, inexplicably, your father.

"Before she died she made me promise that if anything happened to Williston, I was to let you know. She knew you wouldn't come home if he was still alive. She wanted me to remind you about the things you left in her house, things she wanted to make sure you recovered."

Sam remembered. His mother had told him as much before she died. And it was true. He would never return home as long as the old man was alive.

"She said she'd added to them since you'd left, and you must come home and get them. I wish I could tell you more, but I think that was the sum of it.

"For what it's worth, Williston was never able to sell her home and it's still sitting vacant.

"Your mom told me some of the details of why you disappeared and changed your name. I didn't like your father before I learned about it. Afterward, I liked him even less.

"Now you can come back for a visit, Sam Rivers. When you do, please stop by. Here's a link to the business about your father.

"Oh, and his funeral will be at 3 p.m., February 1, Defiance Lutheran Church. Interment 4 p.m., Defiance Cemetery, in case you wanted to attend.

"All the best,

"Diane Talbott"

Sam remembered every detail about what he and his mother had hidden in her house, minutes before he fled. And she'd added to it? He couldn't imagine what, wasn't really sure it mattered, though he was definitely curious.

He clicked on the link and opened an article to the online version of the *Vermilion Falls Gazette*. He'd forgotten Diane was a reporter.

Local Attorney Dies in Hunting Accident
Diane Talbott
Vermilion Falls Gazette, Jan. 27

Sam stared at the screen and reread the article twice, in disbelief. A hunting accident?

He remembered his mother's friend Diane. She was closer to Sam's age than his mother's. When they canoed into the Boundary Waters, Sam was around 15 and Diane probably in her late 20s. He had been impressed by her ability to paddle and by her appearance. He couldn't help admiring the woman, who was both wilderness savvy and attractive.

After his last battle with the old man, Sam stayed away from Defiance because you never knew when a man like Williston Winthrop would make good on his promise to charge him with attempted murder and make it stick.

Sam returned to his email and opened the message from canislupustruth. This time there was no note, only an attachment. He opened the PDF and read "Will & Testament" printed across its top. It was a copy of the old man's will. The list of items included the 300-acre farm, all of the farm's machinery, three feeder calves still in the barn, one truck, a car, his mother's house (apparently vacant), and her car. And money, lots of it.

The old man had over $2.3 million in various TD Ameritrade accounts, and over $50,000 distributed throughout money market, checking, and savings accounts at the Vermilion Falls State Bank. An additional $2.5 million term life policy was listed in his father's name. Everything else was tied up in personal property. Winthrop's signature was dated almost two years earlier, not long after Sam's mother's death. At the line marked BENEFICIARY(IES) he had written: "The members of the Iron County Gun Club, to be divided equally: Angus Moon, Bill Heins, Hank Pederson, and Hal Young."

Sam was shocked by the size of the old man's estate. Maybe legal work on Minnesota's Iron Range was more lucrative than he'd imagined. More likely, the old man had figured out a scheme for bilking clients.

The absence of his own name on the list of beneficiaries was no surprise. Sam Rivers's connection to the old man had ended with their last disagreement, the one that broke three of Sam's ribs and knocked him sprawling into North Dakota's emptiness.

Why would the old man carry a $2.5 million policy on himself? For the benefit of his club? They'd been that close? Sam remembered their frequent meetings, their out-of-season hunting excursions, even their talk of building a remote, isolated cabin in Skinwalkers Bog.

The man who'd suggested reinstating wolf bounties—that was the man Sam remembered. He could imagine the old man standing at a public hearing and arguing, vociferously, that wolves should be delisted, hunted, even exterminated. Bring back the bounties.

Winthrop's perspective was a minority opinion, but there were plenty who shared it.

Sam leaned back from the computer screen, contemplating

his mysterious messages from canislupustruth. After a while, he refreshed his glass of wine. Then he took a dinner out of the freezer—a bachelor's simple repast—and stuck it into the microwave. While the timer wound down, he leaned back against his kitchen counter, sipping more wine and recalling scenes from his childhood.

He remembered the way the old man cooked breakfast. He remembered his fixation on hunting, and the way he instilled in Sam, who did not have the heart for it, hunting's commandments.

"Surprise," the old man said, "is what you hunt. Not the animal. Look for the unexpected place they feel secure, where you can smell it in their blood."

"You've got to put it down," the old man told him, on one of the occasions he'd tried to teach him trapping. They were laying baits around foothold traps on the outside of a wolverine's den. The rancid meat smelled awful, and Sam turned up his nose and held it at arm's length.

"If you don't put it down, they won't come around. The worse it smells, the better. Distracts them from the traps."

It was one of many things the old man tried to teach him. And though Sam was a capable student and learned the lessons easily, he chose not to use them, at least for the kind of trapping the old man pursued. But he was surprised by how easily he recalled the lessons.

His father's death was sudden and unexpected. It was amazing how a single afternoon could change life suddenly, entirely.

The microwave's ding brought him back to his kitchen. He took out dinner and set it aside to cool. Then he returned to Diane's message.

"Thanks for the information," he wrote. He thought about what else to say. "I hope you're well," he concluded.

Then, "More, later."

"—Sam"

He dialed his supervisor. At the voice mail's beep he told her he needed to take some time off, but he'd make sure Rutgers's place was tended in his absence. He thought he'd be back in a week.

The funeral wasn't for four more days. He thought he might like to be there when the old man was dropped into frozen ground. He'd enjoy seeing the look on the club members' faces. If they were still the raw group of outdoorsmen he remembered, he would relish making them squirm. They had been the kind of men who would harass anyone they thought might threaten their claim to the old man's estate. If his father had ever filed an attempted murder charge against Clayton Winthrop (Sam's childhood name), Heins would have reason enough to give him trouble. But Sam never heard about any charges, and besides, the difference between Sam Rivers and Clayton Winthrop was 20 years and a lifetime.

Sam knew Northern Minnesota weather could be dicey this time of year. He checked his weather app. A major winter storm was forecast for Wednesday. That gave him plenty of time to drive to Defiance. And a storm in the middle of the night could be perfect cover. If nothing much had changed in Defiance, it could work.

For the first time in a long while, Sam was looking forward to first light.

CHAPTER FIVE

The five men walked out of Angus Moon's cabin into the woods where the dogs' houses stood. It was late Wednesday, January 29, and the weather was beginning to turn. Winthrop held the lantern. The others followed him up the ice-covered path through the trees. When they reached the houses, Winthrop peered into the black sky. A few thick snowflakes filtered down through the lantern's light.

"It's starting," Winthrop said.

"Gonna be a hell of a storm," Moon said.

"It just gets better and better," Pederson said, chuckling.

They'd spent the evening in Moon's remote cabin, playing cards and being liberal with the juice, waiting for midnight and the forecast onset of the storm. The wind-driven pines and the first light dusting of white told them it was time. Now Winthrop carried the lantern into the wooded enclosure. He lifted it to show the first dog's house, then turned to look at Moon.

"You sure they're ready?"

Moon nodded. He stepped up to the side of the closest house. The five houses stood at different angles in the narrow enclosure. They were fashioned out of scrap lumber. Large pieces of plywood had been nailed over each door. A thin opening at the bottom allowed a shallow bowl of water to be shoved through. As the men got closer, the pungent odor of the dogs' confinement was nauseating.

"Christ," Heins muttered.

"Jesus, Angus. Sure ain't the Duluth Radisson," Pederson said.

"That'd be for us, later," added Heins, smiling.

Pederson and Young chuckled, but Winthrop knew there was work to be done.

A small wolf head peered out from behind the nearest house. The visage startled Young and Heins.

"What the hell is that?" Heins asked.

"What's left of the last litter," Moon replied.

"Couldn't sell it?"

"Not yet. And gettin' a little old. Might have to keep it for breeding stock. But that one's got more dog than I ever seen come out of a match between the Arctic sire and malamute bitch. Not sure the others'll accept it. Might just have to cut the little shit loose. Or use him for target practice."

The youngling cowered behind the house.

"Git," Moon snarled, and the dog disappeared, its chain jangling into the dark.

Moon brought his steel-toed boot back and kicked the nearest house. There was an explosive growl and the sound of teeth gnashing against the plywood wall. It captured Young's attention like a face slap. He stepped back, afraid the boards might break.

Moon turned and smiled, watching Young's retreat.

There was nothing in Moon's unshaven face, or in the intent focus of his gray eyes, that betrayed his role in what happened last Sunday night on Winthrop's farm, though all the club members knew it was Moon who had brought on the vagrant James T. Beauregard's doom. When the scheme was conceived, unanimous decision appointed Moon the executioner. Now, comfortable with his new stature, he spit across the path, sending a wad of brown saliva directly behind the tremulous Young. "They'll keep," he said.

"How long they been in there?" Young asked, more to make conversation than out of curiosity.

"Two days," Moon said. His tongue moved to resettle his chew. He grinned, revealing two rows of stunted yellow pegs.

The five hybrids now penned and starving had been kept for breeding and the club's amusement. They could run down deer better than their wild brethren. And a hefty wooden club let them know Moon was their unchallenged leader. They touched no part of a downed animal until Moon gave them the nod. Now the prolonged absence of food had caused their lupine instincts to surface like an ancient muscle group.

In the growing snowfall, the first dog's howl triggered a chorus of low snarls. The other four houses vibrated with the noise.

"I think they're all just about ready for a little meat," Moon added.

He turned and stepped up to each house and kicked it, eliciting the same whipped fury of teeth and feral growls. Under the force of one of the dog's snapping fangs, a plywood board bowed out. Young stepped back. Winthrop heard his shuffle and raised the light to look at him.

"They won't get out until we let them out."

"No need to rile 'em, Angus," Heins admonished. "They're ready."

Winthrop raised his lantern. At the edge of the trees, there was a black tarpaulin thrown carelessly over stacked metal cages. Moon threw off the tarp and hauled a cage to the nearest house.

"Come here, Young. Give me a hand."

Young hesitated. Then he stepped to the opposite side of Moon. Young was 5'10" with a slight build. He wore a heavy down coat that accentuated his flaccid pudginess. Over his right breast, stenciled yellow letters declared HAL YOUNG INDEPENDENT INSURANCE.

Standing across from Moon, he appeared to be the same height and build. But where Young had narrow shoulders and an upper body molded to the contours of his desk, Moon, who spent most of his life outdoors, was weathered, compact, and powerful.

"All of them part wolf?" Young asked, distractedly.

"Half wolf. Every one of 'em. But some of them act more wolf than others." He nodded toward the cages and said, "Grab a couple of those pine poles. We don't want our hands to get bit off."

The others watched Young retrieve the poles, and he and Moon inserted them into the cage's top metal squares.

Winthrop knew his death was an unusual accident for a man with his hunting expertise. Unusual, but not unheard of. Once the estate was settled and the insurance claim paid, they'd divvy up the shares. Winthrop was taking half. Given the money he'd squirreled away into Belize banks—client trust money he knew he would eventually be at pains to explain—Winthrop figured he could be generous.

Over the next five years the club had planned two more staged deaths. Moon would go missing in the wild; he would be easy. They'd need to wait a year, settle with the insurance company for a lesser amount. But Winthrop knew they'd clear a million. Heins would be more difficult. But Winthrop hadn't funded club members' life insurance policies to assist insurance companies with their bottom lines. Only Young and Pederson would be left to live out their natural lives. The club needed contacts back on the Range. They couldn't lose complete touch, though on paper

Winthrop, Moon, and Heins would be desiccating corpses.

Identifying his own corpse had been routine. The front half of "Winthrop's" head was entirely removed. Witnesses could only identify his clothes and the shape of his body. The coroner knew Winthrop well enough to recognize what was left of his white hair and the orange hunting cap's torn-away bill. The sheriff had his identification. Besides, Goddard had seen the corpse's outfit only a week before the accident. And he recognized the weapon. What was left of the grisly countenance was the worst hunting accident any of them had ever seen. And while everyone spoke of it as an accident, Winthrop assumed the sheriff told the coroner about the sheriff's investigation into Winthrop's legal practice, and that Winthrop knew about it. Williston Winthrop would not be the first aging lawyer to choose death over a prison cell. And the truth was, they were all anxious to cover what was left of his gruesome head. And they were all thankful to be rid of him.

Prior to staging his own death, Winthrop's brief meeting with the sheriff had been necessary to find out how close the county DA was to Winthrop's illegal activities. And he'd been damn close, closer than Winthrop dreamed. In his own way ADA Dunlap had sealed Jimbo's untimely end. And Sheriff Goddard had been the messenger. Everything about Winthrop's accident had happened perfectly: Goddard's relief, the intense cold, a tough hike, the black middle of the night, and the grotesque wound that made Goddard's investigation perfunctory.

Come Saturday, Winthrop would be laid to rest in the grave next to his estranged wife.

Moon and Young placed the cage in front of the dog's house. Once the plywood was pried loose and slid away, the dog was expected to leap into the cage and the wire door slam shut. When everything was in place, Moon pried the plywood open. There was a low snarl.

"Get ready to drop the door," Moon ordered.

Young slipped off the catch and pulled it open. In the dull light, his face appeared tense and worried.

"Ready?" Moon asked.

Young nodded.

Moon slid back the board and the dog charged out. Young dropped the door. The dog reached the end of the cage, spun around, and bit between a thin wire square, trying to get a piece of him. Young fell back, sitting down in the snow. Moon began laughing.

In the same way, they caged the other four dogs. They used the poles to carry the cages out of the woods, loading each of them onto Moon's pickup. As they worked, the snow began to come down more heavily. By the time they finished, the trail was disappearing beneath a thick film of white.

"You should go first," Winthrop told Heins. "Stay on the radio. You see anyone going or coming, give us a couple of clicks on the CB."

Heins turned and started walking toward his car. He was as medium in stature as Young and Moon, but he moved with an authoritative air.

"Angus and I will be 5 minutes behind you. You others follow us, but give us some time. We don't want a caravan."

"We'll be careful," Pederson said. "Just don't start the show without us." He was a big man. The skin on his face and belly sagged in alcoholic puffiness. His face was clean-shaven and his eyes were bloodshot. "I've got a hundred on the she-devil to draw first blood," he said.

"That's a wager I'll take," Winthrop said. "You always pick the bitch, Hank. That big Arctic will take the lead."

"I guess it'll take a hundred to see who's right."

"I guess," Winthrop agreed.

"It's turning into a pretty good night's work for a dead man and four stiffs." Pederson smiled and turned away.

Winthrop laughed. He and Pederson had known each other since they were kids. When things were tense, Pederson had a way of making him grin.

Heins had been gone over 5 minutes before Winthrop and Moon pulled out of the woodsman's long, narrow drive. There was nothing on the CB. Winthrop sat up, watching the snowfall intensify. Then he motioned and Moon turned onto a side road that disappeared in a rough diagonal through the trees.

For the remainder of the crossing they drove in silence. Winthrop was careful to stay out of sight. There was little chance anyone would be out on roads like these at this hour in the middle of an intensifying storm, but when it came to the law, Winthrop took no chances.

Since Heins had first found Jimbo, the other members of the club had quickly seen what could be done. Everyone except Young, who had reservations. But they needed Young's insurance angle to make it work, so they bullied him.

Winthrop didn't like it. They had bullied Young the same way Moon had forced him to help cage the dogs. Moon was acting on his instinctual dislike for cowardice, but it was the exact thing Young needed to force his participation. Still, Young was the weakest link, and Winthrop worried about him.

In a few short days "Winthrop" would be buried. Into the ground with him would be laid all the unpleasantness from the investigations into his illegal law practice. There had been three investigations, none of which amounted to more than a mild wrist slap. The real crimes, of course, were right under their noses— three client trusts Winthrop had been bilking for years. That was the fourth investigation, recently begun. He needed Moon to clear up one last thing, an office fire engulfing every piece of wayward paper and incriminating computer file. All record of his clients' trusts would go up in flames. And without evidence?

It was a detail he had not shared with any of the club members, because there was no need. Just like the other reason for the slaughter of the calves in his barn.

In a matter of weeks the dead Winthrop would resurrect himself, someplace warm to start, one of those countries south of Mexico, where the dollar ran on forever and no one inquired about your past. He would miss the Range, but he'd spent time south of the border and knew there were places a man with his particular talents could thrive.

As he looked back on it, it had been a satisfactory life. He regretted his dead wife, or perhaps more specifically the $179,000 she drained from her accounts in the months preceding her death.

The day Miriam died, Winthrop went over to her house, located her will, and altered it, forging her signature. She was going to leave everything to the boy. It was a simple matter, changing the will. Young was a notary public. Young notarized the revised document and predated it a month before her death.

After Miriam's death the will was probated. There had been

two inquiries: one from the sheriff and one from that bitch Diane. Diane claimed, so Goddard told him, that Miriam said she was leaving everything to the boy. But Miriam's notarized signature was legal proof they could not refute. And where was the god-damn boy? No one had heard from him in years. Winthrop hoped they might bring him forward. He had a score to settle. In the end the flap over Miriam's 11th-hour change of beneficiaries blew over like a northwestern squall.

When Winthrop finally inquired about her accounts, he found out about the missing cash. Winthrop knew people at the bank. They'd worried about her, about her state of mind. She was frail, and withdrawing that kind of money in $100 bills over the last six months of her life was worrisome. But Miriam knew Bill Radcliffe, the bank president, and convinced him it was for a variety of worthy causes, including her estranged son, Clayton. Radcliffe agreed to keep it quiet. No one at the bank said any-thing to anyone until she died. When Winthrop found out, he exploded inside Radcliffe's office like a detonated propane tank. But Radcliffe showed him the withdrawal records, and again everything was legal.

In the days following Miriam's death, Winthrop had turned the old house inside out, searching for the cash. He assumed she'd somehow gotten it to the boy. But he'd checked with the post office, checked with all her friends. None of them remem-bered anything about a series of large stuffed envelopes or boxes that might be used to ship stacks of bills. Or they weren't talking. He thought about trying to track it from the other end, going after Clayton, but finally decided it would be safer to let it alone. There was still the life insurance money. And he needed her house and share of the farm, no questions asked. He and Clayton had accounts to settle. But he didn't want the insurance money or the farm to be part of them.

If Clayton had another copy of the will, there could be complications. But he suspected the kid would stay away rather than risk his arrest for attempted murder. It was doubtful Heins could make the charge stick, but the boy wasn't stupid. A tree-hugging chickenshit, as Winthrop remembered, someone who wouldn't want to risk his luck, particularly in a Northern Minnesota court. Clayton had been more Miriam's son than his own. But that made it all the more likely the boy wouldn't show his face to enter into a contest over something he would just as soon forget.

After 20 minutes the pickup turned onto the snow-covered ruts that took them down to Winthrop's house and barn. The buildings were dark and barely visible through the snow. The gray outline of Heins's police car waited at the bottom of the drive.

"Go around to the side door," Winthrop ordered, pointing to where a pair of ruts disappeared behind the barn. "It's pretty well hidden. And if wolves came, that's where they'd get in."

Moon backed the pickup to the side door. The intensity of the driving snow was starting to swirl around them. When they got out of the cab, Heins appeared out of the white like an apparition.

"Startin' to come down pretty heavy," he shouted.

"Perfect," Winthrop shouted back.

A gust of snow whipped across them in a horizontal slant.

"Couldn't have asked for a better storm," Winthrop added. "An hour after we leave, there won't be anything left to track."

The entry to the barn had a small holding pen where the dogs were corralled. The cages were hoisted down to the side entrance, their openings set flush to the door. The cage lids were slid away. When the barn door opened, the starving animals charged into the confined darkness.

While they worked, Pederson, and then Young, came down the drive and made their way to the barn.

"Better get started," Winthrop yelled over the wind. "It's gettin' pretty wild."

Winthrop led them around the barn corner, up the rise to the loft door. He was the first through the small opening. He came out above the barn floor. The rest of them followed, leaving the storm outside, shaking off the snow and cold as their eyes grew accustomed to the dark. From the loft Winthrop turned on the overhead light. They could hear the dogs beneath them. They watched the vague shapes of the feeder calves jostling at the other end of the barn. The young fatlings made worried sounds in the dark, low and plaintive.

Winthrop looked down, excited by his front row seat at the timeless spectacle of predator and prey. The men stared over the edge, transfixed by the scene. Winthrop double-checked everything, making certain there would be no doubt that the wolves forced their entry and slaughtered the animals while no one was there to prevent it. Pederson hauled up three hay bales, squaring them like park benches. "Come on, she-devil," he called, whooping for his chosen fiend.

The dogs were jostling in the narrow confines, anxious to be free. The calves, all less than a year old, were ululating fear.

Outside, the winter storm increased. The snow buffeted the roof and the north-facing walls. The barn blustered and creaked.

"Come on, Williston," Heins said. "Let 'em out."

Winthrop reached down, opening the door less than a foot before the first dog exploded through the narrow gap. Then all the dogs were through it, roving in a pack of fast-moving whines toward the cattle stalls, recalling instinctively the methods by which wolves chase down and kill.

CHAPTER SIX

S am crossed into Minnesota around 9 p.m. The first heavy snowflakes drifted down through his headlights. Over the next 4 hours, as he traveled first down US 2 and then up US 71, toward Minnesota's Iron Range, the weather worsened.

By the time Sam neared Defiance, heavy snow gusted over his Jeep and covered the highway in broad patches of white. The radio DJ warned listeners about the first bad winter storm of the New Year.

"We have 4 inches," he barked, "but I'm here to tell ya, that's just the start! We're going to see plenty more. Isn't winter land wonderful?"

Sam flicked off the jocular DJ. He recognized the crossroads he was approaching, east of town. In the tight interior of his car, the heat was turned on full blast, but the icy gusts whipped at his windshield and doors.

He peered ahead, replaying his planned entrance into town, imagining his Jeep's tires speeding and banking over the snow. As he hit the deeper patches of white, he imagined the car making solid *whumps* in the dark. Given his postmidnight stealth and the reason for his return, he couldn't have planned better weather.

He paused at the intersection, considering how little had changed. Even through the driving snow, he could see the crossroads still crowded with black spruce and poplar. He looked to his right, down the dark tunnel of highway disappearing into blowing snow. No vehicles. At this hour, in this storm, he didn't expect to see anyone, hadn't for the last 20 miles. Perfect.

When he glanced left, peering up the northern stretch of highway, he thought he saw headlights. Then they disappeared. He waited, hoping he was mistaken or they'd turned off. Then they crested a far-off rise and shown like a pair of carnivore's eyes. The car was a quarter mile distant, driving slowly over the snow-choked blacktop.

He accelerated across the intersection. It would be better if no one saw his Jeep. He tried to remember some place to turn off. He searched along the tree-lined road and saw a mailbox marking a drive opening. Erickson's field!

Well beyond the drive, a gap in the treeline revealed the narrow entrance to a pasture lane. Twenty years ago old man Erickson hired him to help cut a narrow road next to the highway. Between the road and blacktop stood a solid stand of black spruce. If that car turned toward Defiance, the spruce wall would provide the cover he needed.

Sam turned into the narrow lane, steered left, and parked behind the stand of trees, cutting the Jeep's engine.

He flung open the door, stepped into the snowy tree branches, snapped off a 5-foot branch, and carried it, running, back to the lane opening. He found the place where his tracks left the road and used the tree branch to sweep them clear. By the time he was nearly finished, he saw the muffled glimmer of oncoming headlights, carefully rounding the bend.

Sam tossed the tree branch behind him and ducked into the wall of black spruce.

The car crawled along the highway, searching. Suddenly high beams flashed along the wall. Sam remained motionless, well concealed. As the car approached, he peered through the branches and glimpsed a small outline of overhead lights and a passenger door that read Defiance Police.

Sam wondered if it could still be Heins. He watched the car pass the lane's entrance. It traveled another 10 yards and then pulled onto the shoulder and stopped.

After 15 seconds a second pair of headlights rounded the bend. The police car waited while a new blue pickup crept up beside it.

The two drivers rolled down their windows and yelled over the wind gusts. "Thought I saw something," the policeman said.

"Like what?"

"Thought I saw a car cross that intersection."

"At one o'clock in the morning? In the middle of a storm like this?"

Their voices sounded familiar, but Sam wasn't sure.

"Could have sworn I saw something."

"It's your nerves, Heins. Maybe you need a little more remedy."

"You know I don't drink and drive," Heins chuckled. "Let's wait a minute. If I did see someone, we'll give him plenty of time to get home."

"Suits me."

"It's one hell of a storm," Heins said.

"Nothing like back at the farm."

"We couldn't have hoped for a better snowfall."

"Just so they don't get caught in it."

"With Angus's truck? They're back at his place by now." Then, "It's not like you to worry, Hank."

Sam recognized the names: Angus Moon and Hank Pederson.

"Not worried," Pederson said. "Got the law on our side." He chuckled.

They waited in silence for another minute. Then they both started off down the road.

Sam waited until their taillights disappeared. He stood up and shook the snow off his coat. He wondered what he'd overheard. Angus Moon and someone else. Hal Young? At the farm? The old man's farm?

Sam returned to his Jeep. From the glove compartment, he pulled out a black-handled flashlight. The butt of the flashlight was solid steel, heavy enough to break a window, if it came to that. Or Heins's head. He switched the light on to make sure it worked. Then he flicked it off and tucked it into the lower front pocket of his coat.

When Sam was young, Moon's menacing gaze was enough to make him avert his eyes. Moon noticed the boy's furtive turning away. Sometimes he stared at him just to watch him squirm. Unless it involved cards, hunting, or fishing, Moon had an instinctual distrust for anything civilized. Sam hoped he'd have another opportunity to stare into the rugged man's face. This time he wouldn't turn away.

Pederson owned the local Ford dealership. Or at least used to. He was a big man who 20 years ago drank whiskey like water. Pederson had a reputation for hunting women the way the old man hunted deer. Only for Pederson the season never ended. And instead of a deer head mounted on his wall, he'd pull an undergarment out of his coat pocket, grin with boyish pride, and tell the story of how he'd acquired his trophy with so much lewd embellishment that even some of the gun club members turned aside.

Young's independent insurance agency was attached to his house, not far from Sam's mother's place. Sam had often enough walked in front of it, when he was staying at his mother's. He'd even nodded to the man on occasion, who at least nodded back, more cordial than the others.

Heins, Moon, Pederson, and Young. They were the only friends the old man ever had, if you could call them friends. Now the four of them shared almost $5 million and what was left of his parents' property. "But who's counting?" Sam wondered aloud. It was a lot of money, but he didn't care about the cash. Sam Rivers had come to recover his things.

He stared into the snowy darkness of the road. He would give Heins and Pederson time to settle into their beds.

Sam reached into the back of the Jeep and pulled open his gray metal toolbox. He felt for his crescent wrench and a plastic case of small screwdrivers. He didn't believe he would need them, but he wanted to be prepared. He folded the wrench in a thin wool scarf and pulled a stiff chamois from his glove compartment, wrapping it around the plastic case of screwdrivers. Then he slid them both into the lower front pocket of his coat, arranging them so they would not rub or clank.

Sam knew he would have to be careful. He didn't know what Moon was doing, or with whom. But this storm would give them cover. Sam appreciated it for the same reasons. After he was finished, he'd blow out of town before anyone knew he'd arrived, drive south to Brainerd, establish an alibi, and then—after the storm blew itself out—revisit Defiance, the closest place to a child-hood home he'd ever known.

But if he wanted to avoid getting stuck, he would need to move quickly. He put the Jeep in gear, backed down the narrow pasture road, and edged up to the highway. Then Sam Rivers turned toward town.

CHAPTER SEVEN

Outside the barn there were occasional gusts of straight-line winds. The truck's headlights illuminated a wall of white. The windward side of the truck was already drifting with a high bank of snow. After another half hour of watching the storm and seeing no abatement in its fury, Winthrop started to worry.

He turned off the truck and cut the lights. He opened the door and fought his way into a semi-upright position.

"Angus!" he yelled. The wind tore the words out of his mouth. There was no way Moon would hear him through this howl. If they hoped to make it out to the cabin before dawn, he would have to climb to the loft and fetch Moon.

He pitched forward, feeling along the barn wall. He worked around to the back upper side. He went in through the loft door. A dim light glowed from the rafters.

"Angus!" he yelled.

"What?" Moon finally snapped.

The hybrids were still feeding, their dark shapes shadowy in the poorly lit barn.

"They finished?" Winthrop asked.

"Not yet."

"Can we get them out?"

Moon kept staring. He called to one of the hybrids, but there was no response. He picked up a wood chip and tossed it into the center of the feeding dogs. There was an immediate snarl.

"Not now," Moon said.

The wind blustered against the barn.

"When?"

"When they finish eating."

"How much longer?"

"Don't know."

"When do you think?"

Moon considered. "Hard to say. They've been two days without anything but water. They'll have to satisfy their appetites."

Winthrop peered down at the dogs. For the first time his careful sequence of events was taking an unexpected turn. He began to realize the animals might need to be left behind.

"Goddammit! You think they'll run when they're finished?"

"Leave them?"

"You want to be stuck here with them?"

For the first time since the dogs began, Moon listened to the storm.

"What do you think they'll do?" Winthrop asked.

"Hard telling. Probably stay here until the storm ends. There's plenty of food."

"You think you can catch them?"

"They're my dogs. They'll come."

"Not that we have a choice," Winthrop muttered. "We gotta leave them."

He didn't think the sheriff would come out tomorrow, given the storm and how busy the sheriff would be with emergencies in and around Vermilion Falls. But Winthrop couldn't risk being found here with Moon's animals. They needed to get back to the cabin. Then tomorrow Moon would return to the farm, cage the dogs, and hustle them back to his place before anyone discovered them. Once they were safely stowed, Moon could return to the farm as if to feed the cattle, discover the carnage, and report it.

"Let's get the hell out," Winthrop said.

They fought their way down along the edge of the outside wall. At the bottom Moon noticed the door slightly open. He tried to pull it shut, but the storm had whipped snow into the hinges, widening the 6-inch crack to a foot, freezing it there.

"Come on," Winthrop yelled, getting into the cab. "They'll stay put!"

Moon wasn't so sure. He kicked the door, but it was solid. Then he turned and fought against the wind, leaving the door ajar.

CHAPTER EIGHT

Sam's Jeep skittered over the highway, approaching the edge of town. He watched for any sign of Pederson or Heins, but there was no one. He turned north on Beacon, his mother's street, accelerating up the long incline. As he crested the rise, he cut the Jeep's engine. His headlights faded, and for a moment there was only his car going 40 mph through the darkness of the Defiance town street.

He remembered a dead end at the bottom of Beacon. The Jeep dropped off the pavement and jolted through two large banks before plowing into a black spruce tunnel and braking.

Sam breathed in the darkness. He'd expected at least some of the roads to be different, but nothing had changed.

He had walked halfway up the street when he crossed in front of Young's independent insurance office. There were fresh tire tracks up the driveway, just beginning to drift over. He looked up at the old house-office complex, but its windows were dark. Sam wondered about it, remembering Heins's and Pederson's comments. He had thought Young was with Moon. But if that was the case, Young wouldn't be back at his house so soon. Maybe Mrs. Young had returned late? Or it was someone else out at Moon's. He hurried over the fading tracks.

His mother's drive and walkway had not been plowed all winter. Her bushes were rounded over with high banks of snow. The force of several winter storms had almost buried the front porch.

He felt suddenly nostalgic for the decent part of his childhood, the part of it that redeemed him. Whenever he thought about his mother, he did not like to use the last name she adopted after marrying the old man. When Sam was young, Miriam Samuelson showed him the kind of unconditional love he had come, finally, to appreciate. Time away helped clarify what had been good about his childhood.

He rounded the garage and came up to the snow-covered back steps. Even if the house had been occupied, Sam knew its occupants would never find the articles he and his mother had hidden.

The rear entry was covered like the front. He reached up, found the doorknob at the top of a drift, and turned it. Locked.

He remembered a cellar window to the right of the back door. There was no sign of it now, buried under a high bank of snow. He recalled its approximate location and tunneled into the drift. Near the base of the hard-packed powder, there was a hollow where a small cave had formed. Sam reached in, felt for the window, moved down the pane to its bottom, grabbed the single-handled latch, and tried it. Locked.

The storm and hour prevented anyone from seeing or hearing him. He pulled out the steel-handled flashlight and used its butt to break the frosted glass.

He placed one arm through the broken pane, the other against the front. In one heavy effort he pushed and pulled, and with a sudden jolt the window broke open. Glass sprinkled onto the basement floor and Sam's wrist passed over a shard edge. He could feel the laceration, knew it would bleed, but it was a small cut. He returned to the window, pushed it open, and locked it upright.

He turned around and backed feet first into the wide window well, lowering himself through the tight enclosure and dropping to the floor.

It was quiet in the basement, out of the storm. Quiet and warm. His flashlight pierced the darkness like a blade. Against the far wall he saw a lamp, a sofa, and a table covered in plastic. He turned the beam on his wrist. Drops of blood beaded along a narrow line, but it was only a scratch. He walked over and opened the preserve room door. His light flashed off dozens of stacked jars, everything covered by a heavy patina of dust. Seeing all the jars put up by his mother's hands was like stepping into a mausoleum. He had not eaten since dinner. He hadn't thought of food. But when he saw the jars of pickles, jams, beans, corn, and every other kind of vegetable and fruit, his hunger surfaced like a cork.

He took down a jar of pickles. A piece of masking tape read DILL in his mother's awkward script. Sam set the jar aside and kneeled in front of the bottom shelf. He took a minute to remove the shelf's contents, setting the jars on the floor beside him. Then he tapped under the front lip and the shelf loosened. He lifted and slid it out from its mooring, setting it aside. He flashed the light into the floor-wall crevice and could barely see the heavy wires. He reached in and teased them out, making them taut. They were steel wires, and though they were blackened from being against a basement wall for 20 years, they felt solid. He pulled on them, carefully, and a pair of foundation bricks nudged forward. Once loosened, he brought them all the way out.

He flashed his beam into the dark opening. Tucked into the cave there was a large bag. He reached into the black space and dragged it out. It was heavy and covered in dust. He kneeled in the basement storage room, lifted the heavy canvas bag, and shook it. The air filled with a light cloud and he coughed. He hoisted the bag to his shoulder, picked up the jar of pickles, and turned toward the basement stairs. At the top of the stairs he flicked off his flashlight and let his eyes grow accustomed to the dark. A muted back alley light filtered through the kitchen window. It was enough to find his way down the near hallway. He examined the dining room, living room, bathroom, laundry, and bedrooms. He entered his old bedroom. He could see the windows were covered over with snow.

He closed the door and the room went dark. He flicked on his flashlight and set it on the pillow so it faced down his childhood bed, illuminating the room. The bed was still covered in familiar white chenille. Beside the bed stood the old wooden spindle and faux birch-bark lampshade, the white bark faded to yellow. His rectangular pine dresser was still in the corner. There was a pair of closet doors that opened into a recessed wall space.

After his mom moved to town, the old man refused to let Sam stay here more than a few nights every month. But his mother had made it nice for him, and they had both endured the old man's control. All those years and she'd kept his room exactly as it had been when he was a boy.

He wondered what she felt as she passed it, after he had left for good, maybe waiting for him to return, suspecting and then knowing he would not. He wished things had been different and that he'd been able to breach the chasm between them, to let her know that on occasions her remembered kindness reached out of the past. He recalled her hands preparing a meal, washing clothes, cleaning the house, canning preserves. His mother's heart was simple. She'd loved him without measure, abatement, or conditions, done what she could to raise him right. She'd lived with a kind of purity, and he wished now that she were here and he could tell her how he felt.

He turned to the duffel, loosened the drawstring, and peered inside. Near the top was a thick envelope addressed to him. He set the envelope aside, returning to the bag. He found the 10 gauge shotgun, one of his father's precious Decimators. The old man once told him it would be his, but Sam had never lived up to the shotgun's promise. So the old man hadn't kept his word. Sam felt happy now to see it.

The bag also contained the army-issue camo parka, pants, and boot coverings Sam had used for stalking in snow. And there was a full box of shells, also dusty and old. Sam guessed they were still operational. If powder remained dry, it could hold its charge for decades.

Under it all was a plastic-wrapped shoebox, with the heft of a brick. When he peered through the plastic, he saw the blurry face of Benjamin Franklin. There were four of them, set side by side on what appeared to be thick stacks of bills.

If the entire brick was $100 bills, it was a considerable sum. The unexpected treasure made his pulse spike.

He set it aside, opening his mother's envelope. There were several handwritten pages and another legal document. The legal document was a copy of her will. It was a long letter, dated just days before she died. He angled it to pick up the flashlight's beam and read it in the half-light.

She talked about her health. She didn't know how long she would live. She was starting to feel her age and she didn't think the end was far off. She had spent the last few months converting her retirement accounts to cash, gradually withdrawing the savings from her account, over $179,000. If she had drawn a cashier's check and mailed it, and then died, she was afraid Williston would have found Sam and figured out a way to claw back the money. If she mailed it, she would have to insure it, and Williston might find out where it went and why. "Your father knows a lot of people," she explained. "People who owe him favors."

Neither did she trust Williston about the will. She expected he would alter it, since everything had been left to Sam. So she'd taken the money and hid it in the bag believing, knowing, someday Sam must return. And she knew Williston would never find it, not in their secret place. She'd made sure to leave a second copy of the will, this one dated to be her last, "and notarized in Brainerd, so if the older copy is altered, you'll have proof."

She reminisced about Sam, when he was a boy, their lives together, about everything that happened to them. And she warned him about confronting Williston, if he was still alive.

"Get your things, but be careful about it."

She told him to share nothing with Williston Winthrop, advice he didn't need.

She ended the letter with an apology: "I am so sorry for everything," she said. Then, "When you read this I hope everything finds you well. And please remember that I always loved you— more than you can possibly imagine—and always will."

As Sam grew older, he wondered why his mother never divorced the old man. The first time Williston raised a fist, she should have drawn up legal papers and taken him for every dime he had. There was no excuse for accepting the years of belittlement and abuse. But it was his mother. He recognized her optimism in the face of despair, how she refused to let the old man's wickedness tarnish her goodness. And it was true; his father knew people. It would have been difficult to find justice on the Range.

When he was 12, his mother left the farm and moved into this house, to get away from the old man, not her son. But Sam recognized Williston Winthrop held the power. After a summer spent with his mother, he returned to the farm. Sam was a boy and wasn't expected to live outside his father's rule. When he reread the last lines of her letter, he knew she had lived her life according to her convictions. They weren't his convictions. Never had been, never would be. In the childhood room she'd prepared for him, he regretted not fighting harder against the old man's rule. But he had been a boy, and the old man was his father and a powerful son of a bitch.

He picked up the brick of money and felt its heft—$179,000 and change, a considerable sum, particularly by weight. It must have pissed off the old man. Sam smiled to think about it. He knew his mother smiled too.

Outside, the storm was still howling. He would have to leave soon, or risk getting stuck, maybe even discovered. He carried the jar of pickles into the kitchen. He placed the jar in the bottom of the sink and twisted the lid open. He heard the vacuum seal pop, and the fragrance of dill and vinegar, his mother's special blend, was overpowering. He pulled a pickle out of the jar and tasted it, remembering in a sudden rush the pickles he loved as a boy. It had been a long time since he'd had hunger for anything. The pickle tasted salty, pungent, and remarkable.

He recapped the jar and returned to the basement. He extracted three more jars from the preserve room and slid them with the pickles into his bag. He replaced the bottom shelf and moved the contents on the floor back onto it. Then he crawled out the window, leaving the basement as he'd found it. He piled snow into the window well, covering the broken entry with a bank of white. Then he slung the bag over his shoulder, struggled back over the Defiance streets, and returned to his Jeep. He started the cold engine and in the early-morning darkness managed to back out and plow past the dead end of the street, returning the way he'd arrived, with stealth through the widening winter storm.

Eventually the town cop would discover his break-in. But by then the snow would cover his tracks. Weather reports indicated the heavy blow would drop a few more inches before it was done. That would mean it might be a while before Heins discovered the broken cellar pane.

He thought about his mother's letter and the money. Her hope and heart strength were her best epitaphs. And his mother's will had been altered. The proof rested in his breast pocket, where at the right time he would enjoy making it known. He wondered what the statute of limitations was on probating an estate. He'd have to find some legal counsel. And he would need to do so with care. How he had acquired the will and when to make it known would require some planning.

For the moment it was enough to have the old man's precious Decimator in the back of his Jeep, nestled beside her $179,000 and four jars of her excellent preserves.

PART II

Behold, I send you forth as sheep in the midst of wolves: be ye therefore wise as serpents, and harmless as doves.

Matthew 10:16

CHAPTER NINE

"Are you getting anything?"

"Nothing," Moon answered. "Not a goddamned thing."

Moon sat in front of the cabin's CB radio console, trying to call out. "This is Woods Weasel calling the Defiance Star. Are you reading? Over."

Around them the dawn was just starting to break, bright and frozen. The snow banked to their windows, covering the front door. It lay in piles in the woods, along the few hidden trails leading to the cabin and the remote, abandoned logging roads leading to the trails. The pathways were impassable, and both of them feared it would be more than a day before Moon could snowshoe the 2 miles back to the truck and then dig himself out and return to the farm. Which meant the dogs would be alone in the barn for another day. With the goddamn door open.

"Just keep trying," Winthrop said. "We need to get word to Heins."

Moon peered out of bloodshot eyes. "I know." He was growing weary of Winthrop's repeated demand.

"He has to go over and tend them," Winthrop continued, ignoring Moon. "Heins has to find the kill and report it. And get your dogs," he added.

"I know," Moon agreed. When Winthrop was edgy, it was best to go along.

Winthrop hadn't stopped mulling plans since they'd been forced to leave the farm. Now he was trying to work through all the alternatives, tracking consequences, considering steps. He didn't like where his options led, but he didn't have much choice. The dogs unsettled him. Before anyone could be notified, they'd have to be caged. And what if someone else found them? What if they ran? The goddamn wolf dogs were a nasty loose end, difficult to explain and threatening to unravel his plan. He reminded himself that it was unlikely anyone would visit the farm, particularly after a storm like this one, especially given the roads. But he'd feel a whole lot better if they got word to Heins.

"There's only one answer to this," Winthrop finally blurted.

Moon looked at him, waiting for the next directive.

"Remedy," he said with a smile. "A little remedy in our morning coffee."

It was an unexpected remark. "Now you're talkin'," Moon agreed. "Hair of the dog that bit ya," he grinned.

As Winthrop walked across the room, he heard Moon place another call into the ether. "Woods Weasel to the Defiance Star. Come in, Star. Is anyone out there? Anyone listening? Come in. Over?"

Winthrop was still stunned by the night's random misfortunes. They had been forced to leave the dogs. They had driven at a crawl through blinding snow and were damn lucky to find the entrance to the abandoned logging road. When Moon went to unlock the heavy chain, he'd disappeared in a slantwise fury of snow. It reminded Winthrop of farmers getting lost in blizzards only yards from their front door.

In the dark, the truck's headlights illuminated a sideways howl of white, obliterating his view. At the point where Winthrop was certain Moon had been gone too long, was possibly lost, he saw fingers reach out of the blizzard. Moon's gnarled, weathered hand, accustomed to storms, groped and pulled himself through the blow. He struggled forward in a stumbling lurch. He fought his way into the cab.

"Did you find it?" Winthrop asked, inquiring about the lock and chain.

"Jesus Christ," Moon heaved. "Almost got lost out there."

"Where are your gloves?"

"I had to find the chain by feel, then the lock. Then the wind tore the gloves from under my arm. Had to let 'em go." He was breathless and shaken by the storm.

"Did you get it open?"

Moon nodded, catching his breath. "But I'm not sure we want to drive into it."

After Moon dropped the chain, they had no other choice but to inch forward. Normally Moon would have gone back and reaffixed the chain and lock, but after almost getting lost, he refused to try.

They'd spent well over an hour edging toward the trail point. Fortunately, the abandoned logging trail was narrow and overgrown. In most places a healthy canopy overgrew it and afforded some protection against the storm. It provided them with enough visibility to find the trailhead. And once in the bog, the trees helped lessen the blow. Still, they took an extra hour struggling along the narrow trail to make it to the cabin. Almost immediately they'd started calling out on the CB.

Now the radio crackled and sparked.

"It's the atmosphere," Winthrop observed, returning with whiskey. "That goddamn storm choked the roads, the country, the whole fuckin' Range. Now it's whipping around the air waves, sucking every particle into a black hole."

"Must be right over us," Moon agreed. "I can't get a god-damn thing."

Winthrop topped Moon's coffee with whiskey. After Moon picked up his cup, Winthrop raised his own. "Here's to making mayhem pay."

Moon raised his cup and sipped, still peering at the knobs and dials. He flipped a receiver switch and started moving the volume dial. As he did, a crackle faded into someone's voice. Words. They were barely discernible articulations, vowel sounds and consonants. They couldn't pick up anything clear, but it was a man's voice.

"There's something," Winthrop observed.

Moon tweaked the dials. He edged it left and the voice disappeared. He tried the microphone. "Hello," he said. "This is the Woods Weasel," he began, giving his call sign. "Just trying to find somebody. Anybody there? Over."

The voice came back, still muffled.

"Things are starting to clear," Winthrop said.

Moon barely touched the dial and out jumped a man's voice.

"This storm is not the work of Satan, but the Hand of God! If anyone believes for one moment that God is unaware of the devil's pernicious habits, his unyielding effort to turn men's minds to evil, then it is he who does not know God. For God knows all things. He is all powerful, able to see into your heart, and mine. And yes, He can even peer into the black depths of Satan's puny muscle."

It was some religious nut, Winthrop guessed. Using the airwaves to preach his own personal sermon. And judging from the reference to the storm, it had to be somewhere on the Range, someplace near. "Turn that asshole off," Winthrop snapped, which was fine by Moon.

CHAPTER TEN

S omewhere far out in the woods, the dawn's orange patina began to glow. Last night's storm left a high bank of snow against Diane's northwest walls. Snow covered her driveway in alternating drifts. Snow buried her old Datsun pickup so only the hood and wheels on one side were visible. Snow banked high on her front porch all the way to her bedroom window, which was only now beginning to show the morning's first crimson light.

Diane had gone to bed early because there was nothing to be done about the storm. She was 47, and in addition to hot flashes and mood swings that swept across her like siroccos, she sometimes awoke in the middle of the night. She had friends who had been through it, so she knew what to expect. She'd had two checkups with Dr. Susan Wallace, who told her she could soften the effects with hormone therapy. Diane hated the idea of using a drug to ease a natural aging process. But she was tired of a poor night's rest. So she gave hormone therapy a try, and it had worked. But a side effect had been slightly swelled breasts and an uptick in libido, neither of which did Diane, who had been single and unattached for more than five years, much good.

When she shared her symptoms with Dr. Wallace, Susan told her to keep doing whatever she was doing because all her vital signs were excellent. "You must have inherited some very good genes."

Diane laughed. Longevity ran on both sides of her family. But so did tipplers. "It's good to know that eating like a chipmunk and this exercise regimen is having a positive effect. Now all I need is a loaner."

"Loner?"

"A man."

"You want a man who's a loner?"

"L-O-A-N-E-R," she spelled it out. "A borrowed boy. Someone I can spend date night with. The whole night. He can leave in the morning."

Dr. Wallace grinned. "I don't know any loaners. But like I said, whatever you're doing, keep it up. You look great. And your blood work is perfect."

"I feel pretty good too."

So last night, when the skies around her small cabin were howling like a banshee, she had to pee, regular as clockwork. When she returned to bed, the inside of her small bedroom felt like a cocoon, and she enjoyed just lying in the dark, listening to the storm and thinking.

Finally, she rolled out of bed still groggy and managed to get herself robed and in the kitchen. She flipped on her scanners and started filling a coffeepot, listening. The scanners were a recent addition to her professional life. After speaking with a colleague in the Cities, she'd acquired two of the devices. One she kept tuned to local law enforcement frequencies. The other she used to rove the CB band. The police scanner alerted her to Winthrop's accident, so it had already paid for itself. She was also enjoying the periodic conversation she overheard on the CB, one of which started as she readied her coffee.

"Woods Weasel to the Defiance Star. Come in, Star. Is anyone out there? Anyone listening? Come in. Over?"

Who the hell were Woods Weasel and Defiance Star? Diane listened, thinking the voice sounded familiar. But she couldn't place it, and then it stopped.

When she looked outside, she was startled by the snowfall. It was warm in the cabin, but she could see orange sunlight rising on a frozen world of snow and ice. Her outside thermometer showed –7°F.

"That was one hell of a storm," she said.

She waited for the coffee to brew. She doubled its strength because she still felt the effects of deep sleep, almost like she had drunk too much wine the night before. Deep languor settled into her bones. But there was something else. An old desire: The need to stare into a blank screen and fill it with words. Coffee, she thought. I need coffee.

She kept on the scanners, heard Woods Weasel make one more unanswered entreaty, and then both scanners fell silent.

That's the other thing she believed about staying young, given her age. Diet and exercise helped. But there was nothing like having a purpose and rising to it every morning, anxious to begin anew.

She drank her first cup of coffee. She let the caffeine work. Today, she decided, she would begin by finishing her article. Then dig herself out. Today was one of those surprises given to you when you were both thankful and knew what to do with it. It was like being a kid on a snow day.

After high school Diane attended the University of Minnesota down in the Cities. She had the feeling she would like to write, but she was a poor hand at it. She tried one writing class and then another, but only managed average work. Then her sophomore year she took a Women in Literature class. One of the assigned texts was Margaret Atwood's *The Handmaid's Tale,* a novel she had trouble setting down. The story struck her like a freight train. In the past she had been entertained by novels. Atwood's made her look at her own life with a sudden care she had never before felt. She began to cultivate a sense of defiant independence.

Nothing else moved her like writing. And at the university she was exposed to everything, finally settling on journalism as a more practical degree than creative writing or literature. She also began to enjoy the occasional party with friends, the periodic surfeit of wine, the pleasant afterglow of a good joint. She also learned that defiant independence was a kind of aphrodisiac, when—on the handful of occasions she took a lover—she appreciated as much pleasure as she gave. And that's when she moved back to the Range.

After finishing her degree in journalism, she worked odd jobs, mostly with newspapers doing photography and layout, occasionally penning a story. There was a time she spent two or three years in a party blur, working just enough to scrape by, familiarizing herself with most of the region's Northwoods bars. And people liked her, particularly men. She was almost 5'9", with curves in the right places and an engaging smile. And after a couple of sloe gin fizzes, her laugh was, according to one of her friends at the time, "as seductive as a leopard's."

She got on well with the Range men, careful about her occasional companions. In spite of her reputation, taking a partner happened less frequently than the barmen believed. But the last time, one of those trysts took, at least biologically. Her partner had been a fun, capable lover. But to Diane it was clear as a deep-water lake that he would never be a father. Her miscarriage was painful, but fortunate, considering her options. She lost the baby and was never forced to decide between a loveless marriage and the rest of her life. The stark choice made her reconsider her participation in the Range bar scene and occasionally what happened after they closed.

Not long after Diane's miscarriage, her aunt died, leaving her this cabin and enough money so that for six months she did nothing but write. She also read, heavily, which is how she first met Miriam Winthrop. Over 20 years ago Miriam befriended her and introduced her to a local women's book group, every one of them rabid readers.

The group gave her a social outlet. And the reading improved her writing. She finally took a job reporting with the *Vermilion Falls Gazette*.

When she peered out her kitchen window, she realized it would be a while before she dug herself out. She phoned her boss. It was still early. The office would be empty.

"I'm working from home today," she said. "I'm finishing up that long obit on Winthrop, and if I'm reading your mind properly, I bet you want 7 column inches about this storm, which you'll have by this afternoon."

She hung up. She'd wait for the thermometer to climb to zero before breaking out her snowblower. Meanwhile, she needed to finish that obit. She'd barely known Williston Winthrop. But her research had turned up plenty. Dunlap, the assistant DA, alluded to an investigation, but she couldn't get corroboration or any sense of what it was about. And regardless, the *Gazette* wouldn't have run it in an obit. The *Gazette* believed you should never speak ill of the dead—even though Winthrop deserved every ill word she could conjure. The only people she could get to go on record with a positive remark were the members of that club. And they were the beneficiaries of the man's estate, something that prick

Pederson was quick to point out, when she'd spoken with him at the farm. He was coming into some money. Diane still couldn't believe how the man stared at her breasts the night of Winthrop's accident. There had been times Pederson had more or less propositioned her, but so had a score of men across the Range.

She needed a few more details to finish her obit. She'd try Young first. If Young couldn't help, she could always turn to Pederson, who was clearly willing. She didn't like the idea of calling Pederson, but her other alternatives—Bill Heins and Angus Moon—made her skin crawl. At least she had been able to joke with Pederson, because Pederson was a player. She was hoping she'd have better luck with Young.

CHAPTER ELEVEN

By 8 a.m. Sam was returning to Defiance from the east side of town. He had driven all the way south to Brainerd and made sure he bought gas and had something to eat at a local restaurant, keeping the dated receipts in his car, just in case. He'd come in behind the storm, not in the middle of it. The receipts would support his alibi.

The steeple of the Lutheran church rose above frozen birch and pine, its pinnacled cross encrusted with a thick layer of ice. Sam imagined the view from the cross. He remembered a handful of stores, the lumberyard, the school, Pederson's Ford, the Winthrop Building, the Naked Loon Bar, Opel Grady's Café, and more churches than God had any right to expect in a town with these dimensions.

Defiance was settled when Northern Minnesota was the Northwest Territory and people came here in search of timber, fur, gold, and the absence of any laws but their own. They cut down the original pine forest, and the fur lasted until the fur-bearing animals were slaughtered to near extinction. Instead of gold they discovered iron, much more costly and laborious to extract. But as long as anyone could remember, iron sustained the string of Northern Minnesota mining towns across the Range. Until recently.

For the last two decades Sam had read about the decline of the iron mines. Chinese and foreign imports had gutted the American steel industry, drying up the need for local ore. In the wake of foreign competition, the old pit mines were abandoned, replaced by an effort to eke out a living in the tourist trade during the warmer months, at least for those who stayed.

More recently some of the mining companies had begun to restart their iron mining efforts, while others had begun to develop nonferrous metal deposits. The region was starting to come back, but slowly, and not in Defiance.

At the edge of town Sam was pleased to see Erickson's gas station still open. He pulled into the station and topped off his tank. The clear sky wasn't helping with the cold; the station thermometer read −7°F. He'd blown in with a cold front.

Behind the counter a high school kid looked up from his textbook, waiting for Sam to pay. He had green eyes and a compact frame. Under the boy's insulated shirt, Sam noticed broad shoulders and plenty of muscle. His hands were deft and capable, and his face could have graced a box of Wheaties.

Sam imagined the kid gliding over ice, smashing a hockey puck in Northern Minnesota's greatest pastime. It was the eyes that suggested he might be an Erickson, one of the progeny of the clan Sam worked for as a kid.

"Your name Erickson?"

The boy looked friendly enough. "Yeah."

"That your dad who owns the spread outside of town?"

"My Uncle Paul," he said. He took Sam's card and swiped it through the register's reader.

"Do you know a Diane Talbott?"

The boy placed Sam's receipt on the table, waiting for his signature. Sam watched him glance at the cardholder's name.

"Sam Rivers," he said, referencing the name on the card. "My mother was a friend of Diane's."

"Uh-huh," the boy nodded.

"Sometimes Diane would take my mom and me fishing."

The kid nodded again, guarded.

"If I remember right, Diane loved catching snakes, just for the fun of it." *Snakes* was the local term for the long, aggressive northern pike, one of Minnesota's hardest-fighting fish, but also slimy and difficult to fillet.

"Doesn't surprise me," the boy said, smiling. "She lives outside of town, on the Old Road."

The boy gave him directions while Sam returned the card to his wallet. When he looked out the window, he saw the Ben Franklin five-and-dime closed up. The old painted ads were peeling from its windows. The sidewalks in front of the store were choked with snow. Farther down the street he saw a tavern closed and a church with its windows boarded up. The doors to the old Defiance Library were chained. Beyond it, peeking from around the corner, he caught the edge of the Winthrop Building.

"Defiance Hotel still open?"

The boy nodded.

"It's a wonder anybody's still here."

"I'm gettin' out. Soon as I'm done with school."

Sam noticed the kid's sincerity. He thought about telling him a story, about growing up and getting out. But Sam wasn't ready. Not yet.

He thanked the boy and left.

On the edge of town the Defiance Hotel stood like a sturdy brick fort in front of the abandoned Iron Rail depot and the woods that went on forever beyond it. The depot had been used to haul timber and ore when Defiance was still a boomtown. Now its windows stood broken and empty. The old depot door was padlocked.

The ground around the dilapidated structure was thigh high with new snow.

The hotel's sign was faded and almost unintelligible, but its walks were plowed clean. A faded yellow VACANCY was taped to the window. Sam pushed through the door.

Behind the desk a television blared from a back room. Sam slapped the old-fashioned desk bell. He heard a chair creak, and in a moment an old man stood in the door's threshold.

"Yeah?" he said, eyeing Sam with suspicion.

"Have you got a room?"

The old man's head looked like a cue ball, its most prominent feature a pair of antiquated black plastic–rimmed glasses. He wore a work shirt and gray khaki work pants with black suspenders. His clothes were threadbare, but clean and well pressed. His belly pushed over his belt like a distended watermelon, bulging his shirt buttons and parting the suspenders. Judging from the hotel's quietude, he had plenty of time for meals.

"Got 16 of them," the man finally answered.

"Good."

"I taped that VACANCY sign up over 10 years ago. The only times I come close to bringing it down are hunting season and fishing opener."

Sam smiled. "I'm looking for something with a view," he said.

"You can have whatever room you want, but don't expect a view."

"How about a room that overlooks those train tracks, facing the woods?"

"That'll be seven. Right over my place."

Sam signed his name and completed the registration form

with his Yellow Rock address and phone while the proprietor reached down and pulled a key off an inside cupboard. He handed the key to Sam, glancing at his name. "Rivers?"

"Sam Rivers."

"Elwyn Baxter," the man said, reaching over and shaking Sam's hand. "From around here?"

"A long time ago," he said. "It's been a while. I left quite a few years back."

"Any kin?"

"All dead."

"Seems like all the young ones leave," the proprietor mused. "Can't say I blame them. Nothing for them around here. Everything closing up. I don't remember any Rivers."

"None of them live here anymore."

"Figures."

"Does seem like a ghost town."

The old man laughed. "It's a ghost town all right. Plenty of old ghosts like me still hanging around." The old man leaned on the counter, settling in, and added, "If you don't want much, it's a nice place to live. A person couldn't want for better fishing or hunting, or more beautiful scenery than our lakes and rivers."

Sam nodded.

Outside, a car came down the icy street. They turned to watch Heins's police car slow in front of the hotel, then pass by.

"Wonder what he wants?" the old man asked with unguarded derision. "Not in any trouble, are ya?"

"Nothing anybody knows about," Sam said.

Baxter smiled. "That's Bill Heins, Defiance's police force. Not sure what a town this size needs with a police force, but he's it.

Had the job for years. He likes harassing strangers and rolling bums. Saw him just last week. He was out back." Through his rear office window, he motioned to the abandoned building by the tracks. "Picked up some bum. Big fat old man. Now don't get me wrong, no way I'm for vagrants filling our streets. But if you're down on your luck, the only free shelter in town is that abandoned depot, and Heins is out at dusk harassing him. Made him get into his squad car and carted him off." The old man looked at Sam. "What's a dying town like this need with a cop?" he repeated. "I expect Defiance is keeping Bill Heins around for 50 grand a year when everyone else is out of work. But it's not likely to last." The old man smiled. "What's he gonna do when there's nothing left in the Defiance treasury? And from what I hear that day isn't far off."

The old man continued for a while: mostly talking about Heins's uselessness, though his derision wasn't limited to the town cop.

Sam imagined Heins harassing the homeless. From what he remembered, Heins would appreciate a vagrant's vulnerability. Heins had a predator's instinct for finding the weakest animal in the herd.

From the look in Baxter's eyes, Sam knew he was ready to speak at length about any subject Sam cared to discuss. But Sam was long overdue for a warm bed and rest. A long drive and larceny were exhausting work.

He thanked Baxter, excusing himself with an apology, and went out to his Jeep to recover his bag and the duffel. As a source of information the proprietor might be useful, Sam thought. But he recognized a small-town gossip and knew whatever he told the hotel owner would be fodder for the next guest.

Room seven was as austere as a hermitage. The bed was narrow and flat, and the mattress was as hard as slate. But he was too tired to care.

A nicked-up dresser stood to the side of the window. On the opposite wall there was an old picture in a natural birchwood frame—a Northwoods trapper checking his trapline, the setting not much different from what Sam could see out his window. The bathroom, sink, and shower were behind a door at the end of the hall. Sam, more tired than he could remember, set down his bags, took out his Dopp kit, and went down to brush his teeth.

The simplicity of the place was fine by Sam. He planned on resting here, nothing more. And truth is, he preferred his mattresses firm. Sam lay down on the unyielding spread. His watch said 9:30 a.m. He lay flat on his back with his clothes still on. He lifted his wrist, setting his watch alarm for 4 p.m.

He thought briefly how good the last 24 hours had been. Good, and with unexpected windfalls that left him with more questions than answers. If the next day was anything like the last, he was in for an interesting ride.

Then he closed his eyes and instantly fell asleep.

CHAPTER TWELVE

At the Vermilion County Courthouse, Sheriff Dean Goddard stepped into ADA Jeff Dunlap's office.

Dunlap looked up and said, "Hey, just a second," and then returned to his papers.

Dunlap's office was a 10-by-15-foot rectangle with a window overlooking the parking lot. The long wall was lined with file cabinets. The cabinets were topped with archive boxes. His table was covered with several neat piles of paper, each pile an open case. Illuminating the piles was a green glass desk lamp Goddard figured was standard issue for everyone passing the bar. Other than the desk lamp and files, nothing about Dunlap's demeanor or appearance would have indicated he was one of the best prosecutors in the state.

Dunlap had feather-short brown hair parted on the side. His mustache looked like the frayed end of a worn toothbrush. He wore round, wire-rimmed glasses with tortoiseshell enamel. The sheriff had known him for almost a decade, but the man's appearance never changed.

The assistant county attorney and the sheriff had been friends since their first days in local government. Goddard was born and raised on a small farm outside Worthington, Minnesota, a rural community in the southwest corner of the state, about as far from Vermilion Falls as you could get and still call yourself a Minnesotan.

Dunlap was raised on a small acreage outside Defiance. His parents hunted, fished, guided, subcontracted lumber with the county and local sawmills, and cleared over 4 acres on which they planted Christmas trees. Dunlap had grown up with a cabin roof over his head, and plenty to eat, much of it wild. But it was a season-to-season existence. They survived. He loved his parents, but when he was young, he swore he was going to have more than a pot to piss in, and so he did.

He was one of the county prosecutor's top attorneys and was considered the heir apparent to take over when Percy Lange, the current county attorney, strode into the sunset. And those in the know suspected Lange's departure wasn't far off.

"I believe if Jedd Connors has one more DWI, I can put him away for six months and force him to go through treatment for the second time this year."

"County would be better off," the sheriff observed.

"Think it'll help?"

The sheriff shook his head. "But we can hope."

"I guess." The two men were in agreement on most county law enforcement matters. Dunlap closed the folder, leaned back, and put his feet on the only open corner of his desk. "And I suppose the county's better off without that old crook Will Winthrop, though damned if I'm feeling good about it."

When Goddard entered, he'd noticed a familiar yellow file in the middle of Dunlap's desk. It was the folder containing the draft subpoena he was going to serve Winthrop until Winthrop's untimely accident.

As far as Goddard knew, the only person aware of his relationship with Susan Wallace had been Winthrop. There was a time he'd considered turning to Dunlap for advice, just to have a confidant who could advise him on how best to clean up his awful mess. But instinct told him his good friend would give him advice he wasn't willing to follow: end the affair. Given Winthrop's demise, he was thankful he'd kept his mouth shut.

"What's his death mean for your investigation?" Goddard asked.

"Our investigation," Dunlap corrected.

Goddard was glad to hear it. The best way to search Winthrop's properties was to have the investigation remain open. He needed to find that video and destroy it. The ongoing investigation would give him legal cover.

"It preempts justice," Dunlap quipped. "I wanted to make that old man swing by his thumbs. From what I can figure, that guy wasn't only a crook. He was a cruel SOB capable of just about anything a criminal mind can conjure."

It was a familiar subject, though they only broached it with each other. Rigorous in their pursuit of criminals, they were fair and just, above all else. And that made the sheriff's infidelity all the more painful.

"I guess he got what was coming," Goddard observed.

"I guess," Dunlap said, staring off at the filing cabinets lining his wall. "But that doesn't mean his beneficiaries should enjoy the fruits of his illegal labors."

The file in the middle of Dunlap's desk contained much more information than the names the sheriff had shared with Winthrop, well ahead of actually serving him the paper. The fourth investigation into Winthrop's law practice involved three widowed pensioners: Betty Jo Kalumet, Mary Slavenoh, and Gertie Wendell. The three had been housed in an assisted-living foster-care facility called Pine Grove Estates, just outside Hibbing. Betty Jo died two years ago. Mary had been dead less than a year. Gertie was still alive, but had extreme dementia.

The three women shared several characteristics. The first and perhaps most important was their mental status: impaired. They slipped in and out of history with the ease of time travelers, rarely visiting the present. And they were a little fuzzy about particulars. Their own names, for instance, had been as elusive as everyone else's. They had no living next of kin. And in the sense that a pensioner is someone who lives on a small stipend, generally from a qualified benefit plan, these three only appeared to be financially stressed senior citizens in need of a safe home.

Pine Grove Estates was a Delaware corporation. Beneath the corporate veil of Pine Grove Estates was a Minnesota corporation called Iron County Care. Iron County Care had two limited partners and one general partner. The limited partners were Bill and Matty Harris. The general partner was the general counsel for Iron County Care. Everyone was paid by Pine Grove Estates, which had a corporate address in Delaware, but a working address, a PO box, in Virginia, Minnesota. Beneath Iron County Care there were some additional limited and general partners that made the entire structure holding up Pine Grove Estates one of the most sophisticated and byzantine corporate shell games Dunlap had ever seen. He'd retained a friend in corporate law down in the Cities to help him sort it all out.

Over the years the spinsters not only managed to accumulate considerable estates, but also once they entered the comfortable foster care and assisted living provided by Pine Grove Estates, their stipends, and eventually their entire estates, had cascaded down through several corporate entities until they had finally been signed over to attorney Williston Winthrop, general counsel. Dunlap was still trying to figure out all the angles of the complicated scheme.

Everything had continued to operate well below the radar until less than a year ago. Gertie Wendell had a brief bout with pneumonia, and her regular physician was unavailable. Wallace examined her. What Wallace saw made her wonder if Pine Grove Estates' care was adequate. She mentioned it to the sheriff, who drove over to have a look. He found the place clean, filled with plenty of sunlight, the air smelling antiseptic. And Gertie looked as reasonable as one could expect, considering she seldom got out of bed and was recovering from a nasty respiratory infection.

Still, the sheriff wondered about it, mentioning the place to his friend Dunlap, who started digging. After almost three months of to and fro with the Minnesota Secretary of State's office, and the assistance of his corporate law expert in the Cities, Dunlap had finally figured the broad outline of the scheme.

"So this doesn't end it?" the sheriff finally asked.

"No way. But it complicates how we proceed. God knows we're not going to get any answers to our subpoena."

"Dead men don't talk," the sheriff agreed.

"Not in so many words. But we might yet hear something from his grave." Dunlap said. "For starters, I obtained a copy of Winthrop's will. It's a large estate, considering how he lived. He kept his net worth well under the radar. There's plenty, and those buddies of his are going to make out like bandits."

"Bill Heins?"

"He's one of them. Along with that mongrel Angus Moon. And Hank Pederson and Hal Young. You know them?"

"Moon's an outdoorsman. Lives pretty far out. Off the grid, far as I can tell."

"That's the guy. A hunter, trapper, not particularly pleasant. Tell you the truth, it surprises me Williston Winthrop had anything to do with him. But a lot of things about Winthrop surprise me. Did you know he had a son?"

"Where?"

"Nobody knows. He was ahead of me in school a couple years. He was a quiet kid, kept to himself. Then one day he just disappeared."

"Anybody look into it?"

"Nope. No reason to. He was old enough. Apparently the mother knew where he was. Rumor had it that the old prick beat him up pretty bad and Clayton—that was his name—bolted. Didn't come back, and I don't blame him."

"What about Pederson and Young?"

"Respectable enough. But it's a curious thing about Winthrop's estate. Over $2 million comes from a term life insurance policy. Who in the hell keeps that kind of insurance for a bunch of his buddies?"

Goddard shrugged, but agreed that carrying that much life insurance was surprising. Particularly considering his beneficiaries.

"I've learned a little about that business," Dunlap added. "Life insurance companies do a lot of research to make sure they understand a client's total life insurance picture: the companies, policies, amounts, dates of ownership, beneficiaries, that kind of thing. When people buy life insurance, they're entered into databases. If some guy takes out 10 $50,000 policies on his wife, making himself the beneficiary, they want to know about it."

The sheriff wasn't surprised. Insurance companies were hesitant to part with money, so they took precautions.

"And any policies less than a year old are subject to pretty intense scrutiny," continued Dunlap. "For obvious reasons."

"How old was Winthrop's?"

"You can be Winthrop's age and get a $2.5 million term life insurance policy for a little more than $3,000 a year, providing you took out the paper almost 10 years ago."

"He's been paying on it for 10 years?"

"About eight. Not cheap, but for a man like Winthrop, benefiting the way he did from these lady's estates, it would have been chicken feed."

"But he wouldn't gain anything. Just his beneficiaries. What's the point?"

"That part bugged me," Dunlap agreed. "The policy's beneficiaries are the four men mentioned in this will. I double-checked on who paid the annual premiums. It was Will Winthrop, out of an account set up for gun club expenses."

"Maybe they had something on him? Or he was a better friend than we give him credit."

"I don't for a second believe he was a good buddy. And here's the real kicker. That club has been paying premiums on the same policies for every one of its members!"

The sheriff didn't understand. "You mean every club member has a $2.5 million term life insurance policy?"

Dunlap nodded. "For almost eight years Will Winthrop, through that club, has held paper on every member. The listed beneficiaries for each policy are the same, the members of the gun club. It looks like Winthrop, through the club, has paid the premiums all along. That's over $15,000 a year."

Goddard was surprised. "That's a load of money. You think he was just gambling?"

"First of all, the cost was minimal, if I'm right about how much he bilked out of those pensioners. Second, it could have been an incredible gamble, if any of them died before him."

"Maybe he was thinking about offing one of them? Maybe a couple?"

"Maybe the whole damn group," Dunlap agreed. "Though it'd be tough to get away with it."

"Car accident," Goddard suggested. "House fire during an all-night poker game. Boating accident." He thought about it. From what he knew of Winthrop, anything was possible. "Maybe they got him first?"

"Maybe."

"Maybe it was just something the club decided to do for its members?" Goddard said. "The more I think about it, the more I think it was just a gamble. From what I hear, they were all players. Maybe Winthrop and the other club members were figuring one of them would knock off before the end of the life insurance term. Didn't Percy tell you he'd seen Winthrop down at the Black Bear Casino on more than one occasion?"

Dunlap nodded.

"I guess his old buddies hit pay dirt."

"Two point five mil," Dunlap mused.

"Damn. That's a lotta jack."

After a few moments of silence, during which both of them briefly wondered what they would do with that kind of money, Dunlap said, "I'm not sure there's a whole lot we can do about that insurance payment. But we might be able to pry recompense out of Winthrop's estate, providing we can find paperwork that details his legal maneuvers with those pensioners. Tell you the truth, I'm not even sure we can do that. Our best bet is to try and prove fraud. There seems to be a lot of expense reimbursements for unnecessary equipment and dubious treatments."

The sheriff waited before he spoke, long enough so he didn't betray his eagerness to assist. He didn't like hiding it from his old friend, but he had no choice. "Maybe I should poke around a little," he suggested.

"I was thinking the same thing. Maybe take a look at his office and that Defiance house, for starters. Then his farmhouse. It'd be within your purview to enter the place and nose around. To do a thorough search, we'd need a search warrant. But I can work those details, if one becomes necessary."

"What about Heins?"

"What about him? There's no reason to bring Heins into this. I don't care if he's the town cop. Since he's a beneficiary, there's a clear conflict of interest. If Heins catches you at Winthrop's office or his Defiance home, just tell him the county attorney wanted to make sure an old colleague's property was safe."

"Old colleague?"

"Percy's a lawyer. Winthrop was a lawyer. Colleagues. Call it professional courtesy."

"Percy's office investigated Winthrop three times in the last 10 years."

"Then call it attorney collegiality," Dunlap quipped, vaguely.

Goddard grinned. Finally, he stood up.

"We're going to follow the crooked dead man into his grave, dig around a little, and see if he can throw us a bone."

CHAPTER THIRTEEN

The alarm awakened him. He grabbed his Dopp kit and made his way down the hall to the bathroom, where he brushed his teeth, showered, and washed away two days on the road. He decided to leave his three-day beard growth. His ex-wife Maggie had never liked his beard. She thought it made him look rough. Maybe it was time to grow one.

Back in his room he changed into a fresh multicolored western shirt and a pair of jeans and tried to make himself presentable.

When he looked out the frost-covered window, he could see the abandoned depot, the railroad tracks, and the woods beginning to darken. Darkness came quickly to Northern Minnesota. Frozen woods at midnight could be a sanctuary, when entered at the right time, with the right equipment and the proper frame of mind. When he was young, he liked hiking in pale moonlight, particularly in extreme cold, when he knew he would be alone. But his midnight excursions taught him to be careful about darkness, that sometimes it was better left alone.

Eventually Heins would discover the break-in at Sam's mother's house. And it was only a matter of time before Sam would be recognized. The burial was the day after tomorrow, when he would witness the old man's final interment. Then they'd know him. Once they discovered the break-in and knew he was in town, the obvious step would be some kind of search. That's what Sam would do. He considered seeing Heins cruising by in his patrol car in front of the hotel a warning. It was time to hide the duffel.

Diane was one of his mother's more unlikely companions. She

was an up-north outdoorsy kind of woman. Long dark hair, strong legs that curved up to rounded, perfect glutes, and she had well-defined muscles on her arms, probably from all that time spent paddling. And her chest was proportioned well enough to kindle a 15-year-old's imagination (though at 15 it didn't take much).

Before he left, he reached into his bag and pulled out his cell phone. It had been an unusual two days, particularly since he'd turned off his official phone. He thought he'd better check his messages.

First, he heard his supervisor. Forensics in Ashland had finally finished running the tests on that fur. Judy Rutgers's sheep killer was a hybrid—part Mexican wolf and part coyote. They would have loved to have caught the animal just to see it. It had everyone stumped, since it implied there was part of at least one Mexican wolf in Colorado, or at least one within 500 miles. Unfortunately, it never returned. The traps were going back to storage. "Just thought you'd like to know," he said.

A hybrid, Sam thought. That was a surprise.

Then Magdalen's voice came onto the line. "The plot thickens, Rivers. You apparently decided to take my advice and cash in some vacation time? You aren't in Las Vegas, are you?" she asked, chuckling behind the comment. "Here's the deal," she continued. "You'll never guess who applied for your job."

Magdalen was already referring to it as Sam's job. Typical of Magdalen, who usually got what she wanted.

"I'll save you the suspense. Carmine Salazar," she said. Then she paused, to let him absorb the news. "That's right. Can you believe it? His name is Carmine. Like the color. Like a bruise." She snickered at her own wit.

Salazar was the USFW accountant who was living with Sam's ex-wife.

"No wonder he goes by Sal," she added. "Call me. I need to know what you're thinking. The spot is yours. National special agent on the interagency task force. I want you to have it, Rivers. We both know it's perfect for you. But I can only hold off Salazar so long."

The new USFW commissioner was the kind of inside administrator, a technocrat, who might appreciate Salazar's business and accounting acumen. But a field agent? Salazar? From what Sam remembered, Salazar was a pretty boy, someone he couldn't imagine wading through mud, both the real and metaphorical.

But over the last 48 hours Sam hadn't thought about any of it: the USFW, the new job, Maggie, Salazar, any of it. And that's because he still had work to do.

Magdalen would have to wait. And he knew she would.

A few miles west of Defiance, Sam found Diane's place. The driveway curved up behind the cabin into a thick stand of black spruce. There was a pair of fresh tracks in the newly plowed snow. Looked like she had company.

Sam took the next turn and parked on the side of a gravel road. Then he cut the engine and stepped into the frosty dark.

He needed to check out Diane's home (and Diane) before assuming it was the best place to hide his duffel. Given the contents of his bag and what he was going to ask of her, it was wise to be cautious.

He walked along the side road and highway until he came to Diane's drive. Sam bent to examine the tire tracks. Thick new treads, probably a pickup. There was only one set of them. She had either left and not returned, or she had company. If she had company, he would backtrack the way he'd come, no one the wiser.

He climbed farther up the drive and saw the tail section of a new blue pickup protruding from the corner of the house. He couldn't be certain, but it looked like the same truck he'd seen last night, before entering Defiance. Pederson's truck, a polished powder blue with dealer plates.

Maybe it was Mrs. Pederson, if she was still around. Maybe Pederson's wife borrowed his truck and was visiting? But Sam remembered Pederson's wife as quiet, submissive, and slightly rotund. It was hard to imagine she'd become Diane's friend.

Sam walked up alongside the pickup and peered through the frosted passenger side window. There was a half-finished pint of whiskey on the front seat. Parked on the other side of the truck was an old Datsun pickup, its northwest side banked high with snow. Diane's car, Sam guessed. If he was right about the new truck, he was surprised Pederson was paying Diane a visit. But it had been a very long time and things change. Regardless, it was time to leave.

Then he heard a woman's voice, a few decibels louder than pleasant conversation. He edged to the outside cabin wall, listening. When Diane's voice broke off, he thought he heard Pederson's deep bass, low and measured, vibrating across the porch. He was pretty sure it was the same voice he'd heard last night. When Pederson was done speaking, Diane's voice retorted: sharp, focused, angry. But he couldn't make out the words.

Sam edged farther along the front porch, peering through the kitchen window. Wooden cupboards. Some dishes in the sink. A steak knife lay on the countertop, near a quartered lime. Sam ducked below the kitchen window and edged toward the door. Their voices grew louder. He stopped and pressed his back against the wall. From this angle he could peer around the corner and see a closet inside the front door.

Sam flattened, turning his ear against the outside wall.

". . . arrange a Ford Escape?" the man asked.

"Hank," Diane said, loud enough to make her point. "You need to leave."

"A new Escape could get you around a whole lot better than that Datsun socked in by the storm."

There was a long pause before Diane seemed to turn and face the door. "Get out of my house," she finally managed, cold and direct, louder than any of her previous words.

"What is it with you?" Pederson blurted, ignoring her.

Sam heard him rise. His voice moved as he walked across the room.

"I know people in Eveleth. They told me you were a party girl. That you lived for a good time. And that's all I'm saying now. I'll show you an excellent time."

"I haven't been to Eveleth in 20 years. And what I did when I lived there is none of your goddamn business. Get the hell out of my house, or I'll call the sheriff!"

Sam heard her move as she spoke. Their voices were louder, tense. He edged to the side of the front door and stepped back so he could see through the front door window.

"This here is Bill Heins's turf," Pederson said. "You're still in Defiance."

A tattered sofa and easy chair were positioned in front of a fireplace. Some logs were smoldering in the grate, nearly ash.

Pederson stood in front of the chair. Diane was behind the sofa. Sam saw the back of her head, a thick salt and pepper braid trailing down its center. Her square shoulders were tense and alert. She looked stronger than he remembered, more formidable.

"Go home to your wife, Hank," she said, trying to reason with him.

"I told you about the money," Pederson said, continuing to bargain. "A fair piece of change." There was a pause. "How much would you want?"

Pederson wasn't begging. It was a business proposition. He wanted to know her price.

"What would you do with a new Escape and 500 bucks?" Pederson asked. He started to smile. "How about a grand?"

She ignored him.

Emboldened by her silence, Pederson stepped forward.

And then she exploded. "Get the fuck out of my house!" she growled, pointing to the door.

Pederson's face color changed from a healthy pink (which Sam guessed was the whiskey) to crimson. In the yellow light he looked old. He'd made his final offer.

Diane was steadfast, shocked by the proposal. There was a little fear in her fury. And with good reason. Unless Sam was mistaken, it looked like rage building behind the big man's eyes.

Suddenly Pederson turned, head down, starting around the couch toward the door. Sam jerked away from the wall. Then he broke into a dead run, leaping over a snowdrift, trying to conceal himself before Pederson stepped through that door.

But in midair he heard the door's bolt lock snap shut. Pederson had never intended to leave.

Halfway back to his observation point, he heard Diane scream. As Sam approached he heard another scream and then Diane's "Get the hell out of my house!" accompanied by a heavy crash.

Pederson crouched low to the ground, his big arms outstretched, moving like an upright bear. Diane was in a corner, wielding a pine-based lamp like a baseball bat.

"Come on, Diane." He was smiling.

The big man must be a whole lot drunker than he appeared.

"Get out!" she repeated.

He took a cautious step forward.

Diane blurted something unintelligible and swung. Pederson leaped back and the arc of the lamp brushed his shirt.

He started laughing, ignited by the gesture, as though it was some kind of perverted foreplay. He moved closer and Diane stepped back, boxing herself into the corner.

"You son of a bitch!" She swung and Pederson leaped back, then quickly reestablished his ground. Diane cocked to swing again.

"I'll pay," Pederson said. "You wouldn't have called me tonight unless some part of you wanted to consider my offer."

"Get away!" She swung again and he lurched back, stepping forward as the arc of her swing passed. For a drunk past 60 he was quick enough.

"If you touch me, it'll be assault."

"Your word against mine," Pederson said. Diane swung, enraged. Pederson pivoted and stepped in behind her. His huge arms closed around her and the lamp fell to the floor. "And Bill Heins is a friend of mine," he said, tense, through gritted teeth.

Sam stepped back, made a solid kick, and there was a loud

thwack as the wood splintered and the door swung open.

The bunched pair turned to face him, Pederson holding Diane tight in front of him like a shield. Sam stared, trying to measure the big man's resolve. And then something in the agent shifted. He'd felt it before, in similar tight quarters. An adrenaline rush that if left unchecked made him feel as though he could beat the aging car salesman into unconsciousness. Or dead. Only this time it was personal. This time he would need to channel his building rage.

"Who the hell are you?" Pederson finally coughed.

Sam glanced at Diane, thought he saw recognition, then disbelief.

"An old friend of Diane's." He stared at Pederson.

"Get the fuck out of here," Pederson blustered. "This is no concern of yours."

Sam doffed his stocking cap, loosened his scarf, and unzipped his coat. He took a second to shed the coat and drop it with his scarf over the back of the sofa. Now he was unencumbered. He closed the door. Then he turned around and ran his fingers through his hair, never taking his eyes off Pederson. Beat the shit out of him, he told himself. What he deserves. But all he said was, "I think you should let her go, Hank." Sam's use of the big man's name unnerved him.

If Pederson ever loosened that steel-clasp grasp, Diane was set to uncoil.

"This is none of your goddamn business," Pederson repeated.

But Sam could feel a sudden shift in the battle.

"Rape?"

"I wouldn't have raped her. We were just having fun."

"Fuck you," Diane spit.

Sam held the big man's gaze long enough to convey reckoning. "Yeah," he said. "Fuck you." Then he smiled, but without humor. "Chances are, if we all got into it, you might land a couple of good blows. But to do it, you'll have to let Diane go, and when you come after me, something tells me she's going to finish the job she started with that lamp."

Sam watched Pederson working through the problem, recognizing the change in numbers, how it worked against him. "Who the fuck are you?" he repeated.

"The name is Sam," he said. "Sam Rivers. Like I said, an old friend of Diane's. I was in town and decided to say hello." When he was young, the old man made Sam address everyone as mister. It had been Mr. Pederson. "Hank," Sam finished.

There was another long moment as Pederson pondered his options. Then recognition. "Clayton?" he asked.

"Rivers," he said. "Sam Rivers."

Pederson considered, startled by the realization. Then he kicked the lamp across the room. His arms relaxed and Diane slipped away. She turned as she left. Her fist came up like a prize-fighter's, cutting across Pederson's jaw as she backed away. Pederson's head recoiled as she stepped out of reach.

"You son of a bitch!" She started shaking. "Next time I'll have a gun," she managed.

Pederson stared at her, enraged by her parting shot. His hand rubbed his jaw and his middle finger reached into his mouth, coming out red. His left fist lowered and clenched, ready to charge.

"Go ahead," Sam said. "Maybe you'll get lucky."

Sam's voice was even, measured, calm. Gradually the blood ebbed out of the big man's face. The danger passed. He managed to turn and pick up his coat, made a wide arc around Sam Rivers. At the door's threshold Pederson turned.

Sam could see he'd regained some composure. He looked at Diane. "Maybe I got a little out of hand," he observed. Then his eyes narrowed. "But next time I won't be so nice about asking." He turned to Sam. "My advice to you is get out. There's nothing for you here." Then he turned and disappeared into the night.

CHAPTER FOURTEEN

It was not the first time Heins considered himself an outlaw. It was 9° below, practically mild by Defiance standards but cold enough to make Heins's elevated breath rise in columns through the trees. He wore a black ski mask, black mittens, and a midnight-blue snowmobile suit. If you were an owl, perched overhead and watching for movement across the snow, Heins's dark shadow was as clear as a passing moose. But if you were anyone else, casting a sidelong glance through the dark wood, he was an invisible burglar.

All morning he'd sat in his office, monitoring the sheriff's radio chatter, waiting to hear news of the call regarding the wolf kill at Winthrop's farm. Even if Moon had only contacted the DNR, news would have filtered through the sheriff's office. Steve Svegman, the local DNR conservation officer, would have relayed the information to Goddard. There would be another investigation, this one by Svegman. And then they could file their claim with the Minnesota Department of Agriculture.

But word never came.

It was Thursday. He wasn't due at the cabin until Friday, to celebrate Winthrop's wake. Everything coming in from official channels was business about the storm, power outages and downed lines, a few stranded vehicles. A plow breakdown out of Vermilion Falls. Finally, late in the afternoon, when he was still unable to contact Moon by phone at either his place or the farmhouse, or by CB at the cabin, Heins knew something was wrong. He needed to find out what.

There were five overgrown paths leading into the hidden cabin, little more than game trails, all from different angles, as though the cabin was the center of a huge wheel and each of the trails were twisted spokes. The club members were careful to vary their approach, though after dark Heins took the shortest and most traveled path.

Heins stepped carefully through the snow. From the over-hanging boughs, 20 yards from the cabin's windows, the place looked deserted. Two pairs of snowshoes were stuck upright in drifts beside the front door. The kitchen table, just the other side of the front window—their primary sitting, drinking, and gaming table—was empty. Heins thought it was a bad sign.

He continued to the front door, depositing his snowshoes next to the others. When he opened the door, it creaked on rusty hinges. Then he heard it. A startled grunt, followed by a deep, sonorous snore.

"For Chrissake," he muttered, entering the cabin, shaking himself off. He hung his coat and stamped his feet. It was enough to make the snoring stop. He lit a propane lamp.

The cabin was warm and smelled of wood smoke, bacon, and cigars. It was a simple construction, but large for a hideout carved out of Skinwalkers Bog. They'd had plenty of timber to work with, and they'd used it. There was a great front room, open across a long plywood floor with a couple of dingy woven rag rugs, faded ovals across the scarred boards. Along one wall was a small bunk, and along the back there were three small bedrooms—two with single beds lining each wall, a small dresser, a propane gas lantern, and a narrow walkway to allow a person to walk into the bedrooms with enough space to turn and sit. The third bedroom was furnished with a queen bed, a narrow walkway along one side. There was a large kitchen table in front of a wide pair of windows, frosted over in the cold. There was also a counter with a sink, a gas stove, a gas refrigerator, and along the right front wall some open cupboards with dented pots and dishware. It was a sparsely furnished place, but just fine for gaming, hunting, and scheming. All in all it was a comfortable den. But Heins wasn't feeling comfortable.

On the kitchen table were two coffee cups and an empty whiskey bottle. Heins guessed the rest.

From the room with the queen bed, Winthrop stirred. "What?" he seemed to mumble. There was a long pause before Heins heard him mutter, then swear.

Heins walked over to the room's entryway and said, "What if I was the law."

Winthrop lay across the bed face down. He'd been in deep slumber. "Goddammit," he managed, starting to come awake. He turned and saw Heins standing in the bedroom's threshold. "You are the law," he muttered. "Besides, we almost died last night."

Heins was in no mood. "You died Sunday."

"Gettin' out here was a nightmare," Winthrop said, rolling over. "We tried all night and into this morning to raise you on the radio. Couldn't get a thing." From the next room they heard Moon resume his snoring. "Guess Angus didn't hear you."

"Guess not."

"He almost lost it in that goddamn storm."

"Why in the hell didn't anybody check on the stock?"

Winthrop thought for a minute, trying to come awake. "What time is it?"

"After 6."

"Christ," he managed, turning on an elbow. "When Angus and I couldn't reach anyone, we decided to have a little something to raise our spirits." He could see Heins wasn't mollified. "Don't worry," Winthrop added, waving an arm to ward off the lawman's concern.

Heins backed up and let him come into the front room. There was a large potbellied stove near the center back wall. Winthrop limped over, still waking up, and threw another log into the stove. A wisp of smoke curled out the iron door. Then he turned to a shelf over the sink, spilled two aspirin into his palm, and downed them with a cup of water.

"Those calves'll keep," Winthrop finally said. "At least what's left of 'em."

"I know the calves'll keep. It's the DNR and Agriculture I'm worried about. We need to file that claim."

Winthrop paused for a minute, still coming awake. Then he said, "You don't know the half of it."

"Half of what?"

"We had to leave them."

"You had to leave who?"

"Those dogs."

"You left them in the barn?"

"Yup."

"For Chrissake!" Heins exhaled. "Suppose someone goes out there and finds them?"

"Who?"

Heins considered it. "How in the fuck should I know? Maybe somebody who thinks they can steal something out of a dead man's farmhouse."

"So how would they explain they were there, providing they went out to the barn, found the wolves, and decided to report it?"

Winthrop had a point. "Did you consider the sheriff? Goddard's been poking around. Maybe he'd go back out to have another look at the scene."

"Goddard's the least of our worries. And if anyone pokes around, they'll find wolves. So what?"

"Did people get a lot more stupid in the last 24 hours? Why would wolves be corralled in a closed-up barn?"

Winthrop paused, turning. "We left the door open. Couldn't get it shut."

"What?"

"The door froze open. The storm clogged the runner with snow and ice while those hybrids were killing and feeding. We couldn't shut it. But now that I think of it, that's the way they'd enter. Wolves. When Angus has to explain it."

"What if they ran?"

"Could have. I doubt it, given that storm. And the barn's full of food. And they were damn hungry. We couldn't cage them because they were still feeding. And we had to get the hell out of there, or get stranded. Did you want them to find me?" He scratched his head and yawned. "But think about it. Say they run and someone shoots them. They're wolves, aren't they?"

Heins thought for a minute, not happy about it. But the hybrids definitely looked more wolf than whatever else Moon had bred into them. "More or less." But Heins could tell Winthrop was talking himself into this new perspective, given the turn of events. "So what now?"

"We rouse Angus."

As if in answer, Moon snored from the middle bedroom.

"He needs to get back to town. There's something I need him to do at the office."

"What?"

"Loose ends," was all Winthrop said. "I don't want anyone finding incriminating files. Goddard or Dunlap. I might have forgotten something." He paused for effect. "I want Angus to burn it," he said, knowing Heins wouldn't appreciate a major Defiance blaze.

"A fire?"

Winthrop nodded. "A big fire."

"How big?"

"The Winthrop Building."

"A goddamn building fire? It'll draw too much attention," he said, shaking his head.

"You think I wouldn't do it unless it was absolutely necessary?"

Heins turned away. "I don't like it," he said.

"Neither do I. That's why Angus is going to be extra careful about setting it, and when."

"Williston," Heins exhaled. "Goddamn it. How's it going to look with your office going up in flames less than a week after your death?"

"Shit happens," Winthrop shrugged. "It's an old building. Old buildings burn every day. There's a bad socket with a bad fixture plugged into it, directly behind my desk. That and a little dust should make the place go up like a tinderbox. Besides, it's insured," he said with a smile.

"When's the last time we had a fire in Defiance?"

"It'll happen after midnight. You'll be home in bed, along with everyone else. There'll be an electrical spark from a faulty socket. And you know the place is full of paper. Dry paper, just waiting to burn. And the fire marshal practically condemned the place the last time he went through."

Heins exhaled again, looking away. "I need a goddamn drink," he said.

"Hair of the dog that bit ya," Winthrop said. He turned toward the other bedroom. "Angus!" he yelled. "Wake up! Angus!"

Moon stopped snoring.

"What about those dogs?" Heins asked.

"You and Angus can get them in the morning. First thing. Before first thing," Winthrop said. "Angus! Goddamn it. Get the fuck out of bed!"

Moon moaned.

"What if the dogs aren't around?" Heins asked.

"Would you leave in the middle of a storm when there was food and shelter right under your nose? They aren't going any-where. Even if they do, they're wolves. It would appear to be a wolf pack returning to the woods. That might be better," he said, rubbing one sleepy eye.

"They'll want to trap them."

"Good."

"They're not exactly wolves."

"They look like it, more or less. Angus!"

"For Chrissake," Moon moaned.

Heins continued warming himself by the stove, not exactly calmed by his first heavy draught of amber liquid. He felt unset-tled by the development, and the ease with which Winthrop dis-counted it. Whiskey, he thought. While he contemplated the next morning's efforts, trying to work out the timing, a lone howl pierced the 9-inch walls. It was far off, not loud, but they all heard it. The wail from the deep woods raised hairs on the back of Heins's neck, even though he was used to wolf howls. "That's the first time I've heard them in Skinwalkers Bog."

Moon creaked across the bed, managed to sit upright. "Maybe it's my dogs," he mumbled.

"Just what we fuckin' need," Heins said.

"Maybe they decided to run." Moon wasn't serious, but he could feel Heins's worry.

"You don't think they'll stay?" Heins called into the bedroom.

"You just never know about wolves," Moon said, slowly, getting the words out one at a time. "You saw them take after those feeders," he added, bending over and starting to rise, stepping out of the room. "I didn't know they had it in 'em."

"They were starving," Winthrop observed.

"I know," Moon said. "Smart to keep them hungry so long. They remembered they were wolves."

"Part wolves," Heins corrected. "They still have some dog in 'em."

"Last night they tore into those calves like full wolves," Moon said. "Maybe even something better," he mused, coming out of the room, heading to where the whiskey sat on the kitchen table. "But I know my dogs."

"I hope you're right," Heins said. "Because if you're not, we're going to have one hell of a time catching them."

"Don't worry," Winthrop reassured. "Angus'll get 'em."

"Yeah," he said, agreeing with Winthrop. "I'll get 'em in the morning." Then he considered. "It's good a pack's come into the bog. Just shows how much the vermin are spreading. Helps explain our kill."

As if on cue, a chorus of low howls sounded through the cabin's timbers, far off but distinct. The men listened to their eerie wails.

Moon didn't expect his dogs to run. If they did, he had no idea how he might lure and then cage five dogs that had finally recollected their ancestry.

"Angus," Winthrop said, after the woodsman had a chance to drink. "Before you get those dogs, I've got a little job for you."

CHAPTER FIFTEEN

After dusk Goddard nosed his cruiser into the alley behind Miriam Winthrop's vacant Defiance home. The temperature began dropping with the sun. It was already 12° below, heading deeper.

Good and cold, thought the sheriff, happy about the arctic air mass. It would keep most folks indoors.

He pulled the cruiser to the side of the plowed alley directly in front of the garage. Lights were on in the neighborhood homes. The sky was clear, but the moonrise was still a couple hours off. If anyone looked out their windows, they might see the shadowy outline of his patrol car. Might, over the plowed drifts. Then again, this kind of cold frosted over glass. And it was dinnertime. Most families were gathered around their kitchen tables, taking in the warmth and a little chow.

Just to be safe, he'd driven by the town cop's home. It was a small, nondescript square house with no trees and a white expanse of fresh snow. The drive was newly plowed, and either side was drifted high up with snow. The home's windows were dark, front and back, and Heins's patrol car was missing. A subsequent drive through Defiance neighborhoods yielded nothing. Goddard turned the radio channel to the local police band, but there was only static. Heins was gone.

Goddard pulled down his hat, donned his mittens, and got out of his car. He had thick down mittens with an opening for the thumb and trigger finger, so he could whip his gun from its belt holster, should the need arise. Or grab his can of mace. Or the shiny handcuffs, though he wouldn't need any of them tonight. He struggled through deep snow to the back of the house.

He'd already considered a couple of different means of entry, but knew there'd have to be good reason. He squinted through the dark. In his side pocket he had a small black flashlight. He flicked its beam on the back door. He didn't expect to find anything, was surprised when it appeared as though someone had been there. He trailed the light down and saw old depressions in the snow, what looked like footprints buried over by last night's blow. They were barely visible, but still discernible.

Goddard followed the faint tracks around the side of the house, not 30 feet from the neighbor's outside wall. He flashed the light across the snow and saw a pair of boot prints almost covered over. Someone came and went, he guessed. From the looks of it, he couldn't be sure, but it appeared as though someone had come from the front to the back, turned around the corner to the door, and then started back.

He returned to the rear of the house, had another look. Near the corner, to the right of the back stairs, Goddard saw a small depression in the snow. It looked like a deer had lain down in the snow, curled up in a ball to ride out the storm. He stepped over to it, flicked his boot over the surface, and the space opened. He stepped farther into the hole, and his boot pushed down through the surface of the snow, well beyond ground level.

A window well, he thought. He kneeled in the snow, clearing a place. He reached his arm down and suddenly, surprisingly, the snow fell away and a wisp of warm air rose out of darkness. He cleared more space, flicked on his flashlight, flashed its beam into the hole, and saw the jagged edges of broken glass. A break-in?

He cleared the snow away from the window, piling it around the hole. He could see where the pane had been broken, where the window had been pulled up. He reached in, felt for the latch, turned it, and pushed. The window was frozen. He leaned into the hole, extending his arm through the broken pane, pulling as he brought his other hand down and pushed.

As the window came unstuck, his wrist flicked across the broken glass edge. "Goddammit," he muttered. He brought his arm out and looked at the broken skin. A small line of mottled blood rose from the scratch, but the cut wasn't deep.

The sheriff stowed the light and carefully let himself down, feet first, dropping to the basement floor.

He paused, listening. The furnace kicked on and he jumped. He waited a while longer in the basement darkness, listening. But the place was empty.

He reached back up and dropped the window shut, latching it from the inside. Then he turned and surveyed the rest of the room.

A stairwell rose to the main level. There was some furniture near the far wall, and a storage door. The sheriff stepped to the door and opened it.

The dark room was filled with jars. Dusty preserves covered a series of wooden shelves. Down near the bottom it looked like some of the jars had been recently moved. He kneeled to have a look and saw rings in the dust where four jars were missing.

Goddamn thieves, he thought. Stealing preserves. The idea made him smile, taking the edge off his adrenaline surge.

He moved over to the stairs and started to climb. He stepped silently down the hallway, treading carefully over the worn carpet.

There were two doors down its length. He opened the nearest door and it appeared to be an old bedroom. A white chenille bedspread lay across the bed. When Goddard flashed his light across the spread, it was bunched near the floor, as though someone had recently sat on it. The burglar, he wondered?

He left the door open and moved to the next room. A bathroom, quiet, small, rectangular, and tiled, with a sink, toilet, and shower. He walked down to the kitchen, where the light from the street illuminated the old linoleum. There was something in the air. Something familiar. Food? Pickles? He walked over to the sink and he thought the smell intensified.

Goddard searched through the rest of the rooms. Other than the break-in, there was no sign anyone had been in the house for a long time. He opened the cupboards, cabinets, storage closets, anyplace he thought Winthrop might have hidden some sort of digital storage device. He scoured the old bedroom but found nothing. He sat on the edge of the bed and tried to think.

Why in the hell would someone break in and steal four jars of preserves, nothing else? Particularly when there was plenty of other stuff worth taking. In the living room there was a hutch. Two of its drawers contained silver. There was a television in the corner, old but probably serviceable. At least it would bring a few dollars at a Duluth pawnshop. Goddard guessed there were a few hundred bucks worth of pawnshop pickings. Kids on some kind of lark? Everyone in a small town like Defiance knew Williston Winthrop had inherited Miriam's home. Maybe the recent announcement about his death prompted someone to take advantage? But Winthrop hadn't been dead that long. Less than five days. High school kids ripping off the dead man?

Goddard could ask around, see if anyone over at Vermilion High knew anything. But it didn't make sense. Anyone going to that much trouble would have stolen something. At least something worth more than preserves.

He made another cursory examination of the entire house, searching for any cranny Winthrop might have used to store something. Anything he didn't want people to find. He looked through the linens, bedroom closets, under the kitchen sink, peered with his flashlight behind the fridge. The freezer was self-defrosting, empty. The fridge was still running, but empty.

The sheriff sat down at the kitchen table and squinted at his wristwatch in the dim light. It was already after 7 p.m. He'd found nothing in the vacant house. He guessed Winthrop could have taken the preserves, eaten some of his dead wife's pickles. But it was all too fresh. And the basement window was broken by someone who appeared to have entered the place last night, in the middle of that storm, judging from the tracks. None of it made sense.

Finally, he let himself out the back door, unlocking and pushing on the frozen door until it snapped open. It left a small drift of snow to the side, where the door opened. He locked the door behind him, looked around. Still no one. He shuffled the snow back over the door and did the same to the drift over the window well. Truth was, he didn't have a warrant. He knew the break-in would eventually be found. It would be simplest if he could get out of the place without being seen. He might want to come back and have another look around.

Back at his car he examined the neighborhood homes. It was cold and the frosty weather had covered every window with a thick glaze. No one could see anything, even if they had peered out at the plowed drifts.

He wasn't sure what he'd seen, but he knew what he hadn't found. He replayed the scratchy video in his head, wondering where Winthrop hid it. The two other most likely places were his office and the old farmhouse. He might be able to get into the office later tonight, but thought maybe he should wait. Wait for Dunlap to get that search warrant. He could easily check out that farmhouse, but Moon might be out there, tending to Winthrop's feeder calves. Better to wait on that too. Let those remote roads get plowed.

For now, Goddard thought, as he started his cruiser quietly and eased it down the back alley, it would be best to stay frosty and keep his eyes open.

CHAPTER SIXTEEN

In the wake of Pederson's departure, Diane rushed to the door and slammed it, but it wouldn't catch. She turned, keeping the door closed with her back, as if some part of her thought Pederson might return. Her hand went up to her face. Her knuckles were red from striking him. They both heard his engine start. Diane's head turned, listening. Her face was flushed and her eyes flashed with rage. If she'd had a gun, Sam guessed, Pederson would have been leaving on a gurney with a sheet pulled over his head.

The truck started down the drive, its engine growing fainter through the trees. Sam listened long enough to make sure Pederson didn't turn on the side road where Sam's Jeep was parked. He heard the new blue pickup accelerate down the highway and disappear.

Diane's breathing became more measured. Sam wanted to say something, but until she calmed down, it would be like offering solace to a puma. She stepped away from the door. She walked across the living room into the kitchen. Sam heard the freezer door open. She took down an ice tray and a dark green bottle with a red cap. Akvavit, a Scandinavian twist on vodka. She cracked the tray, and cubes spilled into the sink. She reached in, grabbed several cubes, and dropped them into her glass, focusing to get hold of herself. She twisted the cap and poured. There was a sharp pop as the thick, clear liquid washed over the ice.

She raised the glass and Sam watched her take a long swallow, punctuated by a sharp exhalation. She managed to return the glass to the countertop before reaching a trembling hand to her forehead. Her eyes closed and she turned her head, trying to gather herself. She reached down and emptied her drink. Then she took the bottle and refilled her glass.

"That asshole," she finally managed, her hands still shaky. Diane wasn't the type to choke out a sob, though it would have been warranted. Sam guessed it would take a few moments for her rage to subside. Then Pederson had better start watching his back.

Finally, she turned and Sam looked at her face, still reddened but fading to normal. "Sam?"

"I figured it was time for a visit." He paused. He was still a little surprised by what he'd witnessed. Before he could say anything else, she looked away, continuing to regain control. Gray streaks splintered her black hair.

"You've grown up." She stared at him, then seemed to remember something. "How about a drink?"

"I could use one."

Diane took down a glass and filled it with ice and akvavit, then handed it to him.

"You OK?" he asked.

"Getting there," she said.

"You should press charges."

She paused, then took another sip. "Probably should. But you've been away too long. Out here I'm still within Defiance city limits. And that means the investigating officer would be Bill Heins. Do you remember him?"

Sam nodded. "I remember Heins."

"One of your father's friends. And one of Hank Pederson's buddies."

"You have a witness."

Diane stared at him. "Truth is, if I had a gun handy, Hank Pederson's blood would be staining my floor." She looked away, considering. "And that would be the kind of knee-jerk justice Bill Heins and his Iron Range buddies might understand." She took another sip of akvavit. "But to press charges means eventually we could appear before a judge and jury, and that means a fat ass talker like Hank Pederson would dredge up every nasty detail he could find about me. Nothing much recent, but there was a day I liked to party. It might cast enough doubt, in spite of my eyewitness. And remember, up here men are men, and women are their wives, mothers, sisters, and whores."

"I think it's changed," Sam argued. "I think you'd have a pretty good chance."

She looked down at her hand and rubbed the cold glass over her red knuckles. "Don't worry," she said. "I'm not going to let that son of a bitch get away with it. For now I'll have to think on it. I drew a little blood with that fist to his face." She managed a tough grin. "You can bet if I get another chance, I'll draw more. But not in a stand-up fight. It'll have to be ladylike." She turned to Sam, but didn't smile. "Hank Pederson is overdue for some Range justice."

Sam took a drink of the biting liquid and could feel the smooth, pleasant burn.

"Do you remember akvavit?" she asked.

"I remember. The 'water of life,' " he translated.

"Those Scandinavians know their drinks."

Sam drank the rest of it straight away and set the glass on the counter. He could feel the warmth in his throat.

"Have another?"

"One more might be nice."

Sam walked over to examine the door while Diane filled his glass. He bent to look at the broken lock. He fingered the splinters where the bolt tore away from the frame. He turned to look at her, and she appeared to be much better. "Sorry about your door," he said.

She shook her head. "Your entry was as perfect as your timing."

Sam nodded. Part of him was sorry they hadn't convinced Pederson to take a chance with his fists.

Diane examined the place where the bolt lock broke away. He watched her fingers play over the wood, rub over two vacant screw holes. She picked up the piece from the floor and fit it back into its ragged slot.

"It can be fixed," she said.

That's what Sam remembered about Diane. Competence. The ability to live on her own on the edge of wilderness. He guessed it was one of the reasons his mother liked her so much. That and her willingness to put her whole body into a right fist to Pederson's jaw.

She turned and looked at him. Sam followed the focus of her sharp green eyes. She was still a beautiful woman. She wasn't the 30-year-old he'd paddled and hiked behind, but he could see why Pederson would be interested. What he didn't understand was why Pederson thought he had a chance.

She walked across the room, picking up the lamp from where it had fallen, replacing it on the end table. Then she turned and said, "It's been . . . what—19, 20 years?"

She wore a pair of blue jeans with a gray fisherman's sweater that had a top-heavy sway beneath it. Clearly she had been expecting no one, given her comfortable attire.

"Twenty," he answered.

She looked away, calculating in her head. "Yeah," she said, wistful. "Your mother's death was a sore loss for the Range."

"I should have come back."

"You should have." She paused. "But your mom seemed to understand, though she never quite got over the fact you had to run. She told me what happened, the day you left. Or at least what she knew about it." She walked over to the fire and placed two logs onto it. She stepped over to the front of her couch and tried to sit down, but she was edgy. She leaned over to watch the logs, but Sam didn't think she was seeing them.

He came around and sat down in the chair across from her. He could hear the pine logs pop. He still held his drink. He watched her for a moment, thought he'd give her a chance to breathe.

Finally, she turned and looked at him. "I agree. You look," she paused, searching for the right words, "grown up. Nice beard."

Sam reached up and rubbed his stubble. "I haven't had a chance to shave in a few days."

"You're a man," she observed, eyeing him. "You look fit."

"Unintended weight loss. It's deceiving."

She looked thoughtful about the comment. Then she glanced down at his hand, noticing the absence of a ring. "Your mom said you'd married."

"Ended. Six months ago." For the first time he thought it seemed a lot longer than six months. He thought that was a good thing. "It just took me a while to figure it out."

"Sorry to hear that."

"She's already moved on," he shrugged. He thought it would take a little more time for his heart to catch up to his head, but he felt clear about it.

"Marriage can be tough. I don't know a lot of happy ones."

"Glad it didn't happen when mom was alive. She liked Maggie."

If his mother had been alive, Sam knew she'd stand with her son. A mother's duty. But Miriam was the kind who always forgave, particularly if it was about a woman's relationship with a man.

"They got along," Sam added, "the few times mom came out to visit. Things just . . . didn't work out the way Maggie wanted, I guess."

"No accounting for a woman's perspective."

Sam didn't smile, but he appreciated the comment. All he deserved, he guessed. "The same could be said for a man's."

"No disagreement there. A man like Hank Pederson gets liquored up, with some spare change in one pocket and his dick in the other, and he thinks he's God's gift to women."

Sam smiled. Her comment and the akvavit lightened the atmosphere in the room. "If you ever need any assistance with that Range justice, count me in."

"Like I said, I'll have to think on it. But I appreciate your offer. It's not only about getting even." Diane set her glass down in front of her. "That'd do for starters. But I'd really like to arrange it so he won't, or can't, think with his dick ever again."

Sam thought that sounded dangerous. "You might have to settle for getting even."

"You're probably right," she reluctantly agreed. "I had to call the guy on some background for an obit I'm writing about your father. He said he'd get back to me; he was in the middle of something. Before I knew it, he was knocking on my door. Said he was on his way to Vermilion Falls and he decided to swing by and give me everything I needed." She stared at the logs, which were picking up a good flame. "Not that I was surprised. The man hasn't had eye contact with a woman since puberty."

True enough, Sam thought with a smile. And not just for Pederson.

Diane looked at him and said, "You're here to recover your things," as though she'd just remembered.

Normally, Sam would have been more reticent about his life, particularly since it had recently involved breaking and entering. And theft. But spending a few moments in Diane's presence, and sitting down on her couch, seeing her cabin and remembering how she felt about Heins and Pederson and his father, Sam was reminded of everything his mother liked about her. It wasn't only her perspective, but the sense you had that she was in control. Diane Talbott conveyed fearlessness. He hadn't known a lot of women like her. Certainly not his mother. Maggie was partly like her, but not entirely. The idea Pederson believed, even for a millisecond, he could sleep with Diane Talbott was a testament to the car salesman's ignorance or drunkenness or dick logic or all three.

"Already did," Sam finally said.

Diane smiled, a little surprised. "Your mother would be pleased. In the weeks leading up to her passing, she worried about you. She was happy you'd done well, creating a new life, putting yourself through school, becoming a big deal in Fish & Wildlife."

The idea that his mother shared her sense of pride pleased him, but also made him wonder if she had shared too much information with too many. Someone besides Diane had his contact information. He could almost hear his mother recounting every one of his small successes: to the postman, the grocer, Diane, the entire crowd at Opel Grady's Café. "I'm just a field agent," he corrected.

"You're a wildlife biologist and a wolf expert," Diane said. "Your mother had a big heart and the ability to see the best in everything, even your father. And she had blinders for the uglier parts in all of us. And she knew it. So the fact is when she'd give me updates about your career, I took it as a mother's zeal. But then I saw a write-up about your wolf repopulation efforts in Colorado, in that magazine from the International Wolf Center in Ely."

Sam remembered it.

"You've done well, considering what you had to endure as a kid. A Fish & Wildlife field agent and wildlife biologist. Specializing in wolves, but if I remember right, you've done work on all the American predators. It was the wolves part that made your mom the happiest, considering the Winthrop family heritage."

Sam smiled. "Someone from the clan had to atone for three generations of annihilation."

"Your mother was happy it was you. She didn't have what was required to spit in her husband's eye, but she was glad you chose a different path than Williston's. And hers."

"Did she ever let him know where I was, what I was doing, my new name?"

"Never. At least that I know of. She would have known your efforts would have pissed him off. She might have said something, just to get in a dig. A woman's right and an estranged wife's duty."

True enough, Sam thought. He could only imagine what his old man, if he'd learned about Sam's efforts, felt about it. Now that he was back on the Range and seeing it through the eyes of a different time, a different life, he felt again the regret over not returning earlier and facing the old man. When he'd seen Pederson, seen how he'd put on weight, grayed, had a throat wattle, Sam realized that Pederson, the old man, all of them, were 20 years older. They'd aged, and he suspected some of the bite had gone out of their teeth.

Now that Pederson knew about him, the others would soon find out. It would only be a matter of time before he'd have a chance to face them. He guessed Heins, to start. He was looking forward to it. But even Sam knew he would have to pick his battles.

"About my things," he started. "Now that I've got them, I need to store them someplace safe. My Jeep and my room at the Defiance Hotel don't give me a lot of options. Even Heins might be able to find them."

"How much is there?"

He paused. "A duffel bag about the size of a dismantled 10 gauge shotgun, a shoebox full of money, and four jars of my mother's preserves."

Diane was surprised, then smiled. "Some of us guessed about some money. Your mom never said anything, but after she died, Marlene, over at the Vermilion Falls State Bank, overheard Winthrop in a heated exchange with the bank's president. Something about lost money and getting sued, though we never heard any more about it. Glad to know Miriam put it someplace safe. You can keep that duffel here," she offered. "I can put it where no one will ever find it."

"I appreciate that." He set down his glass and stood up from the couch. "It's so damn cold out there, I'd better go fetch it before those preserves freeze and the jars burst."

"Where'd you park?" she asked, for the first time realizing she hadn't heard his car come up her drive.

"Down off that side road."

"There's plenty of room next to my Datsun."

"Sounds good." He put on his coat, hat, gloves, and wrapped the scarf around his neck. He paused for a moment, thinking. "There was also a note with my things. And a copy of mom's will," he said.

Diane looked at him. "And the will left everything to you?" she guessed.

"Everything."

"I knew it! Your mom told me that's what she was going to do. But there was another will in which she left everything to Williston."

"I know. Someone—no idea who—sent me a copy of that will. In an email. But it predates this version."

"I asked the sheriff to look into it, but at the time everything appeared to be in order."

"I know. She left a letter with the will, worried the old man would change it. I guess she knew him pretty well."

"I guess," Diane agreed.

"Was the sheriff a friend of Williston's?"

"Hardly. At least not that I know of. Dean Goddard, our sheriff, is around your age. And from everything I can tell, he's a straight shooter. If Dean Goddard had found anything, he'd have brought it out. Winthrop had been practicing law on the Range for the last 40 years. He'd seen his share of last wills and testaments. If anyone would have known how to change a will, make it look legitimate, it would have been Winthrop. He had the ability and he had the motive and Miriam knew he'd do it."

"Know any lawyers? I don't know if, after a will's been

probated, it can be reconsidered." He also wanted to know about Williston Winthrop's will. Who would have an electronic copy of the will within a day of the old man's death? If he could identify them, he might discover the identity of canislupustruth.

Diane thought about it. "Didn't you go to school with Jeff Dunlap?"

Sam remembered the name. Then he vaguely recollected the kid, a year or two behind him in school. Defiance was small enough so everyone knew everyone. "Little Jeff Dunlap?" he asked.

"Assistant County Attorney Jeff Dunlap," Diane said. "Like you, Little Jeff has grown up."

Sam nodded. "I remember him," he said. Then he turned. "I'll get my Jeep."

Diane let him out. The idea Sam might be able to wrest Miriam's estate from the club members' hands, particularly Pederson's, pleased her. It wasn't the kind of Range justice she had in mind, but it was a start.

Sam walked back to his Jeep, warmed by Diane's fire and the akvavit. He started the Jeep, turned around, and headed back to Diane's cabin. He was taking a risk, trusting a woman he hadn't seen in 20 years. Yesterday he didn't have a whole lot to lose. Now he had a shoebox full of money and his mother's rightful will.

He decided to take a chance. But he resolved to keep at least one eye open. Considering his subject, it wasn't an unpleasant proposition.

PART III

The caribou feeds the wolf, but it is the wolf who keeps the caribou strong.

Keewatin (Inuit) Proverb

CHAPTER SEVENTEEN

The Goddards' phone rang. Startled awake, Dean wasn't sure where he was, what it was. He rolled over, rising out of a deep sleep, and the phone made another jangle. He reached over and picked it up.

"Yeah?"

"Dean?" It was Deputy Barnes.

"Yeah," he managed. Belinda's bed creaked in the next room.

"Sorry to wake you. Thought you might like to know. There's a fire in Defiance."

"Yeah?"

"The Winthrop Building is going up like a Roman candle."

Goddard's eyes opened. "What?"

"Came into 911 about 10 minutes ago. I was just making sure the volunteers were called up, but I doubt it'll do any good. Happened after midnight and it's an old wooden building."

Goddard remembered. "Who called it in?"

"Old lady Cummins. She lives down off Main Street, above the closed Ben Franklin store. She was in bed having trouble sleeping when she saw a yellow flicker through her window. When she got up and looked, the place was covered in flames."

"I bet," was all Goddard could think to say. "I better drive over and have a look. Heins been called?"

"Yeah. He's on the scene, or should be in a few minutes."

He thanked Barnes and hung up.

On the corner of Main and Second the volunteer fire truck was plugged into a nearby hydrant. Heins's patrol car stood parked across the street, at an angle that prevented traffic from getting through. But there wasn't much traffic, given the early-morning hour and the deep cold. The fire was burning like a blast furnace. There were almost a dozen volunteer firefighters, all dressed in heavy gear. The water that wasn't affected by the heat had frozen solid. The adjacent buildings were covered with sparkling icicles, and clouds of smoke and steam rose into the frosty night air.

Heins got out of his patrol car as Goddard parked and approached.

"We caught it in time," Heins said. "They've got it under control. At least it's contained. The building's gutted, though. Not much left."

"Anybody know what happened?"

"Martha Cummins saw it first. It was late. Fire marshal was home. He's been called and is on his way. But I don't think there's much to see. By the time Martha saw it, it was pretty much ablaze."

"Anybody else see it?"

"Nobody I've talked to."

"Wasn't Will Winthrop's office in that building?"

Heins nodded.

"Anybody get anything out?"

"I got here right after they did. There was no way you could go near it. They started spraying down the fire and the adjacent buildings, trying to keep them wet."

"Or frozen."

"Either way. I think they contained it. But Winthrop's office is ashes."

As Goddard neared the fire, he could feel the heat on his face. The firefighters milled around the edges, spraying down the buildings, staying in that narrow zone between the blistering heat and the deep freeze. It was terrible weather for fighting a fire, but it had to be contained. As they watched, the fire marshal's car drove up Main and parked behind the sheriff's cruiser. Walt Gibbons stepped out of his car, walked over to where Heins and Goddard stood. Gibbons was a roly-poly man just past 60, with a cherub face and a bushy gray mustache. Nothing put Gibbons in a more jovial mood than a big fire.

"Gentlemen," he said.

"How ya doin', Walt?" Goddard said, extending his hand.

"Couldn't be better," he said, staring at the fiery ruin.

Heins greeted him with a nod. "Walt."

"Looks like a goddamn wood flambé with silver icing," Gibbons observed.

The three men stared at the fire. The fire marshal paced to the left, considered the smoldering blaze from a different angle. He walked to the other side and then came back to center. Around and in front of him, the volunteers were doing what they could to both contain the blaze and stay warm and dry.

"Looks like they have it under control. It'll just be keeping it corralled from here on out. Anybody see anything?"

"Not until it was stoked up like a goddamn bonfire," Heins said.

The sheriff was peering into what remained of the caved-in structure. The timbers were still firing, blackened and charred beneath the yellow flames. There was no way anything, particularly anything combustible, could have survived that blaze. He didn't know if it was a good thing. Could be, if the only place Winthrop kept that video was on his office computer, where Goddard had viewed it. If, on the other hand, he'd kept copies elsewhere, they'd still need to be found and destroyed. He glanced sideways at the two men, watching Heins observe the smoldering hulk. If Heins knew about the video, he was damn quiet about it. And if Goddard knew Heins, if he had known about it, he would have already leveraged it. Either that, or he would have been a whole lot more circumspect about watching it go up in flames.

"I'll have to wait until well past morning to get in there," Gibbons said.

"What do you think?" the sheriff asked.

"No way to tell. That building was inspected last summer. As I recall, it needed some serious wiring repair. A sprinkler install. Don't know if Winthrop made those improvements, but probably not," he said, looking at the sheriff.

"Probably not," the sheriff agreed.

Heins was silent, watching the last of the building burn.

"The wife believes bad luck comes in threes," Gibbons observed, staring into the blaze. He turned and with a wry smile added, "I guess that means we haven't seen the last of Williston Winthrop's misfortune."

Heins considered it. "Good thing dead men don't worry about luck."

CHAPTER EIGHTEEN

Pederson could see Moon's truck and Heins's police car in front of the farmhouse garage. He turned into the drive and slid down two deep tire tracks that cut through the heavy snow. A bulging blue tarp covered the back of Moon's truck. The wind lifted the corner of the tarp, revealing a row of empty cages.

"Shit," he said, as if Clayton's return and the Winthrop Building blaze weren't complication enough.

Pederson got out of his cab and examined the empty cages. Heins and Moon came out of the barn. Pederson zipped his coat, pulled on his hunting cap and thick, fur-lined mittens, and started across the yard. It was bright and cold.

Heins and Moon stood in front of the doorway and waited. The snow was deep and their tracks cut a clear line from their vehicles to the barn door. The rest of the yard was buried under a sparkling, deep alabaster.

"Having fun yet?" Pederson managed to put on a smile.

"Looks like the dogs had all the fun," Heins said, indicating with a gesture the inside of the barn. "What're you doing here?" Heins wasn't happy to see Pederson. Coming out to the farm and not finding the dogs was worrisome enough.

"Where are the dogs?" Pederson asked.

"They ran," Moon said, looking away.

"What the hell happened?" Pederson wanted to know. Missing dogs was troublesome news, though Pederson wasn't one to worry about details.

"Into the woods." Moon indicated a broken trail through the

snow that ran from the barn's entrance across Winthrop's side yard over the field to the line of trees. The blowing snow obscured their tracks, but they were still visible in the early-morning light.

"Oh, for Chrissake," Pederson muttered. "How'd they get out?"

"Too much storm," Moon explained. "Me and Williston had to leave."

"You left 'em?"

Moon didn't appreciate Pederson's tone. After a day of drinking, a short afternoon sleeping it off, and his late-night arson in Defiance, his head felt pickled. He stared at Pederson for one long second, conveying his mood. "If we hadn't left when we did, we would have been stuck here with 'em."

Pederson looked away, wondering about it. But he couldn't let it go. "Better to have been stuck here with 'em instead of letting them loose in those woods."

"And if they'd gotten stuck?" Heins interceded. "How do you think they'd explain Williston's presence, just in case someone happened by?"

Pederson chewed on the question, but didn't answer.

"Angus is coming out and finding the kill," Heins said, setting up the scene. "Now we're seeing where wolves got in and what they did. Came in the storm." This conversation was a waste of time. "What're you doing here?"

Pederson paused, looking at Moon, then back at Heins. "I assume you know about the Winthrop Building?"

Heins stared at him. "We know. That was Williston's business and it's done."

Heins was shutting Pederson down. "And did you know Clayton Winthrop's back?"

It had been a long time since either of them had heard the name.

"Clayton Winthrop," Heins said, recalling the Jeep with Colorado plates. "I bet that was his Jeep at the hotel."

"He's a lot bigger than I remember," Pederson started. "He's changed his name. Goes by Sam Rivers."

"No shit. When did you figure all this out?"

"Ran into him," Pederson said, not wanting to explain the circumstances.

They all paused for a moment, letting the information ripple across the frozen yard, wondering about it. "What'd he have to say?" Heins asked.

Pederson thought about it. "Not much. I got the impression he's grown up some. What's it been? Fifteen years?"

"More like 20. Though I doubt any length of time would be enough to surface the man in that boy," Heins said.

"Horseshit as a hunter," Moon remembered. "I expect he wants money. Come around like crow on roadkill."

"What makes you think he's different?" Heins wanted to know.

"He's not a kid," Pederson offered. "We had a few words. I told him there was nothing for him here, and he more or less told me to fuck off."

Heins laughed into the wintry air. "You didn't need to do that, Hank. He may be Williston's kid, but he has no claims on the estate. We're all legal and proper. The will's pretty specific." Then Heins thought for a moment. Something was missing. "Why did he tell you to fuck off?"

Pederson looked away, considering. Then he turned back to Heins and said, "I was visiting Diane Talbott."

"Talbott?" Heins asked. He was trying to see it. Heins knew Diane Talbott. The idea Pederson was hoping to get lucky with Diane was absurd. But if Pederson had been drinking, anything was possible, at least in the old car salesman's mind. "Get lucky?"

"Might have." Pederson smiled, seeing where he could go with it. "But that goddamn kid interrupted us."

A shade fell across the town cop's face, the kind of shadow Pederson had been hoping to avoid. "You just can't lay off, can ya, Hank?" Heins started, carefully, so Pederson would feel the pressure. Pederson was Pederson, and Diane Talbott, some affirmed, had a past. Only her past had been over 20 years ago, and it was in Eveleth, across the Range, miles from Defiance and in Diane's case from a different lifetime. He admitted she still had appeal. But from what Heins heard, she'd never partied for money, and never with an aging idiot like Pederson.

"She called me wanting background on Williston's obituary. So I stopped by. No harm in trying. Once a party girl, always a party girl. It's a matter of timing." Pederson held on to the smile, but it was unconvincing.

This time, Heins thought, Pederson's reliance on his professed pussy knowledge was plain stupid. "It's a matter of intelligence. You think with your dick."

Pederson considered a response, but thought better of it. "Maybe it was a mistake. I just mention it because it was surprising to see him. Clayton Winthrop. Sam Rivers. And he wasn't running scared like he used to."

"We can deal with him," Heins reassured. "The best approach is courtesy. If we have to, we can show him a firm hand."

Moon smiled at the prospect.

"As I recall, it didn't take much to get Clayton packing," added Heins.

Pederson looked away. "He's not a kid anymore."

"Aw shit, Hank. If needed, we can smack the kid around a little, let him know he's still not wanted around here. I'm not worried. Williston will be interested to know he's come around."

"You think he's after the money?" Pederson wondered.

"Of course," Heins affirmed. "I don't know how he heard about Williston's death. I know Williston hasn't heard from him in years. Yeah," he concluded. "He's after the money."

"Fuckin' good luck," Moon said.

Heins agreed. "His presence is a minor distraction. Once he reads the will and listens to probate, he'll hear reason."

"I don't think Diane Talbott was expecting him."

"Was she expecting you?"

Pederson didn't answer. Then, "Seems to me we got bigger problems than Clayton. What about the dogs?"

"We'll get 'em back," Moon said. "They won't run far. It's goddamn cold, and there's still a barn full of food. Not to mention a place out of the wind. What would you do?"

"Truth is, it doesn't matter a rat's ass what happened out here," Heins said. "So far we still have a livestock kill to report, still have the evidence. And wolves would have run. They wouldn't have stuck around. Those tracks are fortunate, if you ask me. They're too drifted over to get any good prints, but you can see there were five of them, and they disappeared into those woods."

"I'll get 'em," Moon said, looking up into the wall of trees. "Then I'll teach 'em a lesson."

"Maybe they've gotten a taste of their heritage," Heins

suggested. "Right now they're out there trying to figure it out." He looked up and recalled how those woods stretched all the way into Canada.

"Right now," Moon argued, "they're probably just inside those trees, couple hundred yards in, sleeping off the gorge. Come night they'll be back. They're good at tracking and killing, but they've never done it on their own."

"Did the other night," Pederson observed.

The three of them finally went into the farmhouse to get out of the cold. After they shed their coats, they began mulling their options. Moon could stay at the farm and wait for his dogs. If they showed, he could return them to their houses, and then call in the kill. Or they could, according to the plan (or at least most of it), report the kill to the DNR.

"I told Williston we'd be out by 4," Heins recollected. "The DNR should be able to get somebody out before then."

"It's Friday," Pederson commented.

"Slow day for a conservation officer. And I checked. Steve Svegman's on duty."

"That's good," Moon said. "He's young, and he don't know shit, specially about me." He smiled. "I should call it in?"

Heins nodded. "Call 'em," he said. "The timing's right. It's early. With luck Svegman'll be out before 2. Just be sure and tell them you've got a wake to attend. Arrange it. We don't want them coming out here when no one's around. And get that truck into the garage. We don't want him asking questions about those cages."

Moon agreed. Svegman's early arrival would be good. If he came out anytime during the day, Moon knew, his dogs would stay put, sleeping off their feed.

"This kill's going to set off some alarm bells in St. Paul," Heins observed. "It's big and different. And I don't recall any others like it being reported, at least in our county."

"It was only a matter of time," Moon argued. "Wolves're comin' back. Some are takin' dogs off porches. Somethin' like this was bound to happen."

"I didn't say it was totally unbelievable," Heins said. "Seems to me I've heard about kills bigger than this out west. Idaho or Montana. Outright slaughters. It's just going to take some care, is all I'm sayin'. We've got to be patient. This is definitely the work of wolves," he said. "Svegman'll see that. Open and shut."

Winthrop was to be buried tomorrow afternoon. They'd all attend. Tonight they'd each make their way to the cabin in Skinwalkers Bog. There would be a party, an unusual celebration. A wake, at which the dead man would play both host and guest of honor.

Heins knew it was time to check Miriam's house.

Moon made the call to Vermilion Falls, since he'd discovered it. The DNR was surprisingly sympathetic. There were increasing kills across the Range, in tandem with a rising wolf population. Cattlemen were angry about it, and the DNR and Agriculture had gotten word to give everyone the benefit of the doubt. They'd get a conservation officer out to Winthrop's place by 2, the dispatcher assured him.

"After you meet with the DNR, we'll see you at the cabin," Heins said.

"Keep my seat warm," Moon said. "It's gonna be colder than a gravedigger's ass tonight."

CHAPTER NINETEEN

S am and Diane had come to Vermilion Falls for breakfast. They sat in the Rangers Café. Their breakfast had just arrived, and they spent a few moments focusing on their food.

The previous evening Sam had decided it would be prudent to bed down on Diane's couch. Diane didn't want to admit it, but she'd been shaken by her encounter with Pederson. She didn't think the man would return, but you didn't know about Pederson. Besides, Sam Rivers felt fine, making sure his duffel was secure and for the time being safe. He shared his mother's instincts about Diane. She was a good human being. And something he suspected his mother didn't notice: she was easy on the eyes.

As they finished their breakfast, they talked about how best to explain the sudden appearance of his mother's will, postdating the version that had been probated. After considering a few different options, they finally settled on using Diane as an excuse. Diane had been holding the will in a sealed envelope, with instructions from Miriam she was to give it to her son when he returned.

"And Miriam was explicit," Diane said, rounding out their story. "Under no circumstances was I to mail it to you."

"Why not?"

"For the same reasons Miriam never mailed you the money. She was afraid, given Williston's wide-ranging contacts, he would somehow discover it. And she wanted to make sure you received what she'd left you."

"But you're not going to mention the money."

"Of course not."

"The story seems a little thin," Sam said, thinking about it. "Why wouldn't she have at least told me about her will? Or why wouldn't she have told you it was a copy of her will?"

"The truth was, Sam, your mom was a little paranoid about Williston. There are any number of reasons why she may not have explicitly told you about the will. It could have been forgetfulness in the last days of her life. But it was more likely fear. She was afraid Williston would find out and put a stop to it, to this second, proper will."

"And you never opened the envelope?"

"Miriam was my friend. It was her dying wish. Of course I wouldn't open it." The more she thought about it, the more she thought Sam had a reasonable shot at wresting Miriam's estate from Pederson and his friends. Bending the truth to obtain the right result was not ideal Range justice, but it was a start.

Sam thought it might work, but he didn't know if an estate that has been probated could be reopened, two years later. It was a question for Dunlap, and he wondered how well the story would hold up under scrutiny.

Diane's cell phone went off. It was another reporter. There was a quick exchange, then surprise. "The Winthrop Building? That's interesting. I finished his obit this morning. Should be in production."

The person on the other end of the line spoke.

"That's right," Diane answered. "I didn't mention it in the story because I couldn't confirm it, but I think he was being investigated. About what, I don't know."

Pause.

"Yup," Diane said. "Couldn't confirm it."

The reporter thanked her and then hung up.

"The Winthrop Building in Defiance," Diane said. "Burned down after midnight. Burnt to the ground."

"That's curious," Sam said.

"Started sometime after midnight. Went up like a dried-out Christmas tree. The place was mostly timber. At least that's what Walt Gibbons said. Apparently he'd warned Will Winthrop about the place a few months ago. Wasn't up to code and needed some retrofitting." She glanced at Sam, curious about his reaction.

"Any idea how it started?"

"Not yet. Walt said it would take a while, sifting through the rubble. But his preliminary guess was electrical. He remembered a lot of bad wiring. His recommendation was to upgrade it and install a sprinkler system, which would have brought it up to code."

They fell silent for a minute, mulling over the news.

It was an odd development, Sam thought. Maybe someone did it out of spite, he wondered. A disgruntled former client? Someone on the other side of the bench who the old man had eviscerated in a legal battle? But what value would there be in setting the place ablaze, given the old man's death and, he suspected, the insurance money that would flow to the estate once the claim was settled? It all made Sam think arson was unlikely. And remembering the building, even if someone had set it off . . . if they'd been careful, it would be hard evidence to uncover. Inconclusive, at best.

"You heard me mention that investigation?" Diane said.

"The old man was being investigated?"

"I think so, but I couldn't get anyone to confirm it. I found out when I was researching that piece I wrote. So I called down to the Lawyers Professional Responsibility Board. They have a database. I'd heard he'd been investigated before. Over the last 20 years there were three investigations, none resulting in more than a warning. If I wanted to know more, they told me I'd have to come and review the files myself. But then the clerk let something slip about another investigation, recently opened."

"I'm not surprised," Sam shrugged, "given the old man's temperament."

"When I followed up on the clerk's comment, he said he misspoke. I took that to mean there was no current investigation, but just to double-check, I asked Jeff Dunlap, and he said they couldn't comment about ongoing investigations. So I think the clerk meant he couldn't say anything and Dunlap was telling me an investigation was ongoing."

They thought about it.

"What good is a burned-down office building to a dead man?" Diane wondered.

"There's the paper trail, if the old man was foolish enough to leave one," Sam suggested.

"But about what?"

"About whatever he was being investigated for?"

"I guess," Diane said doubtfully. "But what difference does it make to a dead man?"

"If the old man was alive, it could have been cause."

"But he isn't."

The more they both thought about it, the more the most likely conclusion was that the building fire was an accident. But the timing, and the fact it involved, at least tangentially, the Iron County Gun Club, made them wonder.

"Maybe it's time to pay Jeff Dunlap a visit," Sam said.

"Maybe it's time to see if our story has legs."

CHAPTER TWENTY

Goddard was snowblowing his drive when Belinda stuck her head out the front door. She waved for him to stop. When he did, she said, "Jeff's on the phone. Wants to speak with you. Says it's important."

Goddard looked up, nodded. He parked the blower and went in to take the call.

"Guess what," Dunlap started.

"I'm in the middle of digging out. Give it to me quick."

"Guess who's back in town?"

"Rudy Perpich."

"Very funny." Rudy Perpich was a dentist turned three-term governor, one of few who came from the Range. He was popular, but dead. "I happened to have liked Rudy."

"I did too. With everything else that's going on these days, I just thought we might get lucky."

"Clayton Winthrop."

"Clayton Winthrop?"

"Will Winthrop's estranged son. Remember me telling you he had a son?"

Goddard remembered. "What's he after? A piece of the estate?"

"Sort of. Turns out he's been in Colorado all these years. Changed his name to Sam Rivers."

"Is he a nutcase?"

"Not at all, from what I remember. Not sure why he changed his name, but he's nothing like his old man. He's a field agent for

Fish & Wildlife. A wildlife biologist. Specializes in wolves. And here's where it gets interesting."

"Yeah?"

"He comes over here with Diane Talbott."

"Nice looking company." Goddard looked over his shoulder to make sure Belinda was out of earshot.

"Turns out Diane's an old friend of Clayton's mother. I mean she was an old friend."

"OK."

"Clayton's mother left a copy of her will with Diane. Said if Clayton . . . Sam Rivers ever returned, she should give it to him."

"What?"

"I know. It's a little strange."

"Why did Talbott wait?"

"She didn't know it was a will. Just a sealed envelope."

"And she never opened it? Never mailed it?"

"Said it was Miriam's dying wish."

"Uh-huh," Goddard said doubtfully. "And I've got a feeling I know what the will says."

"You guessed it. This one's a little different than the one probated two years ago."

"What a surprise."

"It's notarized. And it's dated several days after the will used by probate court to settle Miriam Winthrop's estate."

"Let me guess. In the probated will everything went to the old man. The new one leaves everything to the kid."

"You got it. Only he isn't much of a kid anymore. He's grown up. Serious. Pleasant enough. But he doesn't give me the feeling he's a pushover or a crook. They also had a copy of the probated will. Guess who notarized the one leaving Miriam Winthrop's estate to Williston?"

"Hal Young?"

"You're a hundred percent. You been taking ginkgo biloba supplements?"

"Just naturally intelligent. Is the probated version legit?"

"Appears to be. Miriam Winthrop's signature looks a little fruity, but that could have been her illness. And we can check with the notary. If it's legit, that scumbag Williston Winthrop forged his dead wife's signature and cheated his son out of his mother's inheritance."

"How's the signature on the new will?"

"Pretty damn good. Better than the probated version."

Goddard thought about the break-in at Miriam Winthrop's house. "When did Sam Rivers get into town?"

"Yesterday morning."

The timing wasn't right. Goddard wondered about it. Maybe Sam Rivers was lying. "Why didn't Diane Talbott mail the letter to Rivers?"

"Miriam made Diane promise to hold it for him, not to mail it. Diane says she was paranoid about Williston finding out about it. Even if she mailed it from Brainerd."

They both thought about it.

"So he waits until the old man dies before returning home. I guess there was no love lost."

"None, from what Sam said. And he has absolutely no intention of contesting his father's will. But he wanted to pursue getting probate to change his mother's estate, because he believed it was his mother's wish."

"Can he do that?"

"Not sure. I'm not that familiar with estate law."

"It'd be interesting to see him take something from that club."

"That's what I was thinking."

"So he's absolutely nothing like his old man," Goddard said.

"Sam Rivers is different."

The sheriff still thought Sam's presence, the break-in at his mother's house, and the appearance of a new version of the will were all incredibly coincidental. Though Goddard had to admit, Sam Rivers kept good company—Diane was smart and capable. And attractive. Maybe Sam Rivers was a carpetbagger charmer? Goddard knew some USFW people. They were nature people, not carpetbaggers. He would have to meet Sam Rivers and get his own feel for the prodigal son that had blown in from out west.

"You know anyone who works at Fish & Wildlife?" Dunlap asked.

"Paul Williams over in Grand Rapids is a freshwater biologist and Fish & Wildlife special agent. He does a lot of work in wetland habitat, but in fairness he does plenty of investigations too. You heard about that walleye poaching ring he broke up last year, up by Leech Lake?"

"That was Fish & Wildlife?"

"That was Paul Williams. There was a wetland reclamation project a couple years back that was illegal but plenty complicated. Williams surfaced it. Fish & Wildlife is a little more sophisticated than our local DNR conservation officers," Goddard said. "But their turf is the wild, not towns. And they only take notice if animals are involved, not people. Still, I should meet Sam Rivers."

"You should. I'll try to think of something. Thought you'd want to know."

"Thanks."

The sheriff rang off and returned to his snowblower. He was at it 15 minutes before Belinda stuck her head out the front door and motioned to him again.

"Yeah?"

"It's Smith Barnes," she said, holding up his cell phone.

The sheriff parked the blower to the side and reentered the house, taking the phone.

"What's up?"

"I guess Walt Gibbons was right," he started. "Bad luck comes in threes. You remember the feeder stock Williston had at his farmhouse?"

The sheriff thought about it. He remembered walking by the barn. He remembered the smell of cattle, and someone mentioned it. "Yeah," he said. "Calves?"

"Yeah. Pretty big calves. Wolves got in last night and killed them."

"Wolves went into the barn?"

"Sounds like it. Angus Moon called the DNR. They're sending Steve Svegman out. Svegman remembered about Winthrop's accident and thought we should know."

"That was good of him," the sheriff said, thinking of the young conservation officer. "You ever heard of wolves getting into a barn?"

"Nope," said Barnes. "But I suppose it's possible."

"Maybe I should join our young CO. Just to have a look."

"Thought you might want to."

The sheriff thanked the deputy and rang off.

Goddard returned to his snowblower. Sometimes clearing off long rows of white powder was meditative. He thought about Sam Rivers. He wondered about the will. He considered Rivers's occupation. Special agent with the USFW, a wolf biologist. Maybe Goddard could kill two birds with one stone? When the sheriff finished blowing, he came into the house, stayed in his warm wear, and called Dunlap's office.

"Dunlap," the assistant district attorney answered.

The sheriff explained what happened at Winthrop's farm. After Dunlap conveyed his shock, the sheriff suggested it might be a good time to nose around. Out at the farm. Dunlap agreed.

"Maybe Sam Rivers the wolf expert would be interested," Dunlap said.

"Exactly what I was thinking. The more the merrier. Know where I can reach him?"

CHAPTER TWENTY-ONE

O ut at the cabin the CB crackled and popped, emitted something unintelligible, but with a familiar enough tone to make Winthrop sit up and listen. He came out of the bedroom, walked across the cabin floor, flipped a switch, and managed a voice entirely unlike his own. "Come again?" said a gravelly monotone. "Over."

"You wouldn't believe . . ." started to come in, broken, but unless Winthrop's ear had grown rusty, the voice was Heins. There was a long blank space, a couple of crackling sparks, and then, "over?"

"Come again? Defiance Star? Over."

"Defiance Star comin' across the Range at ya, Range Wolf. Over?" Heins asked.

"Range Wolf picking you up now, Defiance Star. Over." Winthrop lifted the talk button and cleared his throat. This wasn't a popular channel, but thanks to the quirks of the upper atmosphere, you never knew when you'd accidentally pick up a message from Anchorage or St. Paul. The beauty of working with a CB radio was that fewer people were using the technology. Cell phones, much easier to use and with much greater ranges, had taken over the airwaves. But cell phones were useless in Skinwalkers Bog.

Regardless, it would be wise to keep the messages short and enigmatic. Winthrop knew Heins was smart enough to take care.

There was a long pause, then "Heir apparent has returned. Repeat . . . surprising heir in the wind. Checking the weather but wanted to know how you might check it if you were in town? Curious. Over."

Definitely Heins. He appreciated the obscurity, but wasn't
sure he followed. Air? "Repeat in different key," he said. "Over."

There was another long pause. Winthrop was just about
ready to repeat his request, when the radio barked "Prince."
Pause. "Music now being heard all over the Range. Haven't
heard him in what seems like 20 years. Thought the king should
know. Over."

Air . . . Prince . . . King? Heir! It came to him like a cattle prod.
The prince's return. Not entirely unexpected. But still surprising.
He wanted to make sure. "Maybe they listen at the Pit," he said.
"Heard they're hitting clay. Tons of it. Clay-tons. Over."

Another long pause. "Heard the same thing. Clay-ton of it.
Can't believe I heard Prince in our small town. Particularly when
it's so cold out. The weather here is clear, but cold. Haven't begun
checking yet. Not sure where to begin. Thought maybe I should
check around, see if the weather's the same all over town. Try to
figure if there's any bad weather brewing. Over."

Winthrop thought, then depressed the call button. "Weather
checks wise. Beacon a must . . . Hotel . . . Starters. Over."

There was another long pause. "Will do. Over and out."

Winthrop didn't risk goodbye.

Clayton had returned. He was surprised it made his pulse
rise. The kid was a little late, but still in time to see his old man
buried, provided he showed up at the grave. Winthrop looked off
through the cabin window. Through the frost-rimmed glass the
thickets of Skinwalkers Bog were bleary and opaque. There was no
telling where this was going to lead, but he smiled, appreciating
the development.

If anyone could lead him to his $179,000 and stolen Decimator, it was the kid.

Over the next couple hours, Heins made his rounds. First he drove over to Beacon Street. He pulled into Miriam Winthrop's drive, parking in snowdrifts near the bottom, wading through heavy snow to the front porch. Everything was covered. He circled the house.

The snow along the side of the house was broken. Someone had tracked it since the storm. The wind had blown over the tracks, but Heins saw they were fresh. He turned the corner and saw tracks leading up the backyard to the door, and then away from it. There was also the shuffle in the snow beside the door. The area was covered over with white powder, as though someone had kicked snow against the house to build a drift.

He looked around the neighborhood, but the homes appeared empty. It was just after lunch. He knew almost everyone in this neighborhood and knew at this hour they'd be working.

He took out his key chain and fumbled through the options, finally extracting one and gripping it in his gloved hands. Someone had already loosened the ice around the hinges. He'd have to ask Pederson and Young. He used his key to let himself in.

The house was dark, stale, tomblike. He walked across the kitchen floor. He stepped down the hallway, but everything was in order. He examined the rooms on the main floor, and then opened the basement door, throwing the light switch. He walked down into the old basement and was pleased to smell its dank normalcy. But it was cold. His breath clouded in the basement air. He looked around and saw sparkles across the floor beneath the basement window. From broken glass. One of the windowpanes was broken out. There was a mat of frozen crusted snow over the spot, with some frozen lips of meltwater seeping down the wall.

"Goddamn it."

Heins examined the rest of the floor, but everything else looked untouched. He walked into the preserve room and flicked on the overhead light. He looked at the shelves full of preserves. He considered taking one, and then noticed the undusted circles where four jars had been removed. He looked for others missing from their two-year hibernation, but there were only the four. He looked around for the missing jars, but didn't find them.

"Break into a house for four jars of preserves?" He wondered. Didn't make much sense, unless you were feeling nostalgic. Clayton. He'd check the boy's Jeep, or his hotel room. It made Heins smile.

At the Defiance Hotel, Heins waited while Baxter came out of the back room. As Baxter approached, Heins nodded, trying to be cordial. The smile was returned, but the two men had never liked each other.

"Need a room?" Baxter asked. He had a strong suspicion why Heins was here. Sam hadn't returned last night. Baxter hadn't seen him all day. But last night when Sam was checking in, Baxter remembered Heins's slow cruise in front of the hotel.

Heins chuckled at Baxter's question. "Not tonight, Elwyn," he said. "Just some information."

"We got plenty of that."

"Excellent. Has Clayton Winthrop checked into your hotel?"

"No."

"Didn't I see his Jeep out front yesterday?"

Baxter and Heins had known each other most of their lives, and to Baxter there were plenty of things about Heins that didn't measure up, the most prominent his salary, paid for out of waning tax revenues.

Baxter looked down at the hotel registry. He flipped it open to the current page and read the name. "Sam Rivers."

Heins smiled. "That's the name he's going by now. That's Williston Winthrop's boy. Left about 20 years back. Got into some trouble and ran. Now he's returned with a different name. But it's the same kid."

Baxter thought about it. There wasn't much to say. It was an interesting development, and Baxter didn't like Sam's deception, but he'd kind of liked Sam, which is a sentiment he'd never felt for Heins.

"Is he checked into your hotel?" Heins repeated.

"Yep."

"Which room?"

"Does it matter?"

Heins sighed. He suspected it might come to this. There was a time he could have forced his way into someone's room without the proper papers, but he and Baxter were too old and familiar. "I have reason to believe he broke into someone's house. I think he's in possession of stolen goods. I'd like to search his room."

Baxter just looked at him. "Got the paper?"

Heins's eyes darkened.

Baxter liked what he saw. It was enough to make him smile, though he didn't.

"I don't have a warrant, if that's what you mean."

"You aren't talking about doing something illegal, are you?"

"Look, Elwyn," Heins said, trying to adopt a conspiratorial tone. "This can just be between you and me. I need to have a quick look. He's not around. Shouldn't hurt anyone. We would be in and out in less than a minute. It would help with an investigation."

Baxter returned Heins's smile with a grin of his own. "But that would be breaking the law. I don't think I could live with myself. You better get some paper."

Out in the cold Heins contemplated ways to get even. He'd get back to Baxter, when the proper moment presented itself. Any questioning of Heins's authority pissed him off, especially when it was a bug like Baxter. Heins would have to teach him a lesson. But for now there was enough money in the balance to buy out the hotel proprietor and several other Defiance storefronts. For now it would be better to keep his cards to himself.

Heins decided to cruise, keeping an eye out for Sam's Jeep. It wouldn't be difficult to find some pretense for pulling him over. Not much had changed in 20 years. In the meantime it might be useful to head back to the office and start in on the paperwork for a search warrant, though he still wasn't certain it was the best approach, or that he would be able to convince a judge. That might be something best decided by Winthrop, later tonight, when they convened at the club cabin for the dead man's wake.

Heins turned the patrol car toward the other side of town. He'd need to change vehicles. It was a hike to the cabin. Tonight he'd make it easier and use the Cat. He was already starting to feel thirsty.

CHAPTER TWENTY-TWO

After their meeting with Dunlap, Sam was driving Diane back to her place when his cell phone rang.

The number came over the Jeep's Bluetooth. A local number. "Rivers."

"Sam Rivers?"

"Yeah?"

"This is Sheriff Dean Goddard."

"Sheriff," Sam answered. He glanced over at Diane with a question in his eyes, but she shook her head.

In the last 24 hours Sam was guilty of breaking and entering and burglary, and he'd come close to assault and battery. And technically he was driving away from fraud: he and Diane had lied about how they'd come across his mother's will. Dunlap must have given his number to the sheriff, which meant Dunlap called the sheriff moments after they'd left his office. Sam wanted to know why.

"Jeff Dunlap gave me your number," the sheriff confirmed. "He says you were old classmates."

"That's right. Truth is, Jeff was behind me in school. A couple years. But I knew him."

"I believe Jeff also mentioned you were a special agent with Fish & Wildlife?"

"A field agent. Currently stationed out of the Denver office."

"Nice city."

"Yes, it is."

"I'll come right to the point. Seems there was a wolf kill out at

Williston Winthrop's farm. Jeff mentioned you know something about wolves and wolf kills?"

"I've seen a few," Sam said. Judy Rutgers came to mind. "What kind of kill?"

"Your dad had feeder calves. Sounds like wolves got into the barn and killed them. Last night. Were you in town?"

"Came in yesterday morning," Sam said, surprised by the question, which had nothing to do with wolves. "I was down in Brainerd when the storm finally blew itself out, but I've seen enough to know you got hit pretty hard."

"We did. Especially out at your dad's place."

Sam had never called the old man Dad. Son of a bitch, when he was trying to be accurate. But something else the sheriff said was much more interesting. "Wolves got into the barn?"

"That's what I heard. Got in, killed, and fed."

"That would be," Sam said, surprised as hell but trying to be measured, "unusual." What he was thinking was extraordinary. Wolves didn't enter barns. Wolves didn't usually take down calves. Cattle were large enough to fend off a wolf attack.

Not that wolves didn't occasionally try. Sam had seen flesh wounds, gashes and tears along bovine flanks that looked like the work of wolves, but he'd never seen them take down an adult animal.

He'd heard of newborn calves being taken, but they were small and on the edge of a herd and unprotected, at least long enough for an opportunistic wolf or a pack to take advantage. And they were always outside, usually on remote grazing land.

"Angus Moon called it in. You know Moon?"

"I remember him," Sam said. "One of the old man's hunting friends."

"That's it. Apparently he's watching the place. Came out after the storm to feed them and found them all," he paused, searching for the right word. "Dead."

"And they were in the barn?"

"That's what they're saying. I'm getting this secondhand. Moon called the DNR about it. A DNR conservation officer needs to investigate. Once it's verified our Minnesota Department of Agriculture reimburses ranchers for confirmed wolf kills."

"Same out west."

"This CO, Steve Svegman, knows one of my deputies and knows about the accident at your father's place and thought we'd be interested."

When Sam met Dunlap, he liked him. But he'd never met the sheriff, and for all he knew, Dunlap had called the sheriff out of suspicion. Considering his activities over the last 24 hours, the suspicion was warranted. Sam would need to be careful.

"Given what happened at your dad's place. I mean . . . his accident. I guess I better go have a look. That farm is in my jurisdiction."

There was another pause. "Makes sense," Sam said.

"And given your experience with wolf kills, I was wondering if you'd like to come along?"

The offer surprised him. Sam's experience with local law enforcement wasn't often positive. During official investigations he'd rankled local sheriffs. It was a matter of turf. "Sure, Sheriff."

"Just one thing. Jeff mentioned you had no interest in

contesting your father's will. To make trouble. That accurate?"

"I have no interest in Williston Winthrop's will or the dispensation of his property. But I assume he told you about my mother's will?"

"He did. That's your business. I was more concerned about any issues you might have with Angus Moon, who's meeting us at the farm."

Sam thought about it. "In terms of trouble, you never know what might set some people off. I've come back to visit. It's been 20 years, and I was curious to see how the place has changed."

"Fair enough," the sheriff said. "I can swing by and pick you up, say, in an hour?" the sheriff suggested. "Where are you staying?"

Sam had always known he would visit the farm. But he would have preferred visiting alone. "I've got a few errands to run," he lied. "How about if I meet you there? I remember the way."

"Why don't we make it . . ." Goddard paused. "Come to think of it, I think my deputy said Svegman was going to be out there around 2? That give you enough time?"

"Plenty," Sam said.

"See you at the farm around 2."

Sam couldn't have hoped for a more legitimate excuse to have a second look at his boyhood compound, though he would have to step carefully. If what the sheriff said was true, wolves had done something extraordinary. Puzzling. Interesting. And that's when he thought a little diversion might help.

He turned to Diane. "You know the sheriff," Sam said. "What's he like?"

"I told you. I don't know him well, but I think he's a good guy."

"Think you might like to visit the old man's farm, see a wolf kill?"

"Sounds awful, but of course I'd like to see it. The paper would definitely be interested. But I'm not sure the sheriff would appreciate a reporter along."

"I'd like to look around out there. If we both went, it might be," he paused, "easier." With Diane out there asking questions, he might have an opportunity to at least look into corners he wouldn't otherwise see.

"I'd love to," she said, managing a small grin.

The old farmhouse had ghosts. Sam wanted to greet each and every one of them. It was the place where the late Winthrop tried to tutor him, though Sam had never been an apt pupil. Long after he left the Range, Sam's inability to measure up was the subject of hours of introspection, up to a point. He'd reached that point years ago, the one in which he finally understood the old man had been an angry man and an unusually brutal father. And those were the descriptions that easily came to mind. In retrospect Sam was glad he had never accepted the old man's perspective on the world, or his way of living in it. Most of all, he was glad he had run, when he was too young to know better or do anything about it.

But now it was time. He felt ready to meet those ghosts and send them back from whence they'd come.

CHAPTER TWENTY-THREE

At 2 p.m. sharp Sam turned into the farmhouse drive. The clapboard house looked older, more dilapidated. Its sides were weathered, paint peeling like flaking skin. A thin trail of smoke wafted out of a stovepipe into a cold blue sky. The tar paper roof looked more tattered and worn. Sam felt a whirl in the center of his chest, as though some remote spark was starting to burn. The farmhouse was rundown and beat up. If this is what 20 years had done to the homestead, or what the old man had let happen to it, he wondered what the years had done to Winthrop.

"You OK?" Diane asked.

"Sure. Why?"

"You look . . . tense."

Sam could feel Diane's attention. "It's been a while," he said. "There's a lot of . . ." he paused, thinking about it. "There's a lot here. Plenty I'd rather not remember."

Diane reached over and placed her hand on his shoulder, an unexpected gesture. He was surprised by how it felt. It'd been a while since he'd been touched.

"I'll be OK," he said.

"I know."

The sheriff and Svegman were on the front landing. Sam watched the door open and Moon step onto the cement block, threading a wiry arm into his down coat. Sam saw Moon shake hands and then peer toward the Jeep coming down the drive, wondering who else had arrived, unhappy about it.

Sam guessed Pederson had already alerted the others to his return. But Moon would be surprised to see him now, with Diane.

"Showtime."

"That guy creeps me out."

"Me too. Always has," Sam said. "Or did. This time I'm looking forward to our reunion."

Sam parked and they stepped out of the Jeep, zipping up their coats as they walked to the front steps.

The sheriff turned and said, "Sam Rivers?" extending his hand.

Sam nodded and took it. "Sheriff," Sam said. If the sheriff was pissed about Diane, he didn't show it.

The sheriff was the same height as Sam, with a little pudginess beneath his down coat and ear-flap cap. He looked a little countryish, Sam thought. But he thought he noticed something intense in the sheriff's eyes.

"Diane," the sheriff nodded.

"Sheriff," she greeted in return.

"This is Steve Svegman," the sheriff introduced. "One of our local conservation officers."

Svegman shook hands, greeting them, and then said, "Fish & Wildlife?"

"Out of Denver," Sam answered.

Svegman was a rookie. Sam guessed he had a military-style buzz cut beneath his DNR hat. He was a little awkward on the front step.

"You're a field agent?" Svegman asked.

"That's right."

"A wolf specialist?"

Sam nodded. "I grew up with them," he said, glancing toward Moon.

"And you remember Angus Moon," the sheriff said.

Sam peered at the aging woodsman and offered him a hand, for appearances. Moon didn't take it.

"Turns out we're fortunate to have Sam Rivers around, Angus," Goddard started. "Sam's a wildlife biologist who happens to know quite a bit about wolves and wolf kills." He smiled, but Moon wasn't reflecting his good humor. And apparently he hadn't been told there would be another guest to their party.

Moon appeared smaller than Sam remembered. Moon looked older and tougher, but not in a good way.

Their breath clouded the afternoon air.

Moon considered Sam with a dark stare, then said, "This here is Clayton Winthrop."

Sam held Moon's watery brown eyes, happy for the opportunity to engage, even if it was just a look. He could see there was still plenty of fight in the compact hunter. But the years, and he guessed whiskey through plenty of cold winters, had rounded the man's shoulders and thinned him a little. He looked older and meaner.

"Williston wouldn't like it," Moon added, turning to the sheriff.

"Williston's in no place to worry about it," the sheriff said. "Besides, I think we could use his help."

The sheriff turned to Diane and said, "Diane, we've got a little situation here. If I'd have known you were coming along, I might have mentioned something to Sam. The DNR and Agriculture don't want news of this kill getting out. At least not until we finish our investigation."

Diane thought about it. She'd come along for two reasons. Sam, because it had been a while since she'd found any men interesting. But once she discovered what happened, and that it was significant, she was also interested in the story.

"Sheriff," Diane started. "I want to be a good citizen. But this is the kind of story people need to know about."

"I agree. It's just nothing we need getting out until we're absolutely certain what we've got here. Don't your stories need to be accurate?"

"It's a wolf kill, all right," Moon said.

"Then people need to know," Diane reiterated.

"Diane," Sam started. "Now that the sheriff mentions it, I'm tracking with him. Wolf kills are sensitive. If this one is real, and it's in a barn, there could be considerable fallout among ranchers in the state. And plenty of heat for the DNR. But first we have to know for certain what it is we've got here."

"That's right," the sheriff agreed.

"What we got is goddamn wolves," Moon said. "Come into a barn and slaughtered calves."

Diane paused, glancing at Moon before turning to the sheriff. "I appreciate that. All I'm saying is people have a right to know. What if they kill again?"

"Damn right," Moon added.

"That's not how normal wolves operate," Sam said.

"Wolves kill anything," Moon said.

"Wolves kill to feed. And for the record, they don't go into barns," Sam stated.

"Bullshit! Done it right here."

"That's why we're here, Angus," he said with a smile, but without humor. "To have a look at something that's never been recorded in the annals of wolf-livestock predation."

"Wolves kill every day," Moon growled.

"Not in barns." Sam watched a vein swell the side of Moon's neck, a good sign. Before Moon could speak, Sam said, "How about this, Sheriff? We make a thorough investigation of this kill. I can help Officer Svegman sort through the details. If that's OK, Steve," Sam said, turning to Svegman.

"Sure."

"Once Officer Svegman finishes writing his report and files it with the DNR, we give Diane exclusive rights to the story."

Diane frowned. She didn't like negotiating access to a story, particularly when it was in front of her and she wasn't one of the negotiators. She was suddenly a little pissed at Sam. He'd invited her on a charade. And now he'd turned paternalistic.

"We can't be exclusive," the sheriff said. "But I suspect we could give her a good head start on viewing the document. That sound fair, Diane?"

"I'm well within my rights to write any damn thing I want."

Before she gathered a full head of steam, Sam cut her off, turning back to Goddard. "I guess she has a point, Sheriff. But if I'm not mistaken, this is a crime scene, isn't it?"

Goddard knew immediately where Sam was headed, and he liked the tack. "That's right," he agreed.

"And the sheriff has the right to restrict access to the crime scene?"

"That's correct," the sheriff said.

"Bullshit," Diane barked. Sam had bushwhacked her. "This isn't St. Paul. This is the Iron Range."

"Diane, your friend here has a point."

"You can't shut me out."

"Yes, he can," Sam said.

She turned a withering eye on Sam. But Sam was ready for it. "On the other hand, Diane, I suspect the sheriff would be willing to allow the press to accompany us, providing you held your story until you received the final report."

The sheriff thought about it. "That's right," he finally said.

Diane didn't much care for where this was heading. But she wasn't sure, just yet, what she could do about it. Except play along. And when she got the chance, give Sam a piece of her mind. He had bailed her out of a tough situation with Pederson. He'd gained some credit with her. Now he was using some up.

"I don't like it," Diane finally said. "But I'll play along, providing the report doesn't take two weeks to write."

"Clayton Winthrop got no business here," Moon said.

The sheriff turned to the woodsman. "Steve Svegman and the DNR are heading up the investigation of this wolf kill. But if I'm not mistaken, he can invite assistance from any party he chooses," Goddard added, looking to Svegman, already knowing the young CO would play along. "Isn't that right, Steve?"

Svegman blushed a little. "That's right."

"Particularly from a wildlife specialist," the sheriff added.

"Uh-huh," Svegman nodded.

"That's a bunch of horseshit, Sheriff."

"Maybe you should return to the warmth of that farmhouse," the sheriff suggested. "We can show ourselves to the barn."

Moon scowled. There was no way he'd let them walk around in that barn alone.

Sam realized there would be no unaccompanied perusal of the farmhouse, at least today. But a glance at the lintel above the door showed the edge of a thin metal line, barely a half-inch curve. It was the place the old man had kept a spare key, back when Sam was young. Sam was glad to know some things hadn't changed.

Moon led them to the barn, clearly angry about Svegman's posse, but knowing they needed the DNR's blessing. Svegman followed Moon across the narrow, unplowed walk, for now taking the lead. The sheriff stepped in behind Svegman. Sam and Diane followed.

"So give us the details," the sheriff said.

"I been feeding Williston's calves since the accident. Wolves came in last night." He turned and glanced at the sheriff. "Killed 'em. Had a feed."

He paused in front of the sliding barn door. "I don't know nothin' about Colorado. But here the packs are growing plenty," Moon said. "They're takin' dogs off porches."

"Most pet predations happen out in the woods, not on porches," Sam clarified, for the record.

Moon stared at him.

Sam stared back, recognizing familiar meanness. It was unpredictability with a sense that just about anything was possible. But Moon was an aging wolverine. Or maybe a weasel, Sam thought, feeling a pleasant tension spread across his solar plexus.

Moon flung the sliding barn door open, then said, "If wolves don't go into barns, then what the hell is this?"

The first thing Sam noticed was the odor. It was like a frozen meat locker, only a little more fetid, with entrails and terminal ooze covering the killing room floor.

"My God," Diane said.

Sam peered across the threshold and examined the floor. "When did you say this happened?"

Moon turned. "Last night."

The first thing Sam noticed was the state of the carcasses. They appeared to be at least 24 hours old, which meant this couldn't have happened any earlier than the night before last. Interesting, given Moon's assertion. Particularly when Sam could see no good reason to lie.

"This how they came in?" Sam asked. He didn't question the timing, but he remembered the words from the middle of that storm, night before last.

"Nothing like back at the farm," Pederson had said, pulled over on the road near Defiance.

Then Heins. "We couldn't have hoped for a better snowfall."

"Just so they don't get caught in it," Pederson said.

"With Angus's truck? They're back at his place by now."

Heins and Pederson had been somewhere, and there were others who were heading back to Moon's place. And at some point, they'd been at the farm. Were they coming from the farm, or somewhere else?

"This door was unlatched," Moon said. "Must have nosed it open."

"Smart wolves," Sam commented. He peered along the frame, found tufts of gray and black hair. "Steve," he called to the conservation officer, who was behind him. "What do you have in the bag?"

"Digital camera. Evidence kit," he managed, a little shaken by the view and smell.

"Got any baggies?"

Svegman opened the shoulder bag, happy for the diversion. He rummaged through its contents and pulled out a small sheaf of baggies with a rubber band around them.

"Can I have one of those?" Sam asked.

Svegman pulled off his mittens and extracted a baggy, handing it to Sam.

"How about a forceps?"

Svegman returned to the bag and extracted the stainless-steel tool.

"Is this normal?" Diane asked.

Sam leaned down close to the edge of the door. The others were standing just outside the barn, watching him work. He clamped down on the largest clump of hair, shaking it loose into the baggie. He found two or three more samples and dropped them into separate bags. When he handed the bags to Svegman, he said, "Nothing normal about it."

Moon appeared to dislike seeing Sam bag hair. Interesting. "Wolf hair is pretty specific. I'm sure this is it, but it's standard with most wolf investigations. You always want a little physical evidence," Sam lied.

"Got plenty of that," Moon growled.

Sam had taken a sample because he wanted to check it. But he was also interested in Moon's reaction. The woodsman's irritation confirmed his decision to ship the sample to the USFW lab in Ashland. As soon as they returned to town, Sam would FedEx it. They'd determine definitively what kind of wolves they were. It looked like the real thing. Sam just wanted to be certain. And if the sheriff and the Minnesota DNR and Agriculture wanted the final report delayed, giving them time to prepare for the fallout, waiting for the DNA analysis would provide some cover.

Clearly the woodsman was unnerved.

Svegman nodded in agreement, though Sam knew he wouldn't have bagged the hair.

Diane watched.

The sheriff's expression suggested he was pleased Sam was along.

Moon finally reached over and flicked on the overhead light, providing a little more illumination for the scene. The smell and shadowed glimpses were bad enough, but under the dull barn light, the five onlookers were shocked by the carnage. Everyone but Moon and Sam.

"My God," Diane repeated.

One glance was enough, not likely something any of them would soon forget. Svegman looked at it and his stomach did a flip-flop.

"Doesn't look good," the sheriff agreed, though he was cool, Sam noticed. He had probably seen plenty worse, involving people, not livestock.

For Sam it was ugly and unusual but not unnerving. He stepped forward. "Got a flashlight, Steve?"

Svegman reached into his bag and extracted a flashlight. Sam flicked it on and carefully stepped to the largest animal, or what was left of it. Then he turned and said, "There should probably be just the two of us in here, stepping around these animals. Or what's left of them."

The sheriff understood. Crime scene. And it was a chance to get into the house. "Angus, mind if we wait in the house?"

Moon clearly didn't like it. Particularly Clayton Winthrop nosing around the barn uninvited and without an escort. "Be quick," he finally said.

Sam ignored the woodsman, knowing he'd take however much time his investigation needed. He was fascinated by the kill.

Sam didn't turn to watch them go. His beam flashed over the nearest kill. Its head and neck had been partially eaten. Most of the rest of it was stripped, entrails cascading from its belly onto the floor. The upward haunch was almost completely devoured. Sam turned the beam on what was left of the nose. "Got that camera?" he asked.

Svegman stepped closer, ashen. Sam watched him reach into his pack and pull out a digital camera with a built-in flash.

"Focus, Steve," Sam advised. "Just focus on what I tell you. You think you can take some pictures?"

Svegman nodded. "I've never seen a kill like this."

"Neither have I. But for the time being, let's keep that between ourselves. Can you just shoot where I point the beam?" Sam aimed the beam on the center of the calf's nose, what was left of it. There were teeth marks around the snout.

Svegman sucked it up, pointed, focused, and clicked. The camera flashed like a lightning strike. In the same manner they spent the next 10 minutes working around the calves, which were all badly eviscerated.

Twice more Sam reached down and placed fur clumps into

baggies. There were a couple of clear footprints in the barn floor where the wolves stepped in blood and paced over the cement. Sam had Svegman photograph them—wide-angle lens, macro shots. Svegman didn't have a ruler, but Sam could tell they were oversized for gray wolves. He placed the toe of his snow boot beside two of the bloody paw prints, for perspective and later measurement. But he already saw something peculiar; they were oversized, and two pairs of prints had a wider stance than a typical wolf.

"There must have been a bunch of them," Svegman said, the carnage and subsequent feeding so extreme.

"Looks like five," Sam agreed.

Svegman was surprised. "Only five?"

"Wolves can eat almost one-quarter their weight in a single sitting," Sam said, still examining the scene. "They gorge, then they sleep it off. Then they'll usually starve a few days before they kill again. Or return to feed off what they've already killed."

"Feast and famine," Svegman said.

"That's it."

On the way back to the house, Moon ruminated about leaving Sam alone. He was an unwelcome development. And Pederson had been right. He wasn't a kid anymore. But it was damn cold. And there was nothing to be done about it. They needed Svegman to authorize the kill. And there was plenty of evidence, even for Sam.

The sheriff let Diane walk in front of him, and they stepped quickly through the cold to the front door. At first the sheriff had been disappointed in Sam. He'd invited a reporter to a crime scene. And that was a clear violation of protocol, though Goddard wasn't sure how they did things in the USFW. Maybe it was different if you were investigating animals, not people. But something about Sam told the lawman there was more to Diane's invitation than friendly courtesy. He appreciated her for the same reason. Because now he might be able to nose around a little himself, inside the house, while the coarse Moon was distracted by his inquisitive guest.

Once inside, the sheriff glanced around the spare front room. "Might be good to look around," he suggested. "Just get a picture of what's here, in case anyone tries to take advantage of Winthrop's passing."

Moon eyed the sheriff with suspicion but couldn't find the harm. He shrugged and said, "Not much to take, I guess."

"Better to be safe," Goddard said. "You like some water or something, Diane?"

Diane nodded to the offer of water and Moon turned into the small farm kitchen to assist.

The sheriff stepped down the hallway to the basement door, then down the creaking stairs into the dark cellar. It smelled dank, musty, earthen. There was a workbench under a couple of spare bulbs. There was equipment for making ammo, and the necessary supplies. A pegboard with plenty of hooks and tools hung in front of the bench. There was an old furnace at the other end of the room. As he stood next to it, he heard the fuel oil ignition spit and light, the heat firing on.

The sheriff stepped over to the bench, checking it for drawers or some other place Winthrop might have hidden a flash drive, or any records of Pine Grove Estates. He stepped over to an opened box and reached in. A pile of empty shotgun shells. He took one out and examined it.

"Damn big charge," he said.

He remembered it was for the weapon that removed Winthrop's head, or most of it. He returned the empty cartridge to the box, had another look, and muttered, "OK," turning back toward the stairs.

In the same manner he examined the rest of the house.

After fetching water for Diane, Moon joined the sheriff. The place was a typical Range farmhouse, the sheriff thought. Rickety and in need of repair. Other than an old CB in a back room, the place was bare.

"Radio still work?" the sheriff asked. He hadn't seen a CB rig in quite a while.

"I guess," Moon shrugged, then switched off the room light. A little too quickly, the sheriff thought.

In Winthrop's office there was no laptop. No computer equipment anywhere. A few file drawers that might contain something, but when he opened them, they were largely empty.

"What're you looking for?" Moon asked.

"Just trying to get a sense of what's in the place."

"Nothin' but paper in those drawers."

And so it was. Other than the old man's dresser drawers, the sheriff didn't see any place Winthrop might have stowed a flash drive, DVD, or any other client files. He couldn't be certain, but he was beginning to think everything might have turned to ash with the rest of the old man's law office. With regard to the digital video, one could hope. With regard to the incriminating files, the sheriff knew Dunlap would be disappointed.

By the time they returned to the front room, Svegman and Sam were coming out of the barn.

"I guess we're done," the sheriff commented.

Moon watched Sam and Svegman approach. Sam was talking to Svegman, apparently tutoring the young CO on some of the finer points of investigating wolf kills. Svegman listened attentively.

The new Clayton pissed Moon off. Sam wasn't scared, and he wasn't a kid.

Sam and Svegman came into the front door, stamping their feet.

Moon was ready to get out to the cabin. He could use a little remedy. Or a lot. And Winthrop and the others would be interested in his update.

"Damn cold out there," Sam said, shaking it off. "I guess I forgot just how cold it could get up here," he said, smiling at the sheriff.

"We're in some kind of snap, for sure," Goddard remarked. "The bank said 12 below."

"What about the wolf kill?" Moon asked, blunt, ready to be done with business.

Sam glanced at the CO. He pulled off his mittens and blew into his hands, trying to warm them. "What about it?" he asked, turning to Moon.

"Wolves done it," Moon affirmed. It wasn't a question.

Sam looked at him. "Seems so," he said. "But it's peculiar. They killed all the calves and left plenty of food behind. That, and it happened in a barn. I can't quite figure it."

"What's to figure?" Moon asked.

Sam stared at Moon. He remembered this front room. It was spare, with an old sofa next to the wall. The sofa was new, at least that much had changed. There was an easy chair to the right of the front window.

Behind Moon was the walkway into the small kitchen, the room he had stumbled out of 20 years earlier, bruised, bloodied, and barely alive. Back down the hallway was the rear door, and to the right of the rear door the old man's infamous office, a forbidden place. He had made enough surreptitious visits to that office to have found the old man's secret hiding place. He wondered about it now. He ignored Moon, blew on his hands, and finally said, "Plenty."

There was a flight of stairs beyond the old man's office, up to the second-floor bedrooms, one of them his. The hallway was covered with photos of the Winthrop family heritage. There was the news account of his great-grandfather's death from wolves, and beyond it, photo after family photo of slaughtered wolves, some containing entire packs. Sam was surprised to see it restored. Twenty years ago, before he left, Sam had shattered every frame.

"Plenty what?"

Seeing the barn was interesting too. He had spent many boyhood hours in the place, including assembling a pack with winter survival gear, at least enough to escape into the northern wilderness. It was all so long ago, but it opened up so much inside him that he knew he'd need to return. Ghosts, he thought. A lot of spirits with whom he needed to converse.

"Damn odd they nosed their way into a barn," Sam repeated, returning to consider Moon.

"I told you the door was cracked."

"I believe you said 'unlatched,' Angus," Sam corrected.

Moon didn't appreciate the clarification. "Fuckin' open," he said, low and even.

Sam grinned. "It's still curious."

"They were followin' their noses," Moon explained. "Pushed the goddamn door open to get at 'em. You ever been hungry?"

"Sure. Not enough to push open a barn door with my nose and kill feeder calves. But I've been plenty hungry."

Diane was cold and the sheriff tired, but Sam thought they both grinned.

"I'm just saying it's a little bizarre. One for the books."

"I don't know about no goddamn books," Moon said.

True enough, Sam knew.

"What about the money?" Moon asked, turning his attention to Svegman. Svegman withered in front of the woodsman's gaze.

"Full reimbursement," Svegman answered. "I don't think we saw anything to presume it was something other than wolves. Did we, Sam?"

Sam paused. He liked having some kind of say in an occurrence that might benefit Moon. "For now, no," he said. "But if you could keep the place untouched, Angus. That'd be helpful."

"This is no goddamn business of yours."

Sam remembered the old hunter's way. Moon liked to raise his voice. A flash of temper was usually enough to dissuade.

The sheriff interceded. "Like I said, Angus. The state can solicit whatever assistance it needs from capable experts, especially Fish & Wildlife, and particularly in matters of wolf kills, given their sensitive nature." He turned to Sam. "Seen anything, Sam, to prevent Steve here from working up the reimbursement forms?"

"Nope," he said. "But it would be good to keep it open because others in Fish & Wildlife and DNR will be interested, might want to have another look. And Steve will need to set some traps. What's left of those calves might make good bait."

"I'll complete the paperwork as soon as I get back to the office," Svegman offered.

"I can set my own traps," Moon said. "Or shoot 'em if they come back."

Sam considered it. He knew Moon was equal to trapping the animals, if they returned, had probably already done it in the wild, illegally. "I suspect Steve can issue you a shoot-on-sight permit, if that's what you want."

"Damn right."

"Steve can include it with the reimbursement form."

The accommodation seemed to settle Moon, which disappointed Sam. He would have preferred him riled before asking his next question.

"Just one more thing. You said the wolves came in last night?"

"Yeah," Moon said.

"From the looks of it, those calves have been dead for more than 24 hours."

Moon's face flushed, at least as much as could be seen beneath his grizzled countenance. His dark eyes flashed at Svegman, then the sheriff.

"Might have been the other night," he shrugged.

"The night of that big storm?" Sam asked.

Moon flashed again, uneasy. "That's right."

"So you haven't been out here for 48 hours? You haven't tended to these calves in two days?"

"Snow was too high," he said, irritated. "Goddamn couldn't get nowhere!"

"So you were stuck at your place?" Sam asked.

"Yeah," he said.

"And I've got a bad memory. How far away from here do you live?"

Moon waved off the question. "What the hell difference it make? Everyone knows that storm was the worst in these parts. I live close enough," he finally answered. "But not close enough to make it over in a storm like that one."

"How far is it, Angus, exactly?" This time it was the sheriff asking. "I don't think I've ever been out to your place?"

"Five, six mile," he said. "Far enough."

"And yesterday," Sam said, "after the plows started clearing the roads, you still didn't come check on these animals?"

"I was busy," Moon said.

Busy doing whatever he was doing the night of the storm. When he wasn't at home. And Sam knew it.

"So they've gone untended for two days?" Sam asked, wanting to be sure.

"That's right. Two fuckin' days. Not that it makes any difference."

"I think he's just trying to understand what happened," the sheriff suggested. "We all just want to know what happened here and when."

"Goddamn wolves what happened!" Moon said.

The sheriff flashed a look at Sam that told him they'd pushed the man enough. He turned back to Svegman. "Steve'll get you those forms, won't you, Steve?"

"Sure."

Moon didn't answer, just nodded, clearly pissed.

"Then I guess we'll be heading out," the sheriff offered, turning toward the door.

Sam took his time getting into his mittens. "If you get lucky and catch something, keep the carcass for us, will you, Angus?"

Moon only scowled.

Sam finished getting into his coat, then stepped into the cold, preferring it to the tight interior of the house. Diane stepped out behind him. Then Svegman and the sheriff. At his Jeep Sam and Diane turned to look back toward the house. Moon was standing in the front window, watching.

The farmhouse and the immediate area surrounding it was a communications black hole. No cell phone reception. Poor media signals, Sam remembered. The poor TV reception from his childhood jump-started his reading. He'd read all of Jack London and everything he could find on wolves. Until he moved out, books were his only escape. He appreciated outdoor adventures, westerns, survival stories, anything having to do with woods or wilderness.

In the car, Diane was staring straight ahead, mute. It made Sam remember Maggie in a similar state, which became more frequent toward the end. She'd wanted to discuss whatever issue pissed her off, but Sam preferred dodging the issue with silence.

Maybe he'd try something different. "Everything OK?"

"I'm wondering why the hell you invited me out here?"

"I thought you'd be interested."

"But you moved to restrict my story when you could have kept quiet."

"Look, Diane. There are two things going on here. First, I needed to do that kill review without Moon observing our methods. And second, until we know for certain that it was a wolf kill, you shouldn't write anything about it."

"What the hell else could it be?"

"I don't know what it was. Something. There was plenty of evidence of wolves, but wolves wouldn't do this."

They drove a little longer in silence. After a while they reached blacktop, and Sam's cell phone went off. This time he thought he'd better listen on his own. He lifted his phone and answered.

"Rivers."

"Dean Goddard," the sheriff said.

"Sheriff."

"I guess you know Angus Moon is still a son of a bitch."

"I noticed."

"And I guess you noticed I don't give a damn what he thinks. If I had more men, I'd have him tailed."

"I kind of figured, Sheriff."

"I'm willing to back you up on this delay in cleanup. But if Moon starts making calls to the Cattleman's Association, or one of those ranching outfits, we could be in for a little heat. Up here we have a pretty active organization. And Agriculture still has plenty of clout."

"I appreciate that, Sheriff. And for the record, I agree. This just bears a little more investigation. I'm going to FedEx some hair samples to the Fish & Wildlife Forensics Lab in Ashland, Oregon. If I call in a favor, I should be able to get the results by tomorrow afternoon."

"What results?"

"DNA analysis. We're stockpiling a database of wolf DNA samples. I'm not expecting anything other than Great Plains wolf DNA, but it's worth double-checking."

"Great Plains wolf? I thought they were timber wolves?"

"Timber wolves are in Canada and Alaska. What we have here in the Midwest are Great Plains gray wolves. But I have to tell you, I saw some anomalies that made me wonder what they were exactly. Judging from those prints and the remains, some of those animals looked bigger than a gray wolf."

"I don't think we should sit on this mess any longer than 24 hours. Ranchers get wind of this, and there'll be a feeding frenzy in St. Paul. And the last thing we need is one of the local papers running a photo of that slaughter. For now let's keep it contained. And one other thing," Goddard added, pausing so it would register.

Sam noted the change in tone.

"Next time don't bring the press."

"Fair enough."

"I don't know you well enough to know if there was some other reason for her presence. But we're straight shooters up here, Rivers. So in the future, before you pull a stunt like that, you better let me in on it."

"Point taken, Sheriff." Diane was still staring out the window, pissed. "I owe you."

The sheriff agreed. "How's she taking it?"

She was listening, but Sam guessed she could only hear his side of the conversation. "About as well as can be expected."

"That bad, huh?"

"Uh-huh."

"We can't keep this out of the press forever. But if Diane runs it first and we can manage the photo that runs with her story, it would be a whole lot better than the alternative."

"Makes sense."

"Good. Now what did you make of the change in Moon's story, about when it happened?"

Sam thought about it. If he told the sheriff about knowing Moon was out in that storm, he'd have to tell him how he knew, which would make his own story about when he arrived in Defiance a lie. "Not sure why he lied about it. Other than he was shirking his responsibilities. Or maybe he let them alone for two days and couldn't tell they'd been dead for 48 hours. But that doesn't make sense either, because a woodsman like Angus Moon can read carcass as well as any American Indian from the last century. Considered with everything else, it was a little odd."

Up ahead, as they cruised down the blacktop toward town, a small clutch of ravens was pecking at a deer carcass. And that's when Sam remembered. Something else had bothered him about the kill, but he hadn't been able to pinpoint it.

"One other thing," he said. "There were no ravens."

"Ravens?"

"Ravens and wolves have been symbiotic for thousands of years. Not always, but usually. Ravens follow the packs, some speculate to clean up after the wolves have finished gorging. American Indians believed ravens led the packs to wounded or sickened animals. Wherever you see wolves, you usually find ravens."

The sheriff thought about it. "No way ravens would get into that barn."

"True enough, Sheriff. But I didn't see any roosting on the roof or in nearby trees. And I didn't see any sign of them. If they'd been following the pack, at least some would hang around a kill that size."

They discussed the next 24 hours, when Sam might return to the house to have another look in the barn. Right now, Sam was pretty sure he'd be returning, but not with Goddard. The carnage was excellent bait, if the animals grew hungry. They agreed that by tomorrow at this time, they'd let Moon clean it up, maybe visit for one more examination of the scene.

Sam ended the phone call and drove the remaining miles in silence. At the edge of Defiance he glanced at his watch. It was after 4 p.m.

"I think I'm heading back to the hotel. I need to bag it for a couple hours, because after dinner I'm heading back out to the old man's place. Take a closer look. Not in the barn. In the house. And it won't be burglary, since I don't plan on stealing anything. And technically not breaking and entering, since I'll have a key. If I get caught, the most they could get me for is trespassing."

"A key?"

"There was a key on the lintel above the front door. I could just make out the edge of the metal. It's where the old man used to keep a spare."

Diane turned, curious. He had her attention. "And what about Angus Moon?"

"There's an old logging road that comes up through the trees across from the farm. I'll take that to within a quarter mile of the place. Then I can approach it in the dark, see if he's still around. But I don't think he'll be there. Angus seemed in a hurry to get rid of us. And I don't think it was just me. I think he was going somewhere. The man never took off his boots or his coat."

"I noticed," Diane said. She'd also felt curious about the place. When Moon had gone into the kitchen to fetch her water, he kept one ear cocked in Goddard's direction, jumpy about the sheriff's perambulation through the rest of the farmhouse. As soon as he'd given her a glass of water, without so much as a courteous glance in her direction, Moon was off to find the sheriff. It was telling.

"Why would you be going back out to the farmhouse?" she asked.

He didn't want to mention ghosts. But another pair of eyes might be useful, keeping watch while he searched through the old rooms. "It's been a while and I have a hunch nosing through that old place might be . . .," he paused, thinking about it. "Might turn up something. Just a hunch."

"You weren't there, but Angus wasn't exactly comfortable having Sheriff Goddard search through those rooms."

"No way the sheriff would know where to look," Sam said. "But I do. Any interest in joining me?"

Truth was, she still felt pissed about Sam setting her up. But the proposition was so intriguing that it was hard to turn down.

"It's supposed to be 20 below tonight," she finally said.

"Perfect cover for a little trespass."

For the time being, she decided to overlook his indiscretion, maybe considering one of her own.

"Why don't you crash on my couch again? It'll save you a trip."

"That makes sense. So, you're joining me?"

"Sure. It's been a while since I've committed any trespass . . . with a lawman."

CHAPTER TWENTY-FOUR

The southern boundary of Skinwalkers Bog was bordered by an old logging road. The road ran 30 miles in a straight line to remote Libby Lake. Since there was nothing at either end but wilderness, and no bars in between, few snowmobilers used it. Heins hauled his Arctic Cat to a small parking area at one end of the trail. Since the storm, the lot had been used once. Now, at dusk, it was empty. Heins parked his truck behind a line of black spruce. Then he revved the Cat, backed it off the sled, and headed down the remote trail toward the even more secluded Libby Lake, a destination he had no intention of reaching.

He'd come in from the opposite side of Skinwalkers Bog, knowing Pederson, Young, and then Moon would take the northern, more familiar approach. Given the terrain and rugged path, Heins's snowmobile ride and hike to the cabin would take just under an hour, which was fine by him. Heins needed time to think.

In the growing dark his snowmobile's headlight wobbled over the narrow track. He went 3 miles before recognizing the spruce-bough tunnel, a place where overhead boughs formed a tight canopy. The ground under the trees was icy and barren. Most riders skirted the trees, but Heins steered straight into them. Halfway down he appeared to turn into a wall of spruce boughs and disappeared. He was through them in less than a second, the thick branches slapping back behind him. He steered the Cat onto a small side trail leading away from the trees. Fifty more yards of ice-covered ruts brought him to a frozen creekbed. He dropped into the ditch and cut the engine.

Against the left bank a spring torrent had caused a large spruce to buckle and tip halfway over, its flat, broad root structure creating a small enclosure. Heins pushed the Cat into the hold until nothing but its taillights showed under the wattle of tree roots and debris. He pulled his snowshoes off the back, fitted them on, slogged his way down 20 more feet of solid creek flow, and climbed the bank to the start of a path, indiscernible unless you knew where to look and where you were going. It was a damn cold night, but he wasn't thinking about the freeze.

Before Heins had left his office, the phone rang. It was 4:45 p.m., and he'd hesitated, not wanting to pick up the receiver. He was running late and anxious to get out to the cabin and enjoy Winthrop's wake. But official quitting time was still 15 minutes away, so he finally decided to answer. "Police."

"This Defiance?" drawled a woman's voice.

"This is the Defiance Police."

"This is Clement Beauregard," she said, a little gravelly.

"May I help you?"

"My brother was due in Winnipeg last Wednesday night," she drawled. "S'posed to be on the 11:25 Greyhound. But he never showed," she said, emphasizing the last word.

"Your brother's from Winnipeg?"

"I'm in Winnipeg," she blurted, short. "My brother's s'posed to be somewhere down there. Farm outside Defiance, I think he said."

And suddenly Heins recognized the name, and accent. James T. "Jimbo" Beauregard. When Heins had first found him, Jimbo mentioned he had a sister, somewhere in Canada, and that he was on his way to see her. It was the only time Heins heard Jimbo's last name, and it took a second to register. Beauregard was the bum, their victim, the guy who was a substitute for Winthrop's body.

"Yeah?" Heins asked, wondering how in the hell she'd figured out to call Defiance. "And he was supposed to be in Winnipeg on Wednesday?" Heins feigned interest, buying time.

"Thas' right. Wednesday night."

"Where did you say he was?"

"Last I heard from him, some farm outside your town. He called me las' Saturday mornin'. From a farm."

"What's his name?" Last Saturday the only place he could have called from was Winthrop's.

"James Beauregard. Folks call him Jim, or Jimbo."

"Jimbo?"

"Thas' right. Uh-huh. Jimbo. Jimbo Beauregard."

"Can't say I've seen him. He from around here?"

"Course not. We're Cajun. Bayou. Down Louisiana," she said, the s like a lazy z. Like teeth on a saw blade.

"But you're in Winnipeg? Manitoba?"

"Thas' right. My cousin Emil started a Cajun café, and I told Jimbo we could use a little help. He was s'posed to be here Wednesday," she repeated.

"Did you say he was taking the Greyhound?"

"Thas' right."

"We don't have a Greyhound bus that comes through Defiance."

"Bemidji," Clement answered, without a beat. "He was takin' it from a place called Bemidji."

"But he said he was in Defiance?"

"Uh-huh," she affirmed. "Stayin' at a farm."

"Did he give you any names?" Heins tried to ask the question normally, but was buzzing inside.

"Huh-uh," she answered.

He breathed. "Did he say how he was getting to Bemidji?"

"Huh-uh," she said. "A ride, I s'pect."

"We had quite a storm the middle of the week. Maybe he got caught up in it?"

"Maybe," she guessed. "I jus' thought I'd hear from him by now. It's not like Jimbo."

"What's he look like?" Heins asked.

"He has a mark on his face. Birthmark. Reddish."

Heins remembered well, listened as Beauregard described her brother in more detail.

She finished by saying, "He's had run-ins. With the law, I mean. He never done nothin' bad. Just a little liftin', time and agin."

"We haven't arrested anyone recently, Ms. Beauregard."

"Glad to hear it." When he called, Jimbo had told her he'd won the money for a bus ticket playing cards, fair and square. She'd been worried about the money. She was happy to hear he wasn't in jail, at least in Defiance. She made a note to call the county sheriff's office. "But I'm worried," she added. "Jimbo was a lot a' things, some of them trouble. But if he said he was goin' to be somewhere at a certain time, he shown. I never known him to be late like this, without word," she wondered aloud.

Hard to know what else to do but play along. He took down the information and assured Ms. Beauregard he'd look into it, let her know what he found. He inquired again after the farm, if she could tell him anything else about it, since the country around Defiance was settled with many farms. But she couldn't. Heins eased a little.

"We'll keep an eye out," he assured her, friendly as he could manage, concerned. "I'll put out a missing person report on him." He took down her number and told her he'd call her Sunday evening, or Monday the latest. It was the weekend, and he was heading out himself.

"If you see him, tell him his sister's askin' after him, and please call."

"We sure will, Ms. Beauregard," Heins said, and rang off.

Heins approached the cabin quietly, snowshoes swishing through deep powder. He thought about the conversation, worried over it, wondering how and when Jimbo had called his sister. Jimbo had been planning to leave. That was a goddamn surprise. The Greyhound out of Bemidji. They were fuckin' lucky he neglected to mention the farm's name, or the rancher who owned it. Mentioning Defiance was bad enough. And it was good she'd phoned Heins. Let's just hope she stopped there.

The cabin lay 20 yards ahead through the trees. Heins slowed.

And then in the dark, from his right, a metallic ping silenced his reverie.

Heins turned, startled, to see Winthrop holding his .45 automatic. He gripped the slide with his gloved right hand and pulled it back to reset the trigger. If there had been a shell, it would have ejected. Instead, he clicked a second time and the firing pin ratcheted down on another empty chamber, making another hollow ping.

"You're dead," Winthrop said. "Sounded like a goddamn moose through those trees."

"That's a good way to get yourself killed, Williston."

"Not if I get you first," he said, stepping forward, reaching and slapping the startled Heins on the back. "Besides, I'm already dead." They chuckled in the dark. "Did you bring those Cohibas?"

With everything else that had happened, Heins had forgotten Winthrop's cigars. "Goddammit. I forgot. I was preoccupied."

"You know how I get when I run out of smokes."

Heins nodded, knowing once Winthrop heard why he'd forgotten the cigars, he'd understand. "I know."

"Promise me you won't forget tomorrow."

"You'll have your cigars, Williston. Right now we got bigger things to worry about."

"What's that?"

"Let me get in out of this cold and I'll tell you about it."

Outside the cabin he took off his snowshoes and stuck them in a drift beside the door. Winthrop went in before him and announced, "The law finally arrived!"

Young and Pederson were at the table, playing cards and sipping whiskey. They looked up at the cold entry, grinning. "Told ya I heard him," Winthrop said.

"Looks like you could use a drink," Pederson said.

"I'll pour him one, man as deserving as the law," Young laughed, getting up and crossing the room.

Once they settled down and Heins had a drink, he turned to them and said, "Guess who called, just before I left?"

"The DNR," Winthrop said.

Heins shook his head.

"Ag?" he guessed.

"They won't call, Williston," Pederson said. "They'll just write the check." He turned to Heins. "The insurance company?"

"Clement Beauregard."

No response. None of them knew a Clement, but a look of surprise spread over Winthrop's face. "Christ," he hissed. "One of Jimbo's relatives?"

"A sister," Heins said. "Remember him saying he was heading up to Canada?"

Winthrop nodded. The others waited for Heins's story. He told them the details of what he knew, including double-checking bus schedules out of Bemidji. Sure enough, on Wednesday nights a bus left Bemidji at 2:50 and arrived in Winnipeg at 11:25.

Now they all shared Heins's worry.

"Ol' Jimbo made a call," Winthrop finally breathed. "Wonder if he used my phone?" That wouldn't be good. Calls could be traced. The number could be on Beauregard's bill and his own, if they decided to inquire at the phone company. He had to think about it.

"Had to be your phone," Heins said. "After I picked him up at the old rail depot, I took him straight to your place. And he never left, far as I know. She said it was Saturday morning. He was at your place, wasn't he?"

"He was out there by himself a couple times. That was one of them. He could have used the phone to call when I was out."

"Maybe he had a cell?" Young wondered.

"Jimbo?" Pederson laughed, no humor in it. "Didn't have a pot to piss in."

They all considered the news, wondering what could be done.

"Goddammit," Winthrop repeated, unsettled. He took a long

swallow of remedy. It seemed to help, but he felt tension winding tight as a trigger spring. "All she's got is a number, maybe. And given she's calling Heins, we got it contained. And she hasn't yet figured out anything about the phone. Hell, maybe the Canadian phone company doesn't keep a record of phone numbers."

He knew it was wishful thinking, but he was trying to ease everyone's concern. There was no goddamn sense getting worked up over something out of your control. But that didn't prevent him from trying to figure out ways to manage it.

"Even if she figured it out, got my number from the fuckin' phone company, so what?" Winthrop said, trying to reason through it. "I'm dead, and Jimbo's disappeared. Nothin' to say I wasn't helping out a vagrant. Or maybe he broke into my place?" Though Winthrop knew that was doubtful, given the remote location of the farm and no easy way to get there.

"Even if he called from my place, there's nothing to say he didn't light out after my accident. Could make them wonder if this vagrant might have pulled the trigger."

The others chewed on it. A pall began to settle over their celebration.

Then Heins remembered more bad news. "And someone broke into the Defiance house."

Winthrop's eyes darkened, a bad sign.

"Hold on, hold on," Heins said. "Far as I could tell the only thing missing was some preserves."

The observation didn't lighten Winthrop's countenance. "When?"

"I found it this morning. I think they got in the night of the storm."

"How long's the kid been here?"

"Checked in at the hotel yesterday morning, after the storm."

Winthrop had little doubt it was Clayton who broke into the house. He just wondered what he managed to steal.

"The timing's off for Clayton to have done it," Heins argued.

Suddenly Winthrop's glass flew across the room and shattered against a timber. The splintered glass brought an even deeper pall to the cabin.

"Who the fuck do you think it was? It was the goddamn kid for sure. And I bet he got a whole hell of a lot more than preserves."

No one in the room commented on Winthrop's guess. There were a few long moments during which the unease in the room was as palpable as a winter storm blast. Young finally pushed out his chair and stood. He walked to a corner and picked up a broom and dustpan. Pederson looked back at the table. Heins kept an eye on the dead man.

Winthrop worried about it all. The damn call and now Clayton, who had very likely recovered $179,000 and who knew what else. "The minute you get a chance," Winthrop ordered Heins, "you pull over that little son of a bitch and search his car, his room, every other place he's been."

"That's my intention."

"The woman's place too," Pederson added.

"Her place too," Heins agreed.

Moon came through the door with a blast of icy air.

"Shut the goddamn door!" Winthrop bellowed.

Everyone was startled by Moon's entry, testament to their preoccupation with Heins's news.

Moon turned and slammed the cabin door.

"Where the hell have you been?" Winthrop started.

"Gettin' thirsty," Moon answered. "And tendin' to business. Settin' traps for my dogs." He pulled off his woolen ski mask and flung it onto a bench beside the front door.

Winthrop and the others were at least glad to hear Moon was doing what he could to recover his dogs. The news finally made Winthrop ease a little, congratulating Moon on his efforts. For the moment, the squall passed.

Heins handed Moon whiskey in a plastic glass. He drank it off in two long swallows, exhaling deeply when it was done. "It's damn cold out there," he said.

"Well, it's fine and tight in here," Winthrop managed, recovering some of his equilibrium. "See any more sign?"

Moon shook his head. "Not exactly. I suspect it'll be the middle of tonight, more likely tomorrow night."

"What makes you so sure they'll return?" Pederson asked.

"They're hungry and cold," Moon said. "They can probably stand it another night, might even get lucky and catch some mice or a hare. But they'll be back. I know my dogs."

"Guess who called?" Winthrop said.

Moon looked up. He turned and began to pour himself more whiskey. "Clayton."

"We know all about the prodigal son."

Winthrop explained about Clement Beauregard, who she was, what she wanted, and what it meant.

Moon reached into his side pocket, extracted a round tin of Timber Wolf chewing tobacco, carefully opened it, and placed a pinch inside his lower lip. "What're we gonna do?"

Winthrop considered. "Nothing. Heins will sit on it. Hope she doesn't call anywhere else. Heins can call her back tomorrow or the next day, and let her know the Defiance Police have come up empty. It should end there."

"Unless she calls the sheriff," Heins said.

"Not even sure that's bad. Nobody else knows. Just call her sometime Sunday or Monday. Tell her you put out a BOLO, but no one reported anything."

BOLO was a "Be on the Lookout" report. If he completed one, it'd have to go through the sheriff's office, which worried Heins, but he nodded. He liked the idea for the same reason: might throw her off the scent. "I told her I was going to."

They were silent for a few minutes, ruminating. Pederson and Heins poured themselves more remedy. Young finished sweeping up the glass.

Moon positioned the chew, tucked it back in his mouth, took another long sip of whiskey. "I seen Clayton," he said.

They turned to him.

"Sam Rivers," Moon said. "And Hank's right. He ain't no kid anymore. Asked a damn lot of questions about the kill. Seems to know somethin' 'bout wolves."

"He was at the house?" Winthrop asked. This surprise he knew he could handle, might even be a good thing, if it surfaced his missing $179,000.

"At the house and lookin'," Moon answered. "Some kind of expert on wolf kills."

"I'll be damned," Winthrop said. "I knew he worked for Fish & Wildlife. He always liked the animals." Winthrop wondered about it. They'd have to keep an eye on the boy. "Anything in particular we need to worry about?"

Moon thought on it, poured himself more whiskey. "He said it was damn strange, never seen anything like it, wolves gettin' into a barn and killin' everything."

"What about Svegman? Did the DNR weigh in?"

"Svegman was there. But he followed Clayton's lead." Moon picked up a second plastic cup and spit.

"What about the forms?" Winthrop asked.

Moon nodded. "Svegman agreed. Rivers didn't stop 'im. We'll be gettin' paid."

The favorable news rippled through the room. They needed some. Pederson, over by the potbellied stove, raised a plastic glass and clicked it against Young's drink, winking and nodding.

"Now that's what I was hoping to hear," Winthrop said, pleased. "Let 'em ask questions. If they're fillin' out the forms, we're gettin' paid." Then he thought of something, a corroborating issue. "They wouldn't dare not pay. Every rancher in the region would make a stink that'd smell all the way down to the Cities." He'd done work for the local cattleman's association. He knew them.

"That's what has the DNR worried," Moon agreed. "That it's genuine. Reporter from the local paper was there. That bright-eyed bitch. She wanted to run with it, but Goddard kept her from it. And Sam Rivers agreed with the sheriff, far as I could figure."

"The sheriff was there too?"

"And the reporter," Moon added, with a glance in Pederson's direction.

"What about the remains?" Winthrop asked.

"What about 'em?"

"Clean it up?"

"Sam Rivers wanted to leave it. Said he wanted to mull on it. Said it'd be good bait, case they returned."

"Don't let Clayton get under your skin, Angus," Winthrop said. "We can deal with the boy."

Moon looked up from his glass. "He ain't actin' like your boy, Williston."

"Why did he want to mull over the kill?" Heins asked.

Moon looked at him. "I guess it don't smell right."

Winthrop could feel their concern. Young and Pederson stood beside the potbellied stove, warming themselves, listening. "Fuck 'em," Winthrop blurted. "We're gettin' paid and that's all that matters. What about the insurance check?" he growled, turning to Young.

"No questions," Young said, shaking his head. "At least not yet. I don't expect we'll get any. They're getting the coroner's report, which will clearly state it was a hunting accident."

"Damn right," Winthrop said with a smile. He walked across the room to where several liquor bottles were stacked on a shelf. He took down a bottle of Crown Royal. "Time I had a proper drink. Don't forget, boys," he said, turning around the room, raising the bottle. "It's my wake!"

Heins smiled. Pederson came over to the table with an empty glass. Young grinned. Moon seemed to require more convincing.

"The DNR thought it was unusual," Winthrop said, talking to him. "So what? If they were that suspicious, why are they completing the forms?" It was rhetorical, and Winthrop didn't wait for anyone to respond. He dismissed the notion with a wave of his hand, pouring whiskey over large square cubes. The liquid sputtered and cracked. "Take them off our trail," he added. "They just don't want it to get out. That's all. Let's have another drink."

As he poured, a distant howl sounded through the cabin wall.

"Quiet," Moon said. The others hadn't heard it.

They paused, listening. Winthrop was about to continue pouring when they all heard the howl, faint and far off.

"Wolf," Moon said.

"Christ," Winthrop started laughing. "Forgot to tell you," he said to the others. "We heard them yesterday. They've finally made it to the bog. What'd I tell ya?" he said, pouring. "They're breeding like rats. Pretty soon they'll be settling on the outskirts of Defiance."

There was another howl, this time from a different set of jaws.

"There's two," Moon observed. The sound of wolves, particularly in this kind of cold, conveyed an absolute wildness Moon had always appreciated.

"There can be a whole pack for all I care," Winthrop said.

"Any chance they'll check us out?" Young asked.

"Fuck no," Moon spit.

"Wolves?" Winthrop laughed. "Goddamn fools if they do. We'll bag 'em and tag 'em and they know it. Besides, you heard the DNR boys. Wolves don't like the smell of man. Let's cut a deck and deal."

Moon paused long enough to hear three more howls. There was something familiar about them, but they couldn't be his dogs. For starters, his dogs rarely howled. He'd wondered about it when they were growing up. He'd tried to get them to howl, but they seldom opened their mouths, except to whine. Too much dog, he'd guessed.

And Skinwalkers Bog was 15 miles from Winthrop's farm, as the raven flew. Probably much farther, if the wolves came cross-country. His dogs wouldn't travel that far, not away from all that food. They could handle the cold, but they weren't used to starvation. He'd catch them in his traps. Probably have them by morning.

He turned to join the others.

As they sat down to play, there was one last long chorus of hungry howls, this time more than three, and closer. But the men were no longer listening.

CHAPTER TWENTY-FIVE

S am tried to sleep through the early evening, with limited success. He was wide awake when his cell phone went off.

"Rivers," he answered.

"Sam," Kay Magdalen said, he thought with a smile. "So glad you picked up."

"Isn't it Friday night?"

"Clarence and I are sitting here watching *Gladiator*." She ignored his comment. "Ever seen it?"

She also sounded . . . different. Maybe a little drunk. "Yeah, I saw it. Good movie."

"Russell Crowe kind of reminds me of you."

"Too bulky," Sam said, ignoring her unusual attempt at flattery. "What's going on, Kay? You've never called me on a Friday night. Someone die?"

"Not exactly. You'll never guess who called me this afternoon."

"The governor?"

"Bigger. The commissioner," she said.

Sam waited.

"Seems he's got a burr on his butt about this interagency task force. He was asking about progress. He thinks we need to move on it sooner, rather than later."

She paused, but Sam didn't take the bait.

"Wanted to know the candidates," she finally added.

"So what did you tell him?"

"You and Salazar, for special agent."

"Did you tell him Salazar's sleeping with my wife?"

"Ex-wife. I left that part out because it's nobody's business. That's what *ex* means."

She was right, but he didn't have to like it or admit it.

"He doesn't know anything about Salazar," she continued. "Except that he has an accounting background, which made him snort. You know what it means when the commissioner snorts?"

"No idea."

"He doesn't like something. Thinks it smells."

There was another pause, before she finally continued. "He thought the position called for a field agent, not a bean counter. And here's the good part. He remembers that article about you in the *Denver Post*. The one about the Key deer. He thought you were probably the better candidate. So you've got a leg up."

If he wanted the job, Sam thought. He still hadn't decided. "Is that it?" he finally asked.

She hesitated. "He thinks there could be a little extra money in it for you. Some kind of promotion. Only thing is, he wants us to decide sooner, rather than later. Like Monday. Tuesday, the latest."

"Did you tell him I was out of town?"

"I did. Know what he said?"

"What?"

"Find him. Tell him. Light a fire under his ass. We need to move on this thing while the funding's still there."

Sam waited. It was dark outside. Even in the comfort of Diane's small living room, he could feel the intense cold, like a low-pressure ridge. "OK," he finally said.

"OK, what?" Magdalen pushed.

"OK, I'll let you know. Tuesday, the latest."

There was a long pause during which he could hear her heavy exhale. "Just don't push your luck, Rivers," she said, gravelly.

"I appreciate all you're doing, Kay." He thought that sounded a little better, though he knew her efforts wouldn't have much to do with his final decision. "Maybe you can do me a favor?"

"Quid pro quo?" she asked, looking for an angle.

"It's not that big a favor. I'm wondering, since you seem to be working late on a Friday, if you could call Ashland? The Minnesota DNR FedExed a wolf hair sample to forensics with my name on it, and I need them to look at it as soon as they get it."

Sam could call, but he thought they might be more responsive to Magdalen. And besides, he might need another favor from forensics and he didn't want to waste the one he had, if he could help it.

"I thought you were on vacation?"

"I am."

"So what are you doing FedExing hair samples on your vacation? Can't it wait?"

"Professional curiosity," he said. "I've got a hunch a wolf kill isn't a wolf kill, but I need forensics to weigh in."

"This personal?"

"Isn't it always?"

"That's why you belong on the team," she said.

Sam didn't respond.

"So let me get this straight," she said. "You're using service resources for your own investigation?"

"I'm helping out the Minnesota DNR on an unusual wolf kill," he clarified. "It's a goodwill thing. If you need a personal angle, consider it an interagency thing."

Magdalen snorted. She must have learned that from the commissioner, Sam thought.

"I'll call," she finally said. "Saturday morning, first thing. You'll get your results in record time. But consider it a big goddamn favor," she said, and then hung up.

Sam chuckled in the dark. Just like her, he thought. She'd help him, but was pissed about it because she knew it wouldn't affect his decision one way or another. He liked Magdalen.

He went into Diane's bathroom and washed up. Her toothbrush, hairbrush, and a few other items were spread across the narrow tiled countertop. Women's things. It'd been a while. He felt a flash of domesticity and thought he missed it. Then he put it out of his mind. It was after 10, time to roll. On his way back to her kitchen, he knocked on her door.

"Come on in," she answered.

Sam hesitated, then opened the door. She was sitting in bed next to a desk lamp, propped up on pillows, a book opened in front of her. She wore a black sweatshirt with, Sam guessed, nothing underneath, judging from the way it moved when she leaned to set down her book. The bed looked comfortable and so did she.

"You ready?"

"Of course." She stared at him, her long hair falling over her shoulders like a mane. "Any chance we'll see those wolves?"

"They could return. But it would probably be later. Probably the middle of the night, given what I saw of that barn and the natural distaste they have for anything civilized."

"I'd better put on something more appropriate."

Her tone left no room for interpretation, but it was an interesting choice of words.

Before he could think what to say, she added, "How's your car
battery? It's going to be pretty damn cold. I don't want to get stuck
out there."

"Practically brand new."

"I'll be ready in 5 minutes," she said.

He turned out of her room and shut the door.

They drove to the farmhouse, talking about Winthrop, the wolves,
county politics, Denver, and wherever else the conversation led
them. It was a comfortable ride. It was around −20°, and they
were dressed in enough layers to make moving a little stiff and
awkward. But it kept the cold at bay. They passed one or two cars
on the highway outside of town, and then nothing for the next 11
miles. Sam drove until he reached a place almost parallel with the
old man's farmhouse. They were about a quarter mile south of the
house. Between them and the farm a large spread of black spruce
and poplar topped a brief rise. A rutted, snow-covered logging
road climbed into the trees. Its surface was pristine.

"Nobody's been here," Sam observed, pulling the Jeep to the
side of its snow-choked entrance.

"Where the hell is here?" Diane asked.

"Close to the farm. Up over that rise through the trees you can
come to a place, if I remember right, where you can look down the
path and glimpse the farmhouse through the woods. We should
be able to see most of the farm, at least enough to see if Angus is
still there."

"Or those wolves," Diane added. "I'd rather not run into either."

"Might be a little fun," Sam disagreed. "But we'll have to be careful. Angus is definitely the type to shoot first and ask questions after the smoke clears. If he's still around, we'll head back the way we came."

"Would the wolves bother us?"

"No. If we were lucky enough to sneak up on them, they'd turn the minute they saw us. Or should."

They got out of the Jeep, fitted their snowshoes, and started up the trail into the trees. The snow was heavy, but the evening was still and cold, and it felt good to be hiking on the old road, generating a little warmth against the subzero weather. Their breath rose in clouds that mingled over the path. They reached the point in the woods Sam remembered. From the seclusion of an abandoned logging trail, they could barely make out the farmhouse, less than a quarter mile distant. They watched for any sign of movement, of light, or anyone awake or stirring, but it was quiet in the dark. And Moon's truck was gone.

"Let's go," Sam whispered.

"Wait a minute. What if he parked in the garage?"

"Probably did, if he's still around. It'd be stupid to leave your truck in this kind of cold, unless you had a plug-in." Sam kept staring at the farmhouse. Nothing. "But there's only one way to know for sure." He started moving again along the overgrown trail, descending through the trees to the road and farm.

The partial moon was high, and the house, garage, and barn were bathed in pale light, giving everything a ghostly hue. They wore ski masks that covered everything but their eyes and mouths.

The only movement was their breath, the only sound an occasional grind of dry powder as they steadied themselves or shoed across the snow.

"Let's check the garage first," Sam said. "If Angus's truck is in that garage, we'll leave. Quiet, like we came," Sam whispered.

"And what if he returns while we're in there?"

"If he's not there now, he won't be back. At least not tonight. Too late. And too damn cold."

She hoped he was right.

The two figures took off their snowshoes and were careful to walk down the driveway's frozen tire ruts. They approached the garage, and Sam walked around to the side window. There were two pines growing beside the outside garage wall, and he pushed in behind their boughs. When he peered through the glass, he saw the pale gleam of a four-door sedan, probably the old man's. Moon's truck was gone.

He returned and said, "Ready?"

"No truck?"

"Just the old man's car. Angus must have gone back to his place. And why not, considering there's no more livestock. And the old man's ghost is still walking around."

"I hope he doesn't mind us poking around his place."

"I hope he does."

They came around the front of the house, stepping along the worn path where their footsteps blended with others. Sam turned toward the front door. The farmhouse was locked. Sam peered through the dark window, but it was opaque with frost. He knocked, heavy and loud. The percussive sound echoed across the road and into the trees.

"Jesus. You trying to wake the dead?"

"Yup," Sam said. "Besides, nothing but trees will hear that knock, no matter how loud I make it. And if someone's still in the place, I want to know about it."

Diane looked at him. His eyes peered out of his ski mask, dark and intense. This wasn't exactly breaking and entering, but close enough to give her a rush high up in the center of her chest. She noticed Sam smile and answered with a smile of her own.

Finally, Sam took off his right-hand mitten, reached up in the dark, and felt along the lintel. The key was where he remembered it. The sharp freeze bit his hand. "And here it is," he said, ignoring the cold, inserting it into the lock.

They opened the door and went in. The smell of the house was familiar, with a little more stale and age thrown in. The old man had been 62, still young by Winthrop standards. Sam pulled off his ski mask and stuffed it into a coat pocket. Diane did the same, her long hair falling across her shoulders.

"Leave the lights off," Sam said.

He fished into the lower front pocket of his coat and brought out the steel-handled flashlight, flicking on its beam. Diane reached into her coat pocket and brought out a small handheld flashlight. They examined the contents of the living room, then walked into the kitchen. The table and chairs were unchanged.

There was a gas range and a newer refrigerator next to the stove. Sam remembered the day he'd almost shot the old man. Sam had forgotten to load the weapon. When Sam pulled the trigger, it snapped on an empty chamber. Winthrop, drunk, pulled the empty gun out of Sam's hands. Sam had been so startled by his trigger pull, by the certainty he wanted to kill his old man and would have, if the gun had been loaded, that he retched. It was the last time Sam had been in this kitchen.

"One thing I do need to take out of here," Sam said, remembering.

"I thought you said we were just looking around."

"I need more shells for my shotgun. It's an odd gauge, and if I'm not mistaken, the old man kept shells for it in the basement."

"Why take them?" Diane asked. "Why risk it? Why don't you just go buy some?"

"These were specially made shotguns," Sam said. "They take an unusual load. Besides, no one's going to miss them. They'll just stay down in that dank basement collecting dust."

"It's your show," Diane said.

Sam turned out of the kitchen and started down the hallway.

"Just a minute," Diane said. She'd paused in front of the start of the Winthrop glory wall. "I noticed this when I was here before." She was curious.

"Here's where it begins," Sam said, pointing his light onto the first clipping. He was too far away to read, but he started reciting it aloud from memory.

FEARED EATEN BY WOLVES
Searchers Discouraged in Hunt for W. H. "Gray" Winthrop

Jan. 5, 1905, Defiance, Minn.—The search for W. H. Gray Winthrop, Defiance attorney, avid fisherman, and hunter, has been abandoned. Winthrop was last seen entering the remote wilderness at mile marker 76 on the Iron Line, where he was hunting wolves. For two weeks nine men and a half-dozen

hounds have been scouring the country. They recovered his
shotgun and the torn remnants of one snowshoe, both identified as Winthrop's, and both scarred by fang marks.

Theodore "Doc" Dunlap, who headed the search party,
returned yesterday with news that the country for miles
around has been thoroughly covered. Other than the shotgun and snowshoe, searchers' efforts have been in vain.
Wolves in that vicinity are plentiful, and chances are the
man's body was entirely devoured.

When he was finished, Diane turned. "When was the last time
you read that?"

"Twenty years. Some things you just don't forget."

"Guess not. That was verbatim. You must have a pretty good
memory."

"Average," he said. "Just one of the old man's games. He made
me memorize it. You'd be surprised how much you can remember
when the punishment for getting a word wrong is a smack upside
the head that rattles your teeth."

"Oh," she said. But as bad as she knew that sounded, she was
still interested in what the other pictures portrayed. She cast her
small cone of light on the next picture along the wall. In the old
photo two men stood over five wolves laid out in front of them
on the snow. The next photo showed even more wolves, some of
them hanging from a game pole, others laid out in front of the five
hoisted wolves.

"I'll leave you to it," he said. "I'm going to get those shells."

"OK," Diane said, absorbed in the pictorial legacy of the Winthrop family clan.

In the basement Sam's beam flashed on two full boxes of

10 gauge shells. He was surprised to find the fresh makings for more shells on the workbench, as though the old man had been in the middle of stocking up before his accident. It supported those who believed the old man hadn't pulled the trigger on purpose.

He placed the two boxes of shells into the back lower pocket of his coat. They were heavy behind him, but their awkward weight felt familiar, reassuring. There was something that felt good about taking ammo from the old man's basement, particularly ammo Winthrop would never be able to use.

By the time he emerged from the basement, Diane was at the end of the wall.

"That's a lot of wolves," she said.

"I counted them once: 417. After my grandfather and the old man cleaned out this area, they began hunting farther afield. Went up into Canada, even Alaska."

"Incredible."

"More like a demented obsession. But that was the old man's way."

On the main floor, at the end of the hallway, was the office Sam was never supposed to enter. He remembered it, the smell of cigar smoke still thick in the tight interior of the room. When he was very young, his father told him the room was off-limits. Innocent and compliant, he obliged. But for Sam the forbidden, at least in this context, pricked his curiosity like a bug itch. The door was usually closed, but whenever he heard the old man working at his study desk, Sam would pass by the room slowly, listening. Sometimes, when the old man was away, Sam opened the door and peered inside. When he realized he could open and peer without being discovered, at least when he was certain the old man was

gone, he lingered at the opening. His curiosity grew. He was surreptitious in his efforts. He was careful—knowing the old man—
to leave plenty of time between explorations.

Not long before he fled, Sam had been in the kitchen when
he heard a clattering from the nearby office. Standing in front of
the sink, he swore he felt the floor vibrate along the floorboards.
At the time he wondered about it. Then on one of his perusals
of the sacred chamber, he carefully examined the floor. Under a
corner of a corded throw rug, he found a section of the boards
with slightly larger gaps between the slats. He inserted the edge of
a paper clip into one of the narrow gaps, prying up a foot-square
section of floorboards to reveal a secret hollow. Nothing much in
it. Papers, a couple of folders, a small metal box.

He'd just turned 17. The papers didn't interest him. Knowing
about it was enough. There were coins in the metal box, old and
tarnished with age.

Now Sam reentered the office. He smiled to remember the
trepidation that first accompanied his perusal of this room—the
way his heart was hammering in his chest, his fear the old man
would catch him nosing around his private stuff. Now he was simply curious again, hoping the old man had left something interesting in his secret space.

Diane watched him cross the room, raise the corner of a rug
(this one different, but used for the same purpose). Sam left the
rug turned over, moved to the old man's desk, found a large paper
clip, and used it to pry up the edge of the floorboard. Just like
when he was a boy.

"A secret stash?"

"Some place the old man thought was secret. He never let me

come into this room. Said his study was off-limits, which in the end only made me curious."

Diane grinned. She could relate.

Sam flipped up the foot-square piece of floorboard, revealing a small cavernous opening. There was a flash drive sitting on top of several file folders. He reached in and pulled out the flash drive and said, "I suspect whatever this contains should be interesting, if the old man was hiding it here." He extracted the files. "Pine Grove Estates?" he wondered, reading the tabs. "Ever heard of it?"

Diane shook her head. "Never. Maybe the drive has something. Did your dad have a computer?"

"I haven't seen one." The rest of the hold was empty. "We'll just keep these," he said, returning the wooden covering to the floor. "Maybe they contain something worthwhile."

Diane made a note of the folder's subject. She'd never heard of Pine Grove Estates, but knew she'd be searching for it as soon as she returned home.

"We can check out the flash drive at my place."

Sam looked at her. He recognized her reporter's interest. He thought he'd better have a look at the drive before she put it on the pages of the *Gazette*. "Let's check upstairs," he said.

They climbed to the second floor and continued nosing around the old house. In 20 years Sam was surprised to know nothing much had changed. When he opened his old bedroom door, he found everything the same. The bed sat in the corner. The overhead light was exactly as it had been. There was a small desk in the corner with a dresser beside it. On top of the dresser was a piece of macramé his mother made for him when he was a boy, a foot-square black rose. Above his bed, hanging on the wall, was the gun rack he'd made in eighth-grade shop, empty.

It was all carefully preserved, clean, the bed still made as though his return was expected. He was surprised to feel nostalgic for his boyhood room, where so much had been wrong for so long.

He walked over to the mattress and sat down. Same give, same resistance, even the same bedspread. He wondered if anyone had slept here since he'd left.

"It's all the same," he said, surprised.

Diane came over and sat beside him.

"It's weird," he added.

"What's so weird about it? What did you expect?"

"I don't know. Guess I hadn't thought about it. I suppose I expected to see storage, or a study or something."

"He has a basement," Diane reminded him.

"Had," Sam corrected. "I know. I just didn't expect it to be exactly the same. I thought maybe there might be something here. It's a little eerie, like visiting a grave and feeling a presence."

"Your dad had a scary feel to him, the few times I met him."

"He had an interesting perspective about women."

"I wouldn't call it interesting," Diane said, remembering. The Range could be a tough place for single women, where some men had a perverse sense of sex roles. "More like, if we didn't have sex, there'd be a bounty on us."

The harsh comment made Sam grin. "That's about it," he agreed.

They were quiet for a moment, sitting on the bed.

"What's your perspective about women?"

The way she asked felt suddenly different. But it had been a very long time since he had tried to parse a woman's interests, so he hesitated.

"I love women the same as men." Then he thought that didn't sound right. "I mean, we're equal, but different. And sometimes, vive la différence." Sam was trying to be suave, but it sounded awkward.

It was Diane's turn to chuckle. But what she was thinking was, How did a man as awful as Williston Winthrop have a son like Sam Rivers? She knew Miriam deserved some of the praise. But Miriam had her faults. Miriam was sweet without the willingness or ability to make difficult choices, like divorcing Will Winthrop, for starters.

"What happened to you?" Diane finally asked. "I know Williston beat you up pretty bad. But what finally made you leave for good?"

Sam had never told anyone. "I tried to kill my father."

Diane paused. "I suspect you had motive."

"You didn't see me when I left. I had a black eye, a bruised cheek, three broken ribs. But I didn't find that out until after I thought it was taking too long to heal."

"Where were you?"

"Sisseton, South Dakota, just across the border. I didn't run very far at first, because I wasn't sure about leaving. I wasn't sure where I was going. I wasn't sure about anything."

Diane thought about it. "That was the middle of winter, wasn't it? I remember your mom being pretty upset. But she didn't talk about it much."

"Yeah. It was winter."

It had been 20 years, but remembering it like this, Sam could still feel a vestige of the tension he'd felt as a boy. He took the next few minutes relating the story to Diane, including the part about almost killing the old man and then the old man's departure. Now, two decades later, it all sounded surreal, like a nightmare.

Diane was quiet. Sam guessed she wasn't sure how to take it—the beating that started in this room. Unexpectedly her hand moved to his thigh. While he was wondering how to take it—just consolation?—it squeezed.

Maybe not just consolation, he thought. But while he was wondering how to take that, she turned her head, just so. Then she reached up and placed her right hand along Sam's neck, threading her index finger under his ear. The touch startled Sam, but its sentiment was obvious. He placed a hand on her thigh and turned his head to kiss her. She came into his kiss, opening her mouth. Sam raised his hand to the other side of her head. She reached up to press his hand more firmly against her, affirming it. And after a few long moments with their lips fastened together, neither of them wanting to stop, she pulled his left hand away from the side of her head and moved it to her breast.

CHAPTER TWENTY-SIX

S uddenly a piercing, lonely howl came into the room.

Sam's hand on Diane's breast was having the desired effect. For both of them. She didn't want him to take his hand away, unless it was to reach up under her clothing.

"Did you hear that?" he said.

Then another howl.

Reluctantly, Sam got up off the bed and turned to the window.

"Goddamn it," Diane said.

Sam smiled in the dark. He thought about turning back to her, but another howl changed his mind. "Ditto," he said, turning toward the window. "Let's just hold that thought."

"Hold something," she murmured.

It'd been too long. Probably for both of them, Sam guessed. But the wolves had returned and they would have to wait. Given the circumstances, a little tension could be a good thing.

Another howl.

"The wolves are back?"

"Yeah," Sam said. "Sounds like right at the edge of the woods."

Just inside the woods a wolf raised its head and howled a second time. There was a small clearing in the trees. Pale moonlight shown down through the trees and the wolf looked up, parting the air with his belly cry of hunger. The sound reached through the night air into the farmhouse bedroom. Wolves at night, particularly in cold like this, could make a wail that resonated through the frozen dark, as though the wolf were inside the house instead of a quarter mile behind it.

Diane tensed. "That was incredible," she whispered. She'd heard wolf howls, but never this close. It was a thrilling, wild, frightening sound, one that made you happy there was a wall between you and whatever animal made it. She was disappointed by the interruption, but a wolf howl was genuinely distracting.

"Gotta be the pack that went into the barn," Sam said.

"You think so?"

The next low chorus of howls made Diane grow more tense. Sam waited by the window, watching the treeline. He heard another wolf call, closer than the last. There was a large expanse of white where the rear field disappeared over a small rise to the woods, but it was empty.

"Do you think they'll come near the house?" Diane wondered. She moved a little closer.

Sam sensed her shuffle. Touching her breast opened a forgotten well of desire. Sam was focused on the wolves, but part of him wanted to turn and finish what they'd started on the bed.

Another howl snapped his reverie. "Wolves hate anything human. They'll give us a wide berth. If it's them, they're back to feed."

Then they saw movement at the edge of the trees, though it was too dim to see clearly. One hundred yards across the field, first one, then another, then all five stepped out of the trees, making the pale moonlight come alive. The first one to come out of the woods raised its head and howled.

"They're so close," Diane said.

"Any closer and . . ."

Sam could hear her breathe beside the opposite stretch of

window. He'd noticed this before, how the close proximity of wolves (or any predators, for that matter) made him hyperattentive. Then again, maybe it was the kiss. He listened to his heart beating in the old bedroom. And then the wolves again.

"What?" Diane said.

"Any closer and we could see their yellow eyes," which made him think.

The wolves were tentative with each step. After a few yards they paused and sent their call into the night sky. Sam had observed wolves often enough to notice their clear shapes and markings even in the moonlight. These wolves were big. Unnaturally large. He couldn't be certain. Their coloring wasn't clear in the dark. But their shapes were more the size of timber wolves or Arctic wolves than Great Plains. If they were Great Plains wolves, they were the largest he'd ever seen. He needed a closer look.

All those years ago it was wolves that awakened him. Since then he had observed countless packs and examined plenty of individuals up close. And in all that time the thrill of seeing a pack in the wild never abated.

"Why howl and alert everyone to their presence?" Diane wondered.

"It's a warning. Mostly to other wolves. They're making sure everyone in the neighborhood knows it's their kill. Would you go near a howl like that?"

The animals appeared more emboldened than a normal pack. There was something familiar and unusual about them. They moved as a pack, paused to howl, but kept driving toward the barn, where the rest of their kill remained.

The last animal came cowering, taking up the rear. It appeared the least wolf. Its legs were a little too thick. Its coat a little dark. Its tail, ears, snout, all of its proportions a little skewed.

"Goddamn," he said. "Got to be a hybrid." It made him wonder about the others.

As the wolves neared, they began to move with cowering, tentative steps, testing the air. It was an unusual gait. Wild wolves only cowered before other wolves, or other members of the pack, if they were bested, or if their pack position ordained it. These wolves lowered their heads and smelled the air with suspicion.

"Let's just watch, see what they do," he said.

One wolf was out in front, leading. The others followed from a comfortable distance. It took them less than 5 minutes to approach the house and barn.

They paused, their noses in the wind. When they felt certain nothing in the yard stirred, they came on more quickly.

Sam and Diane were hypnotized by the way the pack moved together, one wolf in the lead, the others following: a web of tooth and claw that could be focused, Sam knew, in an instant.

They visited like ghosts. And while it was the middle of the night, the right time for wolves to approach, a normal pack would have been more reticent. A normal pack would be approaching from behind the barn, from the safety of trees and bush that hugged outlying buildings.

The lead wolf neared the cracked door. He paused, sniffing the night air. His nose bent to the ground. In the moonlight he peered around the door. Sam thought he saw something. Probably Moon's traps. Setting wolf traps in snow was almost impossible.

Any fraction of displaced powder, any crease or depression in the snow's surface, and the animals sensed something awry, gave it a wide berth.

But the smell of food was compelling. The lead wolf stepped carefully through the snow toward the cracked barn door. He placed his muzzle through the opening, which was just wide enough to permit its entry. And then he disappeared inside.

"Incredible," Sam said. "No wolf would do that," he whispered. "These animals have some familiarity with buildings." Again, hybrids, he guessed.

The other wolves followed the same zigzag path toward the door, stepping carefully over the snow, avoiding the delicate surface anomalies where Sam guessed Moon had set foothold traps. And then they were through the opening and gone.

Diane turned to look at him. "What now?" she asked.

He wanted to pull her back into bed but knew it could wait.

"We trap 'em."

"How in the hell are we going to trap them?"

Sam peered at the barn door. He wondered why Moon had left it partially open. It wouldn't have been normal, but Moon was a born trapper. He was baiting them.

From this distance the black rectangular opening was large enough to permit a wolf to squeeze through it. Sam could barely discern the shadowy opening against the grayer exterior of the barn. Trying to get a fix on the door's details from the bedroom window was impossible. "We can trap them in that barn."

"You want to go out there while they're feeding?"

"You have a better idea?"

"Yes. Sneak back the way we came. Give them the widest possible berth and hope they don't hear us."

"And lose this opportunity to catch them alive, study them?"

"And avoid the opportunity to be attacked, killed," Diane corrected.

"They're busy feeding. We can sneak out and slam that door shut before they hear anything."

"Supposing you can't get the door shut?"

"There's only one way to find out," he said.

"But they're wolves!"

"This may be our best chance to trap them, have a closer look. If I'm right about these animals, we'll need one to corroborate what I suspect will be the results from the DNA analysis."

"They'll hear you coming."

"In this powder we can be quiet."

"We?"

"You wouldn't have me going out there alone, would you?"

"This is crazy."

Sam smiled. "It is crazy," he agreed. "Normal wolves would scatter. But a normal pack wouldn't have entered a barn to feed, let alone kill. They would have fed on their capture someplace safe, eating it in a thicket. I don't know what these wolves would do if they were cornered, but I'm not passing up a chance to trap them in that barn. If I'm right, it could explain plenty."

"And what are we going to do with them?"

"Leave them here. Go back to the car. And in the morning, alert Svegman so he can get out here and secure them."

"And then?"

"Examine them," Sam said. "We need to understand this pack,

this kind of carnage. If they are wild, it's a whole new level of wolf behavior. It's a whole new breed of wolf."

"And if someone comes back, like Angus, and happens to open the barn?"

"He'll see the tracks. He'll notice they only go one way."

"And he'll know someone was here, to shut the door?"

"Not that I care. He won't know who was here."

They had two options: leave the house and return to their Jeep without disturbing the animals and their middle-of-the-night meal. Or try and trap them. Twenty years ago Sam fled. Today he didn't think twice.

"Let's go."

Diane wanted no part of it, but didn't feel like she had a choice. Eventually she'd have to head back to the Jeep. If the wolves were trapped where they couldn't follow, that would be a good thing.

They bundled up for the cold. Then they moved to the front door, opening it without a sound, stepping carefully into the cold.

Their earlier work had worn a path to the barn's entrance. They stepped onto it and, slowly, carefully, approached the barn in silence. Sam stopped 10 yards short of the door. He examined its exterior. Normally the door could be slid shut and fastened. Now that he could see it more clearly, Sam recounted the way he'd done it before, absent about the process, automatic. He looked up at the handle, and then along the top sliding door runner. A small pile of snow drifted across the entrance. It had been partially tamped down by the wolves, enough to prevent the door from closing completely.

Diane stood behind him. He turned and pointed to the snow-choked entrance. He made a clearing motion with his hand, pointing again to the bottom of the door. Diane understood and nodded.

She took off her mitten, placing it in her front parka pocket. She wore a small cotton glove beneath it, one that would allow the unencumbered positioning of her finger inside the trigger guard of the door handle.

Sam stepped carefully toward the entrance. He could see where the wolves had skirted Moon's foothold traps. Moon had done an excellent job concealing them, knowing wolves had a preternatural sense for anything awry. But the wolves had either recognized anomalies in the snow or smelled Moon's scent. Now Sam kept to their paw prints, glad they'd forged a path for him.

He concentrated on slowing his movement. The rectangular opening was a deep black gap. He tried to listen in the cold, but could not hear into the barn. He assumed the wolves were feeding. He knew their preoccupation with food would be a good thing, though it could cut both ways. If they were feeding well away from the door, they might only rise to snarl a warning. But if they were close, or if they felt their feeding was threatened, they could attack.

The wolf tracks moved to the right of the trail, entering the barn door from the side. He followed their tracks, stepping to the right of the barn's entrance, careful his shadow didn't cross the threshold. The powder enveloped his feet, as though he were stepping into fine dry sand.

To shut the door he would have to be directly in front of the threshold. He would stay to the side so as not to forewarn them. He imagined it, stepping over the doorway, one foot into the barn as the other kicked the snow free. Then he'd pivot and pull the slab of wood across its runner. It would have to be done in one fluid motion. Wolf jaws could exert over 1,000 pounds of pressure. If they were lucky enough to reach him, they could snap his forearm like a matchstick.

Adrenaline heightened his senses. He could feel his muscles tighten. Over the door handle there was a latch. He imagined driving it into its metal catch. He imagined the sound it would make as it fell into place.

And then he sprang.

Sam took hold of the door handle and began kicking snow across the threshold. He looked up and saw a spray of snow enter the barn. Ten feet away a startled wolf leaped from its feeding, cowering low, snapping in a startled growl, ready to spring. Sam pivoted, jerking the door shut. But there was still too much snow in the narrow gap. He held the door handle with both hands, peering through the crack. The wolf was still recoiled 10 feet from the opening, watching him, waiting for his next move.

"Now!" Sam said.

Diane stepped forward and placed her hand beside Sam's on the door latch. Sam kicked at the snow.

The wolf stayed in its low crouch, ready to uncoil.

"Shut it!" Sam said, and they both pulled hard on the handle. It swung into its slot with a solid *thwack* and Sam closed the latch.

They leaned against the door, breathing heavily in the cold night air, their pulses rocketing. After a few moments, Sam stepped away, turned, and started back toward the farmhouse.

"Watch those traps," he said, pointing to the ground, stepping carefully to avoid them.

"What now?"

"We'll call Svegman when we get back to town, leave him a

message. These wolves'll keep. I'd guess Angus Moon is sipping on his inheritance, not that he ever needed an excuse," he said, turning to wait for her. "I doubt he'll be out before noon."

Once they were beyond Moon's traps, Diane hurried up behind him.

Sam checked his watch. "1:30."

"That gives us some time. I could use a drink," Diane said.

The moment wasn't right. Or rather, he didn't know her well enough to say it, but what he thought was, 'Let's continue what we started upstairs in the farmhouse.'

"Me too," he finally said.

But they both thought the drinks were a preamble to something much more intimate with each other.

PART IV

We have the wolf by the ear, and we can neither hold him, nor safely let him go. Justice is in one scale, and self-preservation in the other.

Thomas Jefferson

CHAPTER TWENTY-SEVEN

In the early-morning light, Moon approached the farmhouse.

He'd been up before dawn, wakened with the others by Winthrop, who had stood in the front room and bellowed, "Get up, you miserable peckerwoods! Our work isn't done! Get up!" A chorus of groans assured him his troops were on the rise.

"Not even light," Heins commented, from the comfort of his narrow cabin bunk.

"That's right," Winthrop agreed. "Dark's the best time for our kind of work. It'll get you at the farm by daybreak. See if we've had any luck with those dogs. If Angus is right, he'll need help with those sorry animals."

Moon didn't move. Winthrop finally walked into the small cabin bedroom and pulled down the covers on Moon's bed. The room was cold and the woodsman cussed. "Christ, Williston. I went to bed two and a half hours ago."

"There'll be plenty of time for sleep after you get those dogs and the check. And today yours truly finally gets buried. We'll have a fitting celebration tonight. Last night was just a rehearsal. And if I'm right about those dogs, you can take care of them and sleep in tomorrow. Get the fuck up!"

Two hours later Moon turned into the farmhouse drive. He was the first to notice something awry, and he didn't like what he saw. There were more tracks around the barn's entrance, ones he hadn't made. He could see they came out of the woods. But the door was closed and latched shut. Moon left it cracked for a reason.

"Shit," he hissed.

Heins and Pederson followed Moon's rusting truck down the drive. The cages jostled beneath the old bed's tarp. Moon pulled into the yard, backing around so the taillights faced the closed door. He got out of the cab as the others parked in front of the garage and stepped into the early-morning cold.

Sunlight was breaking off the horizon. They'd made good time. The frosty snowshoe out of Skinwalkers Bog was like a draught of strong coffee.

"What do you think?" Heins asked.

Moon was walking toward the barn door, studying everything with a tracker's eye. He could see animal prints coming out of the woods. He watched them approach the barn. He saw other trails cross over the path, step to the side, and approach the barn door. He could see another pair of tracks approach, their kicking brush marks in the snow, the closed door and fastened latch. And not a goddamn trap triggered. Wolves and men, they'd both been observant.

"I'll be goddamned," he said.

"What?" Heins asked.

"Looks like my dogs're back. And they had company," he said, pointing to the tracks.

Heins approached. Then Pederson.

"Walk here," Moon said, pointing to the zigzag tracks left by Sam and Diane. "Less you want to get caught in a trap."

The three of them approached carefully and stood in front of the fastened door.

Moon listened for movement inside. "Somebody's been here. Since last night. And it looks like my dogs come back to feed."

"They in there?" Pederson asked, concerned.

Moon nodded. "Looks like."

"Who in the hell was here?" Heins asked.

"Can't tell," Moon said, looking down, trying to follow the boot tracks. "The snow's trampled and dry. Didn't make any good prints. But whoever was here avoided the traps, just like my dogs," he said, pointing to where the hybrid tracks came down out of the woods, breaking the glistening white plane.

"When did you leave?" Heins asked.

"Soon as everybody else did. I set the traps, careful about it. Then I waited awhile, maybe another half hour. Took off right around sunset."

"So it was getting dark when you left?" Heins asked.

"Just about. I wanted to make the edge of the woods right before dark, so I could see to unlock the chain."

Heins thought about it. "Rivers," he guessed. He looked back toward the house and saw their tracks come away from the back door. "If it was him, he tried to get inside."

Moon peered down at the trail leading toward the barn. "There were at least two of 'em," he said. "And judging by what I can see of the track, I'd say one was a woman."

"Diane Talbott," Heins guessed. He looked toward the barn. "Just what we fuckin' needed."

Moon turned closer to the door, listening.

"You sure they're in there?" Pederson asked.

Moon heard movement on the other side of the door. "Only one way to know for sure."

"What in the hell are we supposed to do now?" Pederson asked.

"Get 'em," Moon said. "Teach 'em a goddamn lesson." He

turned to the door, worked the latch out of its frozen lock, and slid the door open, only inches. A bar of sunlight fell into the barn, just enough for Moon to see a hybrid's paw. There was a low growl, like distant thunder. And then the paw vanished. "Yeah," he said. "They're in there. Couple nights in the woods 'n' they got attitude."

"Sounded wild to me," Pederson said, a little worried.

"We need to think about this," Heins commented. He paused for a minute, looking back to the house. "This could work. Somebody came out to the farm. Found wolves in the barn. Locked 'em in."

"Probably Rivers," Moon guessed.

"Probably," Heins agreed. "Which is even better. Whoever was here saw wolves. You said so yourself, Angus. Nothing different about them. They're wolves."

"Look like it, anyway," he agreed.

"Damn right. More evidence. When we came out to help clean up the mess," he considered, still thinking . . . "Is there another entrance to this barn?"

"Old grain chute, back side," Moon said.

"Perfect. We came out to help clean up the mess, saw they'd been here. But this time they busted out the old grain chute."

Pederson saw the reasoning, thought it was a good idea. "Went back to the woods, where wolves would go," he added. "And whoever came out was trespassin'!"

"Whoever came out better have one hell of a good reason, or they'll keep their mouths shut. That'd be something in our favor. The refusal of someone to come forward."

Moon turned back to the door, getting ready to open it. Heins held him back. "Goddamn it, Angus. Would you wait a minute?"

"Wait for them to come back and get my dogs? We need to get 'em outta there."

"Nobody's gonna get 'em, because they're wolves," Heins said. "You're right about working fast. But caging them isn't the thing." He thought for a moment, rubbing his chin. "At least we got lucky in one respect. It's early. If they think the wolves are caught, we probably got a little time."

Pederson and Moon watched Heins examine the snow.

He turned and said, "Open it up a bit and let's see how they're doing."

Moon reached over to pull the door open.

"Careful, Angus. They've been out in the woods awhile. They might not be ready for a hard hand."

"They'll mind," he said.

He slid the door open a few inches. From inside the barn he heard rustling, then another growl.

"Nothin' a boot won't cure," Moon commented.

Heins looked down at the snow. Tracks were heaviest between the house and the barn's entrance. The rest of the barn was surrounded by an unbroken plane of white. "Looks like they didn't know about the chute. If they did, they didn't check it out. You sure that grain chute is big enough for wolves to get through?"

Moon nodded. "They could get through it."

"Then we open it enough to let them run."

"What?" Moon didn't like the idea of letting his dogs run wild a second time. He didn't think they'd return. "We let 'em go again, they could be gone for good."

"Good 'n' gone's what we want, now that I think of it. What if someone came while we were cagin' 'em, or they even see those cages in the back of your truck, or those pens behind your place?"

"They're my dogs," Moon protested, not wanting to free them. It had taken a lot of hard work to build his breeding stock.

"Think about your share," Heins reminded him, sensing Moon's disappointment. "Share like that be plenty to get you started with whole new stock. Hell, redo your whole outfit."

Moon considered it. Heins was right. But he didn't like it, giving up the dogs he'd bred since birth, all of them a damn good mix of dog and wolf, mostly wolf.

"Seems to me they're just about wild already," Pederson observed.

"Grain chute opens from the inside," Moon remembered.

Heins looked at Pederson. That meant one of them would have to enter the barn and open it. "Shit," he finally growled, rubbing his chin. He looked over at Moon. "Got any ideas?"

"Go in and open it," Moon said.

"You think those dogs'll let you?"

Moon stared back at Heins. "They'll let me," he said.

"Maybe you forgot recent history," Pederson commented. "You just starved them and then sent them killing on their own."

Moon paused, looking at the barn wall in front of him. "I admit they got a taste for it. But they try anything, they'll get a steel toe, somethin' they already know."

"I hope to hell they haven't forgotten."

"They're dogs," Moon reassured.

The three men looked at each other.

"Then let's get it done," Heins finally said. "Before anyone comes and finds us, or sees those cages in the back of your truck. Set 'em free and get the hell out." He looked up over the road, but it was still early and the morning was as quiet as a graveyard.

Moon started for the door, matter of fact, acting as though entering it was without risk.

Pederson and Heins both stepped back.

Moon opened the door wide enough to sandwich through a narrow gap. He pulled it shut behind him, leaving a narrow crack to let in light, and then stepped to one side. His eyes gradually grew accustomed to the dark. A narrow swath of sunlight bisected the barn. In the partial illumination Moon saw carcasses and bloodied humps. To his right there was movement, and then a flash across the light beam, like a shadow flicker in candlelight. Deeper in darkness he heard rustling and then another low growl.

"What's that?" he said, belligerent. He had a cruel, familiar way of handling dogs. He never let them forget he was their unchallenged alpha. Always had been. Always would be. But they had never been out of their cages at the same time, on their own, for two days.

One of the animals answered with another low growl, slightly more pronounced.

"That you, Arctic?" Moon knew him. He was the black-haired one, the biggest. "You'd best keep outta my way."

There was an eerie stillness in the barn, as though the dogs were considering his offer. He could feel their eyes. Moon had been a predator his entire life. The top of the food chain, the unchallenged king of the wild and everything in it. Now from darkness, he sensed wolf eyes staring at him, watching carefully for weakness, assessing him.

Suddenly there was rustling from one of the calf stalls, followed by a low whine. Moon peered into the darkness. He thought he saw one or two animals shift among the carnage. The barn still reeked of it. He could see their shadows in the barn's darkest reaches, positioning, considering.

"Hey ya'!"

He spit tobacco juice onto the floor. He knew they'd smell it . . . remember what it meant. There was quiet again, and then a long, rumbling growl picked up by another growl. Two of them defiant.

"OK," Moon growled. "You had a little taste of wild and you want to keep it! And I'm going to give it to you."

He peered ahead, unable to see more than a few feet beyond the doorway's ambient light. He shuffled his boots forward, feeling his way across the floor's carnage. He entered the darkness, progressing slowly toward the grain chute. Twice he felt heavy objects and stepped to avoid them. There was more growling from the back of the barn, higher pitched and coming from two other positions, as though they were surrounding him. He could feel their intensity, their predatory observation.

In the decade he'd been working with hybrids, he had only been attacked once. He'd had a good bitch he'd used for four years. He'd taken her ice fishing, thinking she could use the exercise and the fish, providing he got lucky. Dragging his sled and supplies across the ice, he'd slipped and fallen. The bitch didn't miss the opportunity. She pounced on the fallen alpha, her wolf instinct returning, her natural inclination for dominance seeing opportunity. She opened her jaws and enveloped Moon's head. Wolf jaws are powerful enough to snap a moose's thighbone and suck out the marrow. In this case, the act was dominance. Moon was part of her pack. She wasn't going to kill him, just let him know she saw weakness and was vying for dominance. He rolled, fought her off, and then beat her until she cowered like the dog Moon reminded her she was.

In the dark interior of the barn, he remembered the slip and fall. He would need to be careful.

"Get it open, Angus," Heins called from the other side of the door. "We got to get those dogs out, clean up this fuckin' mess, and get the hell out of here!"

"Blacker than pitch in here!" He thought he heard movement to his right.

"Hug the wall and feel your way over," Heins suggested. "Hank's on the other side. He can help from the outside when you get close."

Moon was disoriented in the dark. He wasn't certain the dog had moved, but it sounded closer. Maybe it was just louder. He turned to listen and said, "Here now!" taking a step without feeling.

His foot came up against something solid, and he lost his balance. He put his hand out and it slid across gristle and bone, bringing the center of his diaphragm down hard. Air rushed out of him like a bellows. His disorientation was brief but long enough. The wolf dog was on top of him. Moon raised his arm to protect himself, kicked and rolled to his right, feeling a carcass in the small of his back. The animal grabbed hold of his arm, shaking its massive jaws, a demon in the dark. Moon brought his free hand in front of him, striking hard at its head. He struck three more times before it finally let go and retreated. But it wouldn't go far. Moon was still down. He had to rise in a hurry.

"What was that?" Heins yelled.

Moon, on his feet, was breathing hard. "Get the fuck out of my way!" he roared. He found the wall and hurried along it, struggling to catch his breath. He stepped over another carcass and found the chute's door.

"What?" Heins yelled from outside, but Moon wasn't listening.

"Angus," Pederson said, just the other side of the wall. "The door's right here," he said, pounding on it. Moon reached up, felt for the familiar latch, pulled on it, and the square fell open. Sunlight streamed into the barn. Behind him the animals retreated into the barn's shadows.

"Christ," Pederson said, looking down at him. Moon's arm was torn and ragged, blood starting to ooze around the holes in his sleeve. "What the hell happened?"

CHAPTER TWENTY-EIGHT

By the time Sam stirred, it was well after daybreak. He was still half asleep and disoriented. He wasn't in Yellow Rock. There was a feeling of pressure, atmospheric, a dense cold pushing from everywhere but this warm bed, like being inside a shell. The room was lightly shaded. His eyes fluttered, and there was faint illumination, like the kind along north-facing windows toward the end of the day. Shallow half-light without warmth.

And there was the smell. Witch hazel. Ripe. Like autumn woods with an underlying sweetness, with the faint underlying scent of akvavit. And then suddenly he remembered every naked inch of the woman beside him.

Sam smiled. On the long drive from Yellow Rock, he'd had plenty of thinking time. He was 37 and single, still hurting from the bad last year of his marriage. It had taken him six months and the ritualistic burial of his wedding ring to improve his mood.

Magdalen told him the time it takes to get over a divorce is equal to the half-life of the marriage. All things considered, it sounded like a reasonable formula. That would mean three years, for Sam. Five, if you counted the four years they were together before they married. At first, five years sounded like a prison sentence. But on his way over from Yellow Rock, he reconsidered it. From 37 to 42, if Magdalen's formula was right, could be the best five years of his life. If he abided by the formula, that would mean he would run away from any chance of marriage, at least for the next five years, no matter how attracted he was to a woman. Was that possible? Moreover, if he was candid about his refusal to marry and his need to experiment by dating around, would any woman even bother to date him more than once? For now, it was too much to think about. So he decided to be content with who lay beside him.

His evening with Diane was about as unexpected as a January thaw. In his childhood bedroom, she'd felt good. Better than good. Later, during small talk on the return to her place, he wished they could have finished back at the farmhouse, because he thought he knew where this was headed, but was still so surprised by that sudden kiss he wasn't sure. Carpe diem. It should be *carpe momento* ("seize the moment") because he wished he would have seized Diane. Back there. When the moment was like a freshly opened bottle of wine.

But then they returned and each had two glasses of akvavit while they sat on the couch, continuing to unwind. Until Diane stood up, reached out her hand, and led him to her bedroom.

"Diane," he started, following her.

"Don't talk."

It was hard not to recall every heightened moment of what happened when they came into her bedroom. If their limbs had been tinder, they would have set fire to the place.

He turned out of bed, carefully so as not to waken her, and picked up his clothes on his way out of the room.

Diane's bathroom was at the end of the hall. He paced into it, meditative, taking care of his morning ministrations. In the bathroom mirror his eyes appeared intense, his hair unkempt, and his beard shadowed. If the Range had sullied his features, it had done something else entirely to his perspective. For the first time in a long while, he was starting to feel good again.

Last night they'd left Svegman a message about the wolves

out at Winthrop's farm. Now he tried him again, but got his voice mail a second time. When he pressed zero, it rolled over to an assistant's voice mail. Sam left another message. Then he dialed the sheriff.

"Dean Goddard."

"Sam Rivers, Sheriff. You work every Saturday?"

"Every Saturday. Beats Belinda's church services," he said. "She's gone at the crack of dawn and doesn't come home until after supper."

"Saturday and Sunday? That's a long weekend."

"Just the half of it. What's up?"

"We went back to the farm last night. Diane and me."

There was a pause. "Thought you might. Wished you hadn't."

"I had a hunch those wolves would return."

"I assume Angus was gone?"

"Yeah."

"You didn't break in, did you?"

"No. I wouldn't have broken into the house." True enough. "I was pretty sure those wolves would return, and I wanted to see them."

"Did they?"

"Yup. Got hungry and came back to feed. I thought with all the trampling and Angus setting traps, no wolf would come near the place."

"Any get trapped?"

"Not in Angus's footholds. We watched them go into the barn, avoiding those traps like they had a map of the place. Stepped around every one of them. Never seen anything like it."

"Smart animals."

"After they entered the barn, we gave them a few minutes to settle in, then snuck over and shut and latched the barn door. They're still there. Trapped."

"Did you call Svegman?"

"I did. Early this morning we left him a message. But he hasn't gotten back to me. Any idea where to find him?"

"I'll give him a call. Steve's from Vermilion Falls, but he should be able to get out there by noon. I could go out with him." Goddard might like to have one more look at the house, though he didn't think what he wanted was there.

"That'd be great."

"And for the record," the sheriff added. "No more visits without the law. I called you for your wolf expertise. If Angus finds out you were there again, all hell'll break loose."

"OK."

"What did you have in mind . . . about the wolves?"

"Ideally I'd like them captured alive," Sam said. "I know they can't stay in that barn, but I'd like to see them, watch them for a while."

"I'll see if he can get some others to assist."

"That'd be good. Thanks."

"We'll be in touch."

They said goodbye and hung up.

That went about as well as Sam figured it could. The sheriff didn't like their visit, but at least he was following up on the wolves.

Diane's bedroom door opened.

"Morning," she managed, on her way to the kitchen.

"Morning."

She wore a long-sleeved blank sweatshirt, nothing underneath, and a threadbare pair of aqua sweatpants. Her big hair still fell over her shoulders like a rock star. A pillow seam lined her left cheek. She was just waking up. He decided to let her get some coffee, wake up, come to her own terms with the previous evening. "Can I borrow your computer?"

He'd seen it last night in her bedroom, where it had served as a hanger for some of the clothes they'd flung across it.

"Have at it," she said. "I need coffee."

He fetched the flash drive and returned to the bedroom.

Next to one side sat a small table with her laptop. Sam walked around the end of the bed and sat down in front of it. He inserted the flash drive into the USB port, turned on the laptop, and waited. It took a minute for the screen to come up. After the icons appeared, he reviewed the contents of the flash drive. It contained a single video. Sam moved the mouse onto the file, opened it, and clicked play.

Two bodies—and judging from their naked embrace and rhythm, they were having a good time. Then Sam noticed the sheriff's clothes tossed over a nearby chair. The sheriff's gun hung in its holster over the back of a chair. The date appeared in the lower right corner of the video screen. January 2. Approximately one month earlier. It sure as hell looked like the sheriff. Sam had never met his wife, but he guessed the woman on the screen wasn't Belinda Goddard. When he played it a second time and examined the room, he recognized a simple dresser, a counter with a TV, a chair with a table, and a door to a bathroom. A motel room. There was a smaller set of clothes laid over the chair next to the sheriff's. One of the items appeared to be some kind of medical smock.

"That's a surprise," he said.

It was not what he had expected to find in the old man's cache. And it could mean a whole lot more than he wanted to know. Where was Goddard the night Winthrop was killed? If the old man was trying to blackmail the sheriff, the sheriff had motive to get rid of him. But Sam had spent enough time tracking predators to get a feel for their personalities. The sheriff didn't measure up to murder. But you never knew. Ted Bundy was notorious for being thoughtful, articulate, and charming. He demonstrated what psychologists describe as a mask of sanity. But if the sheriff was a murderer, Sam was a rodeo clown. The man was as grounded as dirt and as balanced as an acrobat walking a tightrope. Blindfolded. On the other hand, there was no accounting for what some people were capable of when pushed.

Earlier he'd examined the file folder's contents, finding corporate charters, stock certificates, assumed name filings, and a few bank statements documenting a lot of money. But it wasn't until he noticed Miriam Samuelson's signature on a corporate charter for Iron County Care that he began to take note. His mom had been a generous woman, but on more than one occasion she'd shaken her head and grumbled about her husband's legal work. And when he was a kid, he remembered rumors and comments from the other club members, about how Winthrop was capable of turning the law whichever way he wanted.

Sam was no lawyer, but it was easy enough to guess the old man's folder business was larcenous. And profitable. He suspected Dunlap would be interested in its contents.

But what about the flash drive? And what about the sheriff? And who was the woman?

Sam set the folder on the bed and closed it. He turned to the open door and called out to Diane.

In a moment she was in the doorway, holding two cups. "So, what did you find out?" She came around the bed and handed one of the cups to Sam.

"Thank you," he said. "I'm not sure what I'm seeing. I think I need another opinion, but I'm not sure about that either."

"So what was it?"

"First I need to know if you can keep a secret?"

"Oh?"

"I want you to identify someone in a video. But I'm not sure it should go beyond this room. And you may never be able to tell anyone, or write about it, at least not until we're sure what it's about. But maybe never."

"Never is a long time. What if it's a murder?"

"It's not murder, but it is important. I need to know what I'm seeing, who it is. I suspect you may know . . . her. But if you don't think you can stay quiet about it, so be it. I won't bring you into it."

Diane appeared serious, considering, wondering if she could agree.

And that was a good thing, Sam knew.

"If I see anyone breaking the law or being violent, I can't make any promises."

Sam thought about it. "Are we talking civil law, or biblical?"

She looked at him and grinned. "Now I'm interested." She paused. "OK," she said. "I'll agree to keep it private. But if there's a chance whatever it is should come out, all bets are off."

Sam considered it fair. "Have a seat," he said.

Once she was seated, Sam clicked the play button.

Through the entire 49 seconds, Diane stared. Sam could tell

she was absorbing the video's impact. When it was over, she said, "I'll be damned." She didn't need to see it again. She stood up from the chair and, without looking at Sam, walked out of the room.

He followed.

Diane was shaking her head. "I don't believe it." She went into the kitchen and refilled her cup.

"Who's the woman?" Sam asked.

Once they were in the living room, Diane sat on the couch. She wasn't shaken. She was chagrined, perplexed. "I just wouldn't have . . . guessed it," she said.

"So who's the woman?"

"That's the local doctor. Susan Wallace. She's also our new coroner, at least since last year, when old Doc Chauncey retired."

"Married?"

"Nope. Works all the time. I thought she didn't have time to think about a relationship. Looks like they've been working pretty close," Diane said, looking up at Sam to consider it. "I just," she added, "I guess I'm surprised, but not surprised."

"What do you mean? Why aren't you surprised?"

"Belinda, Dean's wife, turned fundamental. Couple years back, from what I've heard. You pick things up at the paper. Couldn't have children, turned to the bottle, then got Christ and got sober."

"Nothing wrong with that. And sure no reason for her husband to step out," Sam observed, for the moment disappointed with the sheriff, though he knew firsthand that love could be an intoxicating cocktail.

"Gossip has it, part of Belinda's vows involve no sex."

"What kind of Christian heritage is that?"

"The Iron Orthodox Gospel Church," Diane said. "Their

perspective. Or at least the perspective of Bishop Rose, I guess."

"Who the hell is Bishop Rose?"

"The self-appointed bishop of the Iron Orthodox Gospel Church. There's only one. He's minister, priest, bishop, and pope."

"Absolute power."

"Absolutely."

"So what was the old man doing with the video?"

"No idea," Diane said. "And how did he get it?"

"You think he was using it? Blackmailing the sheriff about something?"

Diane looked up. "I can't imagine Williston Winthrop having this and not using it. Though it was recent enough, maybe he hadn't had a chance. Before you go accusing Dean Goddard of anything," she paused, "you might reconsider. I've known the guy a long time. I suspect his," she paused again, "lapse in judgment, however understandable, is tearing the guy up." And now she was staring at Sam. "But Dean Goddard isn't capable of murder."

"But the old man must have been thinking about using it. If you don't know about their relationship," he said, thinking out loud, "probably no one does."

"If I know Dean Goddard, he'd do plenty to keep this quiet. Not because he's a bad man. But he definitely likes his job. But he wouldn't kill over it. He'd face the storm. If he was being black-mailed, he'd out it and then arrest Will Winthrop for extortion. Whatever this is, it has nothing to do with Williston Winthrop's accident." Then she grew thoughtful. "And he has the perfect alibi," she added.

"What?"

"The night Will Winthrop died, the sheriff and just about all other town and county notables were in Vermilion Falls, at the VFW for their annual volunteer firefighters' fund drive."

"You saw him?"

"I danced with him."

"How long was he there?"

"From before dinner to around 10. He was one of the hosts. He set it up."

"So he has an alibi. And I haven't seen anything to suggest Dean is anything but a reasonable guy," Sam agreed. "I just wonder how far he would go to keep this quiet, to avoid a little bad press?"

" 'A little bad press?' You've been away too long. Press like this in a place like Vermilion County would bury the sheriff. Could cost him his job."

Sam shook his head. "I appreciate that, but would the sheriff step over the line to save his job?"

"I think just about anyone is capable of anything, given the right time and place. But I'm not saying Dean Goddard did anything."

"Did you recognize the room?" Sam asked, coming back to the video.

"Pretty sure it's the Vermilion Falls Motel."

"What are those files?" she asked, remembering the folder.

"Looks like some kind of scam the old man was into."

"You think the scam is related to the video? You think the sheriff knew about it but was keeping his mouth shut, because of that video?"

"No idea," Sam said. "Could be. Maybe we should ask him."

Sam wondered about their next step. He owed the sheriff a

favor. But he had to know what the sheriff did, if anything, to keep his relationship quiet.

"That'd be direct."

"I'd like to give him the benefit of the doubt." He thought for a minute. "And there's the problem of these files," he added.

"What problem?"

"They should be shared with someone in a position to do something about them, if I'm reading them right."

"I don't get it."

"I'd bet Jeff Dunlap would love to get his hands on these files."

"So give them to him?"

"Can't. Technically, they're evidence. They should come from the investigating officer. Otherwise they might be inadmissible, given how we acquired them."

"So what if the sheriff gave them to him?"

"That's what I had in mind, providing the sheriff would play along," Sam said.

Diane considered it. "There's only one way to find out."

CHAPTER TWENTY-NINE

The deputy staffing the front office turned around and yelled back to the sheriff through his open door. "Lady from Canada on line 1. Something about a missing brother."

Goddard had been working on some paper. He picked up his phone and pushed 1. "This is Sheriff Goddard," he started.

"Sheriff, Clement Beauregard."

An older woman, judging from the gravelly tone. She didn't sound Canadian. Was that what his deputy said? Canadian?

"From Manitoba," she added.

"Ma'am?" Goddard asked.

"Ah've got a brotha' down there. At least wuz. Outside Defiance, Minnesota?" She had a thick Southern drawl.

He didn't know if it was a question. "Yes?"

"His name's James T. Beauregard," she said, hesitating. "People call him Jimbo." She waited. "Or Jim."

"Yeah?" Goddard said.

"He was stayin' on some farm outside a' town. Said he'd be here by Wednesday, but din't show."

"He's missing, ma'am?"

"Ah guess. Yeah. You know Defiance?"

"Small town west of us," Goddard explained. "Not that far. When was he in Defiance?"

"Not in town, sheriff," she drawled. "Said he wuz on some farm outside a' town."

"There are a lot of farms all over the area, ma'am. Did he give you a name? Address?"

"No sah," she said, cordial.

"And you're looking for him?"

"Uh-huh," she answered. "He was s'posed to be in Manitoba las' Wednesday."

"Driving?" Goddard asked.

"Catchin' the Greyhound outta Bemidji. Said it wuz all lined up."

"What was his business," the sheriff caught himself, "outside Defiance?"

"Jimbo didn't have no biz'ness. Jimbo was comin' here to lend a hand. My cousin Emil opened a Cajun café. We needed help with the place, and I knew Jimbo could'a used the work."

"Was he visiting someone?"

"Said he got a job on some farm."

"How did he get to Defiance?" Goddard asked. He didn't think Defiance had any bus service.

"Thumb, mos' likely," she said. "Or the rails."

Goddard's eyes rolled up toward the ceiling. A vagrant. Chances are he could be anywhere. Maybe he didn't really like working but didn't want to tell his sister, Goddard thought. "I can ask the cop in Defiance," he said.

"Officer Heins?" she asked.

Apparently she'd done her homework. "Yeah," Goddard said. "Have you spoken with him?"

"Ah have. Said he'd look into it. I jus' thought somethin' might have happened somewhere else. Jimbo said he'd be here on the 11:25 Greyhound outta Bemidji. He ain't perticular 'bout much, but he's always punctual. Has been, anyway."

"Are there any other, ah, reasons he might be late, ma'am?" Goddard asked. He needed to know if the man was a schizophrenic or used alcohol or drugs. And Clement Beauregard sounded like the type who wouldn't whitewash a brother's bad habits.

"Whaddya mean?" she asked.

"Does your brother have any mental issues, ma'am? Is he on any medication? Does he drink? Does he use drugs?"

"Jimbo? Lord no. Takes some nips now and agin, but not reglar. He's had bad luck, most his life. Has a mark on his face. A big red birthmark. People have always thought it strange, but we know it's where God touched him."

Another bizarre stroke from God's hand, Goddard thought. He noted the time the man was due in Manitoba, reminded himself to call Greyhound and ask about it, if he got a spare moment. He took down the rest of the information on Jimbo. Nothing much. A big guy, overweight. Prominent birthmark on his left cheek. Maybe Heins would know something.

When the sheriff mentioned the Defiance town cop, Clement Beauregard told him Heins was running a missing persons on him. That would be a BOLO report. If so, it'd have to come through the sheriff's office, and he hadn't seen anything yet. He'd have to get an update from Heins, soon as he got a chance.

Goddard promised Ms. Beauregard he'd get back to her no later than tomorrow afternoon, then rang off. He was back at his paperwork less than 5 minutes before the phone rang again.

"Line 1," the deputy called through his door. "Dunlap."

Goddard picked it up. "Shouldn't you be tending to family matters?"

"I thought you'd be in. You need to get a life."

Goddard heard Dunlap's wife in the background. In conversation with what sounded like his 7-year-old son. Though she might be talking to their daughter. They were out doing something as a family, Goddard guessed. There was something about the imagined scene that made the sheriff nostalgic, longing for what he suspected he would never have.

"Is there more to this call than an office check?"

"Sorry," Dunlap said. "Taking Katie to catechism. Just trying to keep abreast of the important stuff. Like Pine Grove. Any news?"

"Didn't find anything at the Defiance house or Winthrop's farmhouse. But guess what happened out at the farm last night?"

"What?"

"Wolves returned," Goddard said. "Meeting Steve Svegman from the DNR out there around noon."

"Angus trap them?" Dunlap said.

"Nope. Your friend Sam Rivers was out there last night. Said he had a hunch they might return."

"So, he was right."

"Yep," Goddard said. "But if Angus Moon knew Sam Rivers had gone out there in the middle of the night and trapped those wolves, he'd have an aneurysm."

"And then he'd kill something," Dunlap said. "You hear anything else on Pine Grove, keep me posted."

"Dimes to doughnuts the files went up in that office fire."

"I spoke with Walt," Dunlap said, referring to the fire marshal. "Says all signs point to an electrical fire. Another accident."

"When it rains, it pours," Goddard observed. There was plenty gone wrong with Winthrop and his aftermath. A little too plenty, the sheriff thought.

"Whoops. We're here," Dunlap said, referring to the church. "I'll catch you later, maybe at the office."

"Later."

The sheriff hung up. In less than a minute, another call came in.

"Line 1," the deputy called through his door. "Sam Rivers."

"More news?"

"Diane and I have to come over to Vermilion Falls. Any chance you could join us for a cup of coffee?"

Goddard wondered about it. "Sure. I'm about ready for a coffee break. I'm heading out to meet Svegman at noon. What time can you be here?"

"We're practically on our way. We'll meet you at Rangers Café. If you get there before us, get a booth."

"Business, or pleasure?" Goddard inquired.

Sam hesitated. "Both."

CHAPTER THIRTY

Lindy's Tap was a well-known Vermilion Falls establishment. For most Minnesota bars, it was illegal to sell alcohol for consumption off-site, unless you had a special license, which Lindy's did not. But it was an illegality Lindy considered more of a guideline than a rule, especially when it came to Heins.

When Heins walked through the door, Lindy Lewis nodded and said, "William. Coffee?"

"That'd be nice," answered Heins. It had been a long morning.

"Touch of the Irish?" Lindy asked.

Heins let his eyes grow accustomed to the dark. Apart from two overweight beer drinkers swilling suds instead of coffee, the place was empty. The tipplers were focused on a fishing show broadcast on the behind-the-bar TV. "Why not?" Heins grinned.

Lindy poured the coffee into a large cup, leaving a good inch at the top. He lowered the cup behind the bar and surreptitiously topped off the coffee with an inch of whiskey. Technically, Heins wasn't on duty. But appearances were important, he knew. Particularly on the Range.

"Obliged," he said, taking the cup in hand.

"What's new in Defiance?" Lindy said.

"Been nothin' but chaos since Williston's death."

"I read about the fire."

The club members had agreed not to broadcast the wolf kill. Too much unnecessary press might interest the wrong people. The last thing the club wanted were tree huggers from that wolf center nosing around. Clayton Winthrop was bad enough. But a little gossip in the right corners might cloud things up. "Did you hear about the wolves?" Heins asked.

"Wolves?"

"Wolves got into Williston's barn and killed his feeder calves."

"No shit? I didn't read that in the paper."

"Killed all of them and ate their fill. The DNR's being quiet about it. I guess they don't want the bad publicity," Heins said. In places like Lindy's Tap, the DNR was an unpopular governmental entity. If Iron Range residents thought the DNR was covering it up, it would only add to the outrage.

"Jesus H. Christ. Never heard anything like that."

"You know how plentiful they're getting."

Lindy nodded. "Had Buck Withers in here the other day. He said he had to kill a pair that dug a den on the rear acreage of his farm. They were harassing his livestock."

"That's what I mean."

"Said he didn't say anything to the DNR. Just shot 'em and dragged 'em into the woods. Buried 'em."

"That's a logical course of action, unless you need to get reimbursed."

"I'd do it," Lindy said. "Do it in a second, if my livestock were threatened."

"And damn well better do it before any more are taken."

"The fuckin' DNR. And we're payin' for 'em."

"Just ain't right," Heins agreed.

There was a long pause as the two men considered what was wrong with government. Then Lindy said, "It's a shame about Williston." Lindy knew Heins and Winthrop had been close. Sometimes the two men would come into his bar, or buy spirits. Lindy passed along his wholesale price to his friends.

"A definite loss for the Range," Heins said, sincere enough.

"That man had a string of bad luck," Lindy said.

"Not that it'll bother him now," Heins said.

They talked briefly while Heins finished his coffee. It tasted excellent, an hour before noon. Just the thing Heins needed to put the unpleasantness of his early morning behind him.

"Gonna need a few items," Heins said.

When Heins was buying in bulk, or something special, he always turned to Lindy, who gave him better prices than anyplace else on the Range. Given the club's recent heavy partying, he needed to replenish, particularly in light of this evening's celebration.

"A couple bottles of Crown Royal. A bottle of Stoli. Give me that Reserva Del Senor Tequila, the brown stuff. And one bottle of Glenlivet," he said.

"Jesus," he said. "You're gettin' ready to party."

Heins grinned and nodded.

Lindy glanced down at the bar's only other patrons. Their glasses were still half full. They were watching a fisherman stand at the edge of his boat, fighting to reel in his catch. Lindy nodded and disappeared in the back. Heins drained his cup while Lindy filled two large grocery bags. He came out with the double-bagged sacks, the Crown Royal boxes in one of them.

"Williston's drink," he said, remembering.

Heins hadn't thought about it. "Yup," he said. "Me and the boys are toasting Williston tonight, after his burial. We thought the best way to do it would be with his Canadian whiskey. Not very partial to it myself. But Williston would have liked the gesture."

"That man had expensive tastes."

"That was Williston."

Lindy took Heins's money, and the town cop said goodbye. He had a couple more errands to run. He had to go to the hardware store and pick up some ammo and supplies. He had to go to the grocery store. And he needed a carton of Old Golds. Winthrop's Cohibas, too, he reminded himself. He placed the liquor into his truck's back seat, pulled out of the parking lot, and turned toward Walling's Hardware.

Across the street Sam and Diane stared out the tinted windows of the Rangers Café. They were waiting for the sheriff, who was taking longer than he had expected. They watched Heins head into town.

"What do you suppose the Defiance town cop's up to?" Sam asked.

"Having a drink and buying some liquor, I suspect." Lindy's place wasn't a big secret. If serious drinkers didn't know about his lax observance of liquor laws, they had their suspicions. Lindy was careful. He never sold to anyone he hadn't known since birth. He had plenty of customers.

"The funeral's at 3 p.m.," Sam observed.

"I suspect he's stocking up."

"A postburial fling?"

"Why not?" Diane said. "They can afford whatever they want now, can't they?"

"Guess I'd do the same thing."

"You're not going to the party?"

"Wasn't invited," Sam said.

"Imagine that. Doesn't seem neighborly."

"Not that I won't have a celebratory drink," Sam added.

Goddard appeared not long after Heins wheeled out of Lindy's. When he came in, Sam moved over to sit near Diane.

"Sheriff," they nodded. Sam picked up the coffeepot and topped off his cup. Diane's too. "Coffee?" he asked Goddard.

"Sure."

When Sam reached over to fill his cup, Goddard noticed Sam's wrist scab.

"What happened to your wrist?"

"Cut it on some glass."

Considering his own small cut, the sheriff had an idea about where the glass was located. If so, that meant Sam had been lying about when he arrived in town. "Healing OK?"

"Seems to be."

"That's good," Goddard said. Then he pulled up his own coat sleeve and showed Sam his own cut. "Me too."

"What happened?" Sam asked.

"Cut it on some broken window glass. Basement window glass."

He looked at Sam, but the USFW special agent's countenance didn't change.

"Sorry to hear it."

The sheriff shrugged, obviously suspicious, but letting it go. For now. It reaffirmed Sam's sense of him. The sheriff, Sam thought, was reasonable, friendly, professional. He hadn't seen or felt anything to change his mind. Dunlap said he was an excellent lawman. Diane agreed. And he was no friend of Heins. That was four votes in the man's favor.

Sam finally reached down beside him and pulled up a brown legal folder with expandable sections and an overhanging flap. He reached into the folder and pulled out the flash drive. He set it on the table and slid it over to Goddard.

"What's this?" This time it was the sheriff's turn to play dumb.

"I told you I was out at the farmhouse?"

Goddard nodded.

"When I mentioned it before, I left out the part about finding the old man's spare key and going into the house. And I lied about not finding anything. I just didn't know what it was."

The sheriff glanced at Diane. She held his eyes long enough to tell him they both knew.

"The old man had a special place," Sam explained. "A recess in his study floor. Nobody knew about it. When I was a kid, it had mostly old coins. I wanted to see if he still used it. The coins were gone, but we found something we thought we might pass along to you." The sheriff hadn't lost his matter-of-fact demeanor, but Sam could sense his concern.

"Ordinarily I wouldn't have touched a thing," Sam added. "Not coins, anyway. There's nothing of the old man's I need or want. I cut those strings a long time ago. I don't need any reminders of him."

"So what is it?" the sheriff asked, just to be certain.

"A video."

The sheriff looked away. His index finger started tapping the table. Finally he reached over and picked up the flash drive. He turned it over, but there were no markings on it. "And I'm in it?"

" 'Fraid so," Sam said.

"I see," he said, and looked away again. Truth was, Goddard felt entirely different than he thought he would, now that others knew his secret.

"I wasn't sure if you could tell who was on it. I mean," he

paused, "the woman."

"Can't really tell," Diane offered, blushing a little, "except by the clothes hanging over a chair."

The sheriff sat back, thinking. He wasn't sure where to go with it, but the truth was he felt a lot better about one thing: knowing he no longer had to keep entirely silent about something that was gnawing at his insides like a guinea worm. It was odd. He felt embarrassed, like a boy caught in a lie. And he didn't know if he even needed to say anything about what Winthrop wanted, though he would. Because Goddard had told Winthrop almost nothing. But for a lawman who prided himself on his stellar record, the affair and the resulting compromise, small as it was, burned in his consciousness like a scarlet letter.

First he turned to Diane. "You know Belinda," he said.

"Not really, but," Diane paused, "I heard there was some struggle."

"First alcohol, after she lost the baby and found out there wouldn't be another opportunity. Then this church," he said, feeling more comfortable than he'd imagined, telling it. "I'm not making excuses. There's no excuse for what I've done. But you marry one person and one day you wake up to find an entirely different person. And by then you have separate bedrooms and talk maybe once or twice a week." He paused, looking away. "And then you meet someone. Someone who helps you remember what it is you thought you could live without."

"Sheriff, we're not here to judge you. What you do with your personal life is your own business," Sam said. "What I really want to know is why the old man had that flash drive in his file."

That's it, then, Goddard thought. He wasn't surprised. Sam

didn't give a rat's ass about his moral struggles, probably wouldn't have cared less if the affair had come to light in some other public way. It was the location of the evidence. The sheriff understood Sam's perspective, because it would have been his own.

"Your old man," he began, slowly, shaking his head. "Williston Winthrop was a crook and we all knew it. At least Jeff Dunlap and I knew it. Jeff turned him in once before on an ethics violation, but the St. Paul Ethics Board just slapped his wrist. Williston knew people. Jeff didn't like him and didn't trust him and was sure he was up to no good." The sheriff looked away, thought for a minute.

Then continued. "And then Susan . . . Dr. Wallace got a call from an assisted-living facility out of Eveleth. One of their patients needed some treatment. Normally it was handled by a physician out of Eveleth, but he was in South America. The place was nice enough, but an old lady was its only patient, and it was small, and something about it didn't seem right. Susan told me about it, and I shared it with Jeff. I went over to have a look, but it was legitimate. Just to be sure, Jeff started looking into it."

"Pine Grove Estates?" Sam asked.

Goddard looked at him. He glanced at the folder in front of him, thick enough to contain plenty of information. Probably the whole file on Pine Grove. "That's right," Goddard said. "It took Jeff Dunlap six months to get to the bottom of it. And by the time he did, guess what he found?"

"The old man," Sam said.

"That's right. Williston Winthrop was behind everything. He'd been bilking spinsters out of their fortunes for more than a decade."

Sam only nodded, still waiting for the reason Winthrop had the flash drive.

"Couple Sundays back, Williston Winthrop called me over to his office. That afternoon he showed me the video. He told me all he wanted to know was what a person could find out overhearing a conversation in Opel Grady's Café. He wanted to know what Jeff Dunlap knew."

"About Pine Grove?" Sam asked.

"Yeah, though he didn't mention it by name."

"So you told him?"

"Nope. I almost reached across the desk and throttled him. I was too angry to talk. If I'd had a match and some gas, I would have set the place on fire. Burned down the Winthrop Building with Williston in it."

"Maybe someone beat you to it?" Sam asked.

"Maybe. And I wondered. God knows your father had plenty of enemies. But Walt Gibbons says it was an electrical fire."

It was damn convenient, Sam thought.

"I didn't set it, but I was happy to see it burn," Goddard said.

"That much coincidence is hard to let go."

Goddard shrugged. "But you can imagine how fortunate I felt, at the time. I was hoping that was the end of it."

"So did you tell him anything?"

"He threatened to make the video known." It was an excuse, but it sounded as lame to the sheriff as it had every time he'd repeated it to himself. "Here's the deal," he said. "I called Winthrop that night. Called him from a friend's cabin. I gave him five names, including Miriam Samuelson and Iron County Care."

Those were names in the folder. Iron County Care was one of the umbrella corporations of Pine Grove Estates. It would have been enough.

"Then you told him what he needed to know."

"Winthrop was a crook, a thief, and a son of a bitch. But he was smart. I told him enough so he knew Jeff Dunlap was onto him."

The sheriff knew his career in law enforcement was over. He was already trying to think how he could break the news to his friend, Dunlap. He wondered how far Dunlap would pursue the prosecution. Probably hand it over to someone else in the office. Goddard felt relieved, ready to face it. He was glad Belinda had the church; she'd need it.

"That's it?" Sam asked.

"It's enough."

Sam nodded. Then looked away.

"Who knows?" Goddard wondered.

"Me and Diane," Sam said.

Goddard looked away.

"Sheriff, from what Diane tells me and what I know of your situation and your perspective about law enforcement, I'm a little surprised. But that's not to say I wouldn't have done the same thing, given a similar situation. Far as I know, this is the only record of it," he said, glancing down at the flash drive. "And from our perspectives," he looked at Diane, "this conversation is as far as it goes."

"I divulged information that compromised an investigation by the county attorney's office."

"You did. And you committed adultery, if you want to put a fine point on it. But the old man is dead, and as far as I can tell, there's nothing to be gained by releasing what he had on you. The old man was evil, and you weren't the first or only person he tried to swindle or ruin."

The sheriff stared at him. Then he looked at Diane.

"I agree," she said.

"What about the *Gazette?* What about the story?"

Diane looked away. "I have to admit it's one of the juicier stories to come my way. But if I shared it with anyone, Williston Winthrop would smile from his grave. And I couldn't abide by that." She paused. "The paper's not gonna find out about it from me."

"Or me," Sam affirmed.

Goddard paused and looked away. "Then that's it?" he asked, turning back to both of them.

"This is dead," Sam affirmed. "It's not the kind of news that helps anyone with anything."

For the first time the sheriff looked a little wistful. "What I've got to do is set things right with my wife," he said. "Belinda and I don't belong married anymore, regardless how the public will take it."

"She deserves to know," Diane agreed.

"This is the 21st century," Sam offered. "About as many people get divorced as stay married."

"You don't know the Range," the sheriff offered. "But there's no other way."

"That's right, Sheriff," Diane said. "I may not agree with your wife's religious perspective, but she deserves to know."

"Yes," Goddard said, resigned.

"There is something you could help me with," Sam added.

"Name it."

"I think this folder contains everything Jeff Dunlap needs to prosecute his case against the old man."

"That'd be good."

Sam picked up the folder. "But in order for the records to be admissible, it's probably best they come from the investigating officer." He slid the folder over to Goddard.

Goddard reached over and picked it up. "I'll drop it off with Jeff after I get back from the farm."

Sam told him where to find the secret floor cubby. The sheriff could check it out and tell Dunlap about its location.

After Sam and Diane left the café, they went into town. They parked along the street, walking the sidewalk to the grocery. They passed Heins's truck and Sam peered into the cab. In the narrow back seat, he saw two sacks and five bottles. The Defiance town cop had just broken Minnesota's liquor laws. He paused to be sure. There were three bottles in a far sack and up close, two dark blue boxes—Crown Royal. "The good stuff," the old man had been fond of saying.

They kept walking down the block. When they crossed in front of Webster's Tobacco, they caught a glimpse of Heins. He was turned away from them. In front of him, on the countertop, rested a carton of Old Golds, and three boxes of Cohibas.

Sam didn't want to run into Heins, at least not until the cemetery, later today. He'd say hello to the officer over the old man's grave.

They were well down the street when Sam remembered the Cohibas. They were the old man's smokes. Winthrop had always liked the Cuban knockoffs. Especially with a glass of Crown Royal.

CHAPTER THIRTY-ONE

On their return to Diane's cabin, Sam's cell phone went off. This time he used the Jeep's Bluetooth. "Sam Rivers."

"Yeah. Me again," Kay Magdalen said. "This is getting to be a bad habit."

"What?"

"Working on the weekends, making business calls. I need a life."

"Clarence must be an understanding guy."

She ignored the comment. "McCollum didn't have your cell phone number. And now he's off. Want to know what he found out?"

"What?"

"They're hybrids. All but one. An Arctic wolf."

Sam's Jeep veered a little. "Are you sure?"

"Do I stutter?"

He paused, trying to absorb what that meant. "That's interesting."

"I thought so. The hybrids were part Arctic, part malamute."

"A breeder," Sam said.

"Probably."

"Someone's breeding Arctics?"

"An Arctic," she said, reminding him there was only one.

Sam remembered that the animals he saw come out of the woods were big. Bigger than a gray wolf. Where in the hell did they find an Arctic wolf? In the Lower 48 it was an uncommon subspecies. But in Alaska and northern Canada they were abundant and, in many jurisdictions, fair game. Anyone could have obtained one and bred it.

"No Arctic wolf could get into the Lower 48 without a customs declaration," Sam remembered.

"If they brought it in legally."

"Breeding hybrids is legal in Minnesota. The state doesn't even maintain a registry for hybrid breeders. But there would have to be something in customs, at least a destination address."

"If they brought it in legally," Magdalen repeated.

"Can you have someone in audit check the declarations? Say, over the last five years?"

"It's Saturday, Rivers. I can check on Monday."

"Call Gibson. Call him at home. He owes me a favor. And this is important."

There was a long pause.

"Could you? Please." The plea from Sam came off stilted.

"Rivers," she said, irritated.

"It will put you in my good graces." That was going to piss her off.

"Maybe I should call Salazar. He's kind of anxious to please these days."

Sam figured he deserved that. He let the comment pass.

"Call Gibson. I'd call him, but I don't have the directory. He owes me. Gibson'll do it right away. And if I know him, he's home in front of the Golf Channel."

"I'll call him," she finally said, short. "I'll give him your cell, and you can talk with him."

"Thanks, Kay."

"You made any decisions?"

"Monday," he said. "Tuesday, latest. We'll talk then."

"Hybrids?" Diane asked, after he'd hung up.

"Probably bred."

"So someone raised them?"

"There's a good market for wolf dog hybrids, mostly by people who think the animal will make an unusual pet. But hybrids aren't like regular dogs. And they're not the greatest pets."

"People want to buy them?"

"Some people do. People who usually don't know any better. And unscrupulous breeders will give them what they want. As long as they get paid."

By the time they reached Diane's, the afternoon was squeezing out of the day. He had an hour until the funeral. They rested on Diane's couch.

"Do you think a lot of people will attend the funeral?" Diane asked.

"Probably not. The club," Sam answered. "The old man wasn't popular. He had enemies, not friends. He had clients, but from what I've heard, his rates were about as high as you can legally charge. Whatever legal judgments he won for clients, much of it was taken up in attorney's fees and expenses. Even his winning clients were disappointed, according to Jeff Dunlap."

"I didn't really know him. I saw him around town, but not often. Miriam shared plenty that was," she paused, "pretty awful. What makes someone into a man like Williston Winthrop?"

"Greed," Sam answered. He thought for a minute and added, "I think the seven deadly sins sum it up pretty well. And being raised with the belief that you own the wild and everything in it, that it is part of your rightful claim and heritage, and in the case of the Winthrop clan, duty. "

"But why?"

"I don't remember much about my grandfather. I know he killed more wolves than any other man on the Range. He was an überhunter. An alpha, just like the old man. They both reveled in exacting Winthrop family revenge. At least until passage of the Endangered Species Act."

"What about you? Why didn't you grow up wanting to 'exact Winthrop family revenge'?"

Sam thought about it. He'd spent plenty of time wondering why he hadn't become more like the old man. But unlike his grandfather or Winthrop, he'd never felt the need to conquer the wild, to own it. Wild places were his sanctuary, though he had no illusions about wilderness and the animals inhabiting it.

He guessed the old man had Sam figured out. He had his mother in his blood.

"Miriam Samuelson," Sam finally said, remembering how much his mother enjoyed a clear glass lake at sunset with loons crooning in the distance.

"She was a wonderful woman."

They were quiet for a while, sitting together on the couch, remembering Sam's mother, their thoughts drifting. And then Diane closed the space between them and kissed Sam's cheek, which caused him to recollect her swollen lips and the previous night.

"You're a sweet man, Sam Rivers."

Diane started to pick up their coffee cups from the morning.

Sam grabbed her back pocket and pulled her down. She was startled, but her eyes reflected his own sudden interest. They came together quickly, hurriedly. It took only moments for the breathing to pick up, their pulses hammering. Sam slid his hand inside her sweatshirt, cupped her right breast, found the top of her bra, and pulled it down when suddenly Sam's cell phone went off. He ignored it at first, but given current events he couldn't help but glance at the screen. Steve Svegman. The phone rang again and Sam said, "God, I'm sorry." Then he picked up.

"They got away," Svegman said. He sounded irritated.

"What?" Sam was looking forward to examining those hybrids.

"Angus was there and he wasn't happy. He wanted to know who in the hell trespassed."

"The sheriff with you?"

"He came later. Told Angus he'd been there last night, just to check on the place."

"What happened to the animals?"

"We could see their tracks come down out of the woods. But we could also see them return, from around back."

"Around back of the barn?"

Svegman explained about the chute door and how the wolves had somehow got it opened and escaped, returning to the woods. Svegman and Goddard stuck around for another couple hours, helping Moon clean up what they hadn't been able to clean up already. "Not a pleasant job," Svegman said.

"You didn't want to leave it? Those animals might return."

"Angus wanted it cleaned up. Said the animals were too damn smart, missing his traps like they did. Said he couldn't abide the mess for another night."

"At least it was frozen," Sam said.

"It stunk."

Sam knew it did. "One thing about those animals. They're not wolves. Not exactly."

"What are they?"

Sam explained about the results from Ashland Forensics.

"What's it mean?"

"I suspect they were bred. But until I have more information, we'd better keep it to ourselves. For now, anyway."

"Sheriff know?"

"I just found out myself. I'll call him."

He thanked the conservation officer and hung up.

Diane had taken their coffee cups to the kitchen. When she returned, the smolder was out of her eyes.

"I don't have to go just yet," Sam said.

"We need some time," she said.

"Yes," he finally said. "Later."

He reached up and gave her long thick hair a playful tug. Then he left, while he still had the will.

In his Jeep, on the way over, his cell phone went off. It was a 303 number. Gibson? Sam answered.

"Rivers."

"Sam?"

"Gibbs. What are you watching?"

"I was watching the Phoenix Open in Scottsdale. Then Kay Magdalen called. It's Saturday, isn't it?"

"She's giving me a hand."

"I guess that means I'm giving you a hand."

"It's my lucky day."

"It is your lucky day. Because I found it on the first search."

"What?"

"I could only find one Arctic wolf delivered to Northern Minnesota, to Snow Bank Kennels, four years ago. Came in from Manitoba."

"Got an address?"

"That's all I got. The customs declaration and license were all legit. It's a rural route. But I can't read the signature. Got a pen?"

Sam pulled to the highway's icy shoulder and rummaged through his console. He found a black felt-tipped pen and a square of white Post-it notes. He took down the address: Snow Bank Kennels, Rural Route 8, Defiance, MN 55054. He also jotted down the license number.

"What in the hell you doing in Northern Minnesota on February 1? Cold enough for you?"

"About 20 below."

"It's Minnesota. What did you expect?"

"Did I ever tell you I was born and raised here?"

"Never. But it figures. Know what Kay Magdalen told me?"

"What?"

"She told me to tell you, 'Don't be an idiot. Take the job.'"

"Glad to know she's minding my privacy rights."

"You're the right guy for the job, Sam."

Gibson knew his situation. He knew he'd taken a job with local investigations to try and save his marriage. He also knew the divorce was final and the marriage over. If Gibbs knew, everyone knew. Including Salazar. And Maggie. "I'll take it under advisement." But it wouldn't really affect his decision.

"Consider us even. And no more Saturday calls."

Before pulling back onto the road, Sam called the sheriff.

"Did you hear how we spent our afternoon?" the sheriff said.

"I heard. Thanks for covering for me."

"The least I could do."

Sam explained about Ashland's finding and the hybrids, the importation of an Arctic wolf from Manitoba, and the address—for Snow Bank Kennels. Sam asked him if he could look it up.

"I don't have to look it up. Took it down this afternoon. That's Angus Moon's address. He gave it to Svegman when he filled out those reimbursement forms. At least that's his address. He didn't indicate it was Snow Bank Kennels."

It was like a puzzle piece dropping into its slot. "Sheriff," he said. "I think we need to pay Angus Moon a visit."

"Exactly what I was thinking."

Sam told him he was headed to the burial.

"Don't say anything to Angus Moon. After it's over, meet me at the office. We'll give Angus Moon time to get home, and then pay him a visit together."

The remainder of Sam's drive to the cemetery gave him a little time to contemplate current events. Ever since he'd found out about the old man's death, he'd looked forward to the burial. He wanted to greet all of them, what was left of the old man's club, the remnants of Winthrop's avarice and greed. He wanted to look them in the eye, unable to do so when he was a child. But since his arrival, events had taken on a life of their own. For starters, he was no closer to the identity of canislupustruth@yahoo.com than he had been back in Yellow Rock. It could have been anyone. And he was no clearer about the reason for the messages. If he was being summoned, who had done it, and for what purpose?

As he covered the distance, Sam became preoccupied by more than the identity of canislupustruth and his emails. Or her emails, if it was a woman. He had questions. The old man knew he was being investigated. And if the sheriff and Dunlap were correct, the investigation into Pine Grove Estates could put the man away for the rest of his life. Did that prompt Winthrop, a man as tough as boot leather—or Italian leather, given his expensive tastes—to kill himself? The idea was unimaginable, Sam knew.

And hybrids had entered the barn. If Moon owned the hybrids, did they stage the kill? Was the club just trying to get rid of the calves because they didn't want to care for them? Then get the state to pay for them? It would be like Heins and Moon, he guessed. And probably Young and Pederson too. In one well-planned moment they could rid themselves of the need to care for the calves, and the bother of transporting and selling them. And news of the kill would be proof wolves were getting out of hand. The ranchers' outrage over this kill would be heard much farther than St. Paul. Every rancher in the nation would be pointing to it as evidence wolves needed to be taken off the endangered species list.

Except the club hadn't anticipated Sam's return or his particular expertise.

There were plenty of questions. He was looking forward to posing a few to Moon, after the burial.

The drive helped. He had time to think, to mull, and to let recent events percolate through the cold.

On the way through town, he passed the gutted Winthrop Building. It was a frozen black hulk. It was an eerie presence in the middle of town. Like a charred skeleton, Sam thought.

As he thought, other questions arose, but the answers seemed to swim at the periphery of understanding.

He approached the outskirts of Defiance. There was a turnoff for the cemetery. He could see through the gate to the maintenance shed near the front opening. There was a man leaning over the blade end of a backhoe, chipping away frozen clods. Sam glanced at him. He recognized, beneath the dangling Nordic earflaps, Ben Saunders, a kid he knew in school. He'd been a heavy drinker. As Sam passed, Saunders kept his attention on the backhoe.

The main cemetery road was a long drive bisecting two graveyard knolls. At the base of the knoll a few vehicles were already parked: a police car, Pederson's blue pickup, Moon's junker, a Honda CR-V, and a nondescript Chrysler. Sam assumed the CR-V was Young's. Sam guessed the Chrysler was a clergy car, owned by whomever the club had paid to say a few words over the grave. Sam pulled up and parked behind the CR-V. He checked his watch and saw it was a quarter to four. The service must have been shorter than expected. That made sense. And Sam preferred it this way, making his entrance with the rest of the club standing over the grave.

Atop one knoll Winthrop's grave was still open. Behind it the wilderness bush was an impenetrable weave. The other knoll was opened to an arctic wind that had started to come on when the sun was still off the horizon. It was a fitting backdrop for the old man's burial.

A plowed path wound through the tombstones that knifed above the snow. At the top of the hill the five figures gathered around the old man's grave. The casket must have already been lowered into the grave.

At the top of the hill the figures bent and tightened against the cold. They looked up to watch Sam, the man who had been Clayton Winthrop, make his way up the hill.

When Sam reached the top, he came to stand opposite the men, facing the cold wind. The old man's simple wooden casket lay in the bottom of an 8-by-4-by-5-foot rectangular hole. The earth had been chiseled out of the ground. Even burying the old man was difficult, Sam thought. As it should be.

Heins, Moon, and Pederson stared at him. Young looked at him and turned away, as if the winter had blown something into his face. Then Pederson focused his attention toward the grave. The pastor nodded to Sam, a question in his eyes.

Heins and Moon didn't turn away. They fixed their gazes on Sam, and Sam held them. Then he stepped within earshot of the pastor and said, "I'm his son."

The pastor nodded his acknowledgment. "Would you like to say anything?" the pastor wondered, thinking it was odd Sam hadn't attended the service, which had been brief and at which no one spoke.

Sam shook his head no.

Then the pastor started speaking. Sam couldn't hear everything, but it was bits and pieces of words spoken by a pastor who clearly didn't know Winthrop.

"Good man . . . God-fearing . . . Kingdom of Heaven . . . Hell . . ." The wind tore the words out of his mouth. Sam guessed it was the preacher's standard homily, spoken over a man, who as far as Sam knew, had never seen the inside of a church.

Finally, the pastor hurried through the Lord's Prayer and it was over. He bent to the frozen pile of dirt, starting to pick up a mitten full of earth when Sam interrupted.

It was all moving too fast. Sam didn't know what he'd expected, but he was finally at the edge of the old man's grave, and within minutes the ceremony, the ritual, such as it was, would come to a close. It was the cold whipping across the cemetery rise. It was seeing them all here. He wanted to walk over to Moon and tell him he knew about his hybrids. Somehow Sam felt cheated.

The others watched Sam move to the head of the grave. The frozen clods dropped from the pastor's hand.

Then Sam scraped up a pile of frozen earth and held it, thinking over the casket. He wished the old man were alive. Sam wished he had returned while the old man was among them, and given the man a taste of the anger he'd known as a boy. But it would have been hollow. It would have made no difference to Winthrop. He would have laughed at the gesture.

Sam let go of the earth, and the dirt tumbled across the top of the casket like rattling clumps of ice. "May you sleep more contented in death than you ever were in life," Sam whispered. He tried to summon some small vestige of hope for the old man's soul. He tried to summon something like forgiveness, but he couldn't forget what the old man had done to him. He felt sorry for the bitterness of the old man's life. That much he'd worked out. People wanted forgiveness. People believed you needed to forgive in order to move on. Forgive and forget. But could a person really forget that kind of cruelty, abuse, and pain?

Then a powerful blast of icy air broke them up like bowling pins. Young was the first to peel off and go. He struck down the path, hunched against the wind. Pederson followed him, bent, and angled toward his truck. Both of them left without a glance in Sam's direction. The pastor turned to leave, and then Moon shot an angry glance at Sam, turned, and started down the path. Heins was the only one who decided to have a word. Despite the cold he stepped to where Sam was standing at the head of the grave.

"Clayton," he said, nodding. "Heard you was in town."

"It's Sam. Sam Rivers."

"Yeah," Heins said, looking away. "I heard something like that." Another icy blast brought his breath up short. Then, "I know there was no love lost between you and Williston."

Sam remained quiet, holding the lawman's squint.

"Tell you the truth, I'm a little surprised to see you."

"Say what you will about the old man; he was still my father."

"When was the last time you saw him?"

"It's been 20 years."

"You be stayin' on long?"

"Haven't decided." Sam wondered if Heins knew why he had left. If he did, Sam knew, Heins would probably use it to pressure him to move on. But Heins only stared at Sam as if he knew, which Sam remembered was one of his interrogation tactics: feigned knowledge of a transgression until the person grew uneasy and confessed.

"We had a little trouble over at your mom's place," he said, staring at Sam.

"Trouble?"

"Someone broke in the other night. Probably the night of that big storm."

The night Heins was up to some bedlam of his own, Sam thought, remembering the conversation he'd overheard hunkered down in the roadside ditch. It was an age ago. "From what I remember, Mom didn't have much worth stealing."

"That's the peculiar part," Heins said. "Just took some of her preserves, far as I can tell." He was peering at Sam, looking for recognition.

"She put up some mean preserves. Whoever did it had taste, I'll say that for them."

"Do you remember where you were that night?"

"On my way here," Sam said. "I came in the day after the storm. Come to think of it, I stopped for gas in Brainerd early that morning, if you need someone to vouch for me. What were you up to that night?"

A shadow passed over the policeman's face. He looked away. Then he recovered, turned, and grinned. "Any business in town?"

"Yup," Sam said. "But it's private." The town cop was starting to annoy him.

"No reason to get your hair up, son. I still have some responsibilities here. People still pay me to know other people's business."

"But I'm not one of them."

"It's the jurisdiction. Doesn't matter if you live here or not. If you come into Defiance, I worry about you."

"What are you worried about?"

Heins paused. "That some people don't forget the past. Don't let it go."

Sam didn't smile. He kept his pulse even. "Some things are hard to let go."

Heins sighed and looked away. "I suppose," he said. "No harm in remembering, as long as it doesn't lead anywhere."

"Not sure where it'll lead. Still trying to figure it out." Heins didn't like that answer, which was fine with Sam.

The town cop looked at him and managed another steely grin.

"Godspeed, then," he said, and turned, starting down the hill. After a few steps he stopped, turned back, and said, "Any problems with me looking into the back boot of that Jeep?"

Sam returned the look, unsmiling but calm. "Got a warrant?"

Heins's eyes narrowed. "Don't stretch your welcome, Clayton," he said, then turned and kept walking down the narrow path through the graves. On the way down he stopped and peered into Sam's Jeep.

No law against that, Sam thought. At the bottom of the hill, Heins was the last to get into his car.

After everyone left, Sam turned and followed the icy trail to his Jeep. When he was finally inside, he turned the key and the engine ground once, then gave out a small wheeze and stopped. He pumped the gas and tried a second time, and the engine turned over, like an insolent child not wanting to wake up. He thought he'd better wait a minute, let it warm up.

He looked down at the gravedigger's truck. Saunders had gotten into his cab to warm himself. Now that he was warm, Sam guessed he would finish the job. Then he watched Saunders step out of his truck. The man paused with his door still open. He looked up at the grave, as if in consideration, and then cast a glance toward Sam's Jeep.

Sam watched him through the frosted windshield.

There were so many things that were still unclear.

The mystery of canislupustruth.

The old man's accident.

People age, Sam knew. They age and change. And Winthrop had been 62.

His Jeep's heater was blasting, and the inside of the cab was starting to warm. He pulled off his mittens, reached over, and picked up the Post-it pad and the black felt-tipped pen. He searched through his center console for another pen. He didn't like felt tips. He was left-handed. When his hand moved left to right over his fresh writing, the ink from felt tips rubbed off on the heel of his hand, leaving a black smear. But there were no other pens.

Canislupustruth, he wrote. Then underlined it.

Sometimes making a list shook something loose.

The Iron County Gun Club, he wrote beneath it. Then he added the member's names.

Storm, he wrote. *Hybrids,* he added.

He glanced up. In the distance, Sam watched Saunders's hand reach into the cab and pull something out. Sam watched the man raise a pint bottle to his lips and drain its trace of amber liquid. There was only a swallow. The gravedigger's desultory toss of the bottle punctuated his thirst. He guessed Saunders still had a problem.

Crown Royal, he thought, before he wrote it.

Then he pulled the Post-it off the pad and placed it in the center of his steering wheel. There were more questions. He reconsidered the list.

He glanced up again and saw Saunders look to the horizon, perhaps calculating the remaining daylight. The western edge of sky was turning crimson. Then the gravedigger got into his truck, started it, turned around, and accelerated out of the cemetery.

Saunders was fetching a pint, Sam guessed. Something to help him through the labor of filling in the grave. He watched the gravedigger's truck lights disappear around the cemetery road curve.

Sam stared at the tire tracks in front of him. He noticed Young's CR-V tracks as they pulled away from the road's shoulder and blended with the rest of the road. Then Sam reached out with his pen and wrote *Cohibas* after *Crown Royal*. The old man's favorites. He examined the list.

He had seen those tire tracks before. He remembered the night of the storm, crossing Young's place on his way up Beacon Street to break into his mother's house. Young had been home that night, he remembered. He'd thought it was Young's wife, but he remembered hearing she had died about a year ago. So it must have been Young that night, returning to his office home. So who in the hell was out with Moon, attending to the hybrids?

And then it occurred to him, like a jolt from a frayed wire. He reached into his coat pocket and dialed the sheriff.

"You already finished?" the sheriff said.

"Just about."

"Come on over."

"In a bit. Just one question. Did you get a copy of the coroner's report?"

"Came in yesterday, I think." He could hear the sheriff moving papers around his desk. "What about it?" he asked.

"Just out of curiosity, how was the old man identified?"

"I don't need the coroner's report to tell you that. We all recognized him."

"How?"

"Well," Goddard thought, trying to remember. "I'd seen him just a few days prior. He had on his camo coveralls. Boots. Socks. The same damn outfit he was wearing the night of the accident. Even the back half of his orange hunting cap was there, what was left of it," Goddard added. "And his wallet. And there was that cannon of a shotgun."

"That's it?"

"We all knew him," the sheriff explained. "It only took a glance from all of us. Smith Barnes and Susan. That club. It was Williston."

"So it was identification by physical appearance?"

"What other kind is there?"

"DNA. Fingerprints."

Goddard chuckled. "This is Vermilion Falls, not Denver. If we know something for certain, we don't spend extra dollars we don't have to to verify what we already know. It was Williston."

"Yeah," Sam said, thoughtful about it. "Thanks. I'll be over in a bit," he added, and rang off.

Sam placed the Post-it pad and the black pen into his coat pocket. Then he pulled on his mittens, opened the car door, and started running up the path toward the grave.

At the grave site he glanced back to the cemetery gates. He was alone, and would be, for a few more minutes. Then he took one careful step from the frozen dirt edge and dropped into the old man's grave.

He scrambled to the casket's side and wasted little time swinging open the lid. He wasn't prepared for the heavy mound of gauze covering the old man's head, making him look like some kind of space alien. He hadn't thought about the head being covered. He tried to focus on examining the rest of him.

He needed something from the old man. He tried to understand it, the massive lump lying in front of him, exposed to the winter cold. His body had changed, grown larger, Sam guessed because of age. But the sheriff said he'd clearly recognized him. He peered at it.

The hands were folded over the lower chest. They were pale and large, similar to what he remembered about the old man, but there was something not quite right.

He reached into his pocket, pulled out the pen, and levered it under the frozen hands, trying to lift them. They were stuck together, unyielding. He applied more pressure, and a thumb pried slowly into the air, pulled away from the other thumb, as though it was a stiff metal cable.

The thumbs were thick and wide, not how Sam remembered them. But it had been a long time. A lot changes in two decades. People get old, gain weight.

He pulled off his mittens. He needed the finger dexterity as long as he could maintain it in this cold. As soon as he touched the corpse's hands, their clammy foreignness made him shudder. He held onto them, trying to pry them up. His own hands were biting with the cold. He lost his grip, and the hands snapped back into their frozen position, centered over the old man's chest.

He reached down again, gripping the icy appendages as though they were stumps of frozen meat. He pulled hard and the hands rose, begrudgingly, from the chest. It was like bending lead. He let go and both hands remained poised, as though pleading. It was creepy, Sam thought.

Now both hands were lifting up to the sky. The dead man's right sleeve had slid down the raised wrist. Sam remembered the wrist. The old man had a ragged wrist scar, a farming accident. But now the skin was clear.

Sam took the felt-tipped pen and began scrolling its tip over the dead man's right thumb, then his left. He took a Post-it and pressed it against one thumb, then did the same with the other. He examined the paper. Two good clear prints.

Sam had no idea who lay in the grave, but it wasn't Winthrop.

He heard the drone of a truck, slowing before its turn from the highway through the cemetery gates.

Sam put the Post-it notes in his coat's breast pocket, and then struggled to get into his mittens. He slammed the lid and hurried out of the grave, lurching down the hillside. His hands were aching in the cold, but Sam barely noticed, remembering the corpse's hands raised in a kind of entreaty, a dead reckoning.

five bottles, including two bottles of Crown Royal Canadian whiskey, the old man's favorite."

The sheriff wondered about it, but only shrugged.

"I think they were going to party tonight. Did I ever tell you, sheriff, how that club built a cabin in the middle of Skinwalkers Bog?"

"Skinwalkers Bog?" he asked, doubtfully. "Nobody goes into Skinwalkers."

"Think it's haunted?"

"Hardly. A mosquito-infested swamp, more like it. Takes 20 minutes to hike 20 feet. I suppose," Goddard said, looking at Sam, "they first turn into weasels, so they get in through game trails?"

There was a snicker from Barnes over at his desk.

"They figured out a couple entrances down off two logging roads that border the place," Sam said.

"You think they're partying out there tonight?"

"I think so."

"And you know how to get there?"

"I don't. But I think Diane Talbott might."

"How in the hell would she know?"

"I told her about it the other night, and she said she'd been down one of those roads, looking for some rare bog flowers. Not exactly flowers, but orchids."

"Orchids?" The sheriff thought the story was getting more bizarre.

"There are some rare orchids out there, Chief," Barnes chimed in.

"Don't tell me you're an orchid hunter, Smith?"

Barnes looked thoughtful for a minute. "Not Skinwalkers.

Like you said, it's too damn dense. But I'll go over to the SNA bog near Pine Mountain," he said. "Different times of the year."

"Imagine that," the sheriff said.

"They're somethin' to see," Barnes said, defending himself.

"They are," Sam agreed. "Beautiful, exotic plants. Right here in Minnesota."

"So Talbott found the cabin?"

"Not the cabin. Just quite a ways down the overgrown logging road, she found a place where cars had parked, more than a couple times. And beyond it, the other side of some bushes, there was the start of a narrow trail."

"And you think that's the trail to the club's cabin?"

"One of them."

"Why in the hell would they go all the way out there when they could just drive to one of their homes?"

Before Sam could answer, the phone rang. The sheriff picked up. "Sheriff Dean Goddard."

He was sitting at his desk, listening to the voice on the other end of the line. "Yessir," Goddard said. "He's right here." He glanced over at Sam.

Sam stood, ready to take the phone. But the sheriff kept listening.

"Uh-huh," the sheriff said. He looked across his desk for a clean sheet of paper. He found a pad and picked up a pen. His brow turned quizzical. "Uh-huh," the sheriff said. "Just a minute." He tucked the phone under his chin, holding it against his shoulder. He readied himself for writing.

"James T. Beauregard," he said. "Biloxi?"

He wrote them on the notepad. Underlined them. He

recognized the name. "You know, that's damn curious," he said.

Sam and Barnes watched him. If that was the person in the grave, Sam had never heard of him. They watched the sheriff look across the papers on the desk. He shuffled through several, looking for the paper he'd jotted notes on just that morning. When he found it, he read the paper and said into the phone, "I had a call about that guy just this morning."

The person on the other end said something. Goddard thanked him, told him Sam appreciated his efforts, and hung up.

"Who?" Sam asked.

"James T. Beauregard. From Biloxi, Mississippi. He stole a car few years back, got him printed. Served some time. Not much. Want to tell me where you got these prints?"

"I think we need to speak with the coroner." Sam was careful not to say her name, letting him know it was official.

When he shared the reason why, Goddard said, "I was afraid you were going to say that." From the side desk, Barnes took it in fast, knew what it meant.

Then the sheriff made the call. "Susan," he said. "Can you come down here?"

By 9 p.m. Wallace, Barnes, and Sam were assembled in Goddard's office. Wallace verified there was nothing but circumstantial evidence that had confirmed the identification of Winthrop. Because of its location, clothes, the victim's wallet, and other identifying characteristics, and because they all knew Winthrop, and knew the body before them was clearly that man, the coroner had decided further identification—like a print or DNA analysis—was a waste of time and money. Now if they wanted to find out for certain, they'd have to exhume it.

The sheriff's legal pad contained a brief description of James T. "Jimbo" Beauregard, one he'd jotted down from the morning's conversation with Clement. It bore similarities to Winthrop, except for a prominent birthmark on the face. But he hadn't been that particular taking down more details. They'd have to call Clement. But when they tried, they only received her voice mail. The sheriff left his number and asked her to call him. So it sounded like Clement's brother was probably dead. Which meant Winthrop could still be alive. And they knew where they might find him.

The sheriff liked Sam's idea of surprise, which is why he asked two more deputies and Svegman to join him at his office. He told them all to bring their weapons and to dress for a hike through frozen woods. One of the deputies was out on patrol. The sheriff radioed him and told him to come in.

Sam called Diane and brought her up on current events. He suggested she might want to come along, and the sheriff didn't protest. This would be good press for Goddard, and he knew he might need all the good press he could get, soon enough.

Sam asked Diane to bring over the duffel with his gun and night-hunting garb, absent the money. When Diane arrived, she brought it into the sheriff's office. Sam extracted the 10 gauge pieces from the bag.

"Where in the hell did you get that?" the sheriff asked, recognizing the gun.

"It was a present."

"That's the same gun that killed whoever the hell's in that grave."

"Just like it," Sam said. "This one was promised to me when

I was a kid. Then the old man changed his mind, so I took it and hid it before I left."

Goddard thought of Miriam's place. "In your mother's house?"

"That's right."

The sheriff smiled. "I remember Williston mentioning there was another one of those. That it had been stolen and he was going to get it back."

"Not stolen," Sam asserted. "Just hidden someplace safe and reclaimed." Sam took the gun stock in hand. The solid walnut was heavy and large. He affixed it to the barrel. He screwed down the other pieces and raised the shotgun to his shoulder, aiming down the blackened double-barrel. He was surprised by its heft, still heavy, but it felt less substantial than he remembered. He'd added a few years since he'd held the gun. It had been a lifetime. If Sam's childhood had trained him for anything, it was to hunt predators, whether in Skinwalkers Bog, the Jakarta pet market, or the Florida Keys. Sam was made for this role. He'd have to tell Magdalen.

He didn't know what they might walk into, but he knew he had to be armed when they did. Besides, there were wolves in those woods, and hybrids, at least one or more raised by Moon, if he was right. He wasn't sure what they might do when confronted. In almost all known instances, normal wolves would turn at the sight of man and disappear into woods. But hybrids who had lived with men, who had endured a man like Moon and then ran wild, would be different. Sam couldn't imagine them turning and running. They might feel what he did and have a hunger for revenge. It wasn't revenge, exactly, just a sense of how things should be and the power to make things right.

He put on his camouflaged, insulated fatigues. When Diane came into the room, bundled up as tight as a mummy, she looked at Sam and smiled.

"You look like special ops."

"Special agent, Fish & Wildlife."

By the time Svegman arrived, their group grew to seven: Svegman, the sheriff, Barnes and the two extra deputies, Sam, and Diane. It was going to be a ride and hike, the sheriff informed them. Probably at least a couple miles. Wallace would stay behind and provide radio support from the sheriff's office, in case they needed help. They were headed into Skinwalkers Bog.

CHAPTER THIRTY-THREE

The caravan approached the chained entrance to the overgrown logging road. Tire tracks confirmed the entryway to the boundary of Skinwalkers Bog. Diane remembered, then spotted, the road as Sam's Jeep passed in front of the chain.

Sam pulled to the side of the road. Two patrol cars followed behind, then Svegman's DNR vehicle. Sam got out to examine the entrance. The sheriff opened his patrol car door and stood up in the cold.

Sam approached. "Looks like maybe three big vehicles, two trucks and an SUV, entered that logging road, judging from the tracks. Recently."

Goddard leaned down into the nearby patrol car and said, "Smith, can you fetch those bolt cutters from the trunk and take that chain down?"

"No problem."

Diane wore a heavy down parka that hung above her knees. She had a pair of nylon ski pants over two sets of long underwear. Her breath clouded in front of her ski mask.

The sheriff turned and started walking toward the chain. "Can we drive into it?"

"Not with our patrol cars," Barnes said.

"We can squeeze into Svegman's DNR vehicle and my Jeep," Sam suggested. "We should be able to make it."

"That'll work."

Barnes's bolt cutters made an easy snap on one side of the chain. Then he dragged the cut end across the opening.

The group piled into the two vehicles. Then both vehicles turned carefully into the bush-covered lane, following the tire tracks. After a half-hour drive, they came up a small rise and saw the tracks turn left off the old logging road. Sam got out of his Jeep and walked along the narrow ruts, following them another 50 yards until he came up behind Heins's pickup, Moon's battered Ford, and Young's CR-V.

The others cut their engines and waited for Sam's return. When he came out of the trees, he raised one mittened hand and twirled it in a rapid circle. Car doors opened, quietly, and the group got out of their vehicles. Everyone took a moment to examine and secure their weapons. Then they affixed snowshoes and followed Sam's tracks up the ruts.

Sam walked ahead, turning around the club members' parked vehicles. Up ahead there was a small opening in the trees where a shallow pool of moonlight fell down around him. On the other side of the opening, a dark path started through the dense trees. Sam motioned for the others to approach, and in a moment they all stood in the pool, listening.

From the other side of the woods they heard wolves, faint and far off but distinct.

"They're a few miles," Sam whispered. "Sounds like they're waking up."

"Probably going to hunt," Svegman whispered.

"Cold like this would make anything howl," the sheriff added.

"The cold doesn't bother them," Sam said. "They're marking territory. These woods are theirs. Those calls are to let others know they shouldn't come near."

"Let's hope they make an exception for law enforcement," the sheriff said.

There was another chorus of howls from deep in Skinwalkers Bog.

"Problem is, you just never know about hybrids," Sam added. "Which is why it's a good thing we're all armed."

The sheriff pointed to the tracks disappearing through a pair of black spruce boughs. "Looks like we have an easy enough path to follow."

"They may have blazed it for us," Sam said. "But if what I've heard about this place is true, I suspect the way isn't easy."

"If Bill Heins can walk it, so can we," the sheriff observed.

Sam turned and snowshoed four paces before pushing into a wall of black spruce. The others fell in behind him in single file.

On occasion, the woods were so thick Sam had to switch on his flashlight. He covered over the front of the flashlight with his hand, muffling its brightness. When he was certain it was safe, he shined the light on the ground behind him so the others could approach in safety. They made slow progress through the trees.

The evening wore on. They did not hear the wolves again. Sam knew that could mean anything.

The air was particularly cold, but Sam no longer noticed it. His camo coverings added a layer of insulation and his head, like the others, was covered with a ski mask. Tracking carefully along the trail was absorbing work. After an hour they came to a small rise that climbed a few feet. When they walked onto it, Sam could see the path continue at this level. The swamp thicket changed to old-growth woods. The trail was still shadowy, but partial moonlight filtered through the trees, enough to see where others had passed before him.

Sam turned off his light and walked in the faint glow.

They continued less than 100 yards, winding through the island of black spruce, when Sam stopped. The others stopped behind him. Sam noticed a faint change in the light's intensity through the trees, falling down on the path. He motioned to the others, raising his finger to his lips. Then he stepped forward 15 paces, rounded the corner of a large fir, and saw lights up ahead, the cabin set back in the trees.

Sam retraced his steps. "It's around the corner," he whispered. The sheriff nodded, turned around, and passed word down the line. They all stiffened at the news.

Sam turned and started forward along the narrow path. Everyone followed to the corner tree. Fifty yards ahead the cabin lights were barely visible. Sam moved forward another 20 yards, where the path bent through some Norway pines.

Now they were close enough to see through the windows. Not close enough to see details, but they could see blurred movement inside, what appeared to be figures sitting at a table. The windows were frosted over.

The cabin looked large enough for a few rooms. One large front room and two or three rear bedrooms, Sam guessed. It was a typical cabin layout. He suspected there was a rear door that went back into the woods to an outhouse. Ideally one of them should work their way around back and cover the rear. But it would be difficult keeping quiet in the dense bush.

If the club members heard them, Sam worried they would have time to retrieve their weapons, probably deer rifles, he guessed. Surprise gave them a formidable advantage. And he suspected by this hour, their senses would be dulled by plenty of whiskey.

Sam retraced his steps to where Goddard waited in the trees.

"I'll get around back. I suspect there's a back door and we should cover it before we move in."

Goddard agreed.

Inside the cabin, the five men sat around the table, playing cards. The blistered pine top lay covered with red, white, and blue poker chips; cards; a couple of ashtrays; and glasses. Heins's Old Gold cigarette sent a slender trail into the thick cabin air. In the other ashtray Winthrop had parked one of his Cohibas. Since the evening started, he'd had one of the long cigars almost perpetually stuck into the corner of his smiling mouth.

After the burial, all of the club members made their way to Skinwalkers Bog. And Winthrop had been ready. He'd fired thick filets over the grill. He'd baked potatoes and cut a small hole in the center of three large Vidalia onions, filling them with Worcestershire sauce and topping them off with thick pads of butter. Then he wrapped them in foil and baked them with the potatoes. It had been a feast, washed down with plenty of libation. Now, just after midnight, the five men were practically giddy with good humor.

"I'll call you and raise you," Heins said, tossing his chips onto the considerable pile.

They were all still playing the hand.

Winthrop loved the game. He turned to Heins and smiled. "I'll call ya," he answered, adding the necessary chips to the centered mound. The others tossed their chips in after Winthrop's, everyone still in.

They turned to Heins. He was a careful player. But they'd been drinking long enough, and it was, after all, a celebration. As the club members figured, they were all millionaires, give or take a few thousand. Before Svegman had left the farmhouse, he told Moon he'd get the check to them on Monday. Moon figured he'd be sleeping in. He told Svegman to leave it in his rural route mailbox.

Heins laid down two pair, sixes and sevens. He peered at the remaining players and smiled. It was liberating to know money was no longer an issue. Not a real issue. Now they simply had to figure out how to spend it. And paying attention to whatever opportunities came their way.

Pederson laid down his cards. He did it slowly, with flourish, one card at a time.

"A six," he said, setting it down. "And a three." He peered at the others, smiling. They knew Pederson. This was his technique for showing three of a kind. And sure enough. He laid them all down at once, beaming. "Three aces," he said, like a schoolboy, poised to rake in the cash.

Heins cursed and the others threw down their hands. Everyone but Winthrop. He reached over and grabbed Pederson's arm. "Wait a minute, goddamn it." The others watched. You never knew about Winthrop. He looked Pederson in the eye, laid down his cards, and said, "A flush."

Pederson swore, but his curse was drowned out by a howl of laughter loud enough to awaken the phantoms in Skinwalkers Bog.

"I'm out of remedy," Winthrop finally chuckled, rising to fetch what was left of his Canadian whiskey, parked in a snowdrift outside the front door.

Sam snowshoed soundlessly through the crystalline glaze. In another minute he'd cut the distance to the cabin in half. He was near enough to get a good look when he heard the club members erupt. He'd heard it before. Poker. And unless he was mistaken, someone had just won a big hand. Sam peered through the front window and saw someone pass in front of the opaque pane. It had been 20 years and he couldn't be certain, but it looked like the old man.

He felt a whirl of energy high up in the center of his chest, and his whole body tensed. He stood still, his snowshoes planted in the narrow path, squinting through the frosted glass.

Behind him, the others watched Sam freeze.

With what appeared to be Winthrop so close to the front door and window, Sam knew moving might betray his position, so he waited and watched.

Suddenly the front door opened and Winthrop stepped out. He turned to the right of the door, leaning down to fetch a bottle from a snowdrift, where the natural deep freeze was keeping the liquor cold.

Winthrop found the bottle he was after, straightened, and looked up to see Sam standing in the outer rim of cabin light, like an apparition.

For a moment the unexpected body made Winthrop jerk upright. Sam was covered head to heel in camo, carrying the familiar big weapon in front of him. Then the old man focused on Sam's eyes, appearing to recognize him. Then he looked behind Sam, to where he thought he glimpsed others waiting in the trees.

Winthrop backed into the cabin, slamming the door shut behind him. A bolt lock snapped into place. There was a shout, followed by chaos.

Goddard, Barnes, and Svegman rushed forward. Sam turned

onto the perimeter path and struggled around the cabin corner. Diane waited in the trees with the two remaining deputies, who were falling in behind the others.

Barnes and the sheriff came to either side of the front door. Sam disappeared around the corner. Svegman joined Barnes to the side while Goddard yelled, "It's Sheriff Goddard! Open the door!"

Sam struggled to the cabin's rear. When he turned the corner, he heard a loud bang. Sam ducked. Then he realized the bang was a back door snapping shut. He jumped forward along the dark cabin wall. He fought his way through branches, sounding like a bull moose breaking through the trees.

At the front door the sheriff waited only moments before the bolt lock slid open and Heins opened the door.

"Sheriff," Heins said, trying to act normal. "What in the hell are you doing in the middle of Skinwalkers Bog?"

Behind the cabin a well-worn path made a straight line 50 feet to an outhouse. To the right of the outhouse, black spruce boughs wavered where someone had disappeared into the dark woods.

Sam hurried down the path and hesitated in front of the structure. If Winthrop was armed, he'd use the gun. He peered around the corner of the house and noticed freshly broken snow disappear around spreading spruce boughs. The old man was on the run.

Winthrop knew these woods. He could be waiting 50 yards up ahead with the barrel of his rifle aimed at whoever had guts enough to follow. On the other hand, Sam reasoned, he'd probably seen they had force. Sam guessed it would keep him running. And Sam had come too far not to follow. He only hoped Winthrop hadn't had time to pick up a weapon. He turned onto the old man's trail.

Winthrop's face had been gray, unshaven, and he was heavier, his square shoulders gone round. He'd aged, but Sam could see he was still formidable. And Sam thought he saw something he had never seen break across the old man's face: surprise, followed quickly by fear.

Sam moved forward carefully, following the old man's tracks through the snow. The old man's stride appeared long, as though he was running. Winthrop didn't have time to don snowshoes. He was struggling through the drifts. As Sam tracked—moving through the trees, the seconds growing into minutes—he noticed the old man's stride shorten, the steps contract. The cabin light quickly receded until he was surrounded by dark woods and silence. The tracks continued through the trees. The woods were thick, but on occasion islands of larger pines rose into the dark sky.

Sam trailed for several more minutes. He paused, listening for the old man's footsteps, but heard nothing. He carried the 10 gauge, ready to use it. The adrenaline made his senses keen and hyperaware.

He tracked for nearly an hour, wondering how long the old man could maintain this pace. And where was he going? He couldn't have left with much. His tracks showed he was struggling through the deep snow. Sam turned around a thick pine bough and came out into a 30-foot opening, a frozen swamp in the trees.

Across the clear expanse of white waited Winthrop, breathing hard. Sam watched the old man's breath clouding in front of him, trying to recover. He coughed.

"Thought it was you," Winthrop managed, a little wheezy. "Clayton," the old man added, as though speaking his name might soften the boy.

"Rivers," Sam said. "Sam Rivers."

The old man managed to chuckle. The chuckle led to another brief coughing fit. After it passed he said, "Is it, now? And why the name change, son? Unhappy with your heritage?" There was familiar derision in the old man's voice. It reminded him of his childhood, of being Winthrop's son. The comment blew ash off a coal Sam could feel glow scarlet.

"Needed a change."

"A change," the old man wheezed. "Well, isn't that sweet. Do you think a different name is going to do it? Still Miriam Samuelson's boy."

Sam considered raising the 10 gauge and firing. The idea was spontaneous, powerful, not easily resisted. Blow a hole in the old man's chest. Vaporize his heart. At least what passed for one. His finger itched along the trigger guard.

"Take it easy, son," Winthrop said. "We're just having a family discussion here. I think you should give the old Decimator a rest, put it down."

Sam thought about it, about shooting him.

"Maybe you should just give me the gun, Clayton. Here I am out in these woods, unarmed. It's certain I won't be heading back to that cabin. Give a man a fighting chance."

When Sam didn't move, the old man made one step forward.

Sam raised the gun from his waist, pointing it dead center at the old man's chest. Then he pulled back the firing hammer. "This time it's loaded."

His father peered at the narrow black holes, noticed their deadly trajectory. He stopped and raised his hands. "Hold on, son. I'm stepping back," he said. He moved back. "No sense in getting trigger happy. You've handled yourself well to this point." He paused. "I'm about to come into a fair amount of money. That is, if I stay dead. Providing none of your other friends out there saw me. Right now the most that can happen is fraud over that wolf kill. But truth is, that would be hard to prove, without those wolves."

Winthrop was getting warmed up. Sam remembered the monologues, which could go on for hours.

"Just think about it, is all I'm asking," Winthrop continued, making a step forward.

Sam's barrel rose a few more degrees, enough to remove the old man's head.

"OK, OK. Let's just talk about this. It's business, son. Business. You could share in this, if you played it smart. You could have half my share, which is considerable. I'll even let you keep that $179,000," he added.

So he knew about the money. "That was my mother's gift," Sam said. "Like the house."

"That was my money, son."

It was good to see the old man hadn't lost his love for the green.

"Never was," Sam said. "Never will be."

"I knew you'd come back. I knew she hid it somewhere. Why do you think I sent you all those messages? I don't know how you found out about my accident, but for two years I tried getting you back," Winthrop said. "And this is the treatment I get?"

Canislupustruth@yahoo.com. The old man sent him every email, tried to lure him back because he'd wanted his money, and guessed Sam knew where it was.

"That $179,000 I'm willing to let go," Winthrop said, even again, the calm returning to his voice. "Call it the first installment of plenty more where that came from."

Twenty years was a long time, Sam thought. He'd struggled, found his way, made a place for himself, and begun to thrive, at least until Maggie. But even Maggie had been a move toward his heart, not away from it. In all that time Winthrop had continued the natural course of being himself. And it was different now, standing in front of him, remembering the towering presence of his youth, the one who badgered, bullied, and abused. Now the old man looked like an aging, tired crook, standing at the edge of a clearing in the middle of deep woods. And the wilderness he had so long dominated was taking its toll.

"You want this gun?" Sam said.

Winthrop was surprised, nodded. "Well . . . Yeah. I mean, sure, son. I could set you up real nice . . . give you plenty, once everything comes in, gets settled."

Sam flipped open the shotgun's chambers. He pulled the shells from its double barrel. He flung them into the dark, where they disappeared into the cold.

There was a granite boulder at the edge of the swamp, directly behind him, its surface as smooth as a dinosaur's egg. Sam turned the shotgun around, picked up the barrel end of the Decimator, bent, and put his arms into the swing, driving the gun's stock onto the rock-hard surface. It was an ax blow. The walnut stock splintered.

Behind him the old man gasped. "Wait!"

Sam moved one step forward and swung again, slamming the trigger mechanism onto the stone, swinging in three clear, heavy hammer strikes before pausing long enough to bring the battered barrel up and examine it. The fragile metal trigger had broken and flown off into the deep snow. The hollow mechanism was caved in and flattened. The Decimator would never fire again.

Then he flung what was left of the shotgun across the frozen swamp. It landed at the old man's feet.

He watched the old man step forward, like someone either on the edge or nearly broken. Winthrop fished in the snow for what was left of the Winthrop family heirloom. He brushed off the barrel and looked across the swamp to his son.

Sam thought he might charge. The gun's destruction was the kind of violation that at one time the old man would have answered with raging fists. But maybe he finally understood. His son had grown up, changed, become his own man, Sam Rivers.

They were finished. Sam watched the man, who was still breathing hard. Part of Sam hoped he might charge.

Then Winthrop turned and disappeared into the trees.

"Run," Sam said, in a tone he knew the departed Winthrop wouldn't hear. Not that it mattered now. The old man's tracks would be easy enough to follow. But Sam didn't think this time the old man would survive the dark and cold.

CHAPTER THIRTY-FOUR

Back at the sheriff's office, Heins, Pederson, and Moon sat in three separate holding cells, each positioned so they could not hear or speak to one another. Young had been moved to a small basement utility room, a single bare bulb hanging over his head. Large patches of paint peeled over the makeshift interrogation room's cement walls. The floor was the color of tarnished gray metal. In the spare light the insurance agent looked grim.

Goddard sat alone with him, talking matter-of-factly and without abatement.

"I know in time you're going to tell me what happened, Hal. We've known each other a long time. We already have the physical evidence of the alleged wolf kill. We can press that charge and it'll stick. It's the other matters you were involved with that should scare you, Hal. Murder isn't a hanging crime in this state. But people are put away for life. I suspect, Hal, you've never seen the inside of a state penitentiary." He said the word *penitentiary* carefully, like a dull knife blade. It was having an effect.

"Prison is a nasty place," the sheriff continued. "If I were you, I'd do whatever I could to mitigate my sentence."

The sheriff leaned over conspiratorially and softened his tone. "The plain and simple truth, Hal, is that I don't believe you were the ringleader of this mayhem. And I don't believe you were a wholly willing participant. I think the club needed your insurance angle and you were pressured into it until you went along. Don't get me wrong. That's not a ticket to innocence. You'll have to pay.

But if you cooperate, you're likely to receive a lesser punishment than the other members of your club." Goddard had his attention. "We think they were using you. And I know you, Hal. I just don't see you surviving very long in a penitentiary." The sheriff's eyes were calm, concerned.

The sheriff continued in this vein for a while longer. Young's face remained ashen. Unless the sheriff was a very bad judge of character, Young would soon chatter like a songbird at dawn.

In the intense light of Rangers Café, Sam, Diane, Svegman, and one of the deputies sat at a predawn table drinking coffee and waiting for first light. Diane had her tablet out and was asking questions, trying to nail down the facts for the story she was still hoping to submit to the *Star Tribune* down in the Cities before the morning copy deadline, which was an hour away.

The group had long since worked through the details of what they knew. Sam told the others about his father. Everyone who heard the story had the same question: if Winthrop was loose in Skinwalkers Bog, who was buried in his grave? The sheriff told them about James T. Beauregard, and Sam remembered the Defiance Hotel proprietor mentioning Heins picking up the vagrant. It had a sickening way of adding up, much as none of them wanted to admit it.

At dawn they were going to pick up Winthrop's trail. No one expected Winthrop to return to the cabin, but just in case, Barnes and a deputy had remained at the hideout. And they had the CB. The reception was terrible, but they'd been able to make their words known. Winthrop had not returned.

In another hour it would start getting light. The others finished their coffee and began getting ready.

"Do you think he survived the cold?" Diane asked. She started donning a thick down coat.

"He's lived in these woods his whole life," Sam said. "He's probably alive. I'm more worried he found some way to get out."

"Not likely," Svegman said. "We've got conservation officers patrolling those rural maintenance roads, and we've already picked up the other vehicles. If he gets out, he'll have to walk to do it."

Sam knew the old man was tough enough to last until dawn. But he also knew he'd been forced from the cabin so quickly that he'd run without getting properly equipped. "We'll pick up his trail. I suspect we'll find him before noon."

CHAPTER THIRTY-FIVE

The wolf dog hybrids cornered the deer in a thicket. While the hybrids faced the wavering antlers, the Arctic wolf came up behind the animal and fastened his jaws onto its hindquarters. The lead wolf thought the buck would fall, but one powerful hoof kick sent him through the air with his mouth full of deer hair and a piece of torn hide. Then the buck crashed through the brush and was ahead of them. The Arctic managed to rise and in a few minutes assumed the lead again.

The wolves pounded through thick woods, and the leader sensed the deer's tiredness. The snow was deep, and the buck's hooves, unlike wolf paws, were unable to hurry across the white surface. Its torn hindquarter, with a ragged flesh wound, was bleeding as the deer ran. The predators couldn't see the blood, which froze as soon as it fell and was covered over by dry powder. But it left a scent trail through the dark night air that intensified the wolves' yearning.

The Arctic raced at a steady sprint. The hybrids followed close behind. They moved through the trees as one tight pack of hunger and maniacal purpose.

In the darkness Winthrop struggled through the snow, trying to keep his balance. His chest felt raspy, and it was difficult to catch his breath. In the abject darkness spots floated across his vision, and he did not know where to turn. For the last few hours he had been hiking at a good, steady rate, sometimes crawling to get through a wall of black spruce or alder, then stopping long enough to recover, then starting again, until he felt the oncoming need to lie down and sleep.

But not here, he told himself, knowing the desire to sleep was the first sign of hypothermia. He was still cogent enough to know that if he lay down, he would never rise. He continued through the dark, stumbling, reckoning his direction by the stars, heading north. He couldn't return to their cabin. He had to keep moving as far from the cabin and Skinwalkers Bog as possible. His only hope was to find some remote cabin that he could break into, get himself thawed, maybe find some food and something to drink, and figure out a way to get across the border. If he had any hope of bushwhacking through 7 frozen miles of woods to the border, he would have to keep pushing.

Finally, he stopped long enough to listen in the dark. There was nothing behind him. He found a large fir tree and managed to crawl in beneath the lower boughs to where the falling snow had not penetrated. There was a small cave, and he sat for a while catching his breath, listening. He set the shotgun beside him in the dark, careful to keep his full attention focused on the sound. It was then he began noticing the cold and his considerable weariness.

But I cannot stop, he suddenly thought, in an increasingly rare lucid moment. It was the only coherent thought he could manage as he gasped to take in more air.

He clawed at his chest. Under the considerable layers of clothes, he thought he felt warm enough to perspire. He had never traveled through woods like this, hell-bent on escape, with fear driving him like a wild animal. He had been blind, walking in the dark. His face was raw where branches had cut it. But there was no other option. Run into the woods, north to Canada. A long ways, a Herculean marathon, but not impossible. Or was it?

He laughed, but the exhalation of air made him bend over in another fit of coughing. After it subsided he reached up and again tried to take in more air. He was exhausted but knew he had to move.

He crawled out from under the tree boughs and was immediately struck by a sense of warming air. It was getting warmer, wasn't it? He thought maybe it was a southern warm front coming in. Unseasonable, but lucky. He'd been lucky.

He stomped forward not more than 50 paces before realizing he'd forgotten the shotgun, what was left of it, now only the gnarled steel barrel. But what was left of it could still be a formidable weapon in the hands of someone who knew how to use it.

He retraced his steps, stumbling back over them. But they didn't return him to the place he had just been. Was he disoriented? Lost? It was still dark in the woods. In places he had trouble following the tracks. Twice he came to trees he thought might be the one, but both times their understory cave was empty. He started laughing. The laughing brought on another fit of coughing, and he doubled over in the cold.

Now he was tasting blood and wondered if the stream of spittle hanging from his mouth was red.

He stepped forward, wearily entering the dark. He guessed the posse would not follow in the night. Few were man enough to follow Winthrop through Skinwalkers Bog. Moon could do it. Heins, maybe. But Winthrop hadn't known many men his caliber. He stumbled ahead in the dark and knew the abominable cold and deep snow and complete darkness were his friends. Wilderness was trying to set him free, and he was going to let it.

A sharp pain cut across his chest, and he reached up to claw at it. He paused long enough for the pain to subside. He tried to listen in the dark but heard nothing. He hit the side of his head, wondering if he were losing his sense of hearing along with his sight, because he heard a vague high-pitched whine.

After a moment he felt strong enough to continue and took a few more steps through the deep snow.

The Arctic was the first to reach the deer. The large buck was cornered in another thicket, no place to turn. The wolves crept up slowly, watching the deer's breath cloud the frozen air. Its antlered head was bent forward, ready to fend off a frontal assault. Instinctively the hybrids circled. They kept the deer corralled, but were careful to keep away from its horns. Twice the animal bucked forward, looking for a way to break through the menacing gray line. Twice the hybrids came together like a wall.

Finally, the big Arctic worked in behind the animal's kicking hindquarters. He saw his opportunity and leaped forward with purpose, jaws open. He fastened himself near the place where he'd earlier torn flesh. He could smell the bloody wound, taste the small measure of it. He clamped down hard and let his full body weight hang heavy on the deer's backside.

This time, coincident with the leader's leap, two pack members crouched forward on either side of the wavering antlers. The deer hunched down with the big wolf on its hindquarters, too tired to kick. It shifted its horns to the left and right, heaving in the snow.

Then the fourth hybrid lunged unexpectedly and fastened itself on the back of the deer's heavily muscled neck. The deer arched, hoping to catch the hybrid with a thrust of horns. The wolf dog felt the horns cut into the gray fur, and it was forced to let go. But the action of arching left the underside of the deer's throat exposed and another wolf dog moved in.

Under the weight of three wolves, the exhausted animal toppled in the snow. The hybrid fastened on the buck's throat, clamped down on its windpipe, holding firm until the animal ceased to breathe and lay still.

The big wolf licked the blood from the hindquarter wound. He whined. The others whined and worried over the dead animal. They had felled deer before, knowing how to chase down and kill. But until Moon gave the OK, they had never been allowed to feed. Now they worried and their tails wagged over their kill. The Arctic moved in, pulling at the warm hide.

Winthrop stumbled forward. Ahead, he thought he heard whining. He was exhausted, his breathing short and ragged. His tongue was parched, scratchy. Each breath rasped at his chest, the frozen air taken with difficulty, but he continued stumbling forward.

Again, he thought he heard whining. Or was it the sound of small children? He heard them in the dark. The woods were thick, and he moved toward the sound. Where there were children, there would be shelter. And with shelter, warmth. The prospect compelled him, and he pushed through tree branches, lurching ahead.

The lead wolf was the first to hear something breaking through the thicket. There was almost no wind, so they hadn't smelled or noticed the approach. Now the Arctic could sense the familiar, complete stink of the man.

The human moved forward as though he were blind. The

Arctic watched him through intense yellow eyes. The man stumbled five paces until he was almost upon them. The lead wolf sensed the man's weakness. But the other wolf dogs skirted to the opposite side of the deer, moving away from where they'd begun to feed. They were hungry and had their first independent taste of blood, but the man frightened them. The Arctic refused to retreat. He lowered his head, watched and waited.

"Dogs," the man managed, without authority, barely audible.

The leader cowered before the word. But it was a weak sound uttered from a weakened animal. And now the big Arctic leaned into the sound, creeping forward in the dark.

The man wavered, practically walking into the deer. In one easy motion the Arctic struck the man full force, knocking him back in the snow. The man fell over and lay on his back struggling for breath, clearly exhausted, his arms thrashing. The wolf recognized opportunity and with instinctual precision moved in and took it.

EPILOGUE

By late Monday morning three deputies, led by Barnes, stumbled onto Winthrop's body. They found the nearby remnants of the deer carcass and plenty of blood and tracks. But the wolves were gone. Winthrop was a frozen, bloodless hump in the arctic cold.

Barnes climbed to a copse of rock rising out of Skinwalkers Bog, not far from Winthrop's body. Barnes was able to send out a crackling message. They'd found the man. He'd been killed by wolves. Word spread quickly. Sam was with Goddard when the call came in. Sam wanted to know about it, and Barnes told him everything he could. Sam felt certain it was the hybrids. It would be extraordinary behavior for wild wolves. But given that Winthrop may have stumbled onto a fresh kill and he was in the middle of deep wilderness, it was possible, Sam guessed. He asked Barnes to obtain whatever hair samples he could find.

The sheriff's prediction with regard to Young had been spot on. Around dawn the quiet insurance agent began telling them everything. At least everything he knew. Heins discovered Beauregard trying to warm himself in the abandoned Iron Rail depot near the edge of Defiance. He mistook him for Winthrop, thinking it was some kind of prank. When he realized the man was a vagrant, Heins saw what could be done. He told them about Moon and Winthrop getting the vagrant into Winthrop's clothes, and then walking him out toward the tracks until Moon raised the gun beneath the bum's chin and fired. It was all for the insurance. Young didn't know anything about Pine Grove Estates or that Winthrop had been swindling Range spinsters for more than a decade.

The insurance man also explained about the hybrids. Moon had a breeding area behind his cabin, back in the woods. Before unleashing them on the calves, he'd nailed each of them into their dilapidated quarters and gave them nothing but water for two days. The club believed the controversy would cover their tracks and provide actual evidence that wolves were more plentiful and dangerous. Winthrop wanted a return to the days of wolf bounties, or at the very least to have the vermin removed from the endangered species list.

Young didn't know everything, but he knew plenty. After sharing all the details with Goddard and Barnes, he appeared sallow eyed and gray faced. He was beginning to realize he was looking at serious time.

Pederson was the next to fall.

Heins refused to answer any of their questions and had requested a lawyer. Moon was belligerent and threatening and would have likely killed someone, or something, if given the chance.

On Monday morning Sam received a call from Goddard.

"Enjoying our warm spell?" the sheriff asked.

The Canadian cold front had retreated and it was a balmy 25°F, swimsuit weather by Defiance standards.

"Feels like Colorado."

"Where are you?" the sheriff asked.

"Rangers Café, having a little breakfast, plotting my future."

Sam was up to his usual habits, compiling a list of advantages and disadvantages. The college-ruled notebook lay open in front of him, next to the cup of coffee the waitress kept filling. There were several items listed on both sides of the ledger. A few crossed out. A few had lines indicating order changes, while others had been rephrased. He was trying to determine if he should move forward with the national special agent job and the interagency task force. It was Monday and Sam owed Magdalen a call. But he wasn't ready to make it. Not yet. After considering his list, he noticed Diane's name wasn't on it. That was interesting. It led him to remember the previous evening, in which they both spent a good long while enjoying each other, making up for lost time. This morning too.

Sam appreciated Diane. The sex was . . . well . . . the sex caused him to remember what had been missing from his life. Diane made him remember a person's skin was the body's largest organ, though she brought all of him alive. Still, the reason she wasn't on his list was because she wasn't part of his long-term equation. She was part of something, but Sam wasn't sure what. And he knew he had to make the decision about his future alone.

Goddard knew all about Sam's employment opportunity with the USFW. "Take the job," he advised. "You're a natural."

"Uh-huh." Sam appreciated the comment, though it wouldn't impact his decision.

"I wonder if you can do me a favor?" Goddard asked.

"Name it."

"Can you go out to Angus Moon's cabin? I need some physical evidence of those kennels and his work breeding hybrids. And we need some samples we can tie to those hybrids and the calf kill."

"No problem, Sheriff. I'll head out now. I don't seem to be making much headway here."

The sheriff gave him directions. It was at least a half-hour drive involving plenty of remote turns. Sam looked forward to cruising through the Northern Minnesota woods. It would give him time to think.

Moon's place was set so far back into a stand of Norway pines that it was invisible from the road. The entrance was marked by a lone, rusted mailbox with *R.R. 8* scrawled on its side. If you'd been moving down the road with any speed, you would have passed it. The driveway went up through the trees and disappeared.

Sam turned up the drive, genuinely interested in what he was going to find. He couldn't imagine Moon's place. Or rather, none of what he imagined was pleasant.

After a couple hundred feet his Jeep topped a tree-covered hill. At the bottom of the hill rested a dilapidated double-wide. There was a small clearing with two rusted-out cars almost completely covered with snow. There was a small path to some steps that climbed to a scarred white metal door. Above the trailer's faded brown trim, an antenna stuck out like a skeletal hand. Sam followed the driveway down to a closed garage. To the right of the garage there was another snow-covered vehicle, sitting like an old carcass. The fresh snow made it all appear clean and preternaturally white. But Sam could easily imagine the scene in deep summer, dirty and unkempt.

None of what he found at Moon's surprised him. It was a Northwoods hideout more than a cabin. The rusting hulks, the battered, faded double-wide, even the small antenna reaching out of its roof reminded Sam of the desultory woodsman's life. He was a wild, dangerous man, and if a woman had ever seen this place, she would have turned and run screaming through the trees.

As soon as Sam got out of his Jeep, he could smell the pungent odor of the kennel. Judging from the absence of a single whine or rustle, the kennels were empty, or their inhabitants dead. He pulled a few baggies off the front seat, stuffed them into his coat pocket, and walked through the snow to examine the trailer's front door. The aluminum doorknob was locked. He peered through the front door window, but the frosted glass was opaque. He knocked, though he knew no one would answer. While he waited, just to be sure, he took a closer look at the door. If he wanted, he could easily enter the place. A simple shoulder in the top center would break it open. But he didn't have a warrant, and he didn't want to jeopardize any evidence, and besides, the breeding operation was up in the woods behind the trailer. Goddard asked him to check out the kennel, not the man's living space, though Sam was curious.

The trail into the woods was easy to find. He climbed the icy path through the trees. Fifty yards back he saw the small shelters and three or four fenced-in outdoor pens. As he approached, even in the cold, the fetid reek of the hybrids' confinement was nauseating. It was feces, wolf urine, with maybe a subtext of glandular fear, if such a thing was possible; it became more overpowering the closer he came to the dilapidated compound.

Earlier, when he'd heard how Moon had nailed each hybrid into their small houses, he'd been outraged. He couldn't imagine the hybrids' lives, or the Arctic or malamute who bred them. Or rather, he guessed it was similar to his own childhood, only worse. The thought of it made him hunger for a swifter and more exacting revenge than the slow wheels of the criminal justice system. But he would settle for prison, recognizing a cage would be the best punishment for a man like Moon.

Still, to bring a living animal into this world, in these environs, and to know nothing but Moon's ugly perspective on the world would be a living hell. Sam knew life was difficult enough without being handicapped by a man like Moon. He had to remind himself he was here to help put the man away forever, and try and be appeased, if not entirely satisfied with the effort.

He approached the nearest house and saw the plane of snow where it covered a plywood board. Probably the covering Moon nailed over the nearest house, Sam thought. He moved to the front of the house and saw hair along the scarred wooden edge. He bent down and started pulling a sample from the ragged wood.

Something stirred inside.

Sam jumped back. He thought maybe a wild creature had moved into the house to get out of the cold. But what kind of creature would dare venture into a wolf den, when the smell was overpowering and where it would almost certainly be killed and eaten? Some snow shook loose across the threshold, surfacing a heavy chain, angled down over the worn entrance.

There was another move from inside the house, though not hurried.

Sam stepped back a little farther, peering inside. And then he saw the weak, small head turn and peer out of the dark opening. One of its eyes was cobalt blue. The other wolf yellow. Its head was in the shape of a wolf. Something between a wolf pup and a youngster, maybe just 4 months old? Weighted down by a chain, its head hung low as it peered suspiciously into the bright morning.

"Hey," Sam said.

The chain hung from a makeshift rope collar. The animal peered up, but didn't react to his voice. Its face was gaunt, and its forward limb, at least what Sam could see, was thin and spindly.

But its paw was big. If it was a pup, it was going to be a big hybrid, providing it survived the day.

"Come on out here," Sam said, softly.

Something like a glint of recognition came into its tired eyes. Something like hope, though Sam couldn't see for sure. Sam looked around, wondering if the animal had water, wondering when it was last fed. He would have to get it some water and find out where Moon kept the dog food. He remembered the shed beside the garage and was about ready to retreat and get this creature some food when it moved forward, just a little. Its gaunt, large head came forward and peered out of the house opening. It eyed Sam with suspicion, clearly in a weakened state. But it came forward, one step out of the house with its head poised over its paw. Then it grew tired and lay down, unable to continue. Its chain pulled against the rope collar, but it could only lay in submission.

Sam came forward, cautious but feeling pity. He would have to determine if the dog could be saved. It appeared to have a gentle demeanor, which was incredible given its life until now. But the only way to tell for sure was to get it healthy and spend some time with the animal. Sam found the nearby water bowl turned over and covered with a dusting of snow. He kneeled down in front of the young dog. When he did, the dog managed to lift its head. Sam heard its tail lift and drop, lift and drop. Then it grew still.

Sam squinted to the back of the house and saw another dog's body, unmoving, clearly dead.

"Let's get you out of here. But first let me get you some water and food."

On the way back to the trailer, he banged the ice out of the bottom of the water bowl. It shattered against a tree. He retreated down the icy path, retracing his steps to the trailer's front door. He didn't know where Moon kept fresh water, but he was certain he could find some in the double-wide. He did not pause on the front step, setting his shoulder into the door's top center. The latch shattered and the cheap metal entrance swung open.

It was a simple, surprisingly clean trailer, but he did not pause to consider it. He glanced to his right, found the small kitchen, walked across the threadbare carpet, and turned on the sink faucet. He filled the bowl, returned up the path, and laid it in front of the young dog. As soon as it smelled water, it raised its head and came out far enough to bend and drink. At first it was tentative and weak. But once it tasted the water, its tongue seemed to strengthen from the refreshment. Its head bent in earnest, and it lapped and lapped.

"Take it easy. You're going to get sick."

But the dog didn't listen.

Sam retreated down the icy path to the shed. He opened the door and found three large bags of kibble, one of them opened. The shed was filled with an assortment of odds and ends, including several foothold traps hanging from nails in the sidewall. Sam found a scoop in the opened bag. There was a small stack of bowls. He took one and filled it with kibble. On his way out he grabbed a pair of bolt cutters. He wasn't sure where that chain went, but he knew he was going to free the pup.

Back at the doghouse the pup looked energized by the water. As soon as it got a whiff of the kibble, it started whining. Sam set the bowl down in front of it, and the dog took a lunging bite of the food, wolfing it down. Then another.

The chain impaired its ability to eat. Sam took the bolt cutters to where the last link disappeared into the house. He affixed the tip of the cutters into the link, closed the two handles, and the link snapped, the chain freed. As if in answer the pup's head came all the way up, but it didn't hesitate or alter its focus. It returned to the bowl, hurriedly wolfing down more mouthfuls of kibble.

Sam watched the dog eat. It was going to be a big dog, if it survived. He'd never seen such a scruffy animal. And its coat was matted and thick, dirty from being inside the filthy house. He watched it turn around the bowl, no longer impeded or held back by the chain. Sam leaned down and looked into the house and saw what appeared to be a purebred malamute. Probably the female Moon used to breed the hybrids. This one's mother, Sam guessed. It was dead, frozen in the house. The poor, hungry pup in front of him had been chained into the house beside his dying, then dead, mother.

It sickened Sam. It reminded him why he was here. He took out the baggies, and while the pup finished the kibble, Sam turned to the other houses and gathered more hair samples. If he hadn't needed the samples and the evidence, he would have returned to the shed, found some gasoline, and torched the stinking houses.

When the pup finished the kibble, it moved back to the bowl of water and finished it too. Sam waited to see if he'd keep it down. It was a male, and it peered at him with the most beautiful pair of mixed-colored eyes. If Sam was any judge of dogs, this one's demeanor conveyed cooperation. He considered it, and realized it was probably an offspring from a recent litter, but he guessed Moon had been unable to sell it since it appeared to be more malamute than wolf and had heterochromia, two different-colored eyes, a relatively rare condition.

"Come here," he said, bending a little and beckoning with his hand.

The dog came forward, shy, its head lowered, tail between its legs, wagging a little, uncertain.

Sam did not have to tell the pup to follow him. After gathering and marking the fur samples, Sam returned to the shed. The pup trailed a cautious distance behind him. Sam found some brushes in the shed. The dog was remarkably sweet for a hybrid. Perhaps he hadn't yet come into his wolf heritage. Or maybe he had simply gotten more of his mother than his Arctic father. Whatever, Sam spent a half hour brushing the puppy, who seemed to know Sam meant no harm. He enjoyed being groomed. Unusually, he did not whine or turn away, but sat stoically while Sam brushed out the clumps, the matted fur, the pieces of God-knew-what, mixed in with hay and wood chips.

"You're going to need a bath, for starters," Sam said. "And a checkup."

The dog's tail wagged when Sam spoke. Sam smiled. "Your one eye is a lot like Charlie's," Sam said, a little wistful, remembering his friend. The dog's tail wagged again.

Back on the road the dog sat beside him on the passenger seat. Sam rolled down the two rear windows to provide ventilation. He had the heater blasting in the front. The dog sat still, happy to be in the Jeep. Sam guessed it was the first time the pup had ever been in a car, had probably never been away from the compound. It was remarkably calm, had a kind of natural regal demeanor, watching the snowy world go by. It was gaunt but alert now, since it had eaten and drunk.

Near town Sam phoned Diane.

"Sam," she said.

"Finished with that article?"

"Finished the first one by noon. The editor's damn happy about it. Now I'm working on some background pieces, for tomorrow and the day after. People are going to want to know about this. It's a huge story and I have the exclusive. You couldn't make up a story like this," she said, happily.

"Can you do me a favor?"

"Haven't I proved that already?"

Sam smiled. "Do you know any vets in the area?"

"Sure. People tell me Dave O'Connor's a good one. His office is on the edge of Vermilion Falls."

"Can you get me a number?"

"Sure."

He waited while she looked it up. When she found it, he pulled over and wrote it down.

"Why do you want a vet?"

"Found a pup out at Moon's place, needs some tending."

"You coming now?"

"Figured I would. Then I need to go over to the sheriff's office."

"What are you doing later?"

"Later?"

"After the sheriff. I still owe you a drink and a meal. Maybe you should come over and I'll fix you some dinner and we can celebrate?"

"I can do that." He imagined her lips.

"Pick up some akvavit, would you?"

There was a pause. "That's a dangerous mixture."

"I wasn't going to mix anything with it. Just going to have it straight up."

He thought she smiled over the phone. "I'll pick it up."

On the way to the vet's office, he finally phoned Magdalen.

"Magdalen," she answered, gravelly, her voice short.

"Kay. Sam Rivers."

"Of course it's Sam Rivers. I've already got them putting your nameplate on your new office. Don't disappoint me."

Sam smiled. "I want a raise and I need some special allowances."

"Rivers," she said, a little miffed. "Anyone ever told you you're a high-maintenance pain in the ass?"

He could tell she was pleased. "Only you."

"The raise is already in the works. That's a given. What allowances?"

"I'm thinking the office needs a mascot. How do you think the service would feel about me having a dog?"

"At the office?"

"Yeah. At the office. Like in Europe. And didn't the service once look at using dogs in the field?"

"This is Denver. Not Denmark. And I don't remember the service ever using dogs in the field."

"I may need the allowance," he said, matter of fact. So she would know he was serious.

There was a long pause. Finally, she said, "OK, Rivers. We'll look into it. Just get your ass back here."

"The sheriff needs me to stay and clear up a few details. I suspect I'll have to be here at least through next weekend."

There was another pause. This time he could hear Magdalen's exasperation over the phone.

"Consider it community–law enforcement relations," Sam added, but he was thinking about Diane.

"Goddammit, Rivers." There was another pause. "Did you plan on doing any work when you returned?"

"Whatever you need, Kay."

"Damn right," came her gravelly reply.

Sam smiled.

ACKNOWLEDGMENTS

Nearly three decades ago I sped home over lunch to enter into a brief 45-minute writing spell in the rare quiet of my nearby home. The awful pursuits of the Iron County Gun Club fell out on the page. Eventually that story morphed into *Wolves* (the original version of *Wolf Kill*), early versions of which were read by my sons, Nick and Noah; my wife, Anna; Lois and Laurie Sauerbry; and Dorothy Molstad. All provided both encouragement and suggestions and held to the steadfast belief that this novel needed to see the light of day.

Thanks to Nancy Jo Tubbs, chair of the board of directors for the International Wolf Center, who also graciously read an early version of the manuscript and provided valuable feedback. Mary Logue, author, editor, and writing teacher, pored over the first third of the book and provided insight, suggestions, guidance, and encouragement. It was Mary who first heard about Adventure Publications' foray into publishing regional mysteries and recommended *Wolves*. Thanks to fellow writer Pat Dennis for appreciating the book and passing it on.

Much of the wolf biology and related information in this book is based on information gleaned from discussions with wolf experts and various officials from the Minnesota Department of Natural Resources and the U.S. Fish & Wildlife Service. Also indispensable were site visits to the International Wolf Center in Ely, Minnesota, and the Wildlife Science Center in Forest Lake, Minnesota (where you can learn about and view wolf dog hybrids, rare red wolves, Mexican gray wolves, coyotes, and more).

In Minnesota we are not only blessed with the largest population of wolves in the Lower 48, but also a robust public discourse about how best to manage wolves, a conversation that involves hunters, trappers, environmentalists, outdoors enthusiasts, and everyone in between. Our media gives ample coverage to this discourse, and this book has been better informed because of it.

Finally, 5% of the author's proceeds will be divided equally and donated to the Wildlife Science Center and the International Wolf Center.

POSTSCRIPT: *Wolves* was published in 2013. The next Sam Rivers mystery, *Savage Minnesota*, was published serially in the *Star Tribune* of the Twin Cities during the summer of 2014. I always wanted to see *Savage Minnesota* in print, so when the copyright for that title reverted back to me, I approached Brett Ortler, AdventureKEEN's acquisitions and developmental editor, to see if the publisher was interested in taking on another Sam Rivers mystery. Fortunately, it was. Moreover, they decided to reedit and rebrand both books, and publish two additional forthcoming Sam Rivers mysteries. In addition to Brett's work on these titles, they have also benefited from the keen eye of Amber K. Henderson, AdventureKEEN's developmental and managing editor. I know there are others at AdventureKEEN who have assisted with book titles, marketing, and everything else that goes into publishing books. Many thanks to AdventureKEEN for all its support and hard work.

As most readers know, AdventureKEEN publishes primarily nonfiction titles. I own several of its nature guides. Recognizing fiction was outside of its customary genre, they asked Mary

Logue to continue her work on the series. In addition to Mary's numerous other credits already mentioned, Mary is the author of several mysteries of her own, including the recently released *The Streel* (University of Minnesota Press, 2020). Mary read through and seriously edited each of these titles, making many suggestions along the way. All of these titles have been immeasurably improved because of her hard work and experienced hand.

Thanks to everyone who helped make *Wolf Kill* the book you hold in your hands today.

ABOUT THE AUTHOR

Award-winning author Cary J. Griffith grew up among the woods, fields, and emerald waters of eastern Iowa. His childhood fostered a lifelong love of wild places. He earned a bachelor of arts in English from the University of Iowa and a master of arts in library science from the University of Minnesota.

Griffith's books explore the natural world. In nonfiction, he covers the borderlands between civilization and wild places. In fiction, he focuses on the ways some people use flora and fauna to commit crimes, while others with more reverence and understanding of the natural world leverage their knowledge to bring criminals to justice. In both genres, readers are likely to learn something about our relationship to the natural world and the creatures who inhabit it.

"I was 14 the first time I visited the lakes and boreal forests of northeastern Minnesota," says Griffith, "and its beauty struck me."

Griffith is also the author of *Gunflint Burning: Fire in the Boundary Waters* (2018), *Opening Goliath* (2009), and *Lost in the Wild* (2006). He lives with his family in a suburb of Minnesota's Twin Cities.

DISCUSSION GUIDE

ABOUT THE BOOK

In the middle of a bitter winter night, Vermilion County authorities are called out to Williston Winthrop's remote farm, where the aging lawyer has died in a gruesome hunting accident. For differing reasons, everyone is pleased by Winthrop's demise. Sam Rivers, Winthrop's estranged son, can return to recover the heirlooms he secreted in his mother's house when, at 17, his father forced him to flee Minnesota's Iron Range. The four remaining members of the Iron County Gun Club are the beneficiaries of Winthrop's estate, including substantial insurance benefits. And the county sheriff, the victim of one of Winthrop's extortion schemes, no longer needs to worry about the nefarious man's threats and intimidation.

When Sam, a wolf biologist, returns home, he discovers more than he expected. In the aftermath of his father's death, wolves have entered the old man's barn and slaughtered his feeder calves. Relying on his detailed knowledge of wolf biology, Sam recognizes incongruities in the lupine depredation. The boy has become a man, and with the assistance of Diane Talbott, a local reporter, he begins asking questions that start to unravel the wolf kill, his father's death, a vagrant's murder, and the illegal pursuits of the Iron County Gun Club.

In both fiction and nonfiction, Cary J. Griffith writes about wilderness issues and the flora and fauna that inhabit the natural world. In *Wolf Kill,* the author surfaces some of the controversies surrounding local, state, and federal wolf-management programs. Similarly, contemporary knowledge and understanding of wolf biology and behavior play a key role in understanding what happened in the wilds of Northern Minnesota.

DISCUSSION QUESTIONS

1. Near the beginning of *Wolf Kill,* Sam Rivers is investigating a wolf predation at Judy Rutgers's sheep ranch. In what ways does Sam's work at Rutgers's ranch presage (and help) his subsequent investigation of the wolf predation at his childhood home?

2. Sam Rivers had a tumultuous relationship with his father, Williston Winthrop. In many ways, their characters are foils to one another. In what general ways do the two men differ? And in what specific ways (for example, their relationship to wolves) do the men differ?

3. In the novel, wolf dog hybrids are used to slaughter calves. Ostensibly, the carnage is arranged so that Angus Moon will no longer be burdened with the calves' care. What are some of the other perceived benefits of the wolf-calf predation? Does the predation reveal anything else about the motives and characters of the Iron County Gun Club members?

4. The wolf dog hybrids are set free, so they can wreak havoc in Winthrop's barn. Unexpectedly, after killing the calves, they

cannot be corralled and caged. How is freeing the hybrids similar to the actions of the Iron County Gun Club?

5. There are five wolf dog hybrids, and there are five members of the Iron County Gun Club. Are there any other comparisons that can be made between the wolf dogs and the club members?

6. While breeding wolf dog hybrids is legal in Minnesota, the practice is banned in many other states. Does *Wolf Kill* begin to explore some of the reasons the practice is controversial? If so, discuss some of the reasons you would/would not like to have a wolf dog as a pet.

7. Diane Talbott is instrumental in understanding what has happened in Defiance, the surrounding county, and Winthrop's farm. How does her association with Hank Pederson help her understand how the Iron County Gun Club has benefited from Winthrop's death? How does Diane serve as an emotional connection to Sam's past?

8. Under duress, Sheriff Dean Goddard shared important prosecutorial information with Williston Winthrop days before Winthrop's staged death. Was the sheriff's divulgence instrumental in the gun club's murder of James T. "Jimbo" Beauregard? Technically, the sheriff violated the law. Should he be prosecuted? If so, why? If not, why not?

9. When Sam and Diane learn about the sheriff's reveal of prosecutorial information to Williston Winthrop, they agree to

tell no one. Why? What does the agreement to conceal the sheriff's unlawful actions say about Diane and Sam and their sense of justice?

10.   Near the end of the novel, Sam visits Angus Moon's kennel and finds a mangy wolf dog hybrid survivor. How does Sam's reaction to the wolf dog pup differ from how Sam's father raised him? Is Sam's treatment of the pup, and the pup himself, significant, and if so, why? Would you like to see Sam adopt the wolf dog? If so, why?

READ ON FOR AN EXCERPT FROM CARY J. GRIFFITH'S NEXT NOVEL

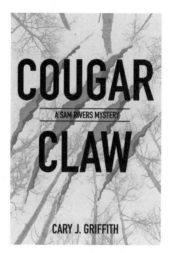

Praise for *Wolf Kill*:

"Griffith's prose makes you feel the winter chill . . . and the twisty plot delivers a chill down your spine. This is a Minnesota mystery with razor-sharp teeth."

—Brian Freeman, *New York Times*–bestselling author of *The Deep, Deep Snow*

AVAILABLE SUMMER 2022 WHEREVER BOOKS ARE SOLD

Prologue

September 2, Savage, Minnesota

Marlin Coots, McGregor Industries' gap-toothed, splay-footed nighttime security watchman, was making his morning rounds of the company's remote shipping facility. He loved this part of the day, when he could step to the edge of the minimum maintenance road and gaze down into the Minnesota river bottom woods. Sometimes he'd see a raccoon scurry into brambles, or an opossum's slow climb up a tree. You never knew what the Savage woods would give up, which is why Coots always took a moment to pause and look down.

The perimeter road was always empty, particularly here, where a huge oak anchored the landward side of the pair of dirt ruts. The other side of the road dropped 15 feet to the bottoms. On this morning Coots was startled to see a large brown animal lying on its side, its neck twisted at an unnatural angle.

A white-tailed deer. The kill was too primitive for a poacher.

Coots backslid down the embankment. The carcass was barely cold. Its chest cavity had a clean incision from neck to belly. The ribs were parted, and its heart and lungs were gone. When he looked around, he noticed a paw print the size of a frying pan.

"What the . . . ?"

His dad told him there were serious predators in the Minnesota River valley. Coots's father had spent most of his adult life hunting and fishing this wild stretch of river, from Mankato all the way up to Savage on the edge of the Twin Cities. Coots didn't share his dad's enthusiasm for shooting game, but he loved seeing the animals in his neck of the woods. So he rigged a motion-sensor camera with a flash, setting it up near the deer kill.

The next day, Coots's camera confirmed the presence of a cougar, with an image clear enough to print. Because this part of the valley was considered an outlying Twin Cities suburb, the local media picked up the sighting. "Big Cat Returns to Minnesota," the *Star Tribune* reported. One of the more dramatic TV news channels asked, "Are you safe in Minnesota's woods?" The coverage reported that over the last 10 years, out west, there had been dozens of human-cougar encounters, "and in some instances people were stalked, killed, and eaten."

The Minnesota Department of Natural Resources tried to place the sighting in perspective. Though cougar attacks were known to happen—even some in which humans were killed—in Minnesota, people had a better chance of being struck by lightning.

The DNR suspected this cougar was someone's rogue pet, though no one came forward. If it was wild, they surmised, it was extremely rare for Minnesota, with only a handful of confirmed sightings in the last 50 years, none near the Cities.

In any case, there was no need to worry. A big cat's customary food source was deer, which could account for why this cougar had come to Savage. Along the suburban section of river, the whitetail fattened on Kentucky bluegrass, backyard hostas, and tulip greens. Deer hunting was irregular or nonexistent, and the deer herd was prodigious.

The kill, the tracks, and the photo made for good TV, which is why, three days later, one station ran a follow-up piece on cougar hunting habits, noting they often returned to feed on kills a second and even a third time, sometimes several days later.

"So if you're heading into the Minnesota River valley," warned the anchor, "be careful out there."

Chapter One

September 23

Jack McGregor pumped hard through the bike's lowest gear, his thighs burning. He neared the top of his 0.25-mile climb, maintaining his bike's progress up this last steep grade. The black coffee he'd finished before 6 a.m. was finally taking hold. He glanced at his heart monitor and watched the numbers spike from 156 to 157. Sweat dampened his tight yellow bike shirt.

Twenty yards, he thought, which was about all he could manage, trying to keep his ragged breathing steady. He rabbit-pedaled through the last short rise and finally crested the hill.

He appreciated the quiet half hour before dawn when the world slept and the late-summer air hung still and pungent. His heart rate peaked at 164, and he managed a stiff grin.

He took in a long breath and smelled witch hazel, he guessed: the odor of weeds heavy with seedpods and a faint wisp of river more than a mile below. It was a wet metallic smell. And maybe there was the trace of something fetid beneath it: a car-struck deer decaying in a ditch, or a snake flattened across the blacktop? Something . . .

Over the last couple days McGregor had felt uneasy. He assumed it was his pending business deal. But there was something else, the vague feeling he needed to be vigilant or wary or just plain cautious. And it was annoying, because Jack McGregor, the 51-year-old owner, president, and chief executive officer of McGregor Industries, was a stranger to unease.

Chester Drive formed a T at the top of Wannamake Circle. The hill dropped down into Savage and the Minnesota River

3

valley, where it connected with MN 13 over a mile below. In another hour the blacktop would be busy with morning commuters, emptying the exclusive neighborhoods up on the hill. But from McGregor's acme, at this time of morning, he had the road almost entirely to himself.

He turned onto Chester and crouched low, reducing his wind resistance so the air coming out of the valley wouldn't pick him up like a sail. Not that there was much of a breeze a half hour before dawn. Jack McGregor liked to feel aerodynamic. He liked to travel fast. As his bike picked up speed, he put his nagging doubts behind him and peered ahead, grinning down the dark thoroughfare.

. . .

The speedometer hit 22. McGregor looked up and saw the road empty all the way to MN 13, not a car in sight. When he glanced down again, the speedometer read 25.

It was still too early for predawn light, which was why McGregor squinted down the path in front of him. At this speed, traveling near the tree edge, it was foolhardy to look anywhere but directly in front of you. Deer frequented the wilder parts of Chester Hill. And plenty of nocturnal animals chose this final hour of darkness to hunt for a safe place to bed down and sleep for the day. Or to search for one last unsuspecting prey.

The wild country was one of the features that had charmed them about Savage. Jack and Carla could have chosen a big house in Edina, Excelsior, Shorewood, or just about any other place they wanted. But Carla liked the unpretentiousness of Savage. She appreciated the secluded, country feel of Wannamake Circle and their remote cul-de-sac, where she wouldn't run into anyone from the club and where she could buy milk at the local Cub Grocery without having to dress up or put on.

Speedometer: 27.

Up ahead something stirred. Under a sumac patch. Not a deer; the movement was too furtive and close to the ground. At his current speed, he would hit it head on in a matter of seconds.

McGregor yelled and the dark creature froze, and he hurtled by in a blast. He glimpsed a skunk hunkered down in the grass.

Just a few seconds either way, rodent or man, and McGregor might have been a stinking pile of . . .

Focus on the tree edge, he reminded himself. It was a brief part of the hill, and he watched as its shadows flew by and opened onto empty pasture. His near brush with calamity rocketed his pulse. His bike speed climbed to 33. He glanced in front of him. The pools of light from the gentrified streetlamps were clear all the way to the bottom, and Jack McGregor flew.

The white Ford Focus—a rental out of Brooklyn Center— approached the entrance to the dirt road.

"Here's the turn," Benedict said.

"I know," John said, tired of taking orders.

They wore dark camo, head to toe. John wore a camo baseball hat with Cabela's emblazoned above the bill. Benedict wore one of those pull-down hats with a ruffled 2-inch brim. They were edgy in the predawn.

John did what he often did, knowing there was bad business ahead. He put himself past it. In 2 hours I will be back at my place . . . showering . . . getting ready for work. Just another day.

But given the task ahead, focusing on what came after was difficult.

This stretch of MN 13 was mostly open country, separated by occasional remote storage facilities and grain elevators. Farther north, Savage gave way to Burnsville and single-family homes, apartment complexes, and a string of busy retail outlets crowding either side of the highway all the way to I-35W. Travel south and you passed more open country until the Valleyfair Amusement Park and Shakopee, the next suburb over. But here, in between the park and Burnsville's stores, the river bottom was vacant and wild, except for McGregor Industries and its potash and fertilizer facility.

John glanced in his rearview mirror. He saw one pair of head-lights, a quarter mile behind him. At this hour there was nothing up ahead. He signaled, turning onto the narrow dirt lane. It was empty and dark and rose to a pair of unmarked railroad tracks. On either side, the weeds were high and overgrown, and the car rumbled over the rails, leaving a faint cloud of dust. The car dropped over the hill, and John turned onto the frontage road, pulled over beside a stand of river maples, and cut the engine. The headlights darkened.

They each glanced at their watches. They would sit in the car for exactly 5 minutes, waiting for the dust to settle and the crick-ets' *screedle-screedle* to return in the dark.

. . .

It took less than 2 minutes for McGregor to rocket down Chester Drive. At MN 13 he pedaled easily across the blacktop, biked 50 yards up the shoulder, and turned onto the frontage road.

He was still a mile from the plant and a little farther to the minimum maintenance road. He could see the faintest start of light in the eastern sky, barely a shadow. He liked hitting the river bottom in that special half-light of dawn. Judging from what he saw off the horizon, he was right on schedule.

McGregor pedaled easily during this part of his morning, saving himself for the hard exercise of the river bottom. He had paid Mountain Cross Bikes to build several private bike trails down by the river. The trails wound through McGregor Industries' low-hung trees and up and down the small ravines leading into the river. Once you got on them, staying on your bike on the trail required unwavering concentration. If you weren't totally focused, you could end up with your torso wrapped around a tree trunk or facedown in the dirt. It was the kind of challenge McGregor liked because it kept him feeling alert and alive.

But here, along the quiet, flat dirt road, he could ease up and contemplate his day.

It had been an intense six months for McGregor Industries. In less than two weeks his sale to Garkill would be final, and he'd have a lot more time for mountain biking. And just about anything else he'd postponed because of work, which was plenty. Best of all, the sale of his company was on his terms. He was getting out from under a business that had occupied 60-plus hours a week for almost 30 years. And McGregor wasn't looking back. First up: a round-the-world trip he'd been holding so close to his vest that not even Carla knew about it. They were going to become reacquainted in some of the finest hotels and biggest beds across five continents.

McGregor kept his bike centered on the poorly lit gravel road. The insects chirruped in the dark. The frontage road was bordered on two sides by heavy autumn bush and occasional trees. You never knew what critters might scamper out of the weeds—could be another skunk or a deer, so it was best to keep to the road's center.

Only five insiders knew about the company's pending sale, and none of them liked it. CFO Spencer Higgins and treasurer Phil Traub had to know. No way around it. McGregor had needed their help. They would both benefit from the sale, Higgins more than Traub.

Madeline Baxter (Maddy), the company's vice president of HR, had to know. Baxter had been around since McGregor was a kid. He suspected she had been his father's plaything, though McGregor was only guessing. McGregor kept the wire-haired old witch around because it had been a promise to his father. But once he was out from under the business, she'd have to fend for herself, and McGregor was pretty sure Garkill would cut her loose.

A year ago McGregor asked Higgins to give Susan Connelly a better job title and more money.

Most people knew McGregor had a problem with women. Sometimes he made bad choices and worse passes, and when Connelly threatened a lawsuit, he'd reached out to Higgins and told him to promote her. You could do that kind of thing when you owned the company.

Higgins made the long-haired blonde a financial analyst. She was good with numbers. After Higgins requested several out-of-season profit-and-loss statements, Connelly figured out the pending sale and had to be brought in on it.

The only other person who knew about the transaction was Angie Sweet, assistant treasurer under Traub. Like Connelly, she discovered the pending sale because of her acumen with numbers.

When there was a lot of excited financial work out of season, she made a rare visit to McGregor's office and confronted him.

You had to admire her. If she wanted something, she pursued it. McGregor misread her ambition and made a play for her in the corporate boardroom. Sweet let him know that less-discreet women could use that kind of thing to file a lawsuit or make a stink. McGregor let her know it would be her word against his. But to placate her, he'd brought her into the fold, with assurances she would benefit like the others from the sale. Not much, really. But enough to purchase cooperation and silence.

Business.

If Carla knew about his indiscretions, she was too savvy to say anything. On the other hand, McGregor had been lucky. In the instances he was fortunate enough to find a willing partner and eventually needed to end things, he'd never had to deal with troubled tears, incriminations, or finger-pointing. And especially no confessions to a spouse, boyfriend, or his wife, Carla.

The truth was, Carla had all the right curves in the best places, and even after seven years of marriage, she still set his limbs on fire. That was why they were going to celebrate her 38th birthday in Bali. It seemed a fitting place for the woman who had agreed to be his permanent concubine.

McGregor kept pedaling easily.

None of the five liked the sale because they all feared the repercussions, and the only one making serious cash on the transaction was McGregor. Higgins, Traub, and Baxter would all lose their jobs once Garkill took over. Sweet and Connelly were both too good looking, too young, and too competent to do anything but land on their feet. But they'd no longer be thinking they were the heir apparent to becoming officers of the company. Besides, Garkill wasn't interested in the business end of the operation. It was clear what it wanted was the company's storage capacity and distribution network, particularly down on the river.

He couldn't blame the five for not liking it. He'd tried to be sympathetic, though it wasn't his nature. Two of them would make good money from the sale. Not enough to carry them into retirement, but certainly enough to tide them over. Baxter was old enough she might retire. He had no idea how she'd managed her money, and frankly he didn't care. For an HR vice president, she'd done what was expected: smiled and forced objectionable policies onto a disgruntled workforce. And whenever the occasional employee with a backbone made a ruckus, she had a knack for cutting them loose.

He came up to the intersection and turned onto the minimum maintenance road. There was a gate up ahead. It was getting light enough to see the shot-up sign, but McGregor had been around it so many times that he dodged right along the worn rut, turned around the steel post, and kept pedaling.

"Hurry up," Benedict hissed.

"Just a minute." John stepped onto the tree limb, unsteady in the near dark. Above him three huge oak branches stretched over the road.

"Give it to me," John said.

Benedict reached up to hand him the 20-pound sandbag.

John took it and tried to get situated.

They knew their rider would be coming from the southeast,